THE
HOUSE
BY THE
LIFFEY

THE HOUSE BY THE LIFFEY

NIKI PHILLIPS

Copyright © 2015 Niki Phillips

The moral right of the author has been asserted.

Apart from any fair dealing for the purposes of research or private study, or criticism or review, as permitted under the Copyright, Designs and Patents Act 1988, this publication may only be reproduced, stored or transmitted, in any form or by any means, with the prior permission in writing of the publishers, or in the case of reprographic reproduction in accordance with the terms of licences issued by the Copyright Licensing Agency. Enquiries concerning reproduction outside those terms should be sent to the publishers.

Matador
9 Priory Business Park
Wistow Road
Kibworth Beauchamp
Leicester LE8 0RX, UK
Tel: 0116 279 2299
Email: books@troubador.co.uk
Web: www.troubador.co.uk/matador

ISBN 978 1784624 156

British Library Cataloguing in Publication Data.
A catalogue record for this book is available from the British Library.

Typeset in Book Antiqua by Troubador Publishing Ltd, Leicester, UK
Printed and bound in the UK by TJ International, Padstow, Cornwall

Matador is an imprint of Troubador Publishing Ltd

To those patient family members and friends who gave me so much help in writing this sequel to The Liffey Flows On By. *They are acknowledged by name in the Author's Note at the end.*

The Butlers and their Relations

Tom Butler: Died in 1946. Father of Milo and Tommy Butler
Aunt May Burke: Tom Butler's widowed sister
Milo Butler: current head of the Butler family and husband of Noola
Mageen, Bill, Harry, Sarah and Izzy Butler: Milo and Noola's children
Tommy Butler: Milo's half-brother and nineteen years his junior
Maggie Flynn: Mother of Noola Butler and Dr Paddy Flynn
Sean Flynn: Nephew of Maggie and cousin of Noola and Paddy
Bob Featherstone: Uncle of Tommy Butler

Friends from the Past

Chuck and Liz Wilson: Friends of the Butlers dating from Milo's days in the RAF
Isabel Wilson: Daughter of Chuck and Liz
Joe Malloy: Milo's ex school-friend and his navigator and partner in the RAF during WWII
Helen Malloy: Joe's wife

Prologue

September 1962

He gazed out of his barred window with a grin of intense satisfaction, more a snarl than a smile. Had he known it, his feelings were those of a predatory animal which, after long hours of hunting, suddenly scents blood. The thoughts went round and round in his head, almost incoherent but always with the one dreamed of target at the forefront of his mind. At long last, after many tedious years of waiting, he was going to have his revenge and, if it all worked out according to plan, it would have been well worth the interminable wait. The red mist grew behind his eyes as his rage increased and with it the old hatred that gave him such a thirst to strike back: to kill. Now, within a matter of hours, this was going to be made possible. He was going to be given the opportunity to hurt Tom Butler where he was most vulnerable. He thought of the supreme satisfaction he would get from that. And he knew he would suffer no sense of guilt or remorse whatsoever, for he believed the evil being planned would be a totally justifiable retribution. He had persuaded himself long ago that Tom Butler was the root cause of all his problems, including being caged up here in this dreadful place for all these years. In his demented state he had also convinced himself that his sister, Angela, had been murdered by Tom. His sense of reason diminished as his rage grew, which always happened when he thought of Tom Butler.

Bob Featherstone was a very dangerous psychopath. He had been in an asylum for the criminally insane for many years, having murdered not only his sister, Angela, but also Billy Flynn, the estate manager at Riverside House, the Butlers' home by the Liffey. In his rare lucid moments, helped by the appropriate drugs, he was well aware that Tom Butler, married in middle age to Angela, had been dead for years. He had been told that Tom had died, suddenly and unexpectedly, from a massive heart attack and he had cheered long and hard at the news, racing and leaping around his cell, punching the walls with delight until his fists bled. He had shouted and yelled:

'At last, at last. Serves you right you bastard, you've got what you deserved!' But once the red mist closed in he lost all sense of reality and his thoughts became totally confused. Mostly he believed that Milo, Tom's son by his first marriage, was in fact Tom, in his muddled state merging the two men into the one character. This made a weird kind of sense, for the two were so alike and he had also hated Milo, believing him to have a shared responsibility for his misery. Now he was confident that Tom was out there waiting for him to take his long-anticipated revenge.

A few weeks earlier Bob had been approached, in a very devious way, by a representative of a group calling themselves The Champions of Justice. They seemed to know all about him and his thirst for retribution and they fuelled that thirst, building on his twisted version of the events which had put him where he was – locked away from the rest of the world, not least from his wife, daughters and parents. His family did visit him but, with the passage of time, his recognition of them had gradually faded, so the visits were now few and far between and made more out of a sense of duty than for any lingering feelings of affection.

The group needed money, a lot of money. It was no secret that the Butlers were exceptionally wealthy, a lot of this tied up in equity, much in valuable property, and the group members believed they had found a way of extorting a substantial sum from the family. They planned to kidnap the most vulnerable child in the family. Someone carefully positioned to do so had helped to collect vital "insider" information for them. They knew the full story about Bob Featherstone. That was no secret either, for it had been splashed across all the daily newspapers at the time. But they also knew where he was incarcerated and they had worked out a way of contacting him and making an offer they were certain he wouldn't be able to resist. He was exactly what they needed. When Angela was alive he was a frequent visitor to Riverside House. Having his own plans for cashing in on his sister's good fortune in marrying into the wealthy Butler family, he had made sure he had an intimate knowledge of the house and the estate grounds. So all that was needed now was for him to be kept lucid for the necessary amount of time to carry out their plans and the member of their group who was a doctor reckoned he could do that with drugs.

Five years after Tom had died, Noola Butler had given birth to a little girl. At the time of Tom's death in 1946, she and Milo had four children and hadn't planned to extend the family further. However, little Iseult, known to all as Izzy, had come along, unexpectedly, and had been born almost two months prematurely. It had been a fight to keep her alive and she was, in consequence, quite a delicate child. Although Milo adored all of his children, Izzy was especially precious to him and his feelings of protectiveness towards her were fiercer than he would ever have believed possible. Almost as though nature was compensating for her fragility, she was exceptionally bright and was also musically gifted. She loved the piano, willingly spending unusually long hours, for a child of eleven years old, playing away to herself. This was open knowledge amongst the Butler family and circle of friends, and so quite easy information to access with some judicious enquiry in the right circles.

It was this child that The Champions of Justice planned to kidnap. This child that Bob hoped he would have the chance to kill. He had never even seen her but she was the daughter of the composite and hated character he thought of as "Tom". That was enough justification for him to do whatever it took so that he could punish his imagined tormentor. With luck he would be able to kill Tom at the same time.

He had been assured that his escape would be easy. They had also promised him that, after he had played his part successfully, he would be spirited away to live in comfort for the rest of his life, where nobody would be able to find him. Nobody would be able to have him brought back to Ireland to resume his existence of misery behind bars. He was being carried along by a feeling of elation that was as powerful in its effect as any narcotic.

xi

Chapter 1

Tommy Butler made a faultless landing in his fighter jet aircraft at the RAF base in Northern Germany. He had just completed a patrol of the border area separating the British zone from the Russian controlled territories. This being the height of the Cold War, it was considered essential to keep an eye on what was now regarded as "the enemy" and to be alert at all times for possible hostile activity along the dividing line between the opposing factions. Things were especially tense just now. The relatively recent construction of the Berlin Wall had finally created a sinister physical division between the two sectors of the city, adding a visible emphasis to the division between East and West Germany. Military personnel were all warned frequently that it wouldn't take much to trigger an incident.

Unaware that his approach to the airfield was being watched by the Station Commander, the sudden release of tension at the end of his watch had resulted in Tommy's execution of a neat dive beneath a high bridge close to the edge of the airfield, followed by a well-executed victory roll, this, almost reflex action, a legacy from his recent days as a member of the Black Arrows. He was one of the most skilled pilots in the squadron and there was little chance that he would misjudge anything and cause a disaster. However, no matter how good any pilot might be, this kind of caper was strictly not acceptable and he knew that, if observed, at the very least a good dressing down would be in store for him.

Tommy was tired and looking forward to having a hot bath and putting his head down for a couple of hours before dinner in the Mess. They all knew that the Station Commander was entertaining the second-in-command of an RAF station further north. The newly

1

promoted Group Captain Wilson was passing through on his way to take up a posting as Station Commander of an RAF base in Cyprus. The Station Commander here, Group Captain Shelly, was an old friend and had offered hospitality. Although no such announcement had been made, it was understood that squadron members would be expected, as a courtesy to the guests, to attend pre-dinner drinks in the Keller Bar. However, before he had time to do anything, Tommy got word that the Station Commander wanted to see him in his office immediately. Tommy groaned inwardly. Why the hell had he pulled that stupid stunt? Typical of him – impulsive, spur of the moment. He knew pretty well by heart the Group Captain's likely comments – he had been at the receiving end several times. He stood rigidly to attention in front of the man who, in truth, he admired greatly.

'Well, Flight Lieutenant, you know why you're here?'

'Yes, Sir!'

'Well perhaps *you'd* like to tell *me*?'

'At the end of my patrol I behaved in an irresponsible manner, showing a lack of self-discipline, Sir.'

'And the possible consequences?'

'Loss of a costly aircraft and a pilot whose training has been very expensive.'

'Anything else?'

'I was also endangering the civilian population, Sir.'

'Precisely. Even you with your considerable flying skills are not immune from making mistakes. You know all this perfectly well and that dangerous stunts are absolutely forbidden. Yet you persist in ignoring the rules.'

'It won't happen again, Sir.'

'Well at least you haven't got the gall to say you're sorry, for I'm quite certain that your only regret probably is that I saw what you did.'

Tommy had the hardest time not twitching a smile but luckily for him controlled his face.

'This has to be your last warning, Flight Lieutenant. One more such misdemeanour and it'll have to be demotion. Dismissed!'

Outside the closed door Tommy let out a long breath. As Maggie

2

would say, "Jesus, Mary and Joseph"! On the other hand he couldn't really blame the Group Captain. The man couldn't possibly overlook such a breach of the very strict rules and he was right, it would only take a hairbreadth's misjudgement for a disaster, especially likely when a pilot was tired. On his way back to his room one of his fellow pilots winked at him and muttered:

'Neat bit of flying, Tommy!' But following the reprimand, and especially the last warning, Tommy's feelings were too bruised to return more than a weak grin.

Later that evening David and Jenny Shelly were joined by Chuck and Liz Wilson with their daughter Isabel for pre-dinner drinks in the Keller Bar of the Officers' Mess. Squadron Leader Bill Welch and his wife Marion also joined them. Bill was CO of Tommy's squadron but had been off base that afternoon. Introductions were made and a short time into the conversation, at a level which could not be overheard beyond their circle, Bill said to David:

'I heard you had to tear a strip off Tommy Butler again!'

'Yes, he really is the limit. He will *not* abide by the rules – performing stunts at the drop of a hat. I really don't know what gets into him. It's as if he's constantly trying to prove something.'

'I know, and of all people he doesn't need to prove anything – he's a brilliant pilot.'

'Not only that; he's very good-looking into the bargain. Has it all: blond hair, blue eyes, tall and broad-shouldered.' Jenny laughed. 'The girls are almost scratching each other's eyes out over him.'

Chuck and Liz had been listening to this exchange with some astonishment.

'Sorry to butt in but is this Tommy Butler by any chance Irish?'

'Yes, he is,' answered Bill. 'Although he's very cagey about telling anything about himself or his background, except for the fact that he is Irish and comes from Dublin.'

'That's true,' agreed Jenny. 'We all do understand that Southern Irish members of the British Forces have to keep a very low profile back at home. Maybe some of them feel a need to be cagey about their background when they're over here too, but he seems to carry this to an extreme.'

'I agree,' said Marion, 'He's open enough about the fact that he's

3

an orphan, but I find it very hard to believe his parents were tinkers. I can't swallow the idea that someone so obviously highly educated could be from a background like that, but he's quite insistent about it and, well, I suppose you just never know!'

'Absolutely. But there's something else. He puts on that Irish accent but when he's caught off guard he has almost no accent at all.'

'Some people are fooled though, Jenny. Last year Nicola Morton fell hard for him and it looked as if things were getting quite serious between them. The Mortons were so worried that Nicola would end up marrying him that they sent her off to Finishing School in Switzerland to split them up. They were concerned that there might be some truth in the tinker story and couldn't bear the thought of their only daughter marrying a poverty-stricken young man from such a background. I suppose you can see their point. If he left the RAF he might want to go back to Ireland and move in with his relatives. Aren't tinkers very clannish?'

By now Chuck and Liz Wilson were laughing so much they could hardly speak.

'One more question about this Tommy Butler. Is he by any chance a good oarsman?'

'Brilliant! He's a member of several RAF teams, and always rows in the various competitions – gets leave to do this wherever he is. He takes himself off to practise whenever he gets the chance. He says his home in Dublin is near a river and he was sometimes able to potter around in boats as a child. That doesn't fit the tinker story either!'

David Shelly smiled and Bill Welch chipped in.

'In spite of the fact that he behaves like an ill-disciplined brat at times, he's quite an asset to the squadron – he's good at other sports too. I just wish he'd stop wanting to break the rules on such a regular basis.'

'Maybe that's just part of being Irish!'

'Now you're stereotyping, David, stop it!' Only his wife would have dared make a comment like that to the Station Commander. 'You must admit though, aside from that cageyness, he's very sociable.'

'Oh yes, good company, highly entertaining and, understandably, popular with the other men, regardless of rank or status. Generous in

4

the Mess too. By all accounts Tommy Butler's no freeloader. But why the questions, Chuck?'

At that point in the conversation Tommy arrived and, on reaching the bottom of the Keller Bar steps, suddenly spotted Chuck and Liz. He stopped in his tracks in complete amazement.

'Good Lord! I don't believe it! I *can't* believe it! Chuck and Liz Wilson – how absolutely amazing! Sir! How? Where? ...' Unusually for him words completely failed him.

Liz, still laughing, although now with genuine pleasure, stepped across to him and gave him a big hug and a kiss, while Chuck gave him a resounding slap on the back. Everyone else looked on in astonishment, but Isabel, aged nineteen, looked at him with undisguised admiration.

'I hope you remember me too, Tommy, because I remember you.'

He looked at her and for a few seconds words again deserted him, for in fine Butler tradition, Tommy fell in love on the spot with this very pretty, and at five foot nothing, petite, daintily-built girl. He recovered his wits quickly, however, and was so glad that a warm greeting would be allowable, for he did remember her as a little girl when the Wilsons had come to Riverside for a visit.

'Of course I remember you, Isabel, and since we're old friends perhaps you'd give me a hug too?'

She blushed but without hesitation reached up to him.

'Now could somebody please explain?' David Shelly was quite bemused. 'How do you come to know each other? How does *Group Captain* Wilson know *Flight Lieutenant* Butler on, what are obviously, quite intimate terms? Christian names no less, though clearly you're not related!'

Tommy turned to Chuck in some agitation.

'Oh, Sir, you're not going to blow my cover are you?'

'I can't imagine why you want to be secretive about your family. And really, Tommy, tinkers! That's going a bit far! Whatever would Milo think?'

'Milo? Milo Butler? You're related to the famous Milo Butler?' David couldn't believe his ears. 'The name Butler is not that uncommon, so it never occurred to me and you carefully kept it under wraps – threw sand in all our eyes.'

Tommy flushed, in fact he felt he was blushing all over. He had so carefully kept his secret because he desperately wanted to make his own way: to have his successes on the strength of his own skill and merits. However, the secret was out now and so be it – it was bound to happen some day, might as well be now.

Tommy *had* made it on his own. Since the age of about six years old he had been determined to follow in his brother's footsteps and join the RAF, and it didn't make the slightest difference that Milo's had been a wartime-only commitment. He had got through his Cranwell training without a hitch and had passed out top of his group. Later, the icing on the cake, he had been selected to fly with the Black Arrows for a short time before they disbanded in 1961, then was sent to his current posting in Germany. Milo, or Lo as he had called him since he first started talking, was very proud of his achievements and he and Noola with her mother, Maggie, had come to his "passing out" parade, but other than that he had carefully kept his two lives completely separate and for more than one reason. There were other aspects of his private life that he definitely didn't want anybody here to know about.

'Sir, I desperately didn't want to take advantage of Milo's reputation and record – succeed on my brother's coat-tails.'

By now everyone else in the bar had stopped their conversations and all were listening with fascination. The Group Captain was delighted. This explained so much about Tommy.

'So he's actually your brother, but quite a lot older obviously. Well, well, well!'

He turned to the assembled company.

'For those of you who may not know the story, Milo Butler, with his navigator and friend Joe Malloy, was shot down while on escort duty on D-Day and the two of them, Joe with a bullet in his leg, rowed all the way home to Ireland in their dinghy. It was an extraordinary feat of endurance for which they were both decorated. Mind you, the fact that they arrived in Ireland was, by all accounts, sheer chance, but nevertheless, quite remarkable. What's more they were members of the same squadron and close friends of Group Captain Wilson. Right, Chuck?'

'Yes, indeed. You can all imagine the excitement when news

6

came through about what they'd done and that they were safely home, not to mention the celebrations we had when they got back to the squadron!'

There was a split second's silence and then a great outburst of excited voices exploded through the bar. At first all Tommy wanted to do was sink into the floor with embarrassment but then he became infected by the general reaction of everyone and started to relax and get carried along on the wave of surprise and delight. Always so proud of his much older half-brother, whom he had hero-worshipped from the time he was a very small child, he now revelled in this huge outpouring of appreciation. To his surprise he didn't at all mind the sense of reflected glory, but tried to answer the bombardment of questions as fascinated friends swarmed around him.

In the middle of all this the Mess Manager arrived down and made his way through the crowd to Tommy. Hans Viberg was apologetic.

'Sorry, Sir, but there's a message for you. I wouldn't have intruded but it seems to be important!'

He handed Tommy a slip of paper which read:

Call this number soonest. Very urgent. Lo. A Dublin phone number was given, one that he didn't recognize.

Tommy was shaken. Something must be horribly wrong for Lo to send such a message. He made his way to where the Group Captain stood with Chuck.

'Please excuse me, Sir, I must go and make an urgent phone call.'

'Something wrong, Tommy?'

'There must be. I've just been given this message.' He handed the slip to David who read it and handed it to Chuck.

'Anything I can do to help, Tommy?' Chuck had seen how some of the colour had drained out of the young man's face.

'Thanks, but I won't know 'til I've spoken to Lo.'

He left to make the call and David said to Chuck:

'I hope it's nothing really bad. In spite of his kicking over the traces so often, I've always liked the boy and now I understand so much more about him. I've never believed that he grew up in a tinker's caravan on the banks of some river, but the information on

7

his documents tells little more than things like address in Ireland. Well "Riverside" could mean anything.'

'I know, and next of kin would be recorded as Miles, not Milo, which wouldn't have rung any bells for you. Same address too.'

'Well what's his home background like then? Do you feel free to tell us?'

Chuck started to laugh again.

'Oh I think it's perfectly in order to tell you – it's certainly no dark secret! The Butler family is one of the wealthiest living in and around Dublin, including Tommy, who is a rich young man in his own right. His father left him very comfortably off. His home, Riverside *House*, is set in extensive grounds which run down to the banks of the River Liffey. As a result, for generations the Butlers have been superb oarsmen and very skilled at other water sports too. The lovely old Georgian house has one wing divided off and this legally belongs to Tommy. Their father died just after the end of the war so Milo, married to Finoula or "Noola", is now head of the family.'

'Well I'll be damned! Did you hear all that, Jenny?'

'Yes, I certainly did and just wait 'til I get my hands on him. I'll wring his neck! But I'm mean enough to have to smile thinking of the Mortons' reaction when they hear all that. Poverty-stricken tinker indeed – and let him ever dare use that fake accent again!'

* * * * *

It took some time for Tommy to get through and when he did he was appalled. Milo answered the phone and, quite uncharacteristically, was barely coherent.

'They've taken her, Tommy, they've taken her and we don't know who they are or where they've gone.'

'Lo, who have they taken and who are "they"?'

'Please can you come home at once, Tommy, we need you here. They've taken her . . . and we know for sure Bob is involved in it somehow.'

'Lo, you're making no sense. You're obviously terribly upset. Please let me speak to Noola or Maggie.'

It occurred to him that whatever was wrong Noola must be

8

equally distraught – unless, of course, it was Noola who had been "taken". Maggie came on the line.

'Hello, Tommy darlin'.'

'Maggie, thank goodness, *please* tell me what's happened. I've never in my life heard Lo in such a state.'

'There's no way I can break this to you easily, darlin', but little Izzy has been kidnapped and it seems that your Uncle Bob is somehow involved.'

'Oh not little Izzy! Please, God, not gentle little Izzy.'

'Yes, darlin', now you understand poor Milo's distress.'

'Of course I do, but *Uncle Bob* involved? He's in an asylum, Maggie, how could that possibly be?'

'Well he escaped and must have had very professional help to manage it. Turned up here with several others, all armed, and took Izzy, in the process badly injuring your Aunt May who tried to protect her.'

'Oh poor Aunt May. Is she going to be all right?'

'We think so. She's been taken to hospital to be patched up.'

'But what on earth is it all about? Who's taken Izzy and why? I suppose it must be for ransom, but who would want to extort money from us? Oh . . . wait! I've suddenly realized who it could be. They're becoming quite active again and always looking for funds – large funds.'

'We must be careful what we say on the phone, but we've not been contacted yet. We're waiting!'

'Okay, Maggie, I understand – we're always being warned that the civilian lines here aren't necessarily secure. I get the picture and that's enough. I'll speak to my "boss" and with any luck should be home tomorrow. Let me have a word with Lo before I hang up.'

'Tommy?'

'Yes, Lo, I'm almost certain I'll get there tomorrow. Chuck Wilson's here on a visit and you know he'll do everything in his power to help in any way possible.'

'Thank God. Give Chuck my best and, if I know when you're arriving, I'll be at the airport to meet you.' He sounded so relieved.

'Thanks and, Lo, we'll get her back – somehow or another we'll get her back – promise.'

9

'God Bless! 'Bye, Tommy.'

Thank goodness they all had Maggie, he thought. Dear, dependable Maggie, adored by the whole family. She had been both Milo's and Tommy's substitute mother when each in turn had been orphaned. Now in her late sixties, she was still as feisty and active as ever. Tommy's thoughts and feelings were in turmoil. He prayed to God that they would get Izzy back alive. He certainly hadn't expected such frightening news.

Chapter 2

When Tommy got back to the Keller Bar he went straight to where the Group Captain, Bill Welch and Chuck were chatting. He addressed the Group Captain.

'Sir, could I please have a word with you in private, and Bill too?'

David Shelly looked at the face now drained of all colour.

'I'll ask Hans if we can use his office, Tommy. Would you like Chuck to come along too?'

'That would be great, if you don't mind, Chuck – er, Sir!'

'Only too happy to help if I can and, Tommy, when we're off duty and out of uniform it's quite all right to call me Chuck. We *are* old friends.'

'Thanks, that means a lot at this moment. Lo sends his best.'

In the small office Tommy then told these three senior officers the story so far as he knew it. David Shelly responded with horror.

'How absolutely appalling! Let's do what we can to help. We'll get you out to the UK as early as possible tomorrow morning, then I'll make sure transport is arranged to take you to Heathrow. From there you can get a civilian flight to Dublin, which is the way I imagine you travel when going on leave. Who do you think is behind this, Tommy?'

'It could be some faction of the IRA. As you know, Sir, they're becoming quite active, skirmishing along the border again. On the other hand, I suppose it could be some other group wanting to make a fast buck, jumping on their bandwagon and letting them take the blame – that's not unknown. But it's hard to say for certain. They've obviously been given some secure number to use at home, one I don't recognize, but nevertheless we've to be *so* careful what we say on the phone. *I* wasn't using a secure line.'

11

'Of course!' David Shelly paused for a few seconds then continued. 'You know, Tommy, we've people based in Northern Ireland who are part of a highly-trained team and very adept at dealing with this sort of situation. I've connections I could use to alert them and have a couple of them diverted to slip over the border and help your family. Obviously they would be completely undercover and I'm wondering what would be the best way to play this so that they don't aggravate the situation. Even when, as we hope, the whole thing is successfully dealt with, it must remain absolutely confidential between you and Milo and, gentlemen, regard this as strictly classified information. For everyone's sake there's no way their involvement must be betrayed. Would that help?'

'It would be marvellous, Sir, but I'd have to get my brother's agreement, although I can't see him objecting to anything that's going to help us to find Izzy. But if they come to stay at the house, which I think is maybe what you had in mind, won't they stick out like sore thumbs?'

'Oh I think they'll see to that – they're used to having to blend into the background. If Milo goes along with the idea the two of you could probably work out some sort of cover story that would stop anyone getting suspicious.'

'Could work, Sir. But what about the Irish authorities: police, army? How would they react if they suspected anything? Milo's wife Noola has a cousin who is very senior in the Garda, the Irish police that is, and she and Milo are bound to want to involve him.'

'You'd be surprised how closely we liaise sometimes with the Irish authorities, quite off the record. Could work very well indeed.'

'This is pretty horrible for you in so many ways, Tommy. Not only has your beloved Izzy been put at serious risk, but your Uncle Bob involved! What a rotten deal.'

'Oh, Chuck, Uncle Bob is such an embarrassment.' Looking at the other two men he explained, 'He's quite crazy and in an asylum: has murdered members of the family, including my *mother*, and is quite capable of doing so again, even a child. That's what's so terrifying in this situation.' Looking at Chuck he added. 'I tell you I never mention anything about *him*. And something else – maybe I could go the same way!'

12

David Shelly understood, more and more, Tommy's reticence in talking about his family and his risk-taking. Did he subconsciously *want* to kill himself off, solve his problem once and for all? Surely not, but maybe without even realizing it?

'Don't worry, Tommy, *we* certainly aren't going to chatter about it.'

'Thank you, Sir.'

They continued to discuss the ways and means, slightly changing some of the ideas as they went along. Eventually Chuck said to him:

'You'll want to go off and pack I know, but come on down and have a drink with us before you go. Liz and Isabel would be so disappointed not to have a chance to say goodbye.' His eyes twinkled. 'I have a feeling that Isabel would be especially cut up if you went off without saying goodbye to her!'

With his fair skin, much to his irritation, Tommy flushed easily. Now some colour came back into his face and he did manage a small but typical Butler lopsided grin.

'I wouldn't want to go without seeing her either. Oh and Liz too, of course!'

'Of *course*, Tommy!' The twinkle grew to a broad grin. He'd seen the young man's face when he looked at Isabel.

They went back downstairs and David insisted on getting a brandy for Tommy.

'Don't argue, boy, just drink it.'

'Thank you, Sir.'

'Is everything all right, Tommy?'

'No, Liz, it's not but, I'm sorry, I can't talk about it here. Chuck will give you the details. I've got to go home though, as soon as possible. It's too late to get all the way this evening, so I'll wait until first thing in the morning. With any luck I'll be there around lunch time and Lo will meet me. He and Noola would want me to give you their love.'

Isabel was listening closely, hardly able to take her eyes off him.

'I'm sorry you've to go so soon, Tommy, when we've only just met again.'

'So am I, but I could write to you. Will you write back?'

13

'Oh yes, and maybe you'd come out to Cyprus to have a holiday with us? Would that be all right, Mum?'

'Now do I really have to answer that? Come out any time you like, Tommy.'

'I'd love to, thank you. Who knows, some day I might get a posting there. I've never been and, by all accounts, it's a beautiful island.'

'Hey, wouldn't that be fun? The rest of your family could come for a visit too.'

'Thanks, Liz.'

Chuck raised an eyebrow at David who gave an almost imperceptible nod.

Chapter 3

Earlier that day, after weeks of miserable weather, the sun had come out and the temperature had risen across the whole of the east coast area of Ireland, with the forecasters predicting the fine weather would last at least a week. It was a Thursday and, regardless of what the weather conditions had been, this was the day that The Champions of Justice had planned to snatch Izzy. However, the warm weather played right into their hands. It meant getting into Riverside would be relatively easy, since doors and windows were likely to be open.

It was the schools' and universities' holiday period. They knew from their informant that Milo would be in his office in the city. His children, Mageen and the twin boys, would be there with him, earning holiday money and learning the stockbroking business, the company having been owned by the Butler family for several generations. They also knew that Mageen's devoted boyfriend and fellow student, Freddie, who spent a lot of time at Riverside in term-time, wouldn't be around. Apparently he had gone home to England for the summer vac.

Younger than the other three, Sarah and her Flynn cousins, with at least one adult keeping an eye on them, would be some distance from the house, pottering around, enjoying some of the water sports so beloved of them all. This was a certainty, for, during the holidays, short of a cloud burst or violent storm, apart from Izzy, the family remaining at home on any day would be down by the river. Here different kinds of boats were kept in a neat boathouse and a dock had been built extending out into the water, facilitating use of the river for a variety of pursuits.

15

Although thoroughly competent in that area, water sports were not Izzy's first choice of leisure pursuit. By preference, she would, without any doubt, be in the large sitting room, playing the Steinway baby grand piano, which, on discovering her talent, her parents had bought for her. House staff should not present a problem. Most should be either in the kitchen area or upstairs cleaning the bedrooms, that being the well-established routine.

The kidnappers knew that they were taking a lot for granted and it was a big gamble that it would work out exactly as planned, but, as it happened, their calculations were absolutely spot on. Their information had been accurate to the smallest detail.

The plan for Bob's escape, like all the best plans, was simple. One of the ancillary staff in the asylum had been vulnerable to a bribe. After breakfast the inmates were usually allowed some supervised recreation, if possible outside. Rory was responsible for the final check that all the relevant doors were locked once the prisoners were back in their cells. It was, therefore, easy for him to unlock Bob's door at this time.

Bob had been agitated since early morning and couldn't wait for his opportunity to slip away. His recent dose of medication would last for some time, so he was still lucid and, in spite of his impatience to be free, he managed to remain controlled enough not to rush out of the door as soon as he heard the key turn in the lock. It had been impressed upon him by Rory that he *must* wait for the signal.

Suddenly from the main reception area came the sound of a fire alarm. Rory, by the simple means of a live cigarette butt and some volatile cleaning fluid, had managed to start a fire in a closet where cleaning materials were stored. This was tucked well away from the main hub of the building and so the fire was not spotted until it had taken a firm hold. Since Bob's block was set quite far from the affected area there was no need to evacuate his part of the asylum, this a policy approved long ago by the fire service and with which Rory was quite familiar. While the usual chaos ensued, with all the associated emergency organisations involved, nobody noticed Bob creeping away around the back area of the complex, wearing a well-worn mackintosh provided by Rory. Neither did anyone spot Rory slipping back to lock the cell door, having ensured Bob had used the

16

almost childish ruse of putting pillows in the bed to look as if there was someone there. It would be some hours before any detailed check would be made and his escape discovered.

Bob followed Rory's instructions to the letter:

'Whatever you do when you get out of the building *don't run.* That will only attract attention. Try to stroll along quite casually and, with that grubby old mack, in the distance you could just pass for one of the gardeners.'

'*Yes*, Rory! You've told me so many times – I've got the message!'

'Fine, but don't let yourself be panicked into rushing things.'

Frequently glancing back over his shoulder, Bob made for the wooded area on the periphery of the asylum. The temptation to run was so strong but he walked as casually as possible, every nerve in his body taut with apprehension. He relaxed slightly when he reached the sheltering trees, then ran until he eventually emerged at the high perimeter wall, topped with rows of barbed wire and shards of glass fixed in a covering of cement. He made his way along this until he came to a side entrance. He had to wait, shielded by the trees, until the two guards there were preoccupied with the excitement of the fire. The moment eventually came when they had their backs turned and curiosity had taken them away from the immediate area of the entrance, so they didn't notice Bob slip through the gates and start towards the main road as instructed. Again there was great temptation to run but he resisted, even when someone called after him from the gates. Turning slightly, he simply raised his hand in a casual wave, and continued walking, so identification was highly unlikely. However, anticipating further challenge, the hairs on his scalp rose and he bit his lip so hard it started to bleed. The challenge never came.

As he approached a side lane a rather shabby-looking van, with false number plates, emerged and came to a stop beside him, and he was bundled into the back. Contrary to its appearance, the van had a high-powered engine and was designed to make a remarkably speedy getaway. There were three others in the van, plus a driver.

Not wishing to draw unwanted attention to themselves, they drove at a sedate pace along the road towards Riverside House and parked outside the estate. The other three in the van addressed each

17

other as Willie, Eddie, and Mac. Eddie was a doctor and had come along to drug the little girl and make the kidnapping as easy and soundless as possible. All three were armed and, including Bob, had donned balaclavas.

'Why can't I have a gun too? I should be armed like the rest of you,' Bob complained angrily.

'Ah would you shut your gob! There's no way we're going to arm you. Just be grateful that we've got you out of that place.'

Only a fool would argue with mighty Mac. He was a big man who looked like a prizefighter. They parked outside the estate entrance.

'Now, Shamus, remember, once we're out of sight, drive *slowly* down that long drive and swing right around to face outwards again. Keep the engine running and, if challenged, pretend you've come to the wrong address to deliver a parcel.'

'Yes *yes*, Mac, you've told me *so* often. I don't need to have it rammed down me throat over and over.'

'Just get it right!' Shamus didn't miss the threat in the voice.

Bob, still lucid for the moment, showed them how to skirt around the east side of the house, through a copse of trees, and so avoid being observed by the grounds staff. As anticipated, they could see, even from some distance, that many of the windows were open. He knew exactly how to get to the terrace behind the house and locate the sitting room. They could hear the piano well before they reached the room and, as quite accurately predicted, the French doors had been opened wide, giving clear and easy access. Jackpot! thought Mac. They crept along, and, at Mac's signal, crouched down behind some potted palms. He crawled along and eased his head around the open door.

Izzy was playing away contentedly, totally absorbed in her music. She made an attractive picture, with her wonderful, strawberry-blond hair, hazel eyes and a skin that was almost transparent. Unlike the other Butlers, who were in rude health, she contracted infections easily and suffered from dermatitis, which broke out whenever she was in any way distressed. All this took its toll and she actually looked really fragile, in fact quite fairy-like, with an almost ethereal aura. She was the darling of the whole family, and

18

they all watched over her fiercely, at times giving the almost tangible impression of spreading protective wings around her. On this occasion it was Aunt May who was watching over her, sitting reading her newspaper, more than happy to keep Izzy company and be on hand should this vulnerable child need help of any kind. They were quite unaware that someone was spying on them.

Mac saw the child and noted her fragility with satisfaction rather than compassion. He was relieved that she, at least, would not be capable of putting up any sort of resistance, although the old woman could be a different proposition. He crept back down the terrace and whispered his instructions.

'Willie, run across and open the door to the hall so we can get out of the front entrance quickly. Eddie, grab the child and give her the sedative. I'll take care of the old woman and, Bob, just stay out of the way, you've done your bit. Then all head for the van as fast as you can. Remember, *no shooting* unless absolutely essential. We don't want to attract attention and at this stage we're not trying to kill anyone!'

However, the effect of his medication was beginning to wear off and Bob's return to Riverside triggered all the old feelings of hatred. He was sure Tom was in there and no way he was going to stay out of things, no way he was going to miss this chance. As the other three rushed into the room he tore off the balaclava and went in after them. Eddie reached Izzy who screamed but the sound was abruptly cut off as he put his hand over her mouth. He jabbed the needle into her and the powerful drug flew through her delicate little body. She collapsed and Eddie threw her over his shoulder and headed for the door, now conveniently opened by Willie. May had jumped to her feet and hurled herself at Eddie, in an attempt to protect Izzy, but Mac intercepted her and hit her hard on the jaw, knocking her out cold. However, just before the blow landed, she had caught sight of Bob. Mac hurried after the others to the front entrance door and suddenly realized Bob wasn't with him. Running back into the room he was just in time to see him stooping over May, with his hands around her throat, trying to strangle her.

'I'll get one of you, I'll get one of you. If Tom isn't here you'll do. I remember you, you old bitch: you're another bloody Butler!'

19

Mac drew his gun and grabbed Bob by the scruff of the neck.

'If I have to use this on you I will. Now get out as fast as you can.'

The sight of the gun did sober Bob and, cursing Mac, he slunk ahead of him across the hall and out into the van, where Shamus was revving the engine impatiently.

They got away without anyone seeing them. In the huge house Izzy's scream hadn't been heard and it hadn't carried down to the riverbank. May lay on the floor until, a short time later, Kitty, the cook-housekeeper, came along to tell her and Izzy that lunch was ready. Kitty stood rooted to the spot for a few seconds as the implications of what she was looking at hit her: no Izzy, piano stool knocked over, music scattered about and May, unconscious on the floor, with a badly swollen jaw and dreadful marks on her throat.

'Oh, Holy Mother, no! Please, God, no! Mrs Burke, wake up, wake up.'

But Kitty couldn't rouse May and so, fear lending her feet a rare turn of speed, she ran down to the river, where Noola and Maggie were sitting watching the children and enjoying the sunny weather. Trying hard not to panic, as soon as she was within shouting distance she couldn't help screaming to them.

'Quickly, come quickly – Izzy's gone and Mrs Burke's badly injured. Hurry, hurry.'

Noola and Maggie leapt to their feet.

'Everyone up to the house – *now!*'

Nobody argued, for they had all heard and were very frightened. They dropped everything and ran, followed by the two women, who felt sick but both were level-headed. In spite of the overwhelming fear that gripped them, they managed to stay in control, realizing how vital this was for everybody else. Maggie called to Kitty as they ran, heading towards the scene of disaster:

'Kitty, take the children to the kitchen. Get someone to find Mickeen and tell him to take some men with him and search the house thoroughly and I don't care what they arm themselves with!'

She knew it was important not to upset the children any more than absolutely necessary, and seeing May injured and unconscious, with Izzy gone, would be horrifying. Noola, she realized, must be in a state of severe shock and she felt she had to take over. She was quite right. Noola was frozen with fear, but the two of them had to get to the sitting room at once.

* * * * *

Noola made a frantic call to Milo. He was out of the office so it was some time before he got her message and called back. He listened to her story, told through floods of tears, and went cold all over. He found it hard to speak.

'Dear God! Our little Izzy! Oh, Noola, what are we going to do? Who has taken her and why? Have you any clue?'

'None at all, Milo, it makes no sense.' Her voice was reaching hysteria pitch. 'Just get here as fast as you can. Bring Mageen and the boys with you. Don't say why in the hearing of anyone else. No police and no press.'

'I'm on my way.'

Before they arrived back at Riverside, Sean Flynn, a Senior Inspector in the Garda detective section, or Special Branch, had set up an Operations Room in the library and had called in one of his very competent junior officers to help him. While waiting for Milo's return call, Maggie had contacted him, addressing him only by his first name. He was her nephew and cousin to Noola. When she told him what had happened there was a moment's silence before he responded.

'All right, Maggie. I'll be there very shortly. Meantime keep this within the household. Explain to everyone no police and no publicity. Spreading the story could be fatal for Izzy.'

Maggie, always quick on the uptake, got the message and passed it on to Noola.

Realising that Milo was badly shaken, Mageen, although devastated at the news herself, had insisted on driving home. It was something of a hair-raising ride for them all. The car screeched to a stop outside the front door and Milo was out and running before it had halted. The others had seen the car careering down the drive and Noola tore out and hurled herself into his arms.

21

'Milo, Milo, what are we going to do? Izzy, Milo, Izzy! Why, Why?'

'Darling, I don't know, but for the others' sake we must try to keep an outward appearance of calm.' He didn't sound calm.

Hard on their heels Paddy arrived also driving very fast. Dr Paddy Flynn, Noola's brother, had also been summoned earlier by his mother, Maggie. He had tried to offer support to everyone and had attended to Aunt May as best he could. Then he insisted on taking her to hospital, on Sean's instructions giving a plausible story to explain her injuries. Once satisfied that she was settled as comfortably as possible he had rushed back to the house, but not before she had recovered her voice enough to tell him that Bob had been there.

'What? Bob Featherstone? You're kidding.'

May's throat was so sore she was hardly able to croak.

'Saw him – three others.'

Paddy wondered if she was suffering from concussion and had imagined it, but when he called the asylum they confirmed the story.

'He's disappeared all right, Doctor. The whole place is in uproar. Garda everywhere.'

Now he ran straight across to Milo and Noola.

'I'm so sorry, Milo. You know I'll do anything that I possibly can to help the family, but,' he dropped his voice, 'I've got some more worrying news for the two of you. Yours and Sean's ears only.'

'Sean? Sean Flynn?'

'Yes. Ma sent for him straight away, careful not to mention his job – we feel the phone line may not be safe.'

'Thank heavens he's here!'

Milo, Noola and Paddy hurried into the library.

'I've an update for you all. Bob Featherstone was here with the men who snatched Izzy. The asylum has confirmed that he's escaped. I'm certain he's the one who tried to strangle Mrs Burke. I reckon he wanted to finish her off but one of the others must have dragged him away.'

'Oh my God!' Milo's voice grew even more agitated. 'We were warned years ago that if he ever escaped this would probably be the first place he'd head for.'

22

'But he couldn't have done it all on his own.'

'That's right, Sean,' answered Paddy. 'Mrs Burke said there were three others. It's surprising she's able to remember so clearly, given she was knocked out and at her age. A remarkable lady!'

'She's obviously a tough old bird – sorry, Milo.'

'You're right. She's a Butler! On the whole we're a tough lot, except for our poor little Izzy.'

'In the circumstances you should phone Tommy.'

'I intend to, Noola. I want him here with us at a time like this and I know darned well he'll want to be here too. Poor Tommy – he'll be appalled at his uncle's involvement in this.'

'No calling anyone until I've set up a separate and secure line for you. I'd say this was a very well-planned crime and your phone here may have been tapped. I'm already working on it. But in any case, the main line needs to be kept free in case they call.'

'I'm glad you're here, Sean. I wouldn't have thought of that.'

'Why would you in your upset state? It's all part of my job.'

Milo managed a bleak smile at him. Sean was so like Paddy that they could have been brothers rather than cousins. Paddy and Milo had been close friends since childhood and Sean had the same red hair and hazel eyes, with the same square, dependable look about him, that engendered trust even before he spoke.

It took time to get it all done. As the day wore on and there was no word, Milo and Noola became more and more distressed and agitated, as did the rest of the family. They wandered around the house unable to settle to anything and never far from the library. Kitty tried her best to persuade them to eat something but none of them, not even the invariably ravenously hungry boys, could touch a thing, except for gallons of tea and coffee. The staff responded magnificently and closed ranks around the family.

Quite soon after Sean arrived he had gathered everyone together and spoken to them.

'It is vitally important that nobody here today talks about what has happened and especially don't tell that the Garda are already involved. It could put Izzy's life in grave danger. Maggie, it was clever of you to call me only by my Christian name when you rang for help and you gave nothing away. I want you all to rack your

23

brains for anything that's happened over the past few weeks that maybe didn't strike you as odd at the time, but now makes you wonder. Anything at all, however small, might be significant.'

Mickeen, estate manager and married to Kitty, responded quickly.

'There was that strange man who came a couple of weeks ago looking for casual work. Looked like a down-and-out, a poor ould fella, so I gave him a bit of tidying up to do outside. Felt sorry for him.'

'Thanks, Mickeen. That's the kind of thing! Can anyone else give us information about him?'

'Well I thought he was a bit inquisitive,' added Kitty. 'Whenever he came into the kitchen for a cup of tea or bite to eat he'd ask all sorts of questions. But I felt sorry for him too. He had a bit of a stammer and I thought maybe he was lonely so I didn't take much notice at the time but now...? I just wonder.'

'Give us anything you can remember about him.'

So Kitty and Mickeen gave every little detail they could remember and built up quite an effective picture of this character.

'Thank you both. I'm certain this fellow is their informer. He was no down-and-out. Just a well-disguised spy.'

Sean used his influence to get the secure line installed by the evening. Milo was peppering to call Tommy but before he made the call Sean warned him:

'Be careful now! Our line here is secure but Tommy's won't be. Don't forget he's got to be careful too, not just because of the situation here but because he's a member of the British Forces. You know how that's viewed in some circles here.'

'Thanks, Sean.'

Milo, with Noola and Maggie close by, made the connection and left his cryptic message. After Tommy's return call and promise to get home so quickly Milo seemed fractionally less agitated.

Sean now gave some strict rules for the next few days or until all had been sorted out.

'Mageen, Bill and Harry, it would be wise for you to go to the office, as usual, tomorrow and try to keep as calm as possible. I know how difficult it will be but it's up to you now not to give the game away. So far as the office staff are concerned, your dad has an upset stomach and won't be in for a couple of days. He wouldn't be able to avoid showing how upset he is and at the moment he looks really rough – even more so than you three.'

'Actually since tomorrow's Friday there's no reason why you shouldn't come home a bit early.'

'Thanks, Dad, we've sometimes done that so it shouldn't raise any questions.'

'But whatever you do make sure you stay together – safety in numbers! Go straight to the office and straight home again.'

'Oh, Uncle Sean!'

'I know, Mageen, I know! You won't be able to see them, I hope, but by now there's a very efficient team of my men hiding around the estate. They're to protect you all. If they've tapped your phone, then so have my people and we might be able to trace any calls from them. On the other hand they've probably thought of that, so it'll be very interesting.'

'We owe you, Sean.'

'Just doing my job, Milo, although this time there's a very personal interest in it. Whoever they are they deserve to be strung up for treating a frail little child like that. And they knew exactly what they were doing, hitting on the most vulnerable person in the family!'

'What I don't understand is that they haven't contacted us yet, telling us their demands. It's driving me mad.'

'That's all part of their strategy, Milo. It's a softening up ploy. They leave people until their nerves are in shreds, then, when people have reached the point of being willing to give them *anything*, they make their demands.'

'We'd have given them anything anyhow, without the wait. It's tearing us apart thinking about what Izzy might be going through – the one of us least equipped to cope with something so traumatic.'

As so often happens where children are concerned, they all dramatically underestimated Izzy, quite overlooking the fact that she too was a Butler. The abductors, in turn, seriously underestimated the dogged determination of Sean and his men.

Chapter 4

Having left Riverside at high speed, the decrepit-looking van slowed so as not to attract undue attention. It made its way at a sedate pace towards the mountain range that forms a picturesque backdrop to Dublin City and continues southwards for many miles to County Wicklow and beyond. The kidnappers had planned meticulously, trying to make sure that nothing was left to chance. The terrain lent itself well to a rapid exit from the built-up area. The numbers of dwellings thinned and then disappeared almost completely as they drove uphill, so there was minimal chance of their presence being readily detected in the quite extensive wilder parts of the region.

Their hideaway had been prepared well in advance. Some months earlier they had found and bought a tumbledown cottage, tucked into the side of a remote valley, saying they wanted to do it up for weekends for the family. It was ideally placed, approached only by a very rough track, barely accessible by a vehicle. Making sure they were not observed, they had prepared the cottage for their scheme. They had done some basic renovations, such as would be expected of anyone creating a weekend getaway for a family. At the same time they had surreptitiously dug a cellar, removing the earth in small quantities at a time. The entrance to this was from above. A trapdoor opened up into one end of the living room of the cottage and the opening could easily be camouflaged by having an armchair pulled over it.

Izzy still seemed to be heavily drugged when they reached the cottage and she was carried down into the cellar where Mac laid her on a truckle bed. Although a fully committed participant in the abduction, as he looked down at her, so pale and fragile, a remaining

26

spark of decency gave him a fleeting twinge of conscience which he quickly stifled.

In fact Izzy wasn't unconscious. Taking her age into account and knowing she was delicate, Eddie, afraid of overdoing it, had given her a very light dose of the sedative, enough, he thought, merely to silence her while they removed her from the house. She had come to a while before they bumped along the track to the cottage. Although quite muzzy she remembered almost immediately what had happened and the plucky child stifled her first instinct to scream for her mother. She decided that she could gain most from pretending she was still unconscious and listening to what was said, picking up as much information as possible. So she didn't move and when she was eventually lifted out of the van remained limp and kept her eyes closed. Mac shouted up through the trapdoor to the room above.

'Eddie, would you come down here and have a look at the kid?'

No answer. Eddie obviously hadn't heard him, so he went back up the ladder, leaving the trapdoor open. Izzy could hear his heavy footsteps crossing the floor and then silence. Making as little noise as possible, she climbed up the steps and cautiously popped her head through the opening.

* * * * *

On Friday morning Tommy made an early getaway and arrived at Dublin's Collinstown Airport in the late afternoon. He had decided that he would take a taxi from there rather than call Milo, which was just as well because Sean Flynn was not keen on the idea of anyone leaving the house. He arrived to find a totally freaked-out family, with an almost equally upset staff.

Tommy had asked the taxi driver to drop him off at the top of the long drive, unsure of the reaction a strange car would get under the circumstances. It was Mageen who suddenly spotted him heading for the house at a run.

'Dad, Dad, it's Tommy. He's here – coming down the drive.'

Milo flung open the door and ran to meet him. Tommy dropped his bag and the brothers gave each other a powerful embrace. Words

27

were unnecessary. Mageen, regarding Tommy more as brother than uncle, and devoted to him since a tiny child, was hard on Milo's heels and hurled herself into his arms.

'Hello, gorgeous.'

'Oh, Tommy, it's so good to see you.'

Milo looked absolutely haggard and the deep shadows under his eyes told that he had not slept since Izzy had been snatched.

'I can't tell you how glad we all are you've come home.'

'No happier than I am, Lo, but what dreadful circumstances! What's the latest?'

'No word from anyone yet. We still don't know who they are or what they're after – except that we're certain they want money. It's so hard on everyone's nerves.'

'Well your security's good and very discreet. I was stopped as I turned into the drive and almost had to produce a passport to convince them I really was a member of the family. They tried to make out they were members of the grounds staff here, looking out for trespassers. One even carried a hoe and the other a rake.'

'Those are Sean's lads – an efficient bunch.'

'I feel dreadful that Uncle Bob is involved.'

'How could anybody attach any blame to you, Tommy? We're pretty sure he was only a pawn in their game anyhow – useful because of his knowledge of Riverside, that's all.'

'But poor Aunt May?'

'Well, yes. It looks as if he tried to finish her off. But again there's no way you could possibly be held responsible. The man's quite mad.'

'I know and that bothers me too. Is it in the blood? It's a very frightening thought.'

'For goodness sake, Tommy, do stop worrying. He's obviously a one-off. You've checked so carefully and told me yourself: as far back as you look there's not the slightest sign of anything of that sort in the Featherstone family. Now, come on inside and see everyone else and we'll bring you right up to date.'

There was little to add to what he already knew but he was impressed with Sean's "operations room" set-up.

'We're just waiting for the phone call now. Sean's pretty certain that's how they'll contact us.'

28

Sean nodded in agreement.

The family spent the evening together, desperately trying not to upset one another by any outward display of their distress. Maggie insisted that they all try to eat something and sitting together around the table helped. They did manage to eat a token meal. They spent the rest of the time wandering around aimlessly, unable to settle to anything and never far away from the library. Like Milo, they all looked haggard from lack of sleep and worry. Having no information whatsoever, their imaginations were running riot, conjuring up the most ghastly pictures as to Izzy's possible fate.

* * * * *

In their mountain hideout, as a priority, the men set up the radio communication system they had been given by "headquarters". They only knew the man running the organization as "Himself". They had been instructed to report to him first thing in the morning and last thing at night, and to keep trying until they made a connection.

Wishing to attract the minimum attention they had not even made any enquiries as to the feasibility of having mains electricity installed, which, although not easy, would have been possible but would have raised much curiosity. They made do with a variety of oil lamps, some candles, a couple of Primus stoves and, lighting a good, big turf fire, they settled in for the evening. They had planned to cook a meal, intending to take a plateful to Izzy in the cellar. When she had popped her head through the trapdoor she had managed to have a quick look around the room above but could see no further before she heard the men returning and had to make a hurried retreat below. They were carrying enough in the way of supplies and equipment to last for several days and it took them some minutes to stow it all away.

She heard one of them coming down the ladder and started to moan, hoping it would sound like someone regaining consciousness. Eddie stooped down beside the truckle bed and spoke to her unexpectedly kindly.

'Are you all right, girleen?'

29

She didn't answer. She had worked out a strategy of behaviour designed to worry them. She kept on moaning. Eddie shook her gently.

'Come on now! I've brought you some food. Try to eat it – it'll help you feel a bit better.'

In spite of her courage, Izzy felt weak and frightened. She started to cry and, hoping it would generate as much sympathy as possible, she took full advantage of it and allowed great sobs to shake her small frame. She was quite right. It really worried Eddie. He sat down on the bed beside her.

'There now, there now. If you eat some of that food it'll help.'

Izzy's stomach had gone into a great knot and the last thing she wanted was food. She just kept up the crying.

'Eddie, will you come up here and leave the brat alone.' Willie sounded irritable.

'She's crying, Willie.'

'So what. I don't give a damn – girls are always crying. Just leave her. She'll shut up soon enough. Tell her if she doesn't behave we'll leave her in the dark. That should bring her to her senses. We need you up here to work this bloody stove.'

'Eat some food, girleen. Keep your strength up. Be good. You heard what he said and he means it.' And Eddie was off up the ladder, leaving an oil lamp for lighting.

'You're not going soft on us, Eddie, are you?'

Eddie heard the threat in Willie's voice.

'No, I'm not, but she's only a little kid and frail with it. Just look at her! It's not her fault that she was the one we decided to snatch. If we're not careful she could become really ill. I don't like the look of her at the moment.'

'Ah give over, Eddie. She's a Butler. I don't give a damn if she does die – that'll be one fewer of them. Leave her to me to look after. I don't mind making her life a complete misery, just like Tom Butler did to me. I just love the idea of the agony of mind he must be going through this minute. I'd leave her in the dark all the time and as far as I'm concerned I wouldn't give her any food, let alone worry if she doesn't actually eat anything.'

'My God, Bob, what a nasty piece of goods you are!' Bad as he

30

was even Willie couldn't go along with that idea. 'I wouldn't do that to an adult that I didn't like, let alone a little kid.'

'Ah you're all soft.' Bob sneered. 'Just leave her to me.'

'Keep away from her or you'll answer to me,' Mac threatened him. 'Aside from every other consideration a dead hostage is no use to anyone. We've got to be able to prove she's still alive so we've got to look after her.'

Izzy had her head as close as possible to the top of the ladder and in the poorly insulated space she could hear some of their conversation. Who was this extremely nasty "Bob"? Why did he hate the Butlers and why did he mention Tom Butler? Her grandpa she supposed – but he was dead. He really frightened her and she hoped he would never be left in charge of her. Bob, on the other hand, was quite determined that he would get his chance to hurt her and as badly as possible. His fingers curled in anticipation of the pleasure he would get from slowly choking the life out of a hated Butler.

31

Chapter 5

On Saturday morning, just as the sun was rising, a car passed the entrance to Riverside. It was nondescript and its number plates were obscured by mud. A brick with something wrapped around it was hurled out, landing on the ground just in front of the firmly closed entrance gates. A member of Sean's alert night patrol team spotted it immediately. Using a large handkerchief from his pocket and careful his hands did not come into direct contact with it, Declan lifted it carefully and took it, at a run, down the drive to the house.

At Milo's insistence, Sean had gone to bed and managed to snatch some sleep. With Tommy staying in support, Milo had kept vigil by the phone and although he had dropped off from time to time, he hadn't had any real rest. Unshaven and with bloodshot eyes sunk into his head, he looked dreadful and felt even worse. The nightmare he had endured when he had been shot down during the war and for nine days trying to row home was nothing compared to this. He had insisted that Noola should take a sleeping pill, arguing that one of them must be fit to keep watch the next day. Now, at long last, there was some communication. He grabbed the brick from the runner while Tommy ran to waken Sean. With supreme self-control he resisted the temptation to tear off the handkerchief and paper attached to it, destroying possible evidence. Declan waited to report directly to Sean and give him every scrap of detail he could about the car.

Sean was on his feet instantly and ran into the library. Milo hastened to reassure him.

'I didn't open it, Sean.'

'Good man! We need to be able to extract every ounce of information from it.'

32

Sean put on rubber gloves. He slowly detached the paper from the brick and opened it up. The note was written on a piece of lined paper, such as could be taken from a school exercise book. It was typewritten and Sean noted that it was articulate and grammatically correct – something he tucked away as significant information.

We know Sean Flynn is there and we know he has the phone line tapped and his men on guard around the grounds, so we will be using other ways to contact you. You should install a radio transmitter / receiver. You were wise not to alert the press and if you do the child will suffer. At the moment she's all right but very upset and finding it difficult to cope. We want a ransom and over the next few days we'll let you know how much and how to deliver. In the meantime you must carry on with your lives as normal and, for the child's sake, you must not give rise to any suspicion that anything's wrong. Keep it to yourselves, Sean and his men, and keep it away from reporters of any kind. If not you'll be sent your girl bit by bit in little pieces. We might even give her to crazy Bob to do as he likes with her.

Sean was almost afraid to read that last bit to Milo and Tommy but knew he couldn't avoid it and Milo's response was predictable and exactly as the kidnappers had planned. He was traumatized and exhausted. He actually broke down in tears and Sean became seriously worried about him. Tommy was devastated too and had blanched at the mention of Bob. He put an arm around Milo, unable to think of anything to say that might bring comfort. He thought maybe it was time to mention the offer of help from over the border. With Sean firmly on the case he hadn't said anything about it so far, but perhaps Sean would welcome help of that kind.

'Lo, Sean, my CO made an offer I decided not to mention unless things became a bit desperate. You seemed to be totally in control of things, Sean, but now we're told they know you're here – I can't imagine how they know but maybe, careful as Maggie was on that first phone call, with the line tapped that's how they found out.'

Tommy went on to explain what had been suggested.

'What do you think?'

Milo was ready to clutch at anything that might help but in spite of his acute distress he recognized the need to be very, very careful.

'I'm willing to try anything that might help us to get Izzy back without her being hurt. What about you, Sean? I wouldn't want to cut across anything you had in mind – you've done a great job so far. If you think it would help I'll go along with it.'

'Just let me think this through carefully. We mustn't let anxiety make us rush our fences.'

He paced backwards and forwards working through the pros and cons in his own mind. Milo and Tommy didn't attempt to influence him, but the possibility of a new and very efficient source of extra help had brought Milo a temporary easing of his distress. He spoke aside quietly to Tommy.

'Your CO is a very decent sort, Tommy. That's an incredible offer.'

'Yes. And Chuck was right in there with him.'

'Good old Chuck!'

Sean eventually stopped his pacing.

'I think we should take advantage of that offer. The lads you're talking about have all sorts of sophisticated tricks that we haven't got access to, you know the usual story, budgets, finance, all that rubbish! I can think of a way of involving them that should arouse no suspicions at all. To have them arrive here as would-be long lost cousins wouldn't work. Something like that's too obvious. The family and house staff would know very well and those fellows out there would see through it too. No! They can come into the city by train mingling with all the other passengers. I'll send someone in plain clothes, very casually dressed, to pick up "a couple of friends" at the station and then they can quietly become members of my force and join me here in that guise. Nobody except us, and my own men, will know they're not what they seem to be. Milo, I suggest you tell Noola only – oh, and Maggie, but strictly no one else.'

'Okay. Thanks Sean. Sounds like a good scheme. I'll use your secure line to call my CO and set the ball rolling. This would be a good time to catch him and get things moving quickly before he goes off for the day.'

The call was made. The wheels were set in motion with impressive speed and the call came back to say two slightly scruffy-looking individuals would slip over the border near Sligo and arrive in Dublin by train that evening, with descriptions added to allow them to be easily recognized.

Milo took a cup of tea to Noola to wake her and put her in the picture and Tommy did likewise for Maggie. The rest of the family and staff were told only the other details given in the note and especially about carrying on as normal. Noola had a hard time not becoming hysterical when told the contents of the note. Mageen's reaction was similar and the twins, Bill and Harry, were at first appalled then became furiously angry; their way of dealing with their distress and feeling of complete impotence. Like their father and grandfather before them they were big, handsome men, with black curls and green eyes, and powerfully built, being exceptionally good at sports. Used to a very active existence they now felt like caged animals and responded accordingly.

'If ever I get my hands on any of that lot I'll tear them apart – and enjoy it!'

'I know what you mean, Bill. Dad, how about we make a call down the tapped line and say to someone like Uncle Paddy, who knows all about it, that I'd be willing to swap places with Izzy? Whoever we spoke to they'd hear!'

'Good idea, Harry, but it wouldn't work. They deliberately took the most vulnerable person in the family to produce just these reactions in all of us.'

'Well couldn't we do that, Uncle Sean, and say that we'll give them anything they want just to get Izzy back safely?'

'Also a good idea, Mageen, but I think we must wait for them to come back to us now and not overplay our hand. I've asked for a couple of especially competent and experienced plain-clothes men, from a special force in another part of the country, to join me here this evening and we'll see what they think.'

They settled in for another long wait, which Sean told them would be part of the strategy of reducing them to the edge of nervous collapse. Fortunately, since it was Saturday, nobody had to go into the office and go through the agony again of pretending nothing was wrong. Then, right on schedule, the new men arrived on Saturday evening, driven quite openly by one of Sean's team. The boys on the gate, alerted to what was happening, gave them a very open and loud welcome, just as if they were old friends and colleagues coming to help with the guard duties. Much to the astonishment of everyone at Riverside they were indeed, in marked contrast to Sean's immaculate appearance, a really scruffy-looking pair.

'Meet Jack and Bertie.'

'How're yez all?' The Irish accent was there but not overdone.

Mageen and Sarah, used to male family members always looking reasonably smart, even in their casual clothes, couldn't believe their eyes. Mageen was the more shaken of the two.

'Good heavens! Don't they look *awful*. They don't even look basically clean! In fact I'll bet they smell. I'm going to keep well away from *them*.'

The new arrivals looked at the two girls and Jack found it hard not to show open admiration of Mageen. With her wonderful, rich chestnut hair and huge dark brown eyes she was an exceptionally attractive young woman. What's more, judging by the absence of rings, she obviously wasn't even engaged, let alone married.

Down boy, he said to himself. Remember – you're not supposed to get entangled with any girl at the moment. Too risky all round *and* you're here incognito.

Sean shooed everyone out of the room except the two newcomers, Milo, Noola, Tommy and Maggie. Then he gave Jack and Bertie a very thorough briefing, including every scrap of detail Declan had been able to observe and remember about the car that had delivered the brick. This wasn't much but given the brief few moments he had to register anything he had done very well. The two men went through every tiny item with a fine-toothed comb, making detailed notes. Before they started to analyse it all Sean, realizing they must be tired and hungry, suggested that they take a break and have some dinner while he and Milo held the fort.

'That'll give us all time to mull things over a bit and see what we can tease out of it all. If there's a call we can get you very quickly – the dining room's just across the hall.'

'Why don't I show the two of you to your rooms now? Dinner will be at seven o'clock, but if you're ready do join us back here in the library for a drink first. I think we could all do with one.'

36

'Thank you, Mrs Butler.'

Carrying their luggage grips they followed her up the elegant, sweeping stairway, their training making sure they registered every tiny detail that they saw: the understated quality and elegance of the furniture and furnishings so far visible to them and later repeated everywhere they went in the house; the antique books lining the library shelves; the original masterpieces on the walls, both oils and watercolours, some of them portraits of what were obviously past generations of Butlers. Bertie couldn't resist a comment:

'What a very good-looking family, Mrs Butler. That lady there looks a little like Mageen.'

'Yes. That's my husband's mother. Killed in a riding accident when he was only eight years old.'

'Oh! How sad! She was really beautiful.'

They were given a room each, intercommunicating through a shared bathroom. They had baths; washed their unkempt, greasy-looking hair; shaved and changed and were ready before the dinner gong sounded. They went back to the library where the rest of the family had gathered, all anxiously waiting, with ill-concealed impatience, for more news. Their wash and tidy up and change of clothes had altered their appearance quite dramatically. As they entered the room again and the family turned to look at them there was a sudden complete silence.

'Good heavens – what a difference! You look positively presentable.'

'*Mageen*! That was really rude. Apologise!' Noola was embarrassed, especially knowing what the two young men were doing for them, but also because it was exactly the kind of response she would have made at Mageen's age.

'Oh! Yes – well I didn't mean to be rude. It was more in the nature of a recognition of the change in your appearance. Sorry, gentlemen.'

The two men were highly entertained. Bertie had often had the same sort of response from his mother when he had returned home from a difficult assignment, looking as awful as he had when he arrived here.

'It's all right, Mageen, we've full sympathy for your reaction. We

37

get the same sort of comments at home.' Jack grinned at her. 'Sean didn't want it to be too obvious that he was having extra muscle in his ops room. We were told to look like casual replacements for the team guarding Riverside so we turned ourselves out in a manner we thought appropriate. Maybe we overdid it a little bit. Just hope it worked!'

'Well, it certainly convinced us. Good for you! What have you done with those revolting clothes? For goodness' sake send them down to be washed. You'll get them back pretty quickly. We've got an extremely competent staff here.'

Typical female, thought Jack. For heaven's sake! Thinking about *laundry* at a time like this. However, maybe for just a few seconds it took her mind off her worry and the girl did look pretty exhausted and seemed so tense. Well, who wouldn't in the circumstances?

After they had all eaten a quick meal, some of them unable to swallow much, Sean gathered everyone, including Kitty and Mickeen, into the library for a brainstorming session. He introduced Jack and Bertie to those who hadn't met them and then got down to business. At that moment the phone rang and everyone froze.

'You take it, Milo, and we'll listen in, and absolute quiet from all of us!'

'Milo Butler speaking.'

'Oh, hello, Mr Butler, it's Freddie Armstrong here. May I speak to Mageen please?'

'Good to hear from you, Freddie. Hold on and I'll see if I can find her – it may take a few minutes.'

Freddie had been Mageen's boyfriend since the previous Christmas. Like her he was reading for a degree in economics and maths at Trinity College. Mageen was seriously smitten and the rest of the family liked him but now was not the time they wanted him to arrive at the house.

'Fob him off, Mageen, he can't come here now.' Milo had put his hand over the mouthpiece. 'I don't care what you tell him, just stop him coming out here.' She nodded.

'Hello, Freddie, I wasn't expecting you back for at least another week.' A pause while she listened.

38

'I'd love to see you too but I'm not feeling well – some sort of stomach bug. I won't go into the gory details.' Another pause.

'No, no, Freddie, thank you but don't come, I wouldn't want you to pick anything up from me. No, honestly, Freddie, better not . . . , Freddie?' She put down the phone. 'He's gone! He said he was going to pop out anyhow. What are we going to do? I can't call him back, he was ringing from a phone box. We can't have him stopped at the entrance and how are we going to explain what's going on here?'

She was close to tears. This, on top of all the stress, was almost too much for her to cope with.

'Don't worry, sweetheart. I can send a message up to the gate to tell my lads to stay under cover. In fact you and the twins could wander up there to meet him. Would it matter so much if Freddie is told what has happened? Can he be trusted to keep his mouth shut? If not then Milo and Noola, you'll have to entertain him for a while and make out that Mageen's too poorly to see him, then send him on his way.

'Actually, Sean, I would trust Freddie. He strikes me as utterly reliable and it might be quite comforting for Mageen to have him here for an hour or so.' Noola sounded confident. 'He might even have some good ideas to add.'

'Thanks, Mum. Actually I'd love to see him.'

Knowing it wouldn't take that long for Freddie to get to the top of the drive, Mageen, Bill and Harry made their way up there and Harry went off into the bushes to find one of Sean's men and explain what was happening. They didn't have long to wait for Freddie to hop off a bus and head for the house. He was quite surprised to find three Butlers waiting for him.

'Well, what a great welcome. Hello beautiful!' He hugged and kissed Mageen. 'I must say you do look a bit peaky, even in this dim light.' He peered through the dusk at her then at the others. 'In fact you all look rather tired. Is something wrong?'

'Hello, Freddie. It's a long story. Let's get up to the house and we can have a talk.'

They arrived and took him into the sitting room. Milo and Noola joined them and all was explained. He was appalled.

39

'What frightful people. Who would be low enough to do such a thing?'

'We're not sure, Freddie. We're waiting to hear from them again. We've got our suspicions but no clues yet. Come on into the "ops room" and meet the detectives who are helping us.'

Freddie was introduced, as a friend of Mageen's, to Sean, Jack and Bertie.

Ah, so there *is* some competition, Jack mused. Well, looking at her I should have guessed there would be. However, all's not lost, they're obviously not engaged. He wasn't introduced as her fiancé, so there's still hope and, oh boy, would she be worth fighting for. But tread carefully boyo!

'The really important thing is, Freddie, that you don't mention this outside Riverside. You heard what they threatened would happen if the story got to the press.' Sean was anxious to reinforce this point.

'I understand, Inspector. I give you my word.'

'Okay, now that everyone's here again, let's continue with our brainstorming session.'

Sean seated them around the large desk and asked them to give all and any information, however trivial it might seem.

'Anyone see the vehicle which they used?'

'I saw a grubby old van moving up the drive very quickly. I was surprised it could shift along so fast.'

'That's the stuff, Mickeen, colour and make?'

'Dirty grey and, I think, a Ford.'

'The most common these days, so a good safe choice for them.'

They went on for a long time pooling every detail that they could think of, however trivial.

'Well that'll do for now. Thanks everyone. We'll put this all together and see if we can come up with any conclusions. Try to get some rest. You're all exhausted both emotionally and physically. I think it would be wise to skip church or Mass tomorrow but, actually, I don't see why the young folk shouldn't go for a row. That at least would maintain an element of "normal" outward appearance.

This cheered the twins. At long last something active to do

40

without going too far from the source of incoming news. They dispersed in different directions around the house. An hour or so later Mageen and the twins walked Freddie back up the drive to get a late bus back into the city. Milo, Noola, Tommy and Maggie stayed in the library with Sean and his two helpers.

'We'll sift through this material and see if there's anything that might help us. We'll share findings with you but keep it just amongst ourselves. I trust them all but it's so easy to let something drop in an unguarded moment.'

Just then Paddy arrived, after a late surgery. He had been to see Aunt May and given her messages from the family, explaining why it was difficult for Milo to get to see her. She fully understood, appreciating that the twins and Mageen had dropped by the previous day during their lunch break. She felt so much better she insisted that she was now quite ready to come home and give all the details she could remember to Sean. Paddy, bearing in mind the trauma she had suffered, wasn't at all happy about the idea.

'It's remarkable what she does remember in the circumstances. She told me that one of the men was a big strapping fellow and the one who grabbed Izzy seemed to jab her in the arm with a needle.'

'Ah, so he may have had some sort of medical experience, and that fits in with something else I should have thought of earlier. It could only have been someone with medical knowledge that would have been able to give Bob the medication to keep him lucid for long enough to be of any help. I'll have the files combed for anyone with a criminal record who has any qualifications of that sort. Anything else?'

'No, that's about it. I'll get off now, unless there's anything else I can do to help?'

'Not for the moment. Thanks for everything, Paddy!'

'See you all tomorrow,' and he was gone.

'Something maybe vaguely related to that has occurred to me, Sean. Amongst my many worries about Izzy, I'm wondering about her dermatitis. It subsided and hasn't bothered her now for a couple of years but it's so stress related it's bound to have broken out badly and must be making her even more miserable. What's she going to do without her ointment? If one of them has some sort of medical

41

knowledge do you think he might care even a little – just enough to help her?' Noola's voice was husky with anxiety and weariness. She was clearly dangerously close to breaking point.

'Well done, Noola. I'll have an alert sent out to all chemists to report anything untoward related to requests for the kind of medication we have in mind. We can emphasise that we're searching for someone who's practising illegally and to keep it under wraps. They'll be discreet. We've worked with them before, looking for people like that.'

'Do you think we should also try to whittle down the likely places where they might be hiding out, Sean? For instance, if they found someone to drive along and throw in that note, they can't have gone too far away.'

'Good point, Jack. What are your thoughts?'

'Bertie and I were looking at the possibilities earlier. Our own experiences of similar situations tell us that they're unlikely to have stayed in the city or in any built-up area. It would be too easy for them to be spotted and it takes only the smallest element of odd behaviour and people do notice. It's impressive how observant Joe Public can be. Our guess is that they'll have moved into an area, not too far away, where very few or maybe no others are living and chances of their being detected are virtually non-existent.'

'Ah, of course. The mountains. But that's going to be like looking for a needle in a haystack.'

'Have you any means of finding out if anyone has been seen recently wandering the hills or has shown an interest in an unusually remote property? Somewhere that would make a really good hideaway.'

'It's a long shot, Jack, and we're talking about a very wide area but always worth discreet enquiries. We mustn't arouse suspicions. But tomorrow being Sunday, and forecast to be sunny again, it would be perfectly reasonable to have hikers out for the day. I'll get a team onto it.' He paused for a few seconds.

'Actually there's another thing which would add weight to the idea of somewhere a bit remote; their stipulation that we install radio equipment here. So far we've assumed that this was to make it difficult to track their calls – even public phones would tell us at least the area they're calling from. Maybe we've been wrong. It could be because they're out of reach of any telephones. As we said: up the mountains!'

'How about we join the hikers, Sean? We're trained to look for the smallest signs of activity in remote places,' Bertie grinned. 'At the risk of outraging Mageen, we can change into our scruffy gear again.'

'Yes, and I've got a couple of very neat little gizmos in my kitbag, one that will help us to communicate with you, transmit and receive, and one that can track local radio signals.' He smiled. 'I won't tell you what we normally use them for!'

'Good thinking, Jack, thanks.'

'Just one thing, Sean, our deductions may be way off the mark.'

'I know that, but it's all we've got at the moment and well worth following up.'

Late as it was, Sean got to work, phoning into his headquarters to get the various lines of enquiry going. He wanted to move in equipment, unobtrusively and as soon as possible, to help locate, even vaguely, any radio calls coming into the house. Just an idea as to whether or not the calls were nearby or far off would help to build up a picture. They set up their night-watch roster and settled in for another nerve-shredding wait.

43

Chapter 6

All through the two days following her kidnap, Izzy lay on her truckle bed and whenever she heard anyone coming down the stairs she pulled the blankets over her, curled up, and turned her face to the wall. She ate none of the food that was brought to her, drank only tiny sips of water and refused to speak. She seemed to be crying continuously. Eddie was the only one who had come down to see her and tend to her wants. He had told her about the small pit they had dug in a corner of the tiny cell which she could use as a lavatory, with some earth to throw into it using a small plastic spade. Conscious of the dangers of infection from such a source he had thrown plentiful disinfectant into the pit. He had also insisted that an air vent must be installed and this had been done by means of a simple tube pushed up through the ground above. Much to the entertainment of the others, and with some difficulty in obtaining them without raising questions, he had even managed to provide her with a basic change of underclothes.

'You must eat something, little Izzy, even if only a bit of bread.'

No answer. This continued into Sunday and he became seriously worried.

'It's been over two days now and she's eaten nothing and not said a word. Only taken some water. It's not good. In fact if it goes on it could be very dangerous.'

'Well you'll just have to work out a way of force-feeding her if necessary. Damn it, Eddie, you're a doctor, of sorts, you must be able to think of some way of making her eat. Just deal with it or one of us will have to. Quite a change to find a female who won't talk. It's usually the opposite problem.'

They had no idea that Izzy, from her perch on top of the ladder, could hear quite plainly what they were saying. It was unbelievably comforting to know that it was important to them to keep her alive. On the other hand she certainly didn't want to be force-fed. She didn't know how this would be done but it didn't sound at all comfortable. She worked out a new strategy.

Not long after that conversation Eddie came down into the cellar again.

'Is there anything at all that you'd eat, girleen?'

In between the sobs, not entirely contrived, at long last she opened her eyes, uncurled and answered him. She saw, rather to her surprise, a kind face. Intensely blue eyes looked at her anxiously below a mop of very dark hair.

'I can't eat anything. I feel too sick.'

He was hugely relieved that she had, at long last, spoken to him.

'There must be something that you could take even on an upset stomach. What do you have at home if you're feeling sick?'

'Ice cream – often nothing else for days until I'm better. But more than food I need something for my rash.'

'Let me have a look at it.'

'*No*! Unless you're a doctor you're not to touch me!'

'I *am* a doctor. Now let me have a look.'

'Well you can see it on my neck and arms and it's all over the rest of me. And it itches like mad. And it's all your fault – you and your friends. I only get it when I'm upset and it makes me very sick.'

This last statement wasn't true but Izzy, noting the kind face, was trying to think of everything possible that might add to this man's feeling of guilt and sympathy for her.

'All right! Now tell me, girl, if I get some ice cream for you will you promise to eat it?'

'Yes, but I'll need lots before my stomach settles. My mum says it's the milk in it that helps.'

That actually made some sense to Eddie. He went back up the ladder.

'I'll have to go and find a chemist. The child has a dreadful dermatitis rash and she's scratched so much it's bleeding in places. If I don't get something to treat it it'll become infected.'

'Did nobody know anything about possible medical conditions?

45

I thought the contact was supposed to give us all that sort of detail, Willie.' Mac sounded annoyed.

'Ah let the spoilt brat suffer. It'll do her good to have to put up with a bit of discomfort.'

'Shut it, Bob. When we want your opinion we'll ask for it. Just remember, keep well away from that cellar. And no, Mac, we weren't told about anything we needed to be prepared for.'

'I'll go to a chemist, but not too close, and get some ice cream too. Apparently that's what she lives on for days when she's ill. I'm not going to even think of force-feeding a little one like that.'

'You're all soft, the whole lot of you. Just let her rot there. I don't give a damn.'

'You'll give a damn if you find yourself back in that place for the duration. And if you touch her that's what we'll do – drop you back there. We need her in good health and able to talk to her parents when we make the call. If she can't talk to them we've a big problem: how do we prove she's still alive?'

* * * * *

On Sunday morning Bertie and Jack left Riverside with others of the night-team going off duty, so that nothing untoward was obvious. At headquarters the two men were given an inoffensive-looking, elderly car, in which they could drive off for the day, completely undetected for what they were. They were joined by a pretty comprehensive team of other well-briefed, plain-clothes police who set off at more or less the same time. They had divided into sections the mountain area which they thought most likely to be the location of the hideout and each team covered one of these sections. The idea was to have a wander around and, towards lunchtime, find a pub on the periphery of the built-up area in their section, drop in for a pint and ask would-be innocent questions.

Nothing useful was forthcoming at lunchtime but on one of the visits to the pubs towards the end of the afternoon a couple of the men struck lucky. Aiden and Brendan had wandered into a down-at-heel pub, most inappropriately called "The Irish Harp", which was more like an old-time shebeen than anything else. It wouldn't

46

have surprised them to have been offered a shot of poteen from under the counter. However, there was a cheerful turf fire burning and a warm welcome from the man behind the bar.

'Good evening, gentlemen. Me name's Mick. What can I get ye?'

'Hello, Mick. Two pints of Guinness would be grand and one for yourself.'

The drinks were poured and there was casual chit-chat, covering the usual social themes for such a venue and occasion: the weather, the scenery and so forth. The two brought the topic around very carefully to where they wanted it to be.

'Well, it's such a grand area I wouldn't mind having a bolt-hole up here, well away from the crowds of the city.'

'But, Brendan, you'd never find a place around here. Shure you'd have to buy a bit of a plot and build on it. I'll bet there aren't any for sale anyway.'

'Yeh, I suppose you're right but I could just afford a small place and the wife and kids would love it. I wish I could find something.' Then turning to the barman he continued:

'I don't suppose there's any hope of finding a little place around about, is there?'

'Well I don't know of anything off hand, but it's always worth asking around. I mean there were two fellas here about six or eight months ago and they were looking for something like that. Liam Nolan sold them a real wreck of a place – couldn't believe his luck. Didn't think he'd ever get rid of it.'

'Oh, looks as if I missed the boat then. I wonder if the people who bought it would sell it on to me. What do you think?'

'It mightn't be what you'd want though, Brendan. Where was this place, Mick? Would it be difficult for us to find?'

'Ah shure if t'was meself I wouldn't try this evening. It's a bit up the mountain from here but, if ye had a car, then I'd say less than an hour's drive should do it. I've never been there so I can't give ye exact directions to the door as it were, but I know roughly the area. 'Tis well off the beaten track, but shouldn't be too hard to find in the daylight. There aren't *that* many places up there.'

'Maybe Liam Nolan would give us the exact location.'

'No chance of that, lads. As soon as he got the money he was off to Australia to join his brother.'

'Oh! Well thanks anyway, Mick.'

Aiden and Brendan were bursting to get more details: Who? How many? Had much work been done on the place? But they didn't want to arouse suspicion by asking too many questions. They deliberately changed the subject and, as soon as possible, careful not to seem in too much of a hurry to leave, they finished their drinks and left with promises to come back and let Mick know how they got along with their quest. They ran back to where they had concealed their car, got back to the local police station as fast as they could and called Sean on the secure line. His warm response was all the reward they needed.

'Well done, lads! You may have got us a vital lead and we'll follow up at once.'

Jack and Bertie were still out in the hills. They had left their car and walked a substantial distance around their designated surveillance area, and their highly trained powers of observation had detected nothing even remotely likely as a hideaway, however well disguised. Sean now contacted them.

'We may have a lead. We could be way off the mark in every respect but it's worth a try.' And he gave them all the information that the others had gleaned.

'Thanks, Sean. Sounds promising. Give us a map reference, close as you can, and we'll get to the area. We'll drop the car and go in on foot and find out what we can. We'll report back before we do anything. The light's going so we won't be easily spotted.'

'Okay, but…'

'We know, Sean. It's a child's life!'

Dear God, thought Sean, I hope we're not barking completely up the wrong tree. We're gambling an awful lot on pure speculation. But we've just got to try anything at all likely.

* * * * *

It had been another interminable day at Riverside. When the word came through about a possible location, hopes were raised amongst

48

Sean's inner circle, but they resisted the strong temptation to tell the rest of the family. Then a short time after Sean's communication with Bertie and Jack, the long awaited, dreaded call came at last and, because it was a radio contact, the others were able to listen in.

'We want one million pounds in *used English notes*, non-sequential numbers, mixed denominations. You've got until midday Tuesday.'

This was all recorded but the muffled voice would be impossible to identify, not helped by the poor quality of the call.

'That's too short a time to get so much used sterling together in cash. It's *Sunday evening*.'

'You're lucky it's not twenty-four hours. If Milo Butler wants her alive then make sure he does it in the time!'

Desperate to keep him on the line Sean continued.

'How do we know the child's still alive?'

'We know what you're trying to do, Sean Flynn: keep us on the line so that you can trace our location. Well you're wasting your time. Next time we call it'll be with the instructions for delivery. We'll have the girl ready to speak to you, but make sure you've got the money. Tell Butler that his child is just about all right but not feeling too comfortable.'

'We'll do our best to get the cash but...' The connection was broken.

'They've gone. Milo, Noola, we'll talk about getting the money together.'

Up to then he hadn't thought either of them could have looked any worse, but he was wrong. They both now looked ready to collapse.

'Well at least we know now that Izzy is still alive and exactly how much they want. And I don't care what I have to do to get the cash, I'll get it somehow. I'm going to call our bank manager now on your secure line, Sean, and put him in the picture. He's a good friend and he'll not spread the story around.'

'Okay, Milo. While you're doing that I'll make radio contact with Jack and Bertie. They might as well come back in now.'

He contacted the two undercover agents again and put them in the picture, finishing up:

49

'Have you had any luck yourselves?'

'No, Sean. We've been using our own detection equipment but nothing. We can't do any more for the moment. They'll have closed down and anyhow it's almost dark. So we'll come in now and listen again to what they said. You've recorded it?'

'Yes.'

'Well maybe we'll be more help back down there.'

Chapter 7

As well as being frightened, miserable and in some distress with her skin problem, Izzy was bored stiff. She had nothing to do, not even anything to read and no one to talk to. So she had ample time to work out ways of arousing the sympathy of the so-called doctor and maybe even some means of escaping from this appalling cellar. She had worked out one particular strategy which she thought would rattle him and maybe the others too. To keep herself occupied she practised some of the ploys that she thought might work.

Like all the others, the call to the family at Riverside had been made outside the cottage to get the best chance of good signal, so she hadn't heard it. However, when Willie got back inside and reported a successful contact, Izzy could hear what was said. She was now really adept at listening from the top of the ladder. The nasty "Bob" was clearly highly delighted.

'That'll give the stuck-up Tom Butler something to think about. A million pounds! I hope it bankrupts him – serve him right. He'll have to sell Riverside and move into some other little place. It'll be the biggest comedown imaginable. And I'll get my share, won't I?'

'You're such a big eejit, Bob. A million is probably chicken-feed to the Butlers and for God's sake stop referring to Tom Butler – he died years ago. You can't have forgotten *that*?' He was making Willie really irritable.

Bob muttered something Izzy couldn't hear, but then someone else arrived at the cottage.

'You're back at last, Eddie. What took you so long?'

'I was afraid to go to a chemist anywhere close, so I drove quite a fair way towards the city. Of course they were closed, so I had to

51

hammer at the door and say it was a bit of an emergency – a child in great distress. After I'd got the ointment for the child's rash, I went to a nearby shop for some ice cream. At least now I've something she'll eat.'

What didn't occur to him to say was that he'd asked them in the shop to wrap the ice cream in newspaper to help keep it frozen, since he had a bit of a journey to take it to a sick child.

Eddie took the ointment and the rather soft ice cream down to Izzy.

'Now, Izzy, we'll put some ointment on the rash and I've some ice cream for you.'

Izzy quite deliberately allowed the tears, never too far away at the moment, to flow freely.

'Thank you, Doctor. But I'll put the ointment on myself. My grandpa told me I mustn't let anyone here touch me.'

Eddie thought he hadn't heard correctly. He made no comment but waited while she ate the fast-melting ice cream and then used the ointment. As she was lathering it into the worst affected areas she turned to the spot beside her on the bed and spoke to the empty space.

'There you are, Grandpa. I've done it myself and it feels better.'

She seemed to be listening and then answered the soundless speaker.

'Yes, I suppose he's been quite kind but he's still one of the people who stole me away.'

By now Eddie was feeling decidedly uneasy.

'Who're you talking to, Izzy?'

'Oh, it's Grandpa Tom. We talk to each other often. He says he'll watch over me. I just call him when I need him and I've asked him to stay with me all the time here.'

'Well... what do you talk about?' An Irishman to the core Eddie couldn't totally dismiss the idea of the supernatural and, although he would never have admitted it, he was deeply superstitious. Now he felt the hairs on the back of his neck begin to prickle.

'We talk about anything he wants to tell me, but sometimes I ask him about things too. Otherwise it would be very difficult for me

52

here, all by myself. No one to talk to and not even anything to read.'
The tears started again. 'So Grandpa and I talk together. It passes the
time. It could get quite serious for me if I didn't have him here. I
could go into one of my fits again.'

'*Fits*! What fits? I didn't know anything about fits. Nobody said
anything about that.'

'How could you know about it – we've only just met.'

'Yes, but . . .' He stopped just in time, before he had given the
game away about an informer who was *supposed* to have told them
all this kind of possible complication.

'What else does your grandpa say?' He strained his eyes, staring
hard at the empty space, actually afraid he might see Tom Butler's
ghost.

Izzy turned to the empty side of the bed again.

'Do you want to give the doctor a message, Grandpa?' There
was silence while she cocked her head to one side, obviously
listening carefully.

'Oh no, Grandpa, he couldn't do that.'

'Do *what*?' Eddie was now thoroughly spooked.

'It's all right, Doctor, it's something quite impossible.'

'What the hell is it? What's he saying?'

'He says I really need to have a walk in the fresh air. It would
make me feel a lot better. But don't worry, I know you can't fix that.'

'No, I can't let you do that but maybe I can find something for
you to read. We're a bit isolated up here but I can find some old
newspapers. Maybe they'd be better than nothing.'

So they were up the mountains! She could have cheered. He
seemed quite agitated and probably didn't realize he had given that
much away.

'That would help. I wouldn't be so bored. And I need some
hankies too. I've had to blow my nose on the blanket which isn't
very nice. I *never* do that at home.' She paused briefly. 'What do all
of *you* do to pass the time?'

'Oh, we play cards, smoke, drink beer, listen to the wireless and
so on.'

'Well some of those papers and a pack of cards would help. Then
I could at least read and play patience.'

53

He turned to go up the ladder and then, looking almost embarrassed, he pulled a bar of chocolate out of his pocket and offered it to her.

'I got this for you too. I thought maybe you'd like a bit of chocolate.'

It was the first time she'd smiled at him and it was like the sun coming out.

'Oh! Thank you, Doctor. I love chocolate. That will help me to feel better too.'

When he went back up the steps and into the main part of the dwelling he tackled the others about the inadequate information they had been given about the child.

'Why weren't we told that she was one of those who hears voices, like that Joan of Arc one? Or that she's liable to suffer from fits? Our so-called "informer" hasn't done too well in many respects.' Eddie sounded really upset and angry, this partly from being unnerved by his latest experience with Izzy.

'What the hell are you talking about, Eddie?'

So Eddie told them blow by blow. Mac and Willie laughed derisively at Eddie's story.

'Give over, Eddie. The kid's pulling your leg. But she's a plucky one and clever with it. I have to admit that. I'll go down the next time and if she tries any of that on me I'll put her over my knee and give her a good walloping.'

'I wouldn't try it, Willie. I didn't know about her fits, just like I wasn't told about the dermatitis. If it's a form of epilepsy and the fit is not treated the right way, she could die. Next time we report in I'm going to complain about not being given full information as to possible health problems.'

'Well, we need to keep her alive at least until she's spoken to her parents. After that if she dies, well so be it. I couldn't care less so long as we get the money.'

'Ah come on, Willie. Poor little kid. You wouldn't really want her to die now would you?'

'I don't give a damn, just so long as we *get the money*. And you watch it! You're getting way too sympathetic. Maybe we should let Bob down there to deal with her after all.'

54

At the mention of the ghost of Tom Butler they all noticed that Bob, whose medication, for the moment, was keeping him fairly well in control, hadn't sneered at the idea. In fact he had turned quite pale. Although he would never have given the others the satisfaction of saying so, he was now determined that he would never go down into that cellar. The thoughts whirled around in his head. He'd have to find an opportunity to get the brat upstairs where he could punish her well away from Tom Butler's ghost. It was one thing to try to kill off the living man but quite another to face his ghost. You couldn't kill a ghost and, what was more, ghosts had strange powers of their own. Oh no! He was going to stay well away from that cellar.

Bob wasn't the only one to have feelings of this nature. Even tough Willie and mighty Mac had some uncertainty about the idea. Although, like Eddie, neither would ever have admitted it, they too were not immune to superstition and each suffered a twinge of discomfort at the idea of a ghostly presence in the house, even if only down there with Izzy. Most strongly affected of all was Shamus, the van driver. He was by far the youngest and so the least experienced of the team. His grandmother told fortunes and predicted future events by using simple playing cards. Although the family pulled her leg about it, she was often uncannily accurate in the way things turned out. Because of this he was strongly susceptible to the idea of otherworldly influences, and so, more than any of them, Shamus was nervous at the suggestion of a ghost. From now on it would take him all his time to pluck up the courage to go into the cottage at all, especially in the evening, and nothing on earth would have persuaded him to go down into the cellar.

In complete ignorance of the fact, Izzy couldn't have chosen a more effective way of making them all feel uneasy.

Chapter 8

Milo and Noola were at the end of their tether and neither was willing to take any of the medication offered by Paddy to help them through. A sleeping pill was the most Noola was willing to consider. Milo wouldn't countenance even that. They were both almost beyond any semblance of rational thought or response and Maggie and Tommy, although in almost as desperate a state, were supporting them as best they could. Sean remained their sheet anchor.

In spite of repeated calls to his home, there was no answer from the bank manager and Milo came to the conclusion that he and his wife must be away for the weekend. He would have to wait until Monday morning to try to contact him again and collecting the million pounds could be an impossible task in the time. So Milo and Sean put their heads together and tried to work out other ways of collecting the strictly specified type of cash without arousing any suspicions. They were joined by Bertie and Jack who made some very helpful suggestions and offered an alternative means of collecting the used sterling for them, one which wouldn't raise any questions. Milo and Noola, with Tommy and Maggie listening, talked around the idea with Sean and then, with relief and enormous appreciation, agreed to go along with it.

The two men asked to make some phone calls in private. They got the hoped for response and explained to the others that they must leave at the crack of dawn the next morning promising to be back by the end of the day with the money.

As soon as he got the opportunity, Tommy spoke privately to Milo and Noola. He looked as awful as they did, for he had the extra distress of knowing now, for certain, that a blood uncle of his was involved in the abduction.

'I want you both to know that I'm willing to give *every penny* I can lay my hands on to help pay this ransom to get Izzy back safely. Please don't refuse me. Allow me to do this for her, for you, for the whole family and . . . for myself.'

Milo and Noola fully understood. Noola looked at the pinched, almost tormented face. She put her arms around him and hugged him tight.

'Thank you, Tommy. We know you would give everything you have to help and we'll talk about it when it's all over and she's home again.'

'That offer means such a lot to us, Tommy. We know you love her as much as we do.'

'As much as if she were my own child, Lo.'

* * * * *

Sean's edict that the fine details should be kept strictly within the narrow group was observed meticulously. It was frustrating for the rest of the family and the equally anxious staff, but they understood his point about it being so easy to let something slip quite inadvertently. So no resentment was expressed, for they were prepared to do anything deemed necessary for Izzy's safe return. They knew about the message via the brick and the phone call with the demand and that Milo was making the necessary arrangements to get the money. Mageen, Bill, Harry and Sarah had been left legacies by their Butler grandparents. When they heard about the ransom demand they had gone together to the ops room to offer everything they had to help collect the sum needed. Their parents would have expected no less of them but, nevertheless, it brought a lump to Milo's throat and Noola dissolved into the tears that, understandably in the circumstances, were hard to keep at bay.

Freddie had insisted on coming out to Riverside again on Sunday afternoon and was there when the call came through. Mageen was really glad of his company. He had a strong personality and managed to cheer her up, even in the face of the depressing

57

circumstances. He seemed to have quite a positive effect on the others too and his support increased his popularity with the whole family. He also endeared himself to the staff by offering to help fetch and carry tea and coffee and other refreshments for everyone, including to the ops room, diplomatically always making a noisy approach to Sean's domain. Most of all he impressed Milo when he got an opportunity to have a quiet aside with him.

'If I had any spare funds I would happily give them to you to help out, but I'm afraid I only have the money from my grant.'

'That is such a generous thought. Thank you, Freddie, but don't worry. We're pretty sure our bank manager will be able to work out something for us.'

Later when he told Noola of this she was very touched.

'He's a lovely young man. I wouldn't mind at all having him for a son-in-law.'

'I'd be pleased too, in spite of the fact that I'm reluctant to give my eldest daughter to any other man!'

'I do love you, Milo. You're a real old softie.' He grinned wearily at her.

'Yes, I suppose I am and I love you too, so much.'

'You know the boys also like him and that's a good sign.'

'Yes. They seem to get on with him really well.'

Freddie was given a warm invitation to stay the night. He politely turned this down but readily agreed to stay to dinner. During the meal Jack tried hard not to watch Mageen too obviously. The more he saw of her the more he was attracted to her. Damn that Freddie, he thought. He tried not to like him, to find fault with him, but he failed. Unfortunately, he seemed to be a thoroughly decent sort. In fact he was very civil to Jack and Bertie, showing what seemed to be a genuine interest in their line of work, obviously in the firm belief, like most of the others, that they were part of Sean's "special force". But they were used to deflecting the kind of questions he asked and painted a convincing picture of the work of the Irish police force in the far north-west of the country. Freddie, however, did detect Jack's interest in Mageen. He certainly had the looks and attraction to arouse *her* interest. He had merry blue eyes with developing laughter lines and the most wonderful smile. His

58

was the healthy aura of one who spent much time in the fresh air and he had the physique to go with it, just topping six feet and decidedly husky looking, but with no suggestion of surplus weight. Freddie was struck by the fact that Jack and Bertie were very similar in build, although quite different in colouring, for Bertie was dark haired and dark eyed.

For her part Mageen had eyes only for Freddie. This, in some senses, was surprising, for unlike successive generations of the male members of her family, and to an extent the women too, Freddie did not have a strong interest in outdoor pursuits. However, she loved his aesthetic looks; his cool grey eyes and unruly fair hair, all of which gave him an aura of gentleness. He could have passed for a university professor and, somehow, this appealed to her. She was seriously smitten, but in the present circumstances she found it difficult to think or talk about anything other than Izzy's plight. All their conversations tended to follow the same kind of pattern.

'I'm sorry, Freddie. It must be so boring for you listening to all of us going on and on about it, but we're all in such a state about Izzy, we just can't think or talk about anything else.'

'*Please*, Mageen, stop worrying. I feel like you do. Izzy seems like a little sister to me too and maybe someday, well… Anyhow, feel free to talk about her as much as you want. I'm more than happy to listen.'

'Oh, Freddie! You're so understanding and sympathetic. Sure you wouldn't like to stay?'

'Thanks, but I do need to get back to do some more revision. The exams are looming and I've still got a fair bit of ground to cover!'

'Yes, so have I, but there's no way I could concentrate on studying at the moment.'

'Course not. But you never have any trouble getting good results anyhow.' He sounded slightly envious.

Although it took them away from the house, given reassurances that they would be told immediately of any new developments, Mageen, Bill and Harry returned to the office in the city on Monday, quite unaware that Bertie and Jack had left a couple of hours earlier, as dawn was breaking. Faithful and concerned, Freddie came home with Mageen at the end of the working day. He stayed as long as

59

possible and joined them for the evening meal but again wouldn't stay overnight.

'It's a lovely invitation and I'm sorely tempted. Maybe . . . but no! I must be strong-minded and keep at the revision. I can still get several hours in before I go to bed.'

* * * * *

While teams of his men were out posing as hillwalkers and hikers on Sunday, Sean had ordered a start to be made first thing in the morning in the search of the records for doctors who had been "struck off". There weren't too many, so the job was done within a relatively short time. Armed with this list of names, his men then started a telephone trawl of the chemists around the city, asking for very strictly confidential information to be returned to them immediately if any of these names turned up as signatory to a prescription. His orders were to start with chemists around the outskirts, especially those fringing the mountainous areas. Because it was Sunday, there was no guarantee of always getting a response, but since time was very tight it was always worth the effort. They might have a quick stroke of luck. They felt quite deflated when nothing had turned up by Sunday evening, but were undaunted in their determination to leave no stone unturned in their quest to find Izzy's abductors, the fact that she was a child adding a substantial boost to their resolve.

It was Monday afternoon before they had a positive reaction. A chemist in an area close to the edge of the city reported being asked to open up and give a doctor ointment for dermatitis, which was needed urgently. Yes, a Doctor Edward J. Conran had filled out a prescription, and yes, they had it in the shop. That was the name of one of the doctors who had been "struck off" and obviously it hadn't occurred to the chemist to check. The young policeman could hardly speak in his excitement when reporting this to his superior and he, likewise, when reporting to Sean.

'It seems this fellow asked them where was the nearest place he could get ice cream too, and as far as they know he went off and bought some. We've asked them to say or do nothing until we get out to see them. Said that it's an emergency we can't discuss at the moment.'

'Well done, all of you. That sounds as if it could be exactly what we're looking for. Go out yourself and get every possible detail and then come straight over here to me. Oh, and take that young Garda with you, he deserves a bit of a reward. We'll arrange for it to seem as if you're coming to replace some of the daytime security guards.'

It was quite late in the evening when they arrived to make their report to Sean and hard on their heels Bertie and Jack arrived back, also in a car belonging to the Garda and carrying large kitbags. They were elated to hear the news from Sean's men and the usual inner circle settled in to hear the full report.

'Medication for dermatitis and ice cream! That *has* to be for Izzy. It's too much of a coincidence.'

At long last Noola sounded slightly optimistic. She even managed a wry smile.

'I wonder how she talked him into getting ice cream for her. Clever girl.'

It was as well she hadn't a remote inkling of the sort of conditions in which her child was incarcerated.

'Well, at least we've substantially narrowed the area where we need to search for them *and* the ice cream had to be wrapped for taking it some distance. In fact, when you add in the information from Aiden and Brendan's friend in the pub and a slight trace we got from their call, I'm confident that we're looking in the right area. You've done a grand job, men. Well done! It's late now so I'll let you go home.'

The two Garda beamed.

'If it's helped to find the little girl we'll be well rewarded, Sir.'

When they had gone Jack and Bertie produced their large kitbags and opened them. They were full of sterling notes. There was a few seconds' silence and then Maggie sat down with a bump.

'Jesus, Mary and Joseph! I feel weak at the knees. I've never in my whole life seen so much money all in one place.'

'I don't suppose any of us has. But how on *earth* did you do it, and in the time?' Milo sounded quite amazed.

'When we alerted our people in the north we gave them the full story as to the demands. They've ways and means the rest of us don't have. They met us at the border. We slipped across and they handed the bags over to us and we made our way back.'

'They *trusted* you with so much money... in cash?'

'Oh yes. In our job there is absolute trust between us all. Has to be if we're to have any hope of working together effectively. Anyhow, we know too well what would happen to us if we tried anything silly.'

'Is it all there?'

'Yes. A team of us helped to count it out.'

'I can hardly believe my eyes, but I'm really impressed. Well done.'

'Thanks, Sean.'

'And how do we even *start* to thank you and your team and what about repayment?'

Jack and Bertie were grinning with delight at the reaction of everyone.

'Don't worry about any of that for the moment, Milo, we can sort it all later. Can the money be locked away where no one will see it? We don't want anyone else to suspect where it's come from.'

'Leave it to me.' Milo knew exactly where he could hide the bags away, with no fear of them being seen.

'Well, we're ready for the call now. Midday tomorrow! We might as well all go and try to eat something.'

Hungry and tired after a very long and difficult day, Bertie and Jack were vastly relieved at this suggestion. It was so late that they didn't even stop to freshen up, knowing that Mageen would have had her dinner long ago and wouldn't be sitting down with them.

Chapter 9

Jack and Bertie were up really early again on Tuesday morning and they set off to search a broad area in which they believed the hideaway must lie. Once again they posed as hikers and wore backpacks. But these were backpacks with a difference, containing an impressive collection of equipment, much of it not readily available on the open market, but rather shades of things to come. Both carried neat but very powerful handguns hidden but easily accessible inside their jackets. They drove as far as they dared and then, using some of their sophisticated detection gear, they walked, traversing a wide area swiftly and methodically. By lunchtime they had covered a considerable area but with no sign of anything remotely like a dwelling, however primitive or tumbledown. They found a secluded spot in the hillside and settled down for a bite to eat, using the bracken as camouflage.

'What time do you make it, Bertie?'

'Just past noon.'

'That's the time they said they'd call back with their instructions, but we're not picking up any radio signals.'

'I know. Shame we've found nothing. We *must* be somewhere close. All the evidence points to this area.'

On the clear air a scream carried across the hills.

'Help me. Someone hel…' the sound was abruptly cut off but there was a cry of pain.

The two men leapt to their feet.

'Where did that come from? That was a child.'

'Behind that hill just above us.'

They ran flat out, almost to the top and then dropped to the ground on their stomachs and crawled the rest of the way, until they could see down to the bottom of the slope the other side, where a small inconspicuous dwelling nestled into a hollow in the hillside. Because they had stopped for a break, they had only just missed it. This was fortunate for, although they had been careful to avoid being observed, they might have run straight into the group now assembled outside the door. They counted five men and, sure enough, a child. The instinct to draw their guns and rush to Izzy's rescue was strong but they were too well disciplined to attempt any such thing, which would have put the child at even greater risk. Bertie produced a Hasselblad with a very powerful telephoto lens and started to take a series of photographs. He and Jack waited until they all went back inside the cottage, then they crawled back down the slope and, using his powerful mini transmitter/receiver, Jack tried to contact Sean.

* * * * *

Just before noon Eddie had taken Izzy up the ladder into the top room. The men hadn't bothered to put on their balaclavas. They were quite confident that they would be well out of the country before they could be tracked down by any information Izzy would be able to give, either of them or the hideaway.

She wondered which of the five was nasty Bob. She shrank back against Eddie, taking huge gulps of the lovely fresh air.

'It's all right, girleen. So long as you behave you'll be fine.'

'She'd better or I'll deal with her. She'll wish she'd never been born.'

She recognized the voice, so now she knew which one he was: older than any of the others, he had short, straight grey hair and faded blue eyes that looked at her with venom. She was terrified but her fear was, to a small degree, tempered by being utterly outraged. On top of all she had suffered, all she had endured, this was the last straw. She managed to garner every last shred of courage she had, drew her small body to its maximum height and looked him straight in the eye, trying so hard to stop her voice from shaking.

'You're a *nasty* person. Grandpa Tom says if you touch me you'll *die*!'

64

Bob turned a dirty shade of grey. Looking at his face, Eddie had the hardest time not laughing outright. Of the others, Shamus had kept well away from Izzy and after that comment moved even further away, glancing around fearfully. Jaysus, he thought, if I see that fella's ghost I think I'll wet meself. Why the hell did I get mixed up with this lot. And that poor little kid . . . !

'We're going to call your parents. They'll want to know if you're still alive so that's why you're up here. You'll have a chance to say a few words to them but no tricks.' Mighty Mac was dangerous looking and would have frightened the bravest. Izzy said nothing.

They moved to where the radio equipment was placed for best reception. That was the moment that Izzy chose to scream her defiance.

'Help me. Someone hel...' Willie hit her hard across the face knocking her to the ground. She cried out. Tears streamed down her face from the pain and blood ran from her lip, but before any of the others could make a more violent attack on her Eddie leapt between her and them, helped her to her feet and put his arms around her. She clung to him shaking all over, while he dabbed gently at her lip.

'Leave her alone, all of you, or she'll not be capable of talking to her parents. In fact judging by the spirit she's shown, she might even refuse to talk to them. What'll you do then?'

Willie sneered at him.

'I keep telling you, Eddie, you're too soft. If she won't talk I'm quite prepared to make her scream – loudly. Oh they'll know she's here all right, I promise you that!'

'If I was too soft I wouldn't be mixed up in this whole dirty business. But I'm not cowardly enough to hit a little kid so hard as to split her lip. Look at her! She's small, she's frail and not well. She has that dreadful rash which irritates her like hell. She's been kidnapped, locked up in a foul cellar for five days, eating almost nothing and she still had enough guts to have a go at Bob. And look at you! You're nothing but an oversized, overweight bully and I just wonder if you've got a fraction of the courage she has.'

Willie raised clenched fists and started towards Eddie, but Mac hastily stepped between them.

'Listen, lads. We mustn't quarrel between ourselves or we're lost. Just let's get on and make that call. It's past midday.'

65

At Riverside they were gathered around the radio transmitter/receiver when the call came.

'Has Milo Butler got the money?'

'Yes, I have.'

'All of it in used sterling?'

'Yes.'

'Right! Take the money to Enniskerry village now and park in the town centre, close to the clock tower. You've got an hour to get there. Any sign of police or any other unusual activity and all you'll get back will be a dead body. Tell that to Sean Flynn.'

Milo's anger was beyond anything he had ever felt. His voice was almost cracking from anxiety and lack of sleep but the steely edge was there.

'We want to speak to Izzy *NOW* or we go no further. But I promise you this. If anything happens to her I'll spend the rest of my life and every penny I have tracking you down. Then I'll kill you myself like the rabid dogs that you are.'

'Watch it, Butler! We've only agreed to return her alive. If you make us angry she's the one who'll suffer. She'll speak to you now.'

'Be careful, brat. One word out of place and I'll shoot you.' Izzy had no doubt whatsoever that Willie meant it.

'Daddy, oh Daddy! I'm here.' She sounded so distressed.

'We love you, my darling Izzy. Are you all right?'

'I'm alive, Daddy. I keep praying that I'll soon be home with you and Mum. I keep saying our favourite psalm, the one we sang at Granny's funeral. Can I talk to Mum?'

Willie pushed her away from the radio.

'That's enough.'

'One hour. You should just make it in that fine big car of yours, but I suggest you move it, and remember, if you value her life, no one else. We'll be watching.'

'How do I know I'll get my child back? How do I know you won't just take the money and run, and keep her so as to make further demands? Or maybe you'll take the money and we'll never see her again.' Milo couldn't bring himself to say "kill her".

'You'll find with the arrangements we've made that won't be possible.'

66

'I need someone to come with me to help carry all that cash for the handover. There are four heavy bags.'

They'd obviously anticipated this stipulation.

'Your brother – no one else.' And he'd gone.

While still distraught, there was some feeling of relief at knowing Izzy was still alive. They all were galvanized into action. Milo and Tommy hurried to collect up what they needed to take with them, Tommy so relieved to be able to do something to help. While they scurried around, Noola was talking about Izzy's brief communication.

'What a strange comment for her to make in the circumstances, Milo. Your favourite psalm! What on earth was she talking about? I expect she's in such a state she's rambling.'

Milo stopped in his tracks. He was so taken up with getting away as fast as possible he hadn't really had time to analyse the comments.

'Good Lord, Noola! You know what she was trying to do? She was trying to give us a hint as to where they're holding her.'

'Whatever do you mean?'

'She was very upset after her granny's funeral. I told her that her granny's favourite psalm was the one we sang at the funeral, the hundred and twenty-first, "I will lift up mine eyes unto the hills". I told her this was my favourite too. We read it again together. That brave little girl was trying to give us a hint as to where they're holding her. In the mountains. Would you believe that, Sean? She's confirmed what we thought.'

At that moment the call came in from Bertie and Jack.

'We've got them Sean, and we know you've just had their call. What's the score?'

'An hour to get to Enniskerry centre with the money.'

'We're quite close to Enniskerry.' Jack gave him their location. 'Lots of detailed photos too so there'll be no difficulty identifying them. When we've got the child back you can spread them all over the papers. You'll get them!'

'Make your way to Enniskerry pronto. I'll get as close as I dare with my men but they'll be watching for us so we'll have to stay well back. I'd love to know how they're going to manage the handover and then get away, with the whole of the Dublin police force looking for them.'

They started down the hillside.

'I wonder where their vehicle is? We know they must have one but I didn't see any sign of it.'

'I bet they've hidden it in the trees at the turn into that track. Let's go and have a look.'

'We haven't got too much time.'

'Neither have they, but we're only about twenty minutes from Enniskerry. Less if I put my foot down.'

They found the van and quickly took more photos.

* * * * *

Milo drove as if Lucifer himself was on his tail, cutting corners; breaking speed limits; smearing tyre marks along the roads and once or twice almost overturning the car, but he didn't care. He kept going as fast as he could possibly manage. Blotting everything else from his mind was the image of Izzy in peril, waiting out there, needing him. Since it demanded his full concentration they spoke little, but something was bothering Tommy.

'How did they know I was there? They must have kept a permanent watch at the entrance gates to the house. But even then how did they know who I was?'

'Well, it couldn't have been the old tramp informant, unless in another guise he was their observer.'

'They had the whole thing very well organized.'

'They'd have to, Tommy, for something like this.'

'Frightening! I'm glad we're armed. It makes me feel a lot safer. Especially knowing they're bound to be.'

And so they mused on, eventually lapsing into silence.

They reached the centre of Enniskerry with five minutes to spare and parked close to the Clock Tower. Being the early afternoon in the middle of the week, there were few people about. In fact it was quieter than Milo ever remembered seeing it. Then the wait began. More psychological torment, but they had expected something like this, designed to stress them out even further and throw them off their stride. Occasionally people strolled past, including a few hikers, not an uncommon sight here. Then, at last, a small boy knocked at the car window and Milo rolled it down.

68

'I've a note here. Are yez the Butlers?'

'Yes. Who gave it to you?'

'Some fella gave me a shillin' to give it to yez.'

'Thanks.'

The instructions were quite coherent, printed in a childish hand, in pencil, on exercise-book paper. It was slightly dog-eared from having been screwed up in the boy's grubby fist but still perfectly legible:

Drive to St Patrick's Church at the edge of the village. Milo Butler alone will carry two of the bags into the church. The door will be unlocked and there will be no unexpected visitors.

Milo would never know or care how they had contrived this.

Many hours had been spent planning carefully. Milo's comments to them had also confirmed what they had deduced, that he would never agree to go alone and unarmed into a remote meeting spot with all that money. So, although quiet, he would realize that the chosen venue was public enough for them not to get away too easily if they tried to do a runner, especially with Tommy, armed, outside. At the same time it was secluded enough for the necessary check. At the early planning stage, "Himself" had also warned them that if they did anything stupid, such as running with the money and killing their victim, they'd never be able to try that method of raising funds again. They'd have lost all credibility and future access to an endless source of finance for the organisation.

Milo followed the instructions and Tommy stayed leaning casually against the car, holding his gun as discreetly as possible under his jacket. He never dreamt he would be so grateful for his ability to use various weapons, started by being taught at Riverside and developed further when he joined the RAF. He was a pretty good shot and wouldn't hesitate if Milo needed him.

'Up to the altar,' a voice directed Milo and two armed men appeared from behind the vestry door, wearing balaclavas. A sound behind made him turn and he saw two more, also armed. One moved up behind him and the other stayed by the open door, looking out at Tommy.

69

'Put the bags on the floor, open them, then step back *and don't try anything.*'

'Why would I? You have my child!'

'But we know you're armed.'

'So are you.'

The voice grunted something incoherent in response.

They counted the money from one of the bags, working extremely fast. They did a very quick, superficial sort through the contents of the other bag and then stepped away.

'Take them out, put them in the boot of your car and bring in the other two.'

Milo followed the instructions and as he zipped up the two bags one of the men stepped forward and, ensuring no deliberate substitution, drew a large cross on each bag with a thick marker pen. Milo swapped the bags, making sure he remained in full view of them, so they could see there was no sleight of hand. He carried the other two into the church and the same procedure took place.

Milo was completely outraged. On top of their many other crimes, so far as he was concerned, to count this money out in front of the altar was an act of sacrilege. He wouldn't have been surprised and would, indeed, have been highly delighted if an Almighty hand had appeared from above and struck the villains dead.

'Now wait for us to pull in behind you and then drive to Powerscourt Waterfall at a steady pace, like tourists out for a day's sightseeing. Park as close to the falls as you can. We'll be right on your tail so no tricks.'

'Will my child be there?'

'She's there.'

'Suppose there are visitors there?'

'There won't be.'

'Okay. No tricks.'

Round and round it went in his head.

'I'm coming for you, Izzy. I'm coming for you. Daddy's coming for you, my darling child. God keep you until I have you safely in my arms again.'

70

Chapter 10

After the call to Riverside had been made, Izzy had been bundled back indoors. She was still quite distraught and Eddie tried to calm and comfort her, while cleaning and disinfecting her damaged lip. He tried to get her to go back down into the cellar and this seemed to be the last straw. The tears ran down her face.

'Please, no. Not back down there, Doctor Eddie – I heard that man call you Eddie.'

'It's all right, girleen, it's only for a few minutes. Then once we leave here it'll soon be over. I'll leave the trapdoor open and you can call me Eddie, that's okay.'

Izzy started to panic. There was no way she could endure this hell, all alone, for one second longer. Since she'd drawn to his attention how bored she was, from time to time Eddie had played a game of cards with her. Realising she had no choice about returning down there, she tried to persuade him to stay with her.

'Please, Eddie, I think I'm going to have one of my fits and I shouldn't be alone when that happens. Could you stay and play a game of cards with me or just talk to me *please*? It might stop the fit.'

'All right, Izzy,' he answered hastily. 'I'll stay with you 'til we're ready to go. They don't need me up here, so don't panic. Come down the ladder with me and we'll have a game of cards.'

Outside a call was made to "Himself" for any last minute instructions. Then the final arrangements were made to move out. There was little to do since they just had to ensure they left nothing behind to tell any tales. Yes, Izzy would be able to give descriptions of them but it would be open to doubt given the age and condition of the child, mental and physical. Anyhow, she might not survive.

71

Better if she didn't Willie thought. In spite of the strict instructions, they all knew Willie wouldn't hesitate to kill her if it would help their cause and Bob would positively relish the chance to finish her off.

'Shamus, go and get the van.'

Willie went and shouted down into the cellar.

'Bring the brat out.'

Eddie and Izzy came back up the ladder.

'Tie her up and get her into the van.'

'You don't need to tie her up, Willie. Surely you're not afraid of what a little kid like that might do. There'll be *five* of us in the van with her, for God's sake!'

'Getting softer all the time are we, Eddie?'

'Just realistic, Willie. Surely you're not afraid of her, or maybe it's that ghost that's worrying you!'

Willie swore violently at him, casting doubt on his parentage and suggesting he did something that, if taken in its literal Anglo-Saxon sense, could be construed as a positively enjoyable experience.

Mac stepped in again.

'Cool it, both of you. No point in falling out at this stage when we're almost there. Now, everybody outside.'

Eddie and Izzy with Bob got into the back of the van. Although Bob was heavily medicated, Eddie made sure he sat between him and Izzy. Bob glowered at her but when she spoke to Grandpa Tom, looking directly at the space beside him, he shrank back glancing around fearfully. She remembered his reaction the last time she had mentioned Grandpa Tom. Willie and Mac put in a very few items which included the radio.

'Pull down the track a bit, Shamus.'

They returned to the cottage with large jerrycans and soon there was a strong smell of petrol. They ran out, tossed a lighted taper through the door and were well clear before the whole place erupted. There would be no evidence.

They made a dash for the van but when they leapt in there was no Shamus. He had heard Izzy's comment to her imagined grandfather and had been completely unnerved. As soon as he had moved the van he got out as fast as he could. While all other eyes were turned towards what was going on at the cottage he ran, hell-

72

for-leather, down the winding track and into the woods at the bottom, disappearing completely from view. No way was he staying in that van. He'd make his way back down to civilization on foot. He knew they couldn't afford to waste time searching for him. He didn't care about the money any more. He just wanted to get as far away as possible.

'Where the hell's Shamus?'

'Don't know. He was standing out there when you were back in the cottage.'

'The big eejit. He's run off on us at a time like this. And we were *all* supposed to get away with the money together.'

'Doesn't matter, Mac. He'll be dealt with. Let's get going – I'll drive.'

'Okay. Straight to Powerscourt Waterfall, but you can take your time. The others have to get to Enniskerry and then the money will have to be counted. That'll take a while.' Mac laughed. 'Anyhow, we don't want to get stopped for speeding at this stage.'

When they got near to Powerscourt Waterfall there was, as they had been told to expect, a notice saying the road and the falls were closed to the public for the day, but not saying why. The area had been hired for quite a considerable sum on the pretense that a film was to be made there. It was explained that those making the movie didn't want curious members of the public turning up to watch them and maybe getting in the way of the work. They wanted them kept well away until the filming was finished.

There was plenty of flat space around the area of the falls and they parked well away from any trees, as instructed. Mac and Willie took out the radio and set it up beside the van, where they thought there should be good reception. Then, lighting up their cigarettes and balaclavas at the ready, they settled down for what they expected to be a bit of a wait.

* * * * *

Jack and Bertie were able to follow the van at quite a distance behind, for when they had found it hidden away they had attached a homing device under it's back bumper. As they passed the turning

73

to the waterfall they could see it making it's way along at a sedate speed. They drove past and well beyond before stopping to call Sean.

'Powerscourt Waterfall, Sean,'

'Got it! I've used side roads to get round and south of Enniskerry, so we're quite close. One of my undercover men tells me that Milo and Tommy have arrived in the main square. Got Noel and Declan with me.'

'If we meet we can work out a way of getting some of us in on foot, through the trees. They were driving quite slowly so I suspect there's no mad hurry. They must be counting the money somewhere.'

'Meet me soonest at Ballybawn. Just drive south on the road you're on now. You're very close to it. I'll see you coming.'

'Right!'

They found the tiny settlement without any trouble. They all squashed into the one car and set off again for the entrance to the waterfall, with Declan driving. They drove past, stopped close to the wooded side of the track and the two of them with Sean and Noel leapt out. The car sped off and all four headed for the trees at a run. Moving through the wood at a pretty smart pace, it didn't take them long to get to the area where they could see the van was parked and, well hidden, they settled down to wait.

Twenty minutes later Milo and Tommy arrived with another car behind them. As soon as they reached the falls the other driver turned around and drove away fast, both men still wearing their balaclavas.

They had heard the cars approaching while they were some distance down the track. Mac had sent off one more urgent message on the radio then got the others out of the van and told them to pull on their balaclavas. He would brook no opposition now to tying Izzy's hands and feet with tapes.

'Don't argue this time, Eddie. We can't chance her trying to run off and jinxing things up altogether.'

'Okay, but I'll do it myself.' Which he did, whispering to her: 'Don't worry, your dad's just about here and I'll not pull the tapes too tight.'

74

Tommy parked the car and Milo, spotting Izzy surrounded by four men in balaclavas, three of them armed, leapt out and started to run towards her calling her name over and over. She had spotted him at the same instant and was screaming to him.

'Daddy, Daddy! You've come for me, oh you've come for me. Daddy *please help me.*'

Being tied up she couldn't move and was being held tightly by Mac, his gun to her head.

'Back off, Butler, or we'll shoot her and you!' Milo stopped short. At that moment, given the chance, he would have tried to kill all four of them with his bare hands.

'Back to your car.'

Milo, Tommy and the men hiding wondered how on earth they hoped to get away with all that money in this van, which would be so easy to track down. They got their totally unexpected answer. There was a buzzing sound from the far side of the waterfall and over the top of the hill came a dark grey helicopter with no markings. They watched in amazement as it settled on the flat ground not far from the van. The door opened but nobody got out and the rotor blades kept spinning.

'Right, Butler, lift the bags out and carry two of them to that lump of rock there near the chopper. Then put them on the ground and back away. We'll bring your child to that point and when we've loaded them, we'll swap her for the last two.'

Milo followed the instructions. Tommy stayed by the car with his firearm at the ready. Willie loaded the two bags and Milo returned to his car for the other two. He stepped forward, this time with Tommy beside him, making no effort to conceal his gun.

All would have gone to plan for them had it not been for Bob. One look at Milo and he had torn off the irritating balaclava. He didn't care whether or not "Tom Butler" saw him. In fact he wanted him to. His moment had come at last.

Unobserved by the other three men he had managed to get hold of a gun. He had seen where Shamus had hidden his in the van and, when the attention of the others was distracted, he had taken it from its hiding place and tucked it under his jacket. He wasn't going to kill Tom Butler first, oh no, he was going to kill his child; that would

75

hurt him much more. Then, oh sweet revenge, he'd kill him too. He ran towards where the exchange was about to take place beside the helicopter. The two bags were put on the ground and Eddie stooped to undo Izzy's bonds. That was the moment Bob shouted his venom.

'Got you! Got you both, Tom Butler.'

Raising the gun he took aim at Izzy but Eddie threw her to the ground and lay protectively over her, so Bob's bullets tore into him instead. Willie didn't hesitate. He and Mac had been instructed not to allow Bob, Eddie or Shamus to survive. Assuming Eddie was dead, he shot Bob twice through the back of the head, then he and Mac grabbed the remaining bags and threw them into the chopper, leaping in after them. Milo and Tommy were too concerned with getting to Izzy to make any effort to stop their escape. At least with Izzy pinned under Eddie they couldn't harm her any more.

Suddenly four men, screaming like banshees, burst from the nearby trees. The helicopter was preparing to take off but the door was still open. At the sight and sound of these unexpected attackers heading straight for them Willie and Mac panicked.

'Move it!' Willie screamed at the pilot holding the gun to his head.

'The door.'

'Just go. We'll manage!'

Bertie and Jack had put hand grenades in their pockets "just in case". They had given Sean and Noel one each and now as they tore towards the chopper, they all, simultaneously, pulled the pins and threw as it started to rise from the ground. Jack and Noel missed and the grenades fell into the stream where they exploded doing no real harm, although the concussion from the explosions hit the chopper. Bertie was a first-class cricket player and Sean a talented hurler. Their throwing arms were powerful and accurate. Both of their grenades went straight through the open door of the helicopter. It swerved as they exploded and continued drunkenly on its course before dropping in flames into the trees the far side of the stream.

In the meantime Milo and Tommy had reached Eddie and Izzy. Eddie was clearly badly injured and in severe pain. They lifted him carefully and Tommy looked after him while Milo took Izzy into his arms.

76

'Daddy!'

'My precious Izzy. Are you all right?'

'Yes. I am now. Can you hold me safely like this for ever?'

'For as long as you want, sweetheart. But let's go home now to Mum and the others. You can imagine how worried we've all been and Mum will want to hold you in her arms too.'

'Eddie saved my life, Daddy. Will he be all right?'

'They'll do their best for him.'

He carried her back to the car while the helicopter burned fiercely. It would be some time before anyone would be able to go anywhere near it. Sean came running over to them.

'Hello there, Izzy. What a heroine you are. I'm delighted to have you back with us all. Are you all right?'

'Yes, Uncle Sean. Where did you come from?' She held out her arms for a hug.

'We'll swap stories when we get to Riverside. I want to hear your story too, so let's wait. Milo, I suggest Tommy drives you and Izzy home. The rest of us will stay here and mop up. I'll call in more help and an ambulance for that injured man. He doesn't look too good.'

'He saved my life, Uncle Sean, when that nasty Bob tried to kill me.'

'I know, darlin'. We'll look after him. Two of the men are with him now, doing what they can.'

'Sean! Thanks…' Milo was too choked up to say any more.

'I know, Milo. See you when we all get back. We'll have a helluva celebration.'

Izzy was surprisingly lively considering what she had been through, but Milo realized that the adrenalin rush of relief and excitement at being rescued must be keeping her going. He knew she would go down like a pricked balloon quite soon. She would probably cry and cry and he wouldn't try to stop her. He knew it would be an important cathartic process. They got to the car and he set her down on her feet. Tommy came running up to them and swept her into his arms swinging her off the ground.

'You came to rescue me too, Tommy!' and then the tears started and she began to shake.

'My sweet Izzy! The whole of the Butler and Flynn families would have come to your rescue if they had been allowed.'

She looked dreadful, worse than he had anticipated, and he tried not to show his shock.

Milo wrapped her in his jacket and held her close all the way home. Sean had promised to call Riverside immediately and let them know Izzy was safe and they were on their way.

Chapter 11

At Riverside the day had crawled by on the proverbial leaden feet. Mageen, Bill and Harry found it difficult to face the idea of going to the office, knowing the call was due at midday, but agreed to go to keep up the pretence that nothing was amiss. They did, however, excuse themselves after a couple of hours on the pretext of approaching exams and revision. So they had all been in the library when the call had come through. After Milo and Tommy had driven away, Noola stayed glued to the phone and radio receiver, with Maggie never straying from her side. Everybody fidgeted around unable to settle to anything, but always staying close to the library. Shortly after the two men had left, Freddie called.

'I wish there was something I could do to help, Mageen. I can't go out there at the moment. My tutor wants to see me at three o'clock this afternoon, but I can get there after that.'

'I'd love to have you here with us, Freddie. If all goes to plan we should have Izzy home around that time and we'll be celebrating in such a big way. We're all just a bit worried as to what sort of state she'll be in. She'll have been through such an ordeal. There'll be lots to tell you when you get here.'

Although dying to see Freddie and tell him everything, knowing the line was tapped Mageen felt that, even at this late stage, she should be ultra cautious as to what she said.

Early in the afternoon there was an unexpected bonus in the shape of Paddy, arriving with Aunt May, still looking rather battered and bruised. Although he thought she should stay in the hospital for at least a week to be on the safe side, she wouldn't hear of it. This proved to be a welcome distraction for they all loved her and she

79

was thrilled to bits at the welcome home that she was given. Maggie had promised to phone Paddy as soon as the call came through, so he had been able to give May the news in the hospital.

'Do you really think anyone would persuade me to stay here when, with any luck, our Izzy will be home later on today? Poor little scrap. I hope she's all right. I'm going straight home to wait for her arrival with everyone else. And if you won't take me, Paddy Flynn, I'll get a taxi.' She grinned at him.

Paddy, also anxious to be there when Izzy arrived, had taken the rest of the day off. He knew it would be essential to give her a very thorough once-over and then to stay close by for the rest of the evening and, if necessary, overnight.

As soon as she heard the news of the expected arrival home, Kitty felt it would be sensible to prepare a really good meal. If all went well, there could be quite a large crowd sitting down to dinner that evening and, for a change, eating heartily. Like so many others, she was praying hard that the little girl would be brought back to Riverside safely.

At long last Sean's call came through.

'She's all right. Milo's got her and Tommy's driving them home.'

'Thanks be to God and thank *you*, Sean.'

'We're all delighted. Got to run. All the details when I get back. Bye!'

'Goodbye, Sean. God bless!'

Noola put down the receiver and, bursting into tears, passed the news to everybody else. Then everyone else started to cry. Even the boys and Paddy found their eyes filling up. The joy and relief was overwhelming.

'Okay everybody, now the huge welcome home. We've all been too upset and apprehensive to think further than getting Izzy back safely so let's get organized. There's lots to do.'

'Good for you, Granny,' and they all ran around, happy to follow Maggie's and Aunt May's suggestions and filling the last waiting minutes very effectively. Except for Noola, who stood outside, pacing up and down. A huge welcome home was wonderful, and was keeping the others occupied, but all she wanted was to have her child in her arms. To her the wait was unendurable, but at least Izzy was alive.

80

Then they arrived, Tommy blowing the horn continuously all the way down the long drive, so that the whole of Riverside would hear. Everyone, including every member of the staff on duty, ran to the front of the house. Each one carried a rose, a flower that Izzy loved and which was in plentiful bloom at that time of the year. The car screeched to a halt and almost before it had stopped, Milo was out with Izzy in his arms. He put her down and Noola was right there, arms open, waiting to gather her child to her heart.

'Izzy, my darling Izzy, you're home in my arms at last. I love you so very, very much.'

'Mum, Mum, I love you too.' But, exhausted by her appalling experience and overwhelming emotion, at that moment she was beyond saying any more.

Then the others all crowded around and Izzy, to her delight, was showered with hugs and roses.

* * * * *

Sitting between her mother and father, and surrounded by the rest of the family Izzy ate her first real meal in days. Kitty had done her proud, producing all her favourite food, including salmon, freshly caught from the river; roast chicken raised on the estate; fresh peaches and grapes from the conservatory and mountains of ice cream. Then she had been bathed and given an extremely thorough once-over by Paddy. As well as the split lip, her face was badly bruised where Willie had hit her and the dermatitis was severe. But everything was treated and she was already feeling a lot better physically and dramatically improved emotionally and psychologically. Everyone was dying to hear all the details of her story but all were acutely aware of the difficulty she would probably have in talking about it. She started to give Milo and Noola a slightly garbled account of some parts of her ordeal, but was asleep before she even got as far as the bed. The only place that she was willing to sleep that night was between her parents in their huge double bed. Feeling exactly the same way themselves there was no argument. Noola climbed into the bed beside her and she too quickly fell into an exhausted sleep, Izzy safely in her arms at last.

81

* * * * *

A good two hours after the others had arrived home, Sean got back to the house with Bertie and Jack. The two would love to have met Izzy but, since she was already in bed, they realized that would have to wait. Having greeted and rejoiced with the rest of the family Sean then took Milo and Tommy aside.

'Sorry about your Uncle Bob, Tommy.'

'Please don't be. It's actually a relief. I was never close to him and any affection I might have had rapidly disappeared when I heard that he had helped with the abduction of Izzy. In the end he was the one who tried to kill her. So don't worry, Sean.'

'Okay, Tommy. Milo, I know you and Noola won't be happy about this but I would like to get as much information from Izzy as possible while it's still fresh in her mind. I'd like to have a chat to her in the morning, after she's had, I hope, a good night's rest. Has Paddy given her a sedative?'

'Yes, he has. Let's just wait and see how she is. She's told us quite a lot already and we can pass that on to you.'

'We still need to be careful. Whoever's behind this will want to eliminate that injured man so that he can't talk. In a day or two we'll possibly release information implying that he didn't survive, simply for his own protection. But we mustn't give away anything about how we came to be on the spot at the point of handover.'

'So we still need to preserve the inner circle?'

'Yes. Oh and, Milo, sorry about the money. The whole lot went up in flames. Nothing left except ashes.'

'Do you know, Sean, I don't give a damn. We've got Izzy back safely and that's all we wanted. If it's cost us a million pounds then it's been worth it. We owe you three and others in your force, Sean, so much. More than we'll ever be able to repay.' He turned to Jack and Bertie.

'I'll collect the sterling as quickly as I can without raising too many questions. The bank manager will wonder what's going on, but I'll work out some plausible story.'

'Oh, I shouldn't bother, Milo.' Bertie grinned at him.

'What do you mean? Of course I must bother. It's a million

pounds that's literally gone up in smoke. And it belongs to your organization.'

Jack and Bertie were both laughing now.

'It's all right, Milo, honestly. You see it was counterfeit.'

'What? My God!' Milo was really shaken. 'Supposing they'd realized that. It would have been the end of Izzy and probably Tommy and me too. Those fellows were really trigger happy.'

'Not a chance. We wouldn't have taken that risk. They were such good counterfeit that it would have taken an expert at the Royal Mint to detect what they were. Not even the bank people would have known – well not too easily anyhow. Believe me we've used the deception very successfully before. But that's not information to go beyond this room, or we could never try it again. The beauty of it is that had things worked out differently and they'd got away with the money, once they'd started spending it they would have left a trail as wide as an airport landing strip leading us straight to them.'

Milo collapsed into a chair. He was silent for a few seconds and then started to laugh. Sean looked dumbfounded, then he started to laugh too and Tommy joined in.

'But what story are we going to tell the family? We can't leave them thinking the million was lost. After all, they all knew we'd got it, although not where from.'

'Don't worry, Milo. A rescue by the Special Branch, which must be kept very hush-hush, might convince everyone. Very few of us know that the money was burnt. Even Izzy can't be aware of it. Maybe we can let it be thought, within the family, that we managed to retrieve it. The only person besides ourselves who would know what really happened would be Noel, who, may I say, is vastly disappointed that his grenade didn't hit the chopper. He's already been warned to say nothing to anybody until we've decided how much, if anything, we're going to release for general consumption. He's a good man. I trust him. We need to think this through slowly and carefully before we come up with an agreed strategy. We're all too tired now and if Kitty could find something for us to eat, that would be great.'

'That won't be a problem. She cooked enough for an army when she knew Izzy was safe and on her way home. Jack, Bertie, how long

83

can you stay with us without anyone realising there's something that doesn't quite fit in your cover story?' Sean stepped in quickly.

'Oh I think I could give anyone reason enough as to why I still need them here. And indeed I do for a few days for a debrief with yourselves and the others in the team. There's an awful lot to discuss.'

'I'd love to stay for a day or two longer and get to know the family under less distressing circumstances. What do you think Bertie?'

'I'd enjoy that too. I'm sure we'd be given leave to stay for just a day or two, if that's all right with you, Milo?'

'So far as I'm concerned stay as long as you like. It would give me and indeed everyone else the greatest of pleasure to have you with us for a bit longer.'

'Great! We must report in though and give an update. They'll be delighted at the way it's turned out.'

'Good. And now I want to get back to the rest of the family and then join Izzy and Noola for a good sleep.'

* * * * *

The family and staff outside the inner circle accepted, without protest, that there was still need for great caution. The feeling of relief throughout the whole household was palpable. They would all have loved to sit with Izzy and hear her story but understood she needed to be whisked away. Noola had never once left her side and Milo only at the request of Sean for further debriefing and planning of strategies.

With Tommy, Freddie, Jack and Bertie joining them, the rest of the family celebrated on for a while, but, feeling emotionally exhausted, some of them started to drift off to bed, thankful that they could now relax and have a decent night's rest. Mageen and Freddie strolled into the conservatory, built onto the lovely old Georgian house during Tom Butler's lifetime. It was originally to house his orchids but there were not many of those left now with only Maggie trying to look after them for Tom's sake.

'Thanks for coming and celebrating with us, Freddie. Having

84

you here from time to time over these dreadful days has meant such a lot to us, especially to me.'

'Well, Mageen, you know I love little Izzy and I'm as relieved as the rest of you to have her back with us again. I'd love to hear her full story. I still can't understand the mentality of anyone who could do such a thing to a frail child.'

'Thanks, Freddie. Would you like to stay the night?'

'No thanks. Got to get back. I'm still *way* behind in the revision and I'm seriously concerned about those exams, but I'll run out again tomorrow morning.'

'But not too early, please.'

They both laughed.

'Mageen, when all this is over and things have returned to normal, there's something I want to ask you.'

'Oh? Why not now?'

'It's not an appropriate moment. I do have some sensitivity towards the family's feelings.'

Mageen's heart was beating so fast. She did love Freddie to the point of distraction and had not been absolutely certain that he returned her feelings.

'I love you, Mageen, so much. You do know that, don't you?'

'Well, I do now that you've told me. And, Freddie, I love you so much too.'

They kissed each other long and passionately and, after a lapse of some time, he told her he must get back to his rooms and they walked up the long drive together. She stayed with him until the bus back to the city arrived. They kissed goodbye and he hopped on.

As she started back down the drive she reflected how lucky she was to have found a kindred spirit like Freddie: they seemed to have so much in common. She was highly delighted that everyone in the family liked him too. Not only that, she had met his sister, Katie, when she came over to have a look around Dublin and she and Mageen had really hit it off. Katie had confirmed for Mageen what Freddie had told her about having been orphaned during the war and being brought up by their grandparents. If Freddie's question was what she hoped, then there would be another cause for celebration and a bonus to add to the safe return of Izzy.

She actually danced along much of the drive. She felt elated. Life was so good again after their nightmare. Izzy was safely home. Freddie was going to propose to her, and it was such bliss to be able to move around freely and without fear again. When she got back to the house Jack and Bertie were having a nightcap with Tommy, Bill and Harry in the sitting room. The twins were bursting with questions, but, bearing Sean's request in mind, managed to contain their curiosity. Mageen put her head round the door to say goodnight.

'Won't you come and join us, Mageen?'

In truth she felt too excited to go to bed just yet. Freddie's declaration had swept away her tiredness.

'Yes, actually I'd love to, Tommy.'

Jack was delighted. He didn't have enough time to attract her away from Freddie, but he was going to make the very most of the time he had. Realistically he knew that it could never go anywhere anyhow, given the job he did and their worlds being so far apart. However, he would so enjoy flirting with her.

Chapter 12

As a special favour, Milo asked Mageen, Bill and Harry if they would go into the office on Wednesday morning and represent the family again, maintaining as best they could a semblance of normality and the fiction that he still had a very upset stomach. Milo didn't need to worry about the business running smoothly without him for a few days. His cousin, Martin, some years his senior, was quite capable of holding the fort in their stockbroking business for a prolonged period. Milo would eventually tell him the story, even if only a sanitized version of it. In the meantime, Milo called him to explain that he would not be back for a day or two and this was accepted with some expressions of concern for his health. It was completely out-of-character for Milo to be even mildly ill.

'I've had a nasty few days. I won't go into the details just now. I hope I'll be back before the end of the week.' And this was no lie.

'Take your time, Milo, all is well here. We've had a few good deals go through. Tell you all when you get back.'

'Thanks, Martin.'

Much later that morning the members of the inner circle gathered around in the library and Izzy, sitting on her father's knee, held firmly in his arms and feeling so safe, agreed to tell about some of her experiences as a prisoner. She was introduced to Jack and Bertie and was told of their part in her rescue, as members of Sean's special team. Everyone was relieved that she looked so much better after a good night's sleep, although her face was still badly bruised, her split lip swollen and her dermatitis angry looking.

Paddy, now accepted as a part of the inner circle, didn't object to his patient being encouraged to talk about it, since he thought

87

talking it out of her system could be a good part of the healing process. But he was adamant that if she started to show signs of distress, they must stop. He knew she should really be in hospital, but he also knew that to take her away from home again would be much too traumatic for her and, anyhow, as an additional and agreed member of the inner circle, he was there watching over her.

So Izzy started to tell her story. She described the horrors of the cellar, her unremitting fear, listening at the top of the ladder and so finding out something of what they were planning. How Bob had raved on about "Tom Butler" and wanted to harm her, because she was a Butler. She'd assumed that must be her Grandpa Tom and so she'd decided to pretend that he was there in the cellar with her, because she thought that might worry them and make them more careful how they treated her.

'What on earth gave you such a clever idea?'

'Granny FitzPatrick! For a while before she died she often talked to someone who wasn't there. I remembered that you said it was spooky, Daddy, and made you feel uncomfortable. I thought if it made you feel like that and you're big and tough, then it might make them feel creepy. I think it really did work, because that nasty Bob went a funny colour when I told him Grandpa had said if he touched me he would die. And the one they called Shamus moved as far away from me as he could. Even Eddie seemed to be nervous when I pretended to talk to Grandpa. He asked me what Grandpa was saying.'

By now they were all laughing which really encouraged her.

'To tell you the truth, Izzy, it would probably make most of us feel uneasy.'

'Even you Uncle Sean?'

'Well, few of us would completely dismiss the idea. You just never know! Strange things have happened.'

'A funny thing did happen. In the end I began to feel that there *was* somebody there with me, trying to protect me. I actually began to talk to him when I was alone. And you know, it really helped me.'

There was a brief silence while they all interpreted this according to their beliefs.

'How fascinating. Maybe Grandpa *was* watching over you, or the Good Lord himself. Whichever, it's an astonishing story.'

88

'I wish I'd known him, Daddy.'

'So do I. And he would have loved you such a lot.'

'Why did Bob hate him so much?'

'Bob was a very sick man, Izzy. It's a long story for another time. But now we want to hear the rest of *your* story. How about your idea to mention the psalm? It was really clever too and did give us a clue as to where you were.'

'Eddie gave me some old papers, like he promised. They were copies of the paper Granny likes, *Ireland's Own*. There are stories and puzzles in it and you're told to look for clues. So I thought maybe I could give you a clue if I got a chance. Something Eddie said made me realize we must be in the mountains. I didn't know until then. I had nothing else to do and plenty of time to think up ways of helping you to rescue me or even escaping.'

'But I'm surprised they didn't realize you were up to something. Didn't anyone say anything?' Noola was amazed.

'No. You see Eddie and the big fat man called Willie kept fighting. They were so cross with each other I don't think they thought about what I'd said.'

'It wouldn't have occurred to them that you might do anything so clever. You've impressive powers of recall, although I suppose it's not surprising you'd remember such horror in detail. After all, some of it only happened yesterday. But what did they fight about?' Sean was intrigued: villains falling out.

'Each time it was when Eddie was trying to protect me.'

'Against what?'

'Willie hit me when I screamed for help. Eddie put his arms around me and wouldn't let anyone touch me again. When Willie told him he was soft he said he couldn't be or he wouldn't have got mixed up in "this dirty business". Then Eddie . . . well he really told him he was a coward and didn't have as much courage as I had. Later, when Willie wanted to tie me up to go in the van, Eddie asked him if he was afraid of me or Grandpa's ghost. Willie was raging and told Eddie he was to "funk off" and that he was a "bustard". He was going to punch Eddie but the other man stopped him. What did he mean, Daddy?'

Everyone in the room had the hardest time not bursting out

laughing again. Trying to keep a straight face Milo did his best to answer.

'Well, a bustard is a very big bird. You don't find them here in Ireland.' Then he started to struggle but Bertie came to the rescue.

'People who are scared stiff are sometimes described as being in a blue funk, Izzy.'

'Oh. So Willie was telling Eddie that he was to go away and be scared stiff and that he was a big bird. It doesn't make much sense to me.' The logical brain was working overtime.

'No, well a lot of things about these people don't make much sense. How they knew all they did is something of a mystery to me.'

'We could find out yet, Sean. Eddie could tell us a lot. How is he by the way?'

'Still hanging in there, Tommy.'

'I hope he doesn't die, Uncle Sean. He did try to protect me and he saved my life.'

'We know Izzy. We know. We're doing our best to keep him alive.'

What Sean didn't say was that he desperately wanted the man to live because of the information he could give about the organisation. As for protecting and saving Izzy – he was one of the abductors for God's sake. But he had heard that sometimes hostages developed quite a close relationship with their abductors. In her perilous situation it was understandable that the child would feel grateful to anyone who had been kind to her.

'You said there were five of them altogether, Izzy. But when we saw you all at the waterfall there were only four men around you.'

'Yes, there were five at the house, but Shamus, the driver, ran away. I think he was frightened about Grandpa's ghost. When we were in the van, before they set the house on fire, I was scared of Bob, so I pretended to talk to Grandpa again. That's when Shamus ran away.'

'We need to find him too. Izzy, it's fine to talk about this within the family but we're not going to spread the story outside just yet. For the moment could I ask you not to talk about Shamus or say that Eddie's still alive?'

'Yes, Uncle Sean, but why?' Sean didn't want to worry her

90

unnecessarily but he felt she could cope with his reasons. Poor little Izzy was having to grow up unduly quickly.

'The people who organized this are evil and they might want to attack Shamus and Eddie so that they can't tell anything about the whole nasty plot. We need to protect them and get as much information as possible from them so as to find those behind the whole thing.'

'You mean they'd want to kill them?'

'Yes!'

'Okay. I won't say anything about them.'

'Good girl.'

After this session Izzy had her parents to herself for a while. She seemed worried about something that she obviously hadn't so far shared with them.

'Mum, Daddy, if I tell you something will you promise, please *really promise* that you won't tell anybody?'

Noola's heart stood still. What had happened that she hadn't been able to talk about in front of the others?

'Of course we'll promise. Just like you promised not to talk about certain things. You would keep your promise, wouldn't you?'

'Yes. Of course.'

'Then trust us to keep ours, my darling.' Milo was just as apprehensive.

'I told Eddie a very big lie and I'm afraid God will punish me.'

'What lie?'

'I lied about my health and you told us we must never do that, Mum, or otherwise God might send us the illness as a punishment for the lie.'

'Whatever did you say?'

'I wanted Eddie to help me as much as possible so I told him I sometimes had fits. He seemed quite upset and said nobody had told him about that or my dermatitis. But it did make him kinder. Will God punish me and make me have real fits?'

'Certainly not, my darling child. God would be the first to forgive you considering the circumstances. That was another very clever thing to do, but that was a strange comment from Eddie.'

'Yes, I thought so too. But you did *promise* you wouldn't tell!'

'No, Izzy, we won't tell.'

91

* * * * *

Sean prepared a statement for the press. The news of the crashed helicopter couldn't be hidden, so some sort of explanation had to be released. The completely accurate information was given that an unidentified helicopter had exploded on take off and that all on board had been killed. Sean hoped this would give protection to Eddie and to Shamus, whom they still hadn't found, but thanks to Bertie's photos they had pictures of him which would make the task relatively easy.

For the family at Riverside publicity was the last thing they wanted. They would much prefer the story was never told and they knew they could trust their staff not to chatter about it. Their big worry was that, since those at the head of the organization hadn't got their money, the younger family members were still vulnerable and especially Izzy. As Sean brought him up to date, Milo voiced his concern about this.

'What can we do to improve our security?'

'They'll know you'll be very much on your guard, so I don't think they'll try anything on any time soon. But you never know. You will, in any case, continue to keep a close watch on Izzy but now watch Sarah too. I'll leave some of my men on duty around the estate for the moment and I suggest you keep your firearms at the ready and easily accessible. It's an appalling thing to have to say to you but necessary for the moment. One of the things I'd dearly like to find is that informant.'

'How that would-be tramp found out so much in the time beggars belief. There has to be some other source.'

'Not necessarily, Milo. These people are professionals, well trained and experienced in this kind of thing.'

'So he was probably another member of the organization. Not just someone bribed on some pretext. Interesting! Tell you what I can do, though. Better than guns from the girls' point of view. I'll make sure all the dogs, including Mickeen's two wolfhounds, stay indoors as much as possible. I know he'll be happy to oblige. The informant knew at that time of the day Mickeen would have them all out exercising well away from the house. "Curiouser and curiouser"!'

'Okay, now sleeping arrangements?'

'Izzy will sleep between us until she feels able to go back to her own bed. For the moment the other four can all sleep in the one room. Not ideal but they won't mind. Won't be the first time. I'll suggest that Maggie, Aunt May and Tommy move in together too. That'll be fun! I can just imagine how all three would have great pleasure in taking a potshot at an intruder.'

'Great!' Sean smiled. 'If only we could find out who's behind this and who their top man is, we could do so much more – maybe wipe out the organization altogether, unless it's… Well, don't let's go there yet. I'm pinning my hopes on Eddie and Shamus.'

'How are you going to handle the information about Bob?'

'We've got that covered too. The asylum and family, including Tommy, will be more than willing to have the minimum of publicity. I feel so sorry for him and for the Featherstones too. I'm hoping they'll accept that Bob was killed in that helicopter trying to get out of the country. We don't know who helped him – true! Or why – not true! As for a body! Well, we can put him in a coffin and seal it up and give some story about the danger of infection from badly burnt bodies so we can't let anyone see the remains. I can't honestly see them wanting to argue. I bet they'll be relieved to accept our explanation, poor people. The asylum won't dispute it either, given that they let him escape. They'll take our word that it's him.'

'It's such a sad end to a sad life, Sean. I'm concerned about Tommy. He's taking Bob's involvement badly. Says he must go and see his Featherstone relations before he leaves. I don't envy him that task, but I think it'll help them. They're all very fond of him. Anyhow, he'll willingly go along with whatever cover-up story you decide to tell.'

Before he returned to his squadron Tommy did visit his Featherstone grandparents and they were highly delighted to see him. Son of their adored daughter Angela, they were so proud of him. He did his best to give support to Bob's wife and family too but the feeling of release amongst the whole family, grandparents included, was evident.

The day before Tommy went, Jack and Bertie, much to the regret of Jack in particular, also had to return to base and left with everyone's huge appreciation for what they had done, not least Sean's. He was also thrilled to bits at being given some of the gizmos that he had so envied.

'You're a grand pair of lads. I'm just sorry I can never openly acknowledge what you've done for us. I'd be more than happy to have you on my team, any time!'

'You're not so bad yourself, Sean. You never know, we might meet again some day and then you can teach us to play hurling.'

Chapter 13

Three weeks later the exams had finished and everyone at Riverside had relaxed, although Milo and Sean insisted that all the security arrangements remained in place. Eddie was still in intensive care but recovering. Curious medical staff wondered why each time he recovered consciousness he asked, "Is the little girl all right?" He said nothing else. "Wanted" notices had been posted in all police stations with pictures of Shamus attached, but so far no luck.

In anticipation that there would be good cause, it had been decided to celebrate following the publication of the exam results and preparations were being made for a very special party. Mageen had been dropping broad hints about a possible engagement, so there would be several things to celebrate.

Two days before the date set for this, the old tramp arrived at the kitchen entrance, closely shadowed by two of Sean's men. There was consternation. Mickeen called to the men to grab hold of him and ran to find Noola.

'That auld fella has turned up, looking for a bit more work. You know the one I mean – the...'

'I know exactly who you mean, Mickeen. Where is he?'

'A couple of the guards are holding onto him and he seems to be frightened out of his wits.'

'I'll phone Sean and see what he says. I imagine he'll want to come out and question him, personally. You don't think he's our informer after all?'

'No. He seems to be terrified and I'm sure it's not put on. And he's definitely not wearing a disguise.'

'All right. Ask the men to stay with him. Take them into the kitchen and ask Kitty to give the three of them a cup of tea. If he really is a poor old tramp we don't want to make his life any more miserable than necessary.'

Sean came out post-haste and gave the man a gentle if thorough grilling with Noola present. With his stammer, obviously aggravated by fright, the story come out agonizingly slowly. It turned out that he was homeless; wandering the roads all over the country; getting the odd bit of casual work; sleeping in barns in the winter or under hedges in the summer. Sometimes the Garda in the country areas were kind and gave him a few pennies to do a bit of sweeping up for them and then let him sleep in a station cell, but he wasn't supposed to tell that and didn't want to get anyone into trouble. He was shaking all over and trying hard to hide the tears which threatened to overflow and drift down his weathered cheeks. Sean didn't doubt his story but just to be certain he and Noola went upstairs to call one of the Garda stations mentioned. It was all absolutely true.

'Yes, indeed. Shure we know old Jockser well. It's a sad story. He's only eleven pence halfpenny in the shilling. Seems to have no family. Honest as the day. Never takes anything that isn't given to him. I wish there was somewhere we could find for him to live but he seems happy enough wandering around.'

Sean relayed the story to Noola who got really upset.

'I feel so awful. Let's go down and talk to him. While you reassure him I'll talk to Mickeen about giving him a bit of regular work. He may be one of those who can't sleep in a house for any length, so I'll tell him myself that anytime he wants to sleep in the stables he's very welcome. I'll get Mickeen to put some sort of a cot in there for him and he can come and go as he likes. I'll ask Kitty to give him a decent hot meal too.'

'So much for our detective work, Noola. I feel a bit uncomfortable myself, but it was the only lead we had. And now the mystery of the informant grows.'

As it turned out Jockser had a magical relationship with animals and eventually became a permanent member of the Riverside community. He helped to look after the horses and dogs and didn't mind how dirty or menial a job was; he did it cheerfully and well.

96

Life changed dramatically for him and from then on he was devoted to Noola.

* * * * *

On the day of the party Mageen was so excited she hardly knew what to do with herself. She was certain Freddie was going to propose. Champagne was already cooling in the fridge so there would be multiple causes to crack it open, for in spite of everything, miraculously, they had passed their exams with reasonable grades. The two of them were in the conservatory again.

'I want to ask you that question, Mageen, but I should speak to your father first.'

'No, Freddie. Please ask me the question. After all you don't know what my answer will be!'

He and she knew perfectly well but he played along.

'My very beautiful Mageen! I love everything about you deeply and sincerely. I would like to ask for your hand in marriage. Would you be willing to accept my proposal?'

The delightful, old-fashioned approach really appealed to her and her heart seemed to fly off into the stratosphere.

'Oh, Freddie, nothing would give me more pleasure. And, Freddie, I love everything about you too, but perhaps, most of all, your kindness and gentleness.'

A long embrace ensued, then Freddie insisted.

'Now I must speak to your father before this can be made official.'

'Wonderful. I'll wait here for you.'

Off he went to speak to Milo. As he asked his permission to marry Mageen his slight nervousness was evident, for he fidgeted and was, uncharacteristically, slightly hesitant in his speech. They chatted for a while as Milo tried to help him to relax and then he finished:

'I want to reassure you that I'm not a fortune hunter. I really love Mageen. I've got nothing to offer her at the moment. I'll finish my degree next year and my prospects are good. I'm confident that I'll be able to support a wife and family in considerable comfort.'

97

'I'm sure you will, Freddie. Reluctant as we are to part with any of our daughters, Noola and I would be delighted to have you as a son-in-law: to welcome you into the family. We enjoyed meeting your sister Katie – liked her a lot and we look forward to meeting your grandparents too.'

'And they'd love to meet you.'

'Well we must get it all set up soon. We'd be happy to have them to stay here.'

The party had got off to a good start before Milo made the announcement. There were whistles and hoots of delight and congratulations and everyone was in the best of spirits. They all wanted to hug and kiss Mageen and shake Freddie's hand or slap him on the back or even give him a hug and a kiss too, not least Izzy, who liked Freddie enormously and was delighted at the way things were turning out. Meantime Mickeen and some of his men, discreetly armed, patrolled the grounds with the dogs.

The evening wore on, the champagne flowed and some of those present became very happy indeed. Izzy was thrilled at being allowed to stay up really late. She and Sarah eventually fell asleep curled up together on the big, comfortable sofa in front of the fire. Behind them the others partied on. Noola stayed close to the sofa and was sitting perched on an arm when Freddie strolled over to join her, glass in hand. He was *very* relaxed and even tripped over the odd word.

'Izzy's looking so much better. The dermatitis seems to have cleared up and the split lip has healed.'

'Yes, young children recover from things remarkably quickly. It's a pity she picks up infections so easily but we're hoping she'll grow out of all these minor ailments in time.'

'That's a relief. Do you think she'll grow out of the fits too?'

Noola, an exceptionally astute person, didn't miss a beat.

'Oh, I expect she will.' She was finding it extremely difficult not to betray her shock and agitation.

'She looks so relaxed, Mrs Butler. You'd never think she'd been through such a dreadful experience.'

'She's a very brave little girl, Freddie. Where's Mageen?'

'Over there with her granny. Do you mind if I go and join them? I mustn't be too late back so I don't want to be away from her any more than I have to, especially this evening. I'm so delighted that she's said "yes" and that you and Mr Butler are happy about it.'

'Of course we are, Freddie. You won't stay the night?'

'No, thank you. I must get back.'

'Off you go then. I'm not so decrepit that I can't remember the excitement of just becoming engaged!'

She called Harry over and asked him to take her place watching over the girls, then strolled over to where Milo was talking to Paddy and his wife, Aoife. She slipped her arm around his waist and he pulled her close.

'You two are still a pair of real old love birds!'

'So we are too, Paddy. Would you excuse us for a few minutes. I need to talk to Milo about something.'

'Of course. We'll go and join your aunt, Milo.' They moved away.

'Milo, I want you to stroll very casually into the library with me, laughing and chatting.'

'What...?'

'Just do as I ask, it's vitally important, maybe a matter of life or death.' Although overcome with horror, she had exercised supreme self-control, so far managing to keep her cool.

She shut the door firmly and told him what Freddie had said.

'Oh come on, Noola. Let's not be ridiculous! *Freddie* implicated in this whole nightmare. No, it's just not . . . Oh, dear God, it could explain so much. But we mustn't jump to conclusions. It's a dreadful thing to think of anybody.'

'But he spoke of *fits* as one of Izzy's on-going health problems. He could only have been told she had fits by the men who abducted her. *They* didn't know she was making it up and nobody else here knows anything about the story. We must do something. And poor Mageen! If he *is* implicated, however marginally, she'll be completely devastated. It'll break her heart.'

'I think Sean's still here. I'll bring him in casually on some pretext. We'll be breaking our promise to Izzy though.'

'Strictly speaking Freddie's spoken about it first, so it's already been told. But anyhow, in the circumstances, I know she'd give us the go ahead. I'm going back now to sit beside her and Sarah.'

99

Milo returned very quickly with Sean in tow. They were laughing and talking until Milo closed the door and told him the story. He looked completely shaken and for a few seconds didn't reply.

'So maybe we've found our informant at last. Oh, Milo! In my job you get the nastiest surprises. I should be immune to it by now but this beats a lot of things I've come across yet. It sounds so preposterous but we can't dismiss it, however unlikely. It's not that late and he probably won't be leaving for a while yet. You know which is his room in Trinity?'

'Yes. It's on the top floor of one of the blocks overlooking Front Square.' Milo gave him the full address.

'I'll get a couple of detectives over there now to search the room. I don't like it but we daren't let it go. Even if they find nothing, the evidence is flimsy but sufficient to take him in for questioning.'

'To tell you the truth, Sean, if you didn't, I'd have a go at him myself and I wouldn't guarantee not to beat him senseless if there was the slightest doubt as to his innocence. I can think of a few others who'd willingly help me too. There have been times in my life when I've been angry almost beyond control, but I feel totally outraged at the idea that Freddie, who was welcomed into this family; who wants to marry my much beloved eldest child, who is deeply in love with him; who has wormed his way into all our affections, could somehow be instrumental in this unbelievably evil crime. A crime against a frail, gentle child, who never hurt anyone or anything in her short life. It was a miracle she wasn't killed – thanks, ironically, to one of the villains. Even worse, Izzy herself likes him. He knows that and could do such a thing to her. Talk about the ultimate betrayal.'

'I can fully understand how you feel, Milo.'

'Can you? Can you *really*? Can you honestly imagine how you'd feel if it was one of your children? I mean it, Sean. I'm ready to kill him if I find there's the slightest shred of truth in this. I tell you something else. I can guarantee that Noola feels just the same way and would help me. Sorry to rant on at you, Sean, you who, more that anyone else, has done so much to help us. It's unfair but I'm beyond being rational. If it turns out to be a false alarm then I'll owe

100

the man a huge mental apology and bitterly regret my lack of belief in him as a decent human being.'

'Leave it to me, Milo. If there's anything at all in it, I'll get it out of him I promise you. In the meantime, use whatever means you can to keep him here for a while. Give my men a chance to sweep his room. He may have been so sure of himself that he hasn't been too careful. Go back to the party and make a supreme effort to be your usual convivial self, entertaining friends and family.'

While Sean got things moving with unbelievable speed, Milo followed his advice and made his way to join Noola beside the sofa. He put his arm around her and drew her a little aside and whispered.

'Sean's getting things going straight away. He wants us to carry on as if there's nothing untoward and keep Freddie here as long as possible while he searches his room. Interesting, isn't it? Now we know why evening after evening recently he's refused to stay overnight, something he's been only too happy to do until now.'

'I'm just as upset as you are, Milo, but let's wait until we've some definite evidence. If it's true then he's taken the whole lot of us for the biggest bunch of gullible eejits ever. Now let's try to carry on as though nothing has happened.'

'You're an amazing woman, Noola,'

'You're still my gorgeous big eejit!'

He managed a weak, reminiscent smile.

'Okay. Here we go!'

Noola managed to be the perfect hostess, without ever moving any distance from Izzy, while Milo circulated, never letting Freddie out of his line of vision and when at last it looked as if Freddie was getting restless and wanting to leave, he took action.

'I hope you're not going to leave us just yet, Freddie. The night's young and it's not everyday you become engaged to someone like my beautiful daughter!'

'Well I mustn't miss the last bus back into town.'

'You could stay, you know. We're not exactly short of space.'

'Thank you but I must get back. I'm hoping Katie will come over to celebrate with us and there may be a message from her. If there is I must call her. She gets worried if she doesn't hear from me.'

Entirely plausible, thought Milo.

'Well don't worry. If you miss the bus I'll ask Mickeen to give you a lift.'

'Thank you but I'll make sure I get to the stop in time.'

Milo was now ready to read evasion into everything that Freddie said and the young man didn't seem too happy at the idea of staying late. Strange since it was his engagement party. Then when Freddie was saying his goodbyes, Sean edged Milo back to the library.

'We've got him! The men found a radio receiver locked into a suitcase in his room. All ready for a quick getaway. Ideal spot for a good signal too, up at the top of that building. There was a loaded gun with it which is not all that surprising. We've got paper evidence too. It was well hidden but my men don't miss a thing. They'll be waiting for him and they'll be armed. He'll be arrested. You don't want us to do that here I'm sure.'

'Oh, please no, for a whole lot of reasons but especially Mageen. Let the unfortunate girl enjoy the rest of her engagement party. I hate to think what this'll do to her. Noola and I will have to tell her in the morning. Good thing it's Saturday and everybody'll be around to help her through.'

'I suggest you wait until I come back to you with whatever information we've found. We'll leave him to cool his heels for a while and, when we've been through the papers, we'll question him.'

'I'm finding it hard to accept the implications of the whole thing. As Noola said, we've been such gullible eejits. I'd give a lot to be there when you question him.'

'I know, Milo, but it would be totally against all the rules. However, we might arrange it that you could overhear some of it without been seen. As far as I can judge he's totally unsuspecting, but, just in case, I'm having him followed all the way back. I have a couple waiting casually up at the bus stop. They'll hop on the bus with him. He won't get away.'

In the end it was remarkably easy. Freddie was still feeling happy after all the champagne and he and Mageen strolled up the drive and waited for the last bus. They joined two others waiting there and when the bus came they kissed goodbye. It was the last time she ever saw him.

102

Chapter 14

The bus pulled into the terminus at O'Connell Bridge. Freddie hopped off with a satisfied smirk on his face. Things had gone well and he was going to be able to regain some lost ground, to get his hands on a lot of Butler money. The fact that people had died in his earlier effort to achieve this didn't worry him in the slightest. The two plain-clothes detectives, posing as an ordinary looking couple, were close behind him. They pointed him out and he stepped straight into the path of two burly Garda.

'We'd like you to come with us, Sir.'

'What?'

'We've got a car across the street and we'd like you to come with us to headquarters.'

'What the hell are you talking about? I'm not going anywhere with you.'

'We have a warrant for your arrest, Sir, so please come quietly.'

They showed him the warrant and he tried to make a run for it but they were ready for such a reaction and had him by the arms, hustling him across the street. He was no match for the two strong and determined men, who knew the bones of the story and especially that he might have been the ringleader of the gang that snatched the little girl, but at least was deeply involved. They weren't too gentle. He was thoroughly frisked then pushed into a cell and left for what was sometimes referred to as "the long wait", but from his past experience he recognized this as a softening up strategy.

'I want to know why I'm here and what the charge is.'

'All in good time, Sir.'

'I want a solicitor.'

'Yes, Sir. Have you got one we can send for?'

'No, but I want one.'

'A good solicitor will be found for you.'

'I want one now.'

'No chance of finding one at this hour, Sir.'

Three hours later, in the small hours of the morning, he was taken to a formal interrogation room where Sean was waiting for him. The Garda pushed him in and took up positions either side of the door.

'Ah! Sean Flynn,' he sneered. 'Perhaps you'd be good enough to tell me what this is all about. I've been grabbed in the street and forcibly brought here and I would like to register my complaint in the strongest of terms. I want a solicitor and will be taking legal action against you and your force.'

'Sit down, Mr Freddie Armstrong, but that's not your real name is it?'

'What are you talking about?' he blustered. 'You know *damn well* who I am. We've both come from the party celebrating my engagement to Mageen Butler.'

'I know *damn well* you're not Freddie Armstrong, but we'll leave that for the moment. It's not the main issue here.'

'Oh, and what *is* the main issue?'

'Your involvement in the abduction of Izzy Butler and holding her to ransom.'

Freddie made a good show of bursting into derisive laughter.

'Now we're in what they call the realms of fantasy. You can't find the ringleaders so you're clutching at straws. Poor Sean Flynn! Defeated in his search for those at the head of the organization, so he's conjuring up scapegoats, frightened at having to admit failure. What a joke! What possible grounds do you have for trying to pin anything on me?'

'You gave yourself away. Isn't it interesting how those who think they've got away with a crime often become careless and make some small slip which betrays them.'

'What the hell are you talking about?'

Freddie was putting on a good show but Sean, well used to

interrogating the guilty, could hear the slight hint of uncertainty creeping into the voice and tiny beads of sweat starting to show in his upper lip.

'Izzy suffers from dermatitis and other health worries.'

'That's no secret.'

'How did you come to know about that?'

'Mageen has mentioned it a number of times. I remember references to it by others in the family. In fact her mother spoke about it during the evening.'

'Saying exactly what?'

Now Freddie was genuinely puzzled.

'She said how Izzy was much better. I had said I noticed the dermatitis had cleared up and the split lip had healed.'

'And you mentioned her fits maybe disappearing too?'

'Yes, and Mrs Butler said she hopes they too will go in time. Look, this is getting more and more ridiculous – talking about a child's ailments. Where's it all leading?'

'How did you know Izzy suffers from fits?'

'I've just told you. These health problems have been talked about openly in the family.'

'No, Freddie. You see Izzy doesn't suffer from fits. She made that story up to create sympathy and worry amongst her captors. The only people she told about this were her parents and she swore them to secrecy because the poor kid thought it was a wicked thing to have done. True to their promise they never told another soul.'

The sweat beads grew and he lost some colour.

'I don't believe a word of this. You're making it all up to pin something on me. You'll have to come up with better than that!'

'There's only one way *you* could have known, Freddie. The abductors must have told you during one of their radio reports from their hideout.'

'Radio reports! Hideout? More fantasy. Mageen *told me.*'

'She couldn't have, Freddie. Even now she doesn't know about Izzy's pretence.'

'I *remember* her talking about it. You need a scapegoat and you're just trying it on to make me confess to something I didn't do. I know all about this kind of police trickery.'

105

'And how would you know that, Freddie?'

'Everybody knows about it.'

'Well, how interesting. I suggest you know about it because you've been through this kind of thing before.'

'Rubbish! Trickery!' The level of the voice was rising, the tone much more aggressive. 'Your evidence is far too flimsy to be accepted. So I suppose your bully boys, who dragged me here, will try to beat me into a confession of some sort?'

'We don't use those tactics but anyhow, even if we did stoop to such methods, in your case we don't need them. Let's go into the room next door.'

Laid out on a table and carefully labelled were all the incriminating items which had been found in his room in college. The two detectives who had collected them were standing by and confirmed the source. Further denial was pointless, but he wasn't giving up that easily.

'I've never seen any of this stuff before. You'll have to prove these items are mine.'

'They were all found in your room. We do have a great collection of fingerprints and incriminating documents in *your* writing. And why would a student at university need a radio transmitter/receiver? One tuned to the wavelength used by the kidnappers. You see we did get their equipment, left with their van at Powerscourt. Denial is a waste of time. You do realize that the contents of this evidence will convict you of responsibility for the deaths of several people and abduction and incarceration of a young, delicate child. We still have the death penalty in Ireland and on the strength of this evidence, not least the kidnapping of Izzy, you will almost certainly be found guilty and condemned to hang by the neck until you're dead.'

That finally seemed to take all the bravado out of him.

'I'm not saying any more until I have a solicitor.'

Sean turned to the other men present.

'Take him back to his cell. There's no chance of finding a solicitor at this time of the night. We'll have to wait until the morning and try to find someone willing to take him on.'

The two men left the room. As Freddie followed, Sean, who had more acute hearing than most, distinctly heard him mutter, in what Freddie intended to be under his breath:

'Bloody kid. Pity they didn't kill her off.'

Sean smiled to himself, pleased this vile creature realized that, when it came right down to it, he had been beaten by a clever little eleven-year-old girl.

* * * * *

Fortunately everyone had slept late so all were still at home on Saturday morning. Bill and Harry had been for a strenuous row and planned to go into town for the evening. A group of friends were celebrating exam successes together, intending to go dancing. Freddie and Mageen had arranged to meet for a special dinner in a prestigious restaurant. She floated around the house in a dream-like state, not quite sure what to do with herself. Noola and Milo watched in consternation. This evil creature had turned their clever, practical and normally down-to-earth daughter into a totally distracted girl, unable to think or talk about anything else at the moment. Conversations with her were now on one topic only. That morning in the kitchen, where, by tradition, Milo and Noola, and often other members of the family too, had coffee with Kitty and Mickeen, she had taken up this well-worn theme.

'Oh, Mum, Dad. I love him so much! Isn't he wonderful? He's so clever and kind. I'm *so* glad that you like him. Everyone in the family seems to like him.'

Mageen didn't seem to notice that her parents' responses were less than enthusiastic. She had that special glow about her that often characterizes a girl in love; her cheeks flushed, her eyes sparkling. Beautiful at the best of times, she now looked stunning. How she had passed her exams was a mystery to them. They were seriously concerned for her sanity when she was told the truth.

'You know she won't believe us, Milo.'

'I know. That's why I think it's so important that it comes from Sean.'

'It's a mercy we found out now and not after they were married.'

'Doesn't bear thinking about.'

107

Shortly after midday Sean arrived.

'It's basically positive news. With all the evidence we found we've actually got enough to convict him. We were hoping to get more out of him but he's demanded a solicitor before he says anything else, and he's entitled. In the meantime we're urgently following all the leads we've got so that we'll have further evidence and, with any luck, catch the whole group. Once a solicitor has been persuaded to take him on we'll be carrying on with the questioning. In fact I made sure I did the questioning myself. My men all know the story. Some of them helped in searching the mountains and the chemists and heard the way Izzy was treated. I couldn't have blamed them if they had been quite rough with him. Even now, in their custody, I wonder how he'll get on. But, in the circumstances, Milo, you won't be able to listen in I'm afraid.'

'Fair enough. Perhaps it's just as well. I'd find it hard to keep my hands off him. But I'm quite surprised he was willing to talk at all. Surely he tried to plead ignorance?'

'Yes, he did, but the evidence against him was too strong. He said it was all a "set-up" and became really aggressive, but finally backed down when I pointed out to him that we still have capital punishment in the Republic and that, given the evidence of his many crimes, he would probably be condemned to hang by his neck until dead. Doesn't sound so great, does it? Then came the demand for the solicitor to be present before he was willing to say any more. I imagine he's hoping for what the Americans call "plea bargaining" – leniency in exchange for the full facts.'

'I wonder what the story is? Where does he fit into the whole picture? Is he one of the leaders of whatever gang it is or just one of their pawns? We really do want to know whatever you find out. Aside from his crime against Izzy we're now going to have a really heartbroken Mageen. What an appalling thing to happen to her. Two of our children! I still want to kill him. Maybe some day I'll get the chance and I won't hesitate, Sean, I can promise you that!'

* * * * *

Milo and Noola decided to ask Maggie to be with them when the

108

news was broken to Mageen. Maggie had lost two men she had loved deeply and was bound to have so much sympathy for what her granddaughter would be feeling. She, of all people, would be able to relate to what Mageen was going to have to live and cope with. What was more, she and Mageen were devoted to each other – as thick as thieves. They all knew that shock would be a huge initial factor.

Maggie, for once, was speechless for a few seconds when the news was broken to her.

'Are you absolutely sure? I mean could there not be some dreadful mistake, Sean?'

"Fraid not, Maggie. There's no doubt whatsoever. We've all the evidence we need.'

'I can't believe it. But then how much did we really know Freddie?'

'I've been thinking about that and the answer is not a lot. Only what he chose to feed us and we believed him.'

'But we'd no reason not to, Noola.'

'Perhaps we really are gullible, Milo.'

'I disagree with you there, Noola darlin'. We're not automatically suspicious of everyone who comes to the house. We trust people and I don't think we should stop doing that. We need to be a bit more careful in future. That's all.'

Just off the main large sitting room was a small room which was used as a kind of den. At Milo's request, a fire had been lit in the big grate there, creating an intimate atmosphere. He brought along some champagne left in the fridge from the evening before, and they assembled there, himself, Sean and Maggie, while Noola went to find Mageen.

'Champagne, Milo? We're not exactly celebrating!'

'No, Maggie, but it's very good for dealing with shock. Ask Paddy!'

* * * * *

Mageen was told the whole story, with Sean describing to her the irrefutable evidence of Freddie's guilt. Knowing she would reject

109

what he said, he had taken the precaution of bringing some items with him, including paper evidence written in Freddie's very distinctive handwriting. He did it as gently as he possibly could in the circumstances but, as they suspected, there was no way he could let her down lightly. Fortunately she was sitting down, otherwise her legs might have given way. At first, much as Sean had predicted, she refused adamantly to accept Freddie's guilt.

'I don't believe any of this. It must be some sort of joke, Uncle Sean. It *can't* be true.'

'Mageen, darlin', not one of us would joke about such a thing. That would be such insensitivity and bad taste! I haven't got the full details yet but, as I've shown you, there's no doubt as to his involvement. He's asked for a solicitor and we've to wait for the rest until that's been arranged.' He hesitated for a moment then decided to tell the part that would prove beyond all doubt that Freddie was guilty as hell. 'I haven't told anyone else this yet but as he was leaving the interrogation room I heard him mutter: "Bloody kid. Pity they didn't kill her off." You know how acute my hearing is – he had no idea that I'd heard!'

She didn't scream; she didn't become hysterical; she didn't even cry. She seemed to become frozen. She was sitting on the sofa beside Noola, who put her arms around her and she laid her head on Noola's shoulder.

'Mum, oh Mum. Whatever am I going to do? I love him so much. I might as well die 'cause I don't think I can live without him.'

'*We* all love *you* so much, my darling, and we want you around for a very long time yet. Dad and Granny and I can all understand something of what you're feeling. As you know, Dad lost both his parents, his mum when he was only eight. I can remember exactly how I felt when I thought Dad had been killed in the war. And Granny has lost two men she loved deeply: Grandpa Billy and Grandpa Tom.'

That produced a reaction.

'Granny? You loved Grandpa Tom? I didn't know.'

'No reason you should, darlin'. On the day I accepted Grandpa Tom's proposal, sitting down there beside the river, he had a massive heart attack. Uncle Paddy tried to save him but not a hope.

110

None of this helps you now, but we do sympathise with you.'

Milo poured a large glass of the champagne.

'I want you to drink this, Mageen. It's said to be good for shock and you've had about the biggest shock anyone could have had.'

'Not only have I lost someone I loved more than life but it turns out he was really evil and I never suspected. I'll never get over this. Losing him *and* being made such a fool of.'

'We've all been fooled. And you *will* get over it. It'll take time, and you'll have to fight, but you're a Butler and you'll win.'

'I don't think so, Dad. I'm not interested anymore. Life seems to stretch ahead of me like a monotonous grey nothingness.'

'I'm so, so sorry, Mageen. I don't know when I've hated more having to tell rotten news to someone.'

'It's not your fault, Sean.'

'That doesn't help, Noola, but I must get back to the station now.'

He gave Mageen a hug and a kiss.

'We're all behind you, girl!'

'I know, Uncle Sean.'

Milo went to the car with him.

'Watch her like a hawk for a while. Don't leave her on her own and especially down near the river. Put Paddy in the picture as soon as possible, he may suggest sedating her.'

'You don't seriously think...?'

'The girl is completely shattered! Heartbroken! What's happened is actually worse for her than if he'd been killed. She's in love with someone who's turned out to be a big-time crook. She's not capable of any sensible thought or decision. Believe me I know. You see it in my line of work.'

'Okay, Sean. When we tell the rest of the family they'll all rally round. And ... thanks again.'

111

Chapter 15

On the understanding that it would help to lighten his sentence, and with the encouragement of the solicitor, Freddie eventually told all. In time Sean gave a summary of it to Milo, Noola and Maggie in his own words and adding his own interpretation in places:

'Freddie has been mixed up in various unsavoury episodes in his life and has spent time in prison. While he was there, he met a member of a group that raised money by various illegal means, including holding people to ransom. They became close friends. Seduced by the allure of vast amounts of money he agreed to join them. It seems crime was second nature to him. Being exceptionally clever and obviously completely without morals or conscience, he was good at it and rapidly become one of the top members of the group. They accumulated impressive resources, but, as so often happens, their greed was never satisfied and they wanted more and more money.

'They realized that they needed to let things cool off in mainland Britain, so they moved their operations over to Ireland. One of the inmates in the prison had been Irish and they had picked his brains about well-known wealthy families that could be worth targeting. Butler was one of several wealthy ones mentioned. They set to work, did their research very thoroughly and discovered that the Butlers were ideal for their purpose. They tapped every possible source of information and soon put a comprehensive picture together.'

'Ah! I see. Then they needed to get someone "inside" to get the maximum information about the everyday running of the house and intimate details about the family.'

'Absolutely right, Noola. Getting the general information was easy, but, for their planned abduction to succeed, they needed to get those kinds of small details that can be make or break. Of the three of them at the top of the organization Freddie was the ideal candidate. They found out that Mageen was at Trinity and so Freddie, with a completely new stolen identity; with false documentation such as exam successes; applied for and was offered a place and set out to ensnare her. He knew how to make himself seem very cultured and attractive to someone from her background and succeeded beyond his wildest dreams. Oh, and incidentally, he's quite a bit older than he'd led you to think. It was almost too easy. Ironically he did come from an educated background and could have done well had he not turned to crime. But he obviously enjoyed the fantastic adrenalin rush created by breaking the law.' Sean paused in his story at this point.

'And the three at the top? Freddie, Ben, the pilot of the helicopter and . . . Katie.'

'No! But why am I surprised? The whole thing is unbelievable.'

'You haven't heard it all yet, Milo! Freddie and Katie, not her real name either, are married.'

'*What*?'

'Yes. She's his wife.'

'So he would never have married Mageen anyhow?'

'Oh, yes. The plan was that if the abduction went wrong, and they lost the money, he would go ahead and marry her. He knew she had inherited quite a lot of money. He was certain that you would give her a very generous marriage settlement too. And he was right wasn't he?'

'Yes! *Very* generous!'

'So one way or another, if not a million, he would get quite a lot of money, enough to make it worth the risk.'

'Commit bigamy? With our daughter! But the money would be hers.'

'He knew that, in her besotted state, she would almost certainly be persuaded to part with it, give it all to him. Then he would divorce her or simply disappear. Well that's what he *says*, but I wonder if he wouldn't have got rid of her some other way! He's evil enough!'

113

'Go on. I'm shaken to the core but we might as well hear it all.'

'The others involved in the kidnap were locally recruited and extremely well trained. But the three had no intention of letting them go alive. They knew too much. Willie and Mac were to kill Bob, Eddie and Shamus on the helicopter and dump them overboard out to sea. Then when it landed Mac and Willie were to be disposed of too. The four in Enniskerry were to wait at a rendezvous to be picked up and given their share. They weren't going to live either. Same fate. You wonder how some of these people can be so naive. Or maybe they think they know too much to be left without their reward. Fools!

'Anyhow we've got the names of all survivors involved and we've already picked them up. They don't know what's hit them.'

'Katie?'

'She and Ben had rented a place quite close to Trinity, where Freddie could hop in and out easily. I suspect he often spent the night there. We've got her in custody too.'

'Brilliant! What about Eddie?'

'He's recovering all right. Until I went to see him he had said nothing except "How's the little girl?". I've been to see him and told him that Izzy is fine, has recovered well. She knows he saved her life and hopes he's all right too.

'It's a sad story. He qualified top of his year and set out on a career as a doctor with the brightest prospects. He started off really successfully but then a family he knew well asked him to help a young girl of fourteen who had been raped by her uncle and was pregnant. He felt desperately sorry for the poor kid and eventually agreed to terminate the pregnancy. Something went wrong: she had to be taken into the emergency department of her local hospital and the whole story came out. She didn't actually lose the baby but, nevertheless, he was taken to court, convicted and sent to prison for five years. He was, of course, struck off.

'Since then he has scratched a living doing all sorts of casual labouring jobs. His family doesn't want to know him. He was the perfect recruit for this gang. That kind of information isn't difficult to come by. There's no question that he bitterly regrets what he did – regretted it from the moment he saw Izzy, but by then it was too

114

late to back out. By all accounts he did his best to look after her.'

'Heavens, Sean, you almost make me feel sorry for him.'

'In a way I actually do feel a bit sorry for him, Noola. I don't think he's basically a bad person. He's just been incredibly foolish and unlucky. I know what he did was unforgivable, but he did look after Izzy; made sure she was as comfortable as possible in the circumstances, and protected her from the others. In the end he risked his own life to save hers. By all the laws he should be dead.'

'Are you suggesting that he's absolved himself to some extent?'

'I suppose I am, Milo. But as you pointed out, how would I feel had it been my child? The answer to that is I honestly don't know.'

'But why did he, once a good doctor, agree to do something so awful?'

'He was desperate to have enough money to go somewhere far away and make a fresh start. Not in medicine but at least a regular job, of some sort, where nobody would know his background. He was living a miserable hand-to-mouth existence here. I'd like to know how you feel about letting him slide quietly away?'

'We'd need to think about that, Sean. At the moment I, for one, feel like stringing up anyone who had anything to do with this whole ghastly affair and I'll be absolutely furious if Freddie gets away with anything less than the death sentence.'

'Well that, at least, I can sympathise with.'

'There's something I'm curious about, Sean. What if they'd got away with all that money?'

'The plan was to leave the country. You'd never have seen him again.'

'And Mageen?'

'He'd have abandoned her without another thought, Maggie.'

'It's such a shame you can't tell him it was counterfeit. I'd love to see the look on his stupid face!'

'We can't even tell the rest of the family, but I've had a thought. How about telling Mageen? She'd not give the game away.'

'What a great idea, Sean. She could do with knowing he'd been duped and would have been caught had they got away with the cash. That he wasn't so smart after all.'

Sean, Milo and Noola grinned.

115

'Would you like to tell her yourself, Maggie?'

'I'd be just delighted. That poor girl could do with something to make her smile, even if only briefly.'

'She'll smile even more when she hears how those two scruffy individuals were instrumental in the whole thing!'

'So she will, Sean. I can tell her that too?'

'Why not? Pity we can never tell the others.'

Mageen did smile, at long last. Since being told of Freddie's treachery, not only had she not smiled, she had eaten almost nothing and had hardly slept, adamantly refusing to accept even the mildest sleeping pills from Paddy. She looked really ill. What worried everyone was she didn't cry. They knew the healing effect of tears, and that if someone can't cry the shock is very likely to come out some other way. The others in the family were equally incredulous when they heard the story and, after the first shocked reaction, had been furiously angry. Izzy did cry, not for Freddie but for her beloved big sister. They all closed ranks around Mageen and did everything they could think of to help her cope with her extreme distress.

Since there was no longer any worry that she might throw herself in, Maggie took her for a walk down by the river and told her the rest of the story. Then came the smile.

'Oh, Granny. I hope Uncle Sean tells him it was counterfeit.'

'I suspect he may not be able to without giving too much away.'

'And Jack and Bertie doing so much for us, and not even members of our own police force. Oh dear! I was very rude to them too. But they really were so scruffy when they arrived.'

'They were, darlin'. All part of the disguise.'

The smile suddenly turned into tears. Maggie took her into her arms and the floodgates opened. They sat down on the riverbank together.

'Granny, Granny, whatever am I going to do?'

'Mageen, darlin', you're going to grieve but, in time, your heart and soul will heal. You're young and you've your whole life ahead of you. Get well and live it to the full. It's much too precious a thing to throw away for the likes of that Freddie! You wouldn't want to think he had the satisfaction of laughing up his sleeve, knowing he had destroyed you?'

116

'No! Come to think of it, I wouldn't.'

'Well come on then. Let's see some of that Butler grit.'

So Mageen began her slow recovery, but it was to be a considerable time before she trusted a man again, other than those in her family.

Chapter 16

1965

Towards the end of his tour of duty in Germany Tommy had been given a posting to Cyprus. He had arrived there eighteen months after the Wilsons, but in the meantime had spent some of his leaves there and by good luck had been sent there for a training session. The relationship between him and Isabel had developed and blossomed, standing the test of separations.

When they had met in Germany Isabel had been in the process of training to be a teacher and in the meantime she had qualified with flying colours. Delighted to be able to stay with her parents in such a beautiful place, she had applied for and been offered a job in an RAF primary school, although she could only be what was referred to as "locally employed". While her job contract gave her no permanence she was more than happy with this arrangement, since it meant that, for the moment, she could stay in Cyprus. With Tommy's posting there, all had fallen into place beautifully.

Once their relationship had become well established, Isabel had spent a couple of Tommy's leaves with him at Riverside. She had been given such a warm welcome and had felt very much at home with the family. Around the same age as Mageen the two girls had become firm friends and Sarah and Izzy liked her a lot too. Her response to Bill and Harry had been very feminine. She found the two young men so attractive, and they flirted mildly with each other but Tommy had nothing to worry about. Emotionally she was fully committed to him. What bothered her was his reluctance to propose to her, although he had told her the full story about his uncle: his history as a psychopath and involvement in the abduction of Izzy.

118

Now it was May 1965 and he had just come back from leave spent at Riverside, but this time Isabel hadn't been with him. Towards the end of his leave, when visiting his grandparents, Tommy had made an alarming discovery about his cousin, Wendy, Bob's younger daughter. She was showing definite signs of mental instability. Before returning to Cyprus he had made an opportunity to have a private word with Milo in the library, a favourite room for both of them. In the relaxed atmosphere and drinks in hand, he put Milo in the picture.

'But this must be a recent development!'

'It seems not. There have been signs for a while but, understandably, her mother and Gran and Grandpa have tried desperately to persuade themselves that she was just a bit temperamental. But it has become more marked recently and her doctor has suggested that she should have treatment for it. On top of all the other problems they've had this is so hard on them and Gran and Grandpa are both getting very frail, especially Grandpa.'

'Oh, Tommy, that's a real blow below the belt!'

'It certainly is, Lo. I had always banked on Uncle Bob being a one-off, like you said. What on earth am I going to do? I love Isabel so much and desperately want to marry her but with this latest development I don't feel I can. There could be no question of children and that's not fair on her. But perhaps even worse, suppose I developed signs of instability? She'd then be tied to someone like Uncle Bob. My feeling at the moment is that I should end the relationship as gently as possible and give her the chance to meet someone else.'

'Oh Lord! I'm so sorry, Tommy, what a dreadful thing for you to discover and what an extremely tricky situation.'

Milo got up and paced around nursing his glass. Eventually he sat down again.

'You've asked for my opinion and for what it's worth I think the fairest thing to do would be to tell Isabel the full story. Then you can decide together what you want to do. I think it would be rather cruel just to end it with no explanation. It could have a dreadful effect on her. Remember Mageen? Rather different situation, I know, you're no villain, but for her the end result would be the same – the man

119

she obviously loves deeply would have let her down. She'd be heart broken. As for you becoming mentally unstable, if there was any likelihood of that I'm quite certain it would have shown itself by now. That, at least, I feel you don't need to worry about. In fact I would say you're exceptionally stable. But I suggest you go and have a chat with Paddy about it. He'll give you a very straight opinion when you tell him why you want to know.'

There was a brief silence while Tommy thought about all this.

'Thanks, Lo. Yes, I'll do that and then when I get back I'll have to find an opportunity well away from the rest of Isabel's family and try to pluck up the courage to tell her. I feel completely shattered by the whole thing.'

* * * * *

To celebrate his return to Cyprus, Tommy and Isabel had gone to Famagusta for the weekend and were having a lovely Cypriot meal together in their favourite taverna, Smokey Joe's, a much loved eating place, with the name originally given by locally based Services personnel. But Tommy seemed preoccupied and when Isabel pressed him to tell her what was bothering him he decided that this was the moment to come clean and be honest with her, as Milo had advised.

'It's the mental health problem in my family.'

'I can understand it being a worry to you, Tommy, but you said yourself that you had checked and couldn't find another incidence of it on your mother's side.'

'When I was home this time I discovered that my cousin, Bob's younger daughter, is showing definite signs of mental instability.'

'This is something new?'

'Apparently not.' And he told her the rest of the story.

'Oh, Tommy. What bad luck. I'm so sorry.'

'Quite honestly I'm devastated. I love you so much, Isabel, and wanted desperately to ask you to marry me but under the circumstances I feel it would be so unfair to you. I'm frightened that I might go the same way, although Paddy tells me that if it hasn't shown itself yet it almost certainly won't. But I would be afraid to

120

bring children into the world with such a time bomb ticking away in their genes.

There was silence for a while.

'Isabel?'

'Yes, Tommy. I'm thinking this through.' She paused again. 'You know that I love you too, Tommy, so much and I've come to the conclusion that, much as I would love to be the mother of your children, what matters most to me is being with *you*. A family would have been a big bonus but not essential. Lots of couples don't have any children. I would be quite willing to say yes to a proposal on those terms.'

Now Tommy was silent for a brief few moments. Then he reached across and squeezed her hand.

'What a wonderful girl you are and what an affirmation of your love. But, Isabel, I don't think I can let you do this. I think we must have a period of separation so that you've a chance to think this through, at a distance, and be quite sure that you're willing to make such a sacrifice.'

'No, Tommy. No! I'll feel exactly the same in one year, in ten years, in twenty years. Please don't do this to me. I can't bear it.'

She was trying so hard not to cry believing this to be a weapon women sometimes used unfairly to persuade men, but there was a decided tremor in her voice.

Again he was silent for a few moments before giving a response.

'All right. I agree on one condition: that we talk this through with your parents. For me that's essential. You're their only daughter and I would be asking for your hand in marriage with this understanding.'

'Yes, I agree to that, but I want to talk to them first.' She was smiling again.

'Well I can hardly say no to that!' He paused, looking at the beloved, sweet face and then continued. 'But I'm quite surprised that you haven't tried to persuade me to change my mind and take the risk of having a family on the grounds that the illness might not show up. The instinct to want children is so strong in most women, I feel sure many would have done that.'

'Oh, Tommy, that would be *so* selfish! And what an appalling

121

thing to do. To risk bringing someone into the world, who we might be condemning for life to such a serious illness, just because *I* want a child, *I* want the joy of motherhood – and I do, very much. Either boy or girl, the child could end up like your Uncle Bob. No! I couldn't do it.'

'You really are a remarkable girl. I would love to take you in my arms and kiss you, but it's a bit too public here. Now let's do justice to these marvellous steaks and then go back to our hotel.' He grinned at her. 'Midnight swim?'

'Oh, you can swim can you, Tommy Butler?'

'Well, I can dog-paddle around.'

They laughed and the atmosphere relaxed. In the background "Smokey" and his wife Ellie, who always worked by his side, smiled in sympathy with the attractive young couple and, with the dish of local fruit they had requested, brought them glasses of Filfar, a Cyprus orange liqueur, "on the house".

Chapter 17

It was almost three years since Izzy's abduction and things at Riverside had moved forward at something of a breakneck speed. Mageen was now twenty-three. She had finished her degree and, in spite of her heartbreak, had pulled herself together with admirable determination and had done very well. From the day she had unburdened herself to Maggie, sitting on the riverbank, she had never again mentioned Freddie's name, not even when the verdict of his trial, the death penalty, was announced. It was later commuted to imprisonment for life with hard labour.

Both her parents were delighted, but especially Milo, when she opted for a career in stockbroking and joined the family firm. Through a business colleague, Milo had arranged for her to spend six months in London, working in the Stock Exchange. She thoroughly enjoyed the experience and rose to its challenge without being the slightest bit fazed. Her enthusiasm had been really fired, confirming for her that this was the career she wanted.

'I loved every minute of it, Dad. The excitement of being in there at the sharp end is fantastic. And London is such a vibrant and interesting place. I had a good time socially too.'

'Yes, you mentioned that there were several of you who became good friends and went out together.'

'That worked so well, with no one committed to anyone else, which suited me down to the ground. When it was time to come home I was quite torn. I wanted to stay longer but I missed home so much that in the end there was no real contest. Anyhow, there's nothing to stop me from going back there now and again for a kind of refresher course, is there?'

'No, indeed. You know we wouldn't have tried to stop you if you had decided to stay and live in London, but Mum and I are delighted that you wanted to come home. We've missed you such a lot. I'm very impressed with some of the business ideas and practices you've brought back with you too. We'll look at introducing some of them here.'

'Can I be involved?'

'But of course!'

'Great!'

Milo smiled. He adored all of his children, each for different reasons. Mageen was his firstborn and he remembered so clearly the first time he held her in his arms: the sense of overwhelming joy and protectiveness that had surged through him. Then, too, she looked so like her mother in features and in the huge eyes, so dark they were almost black. The only difference was his beloved Noola had black curls whereas Mageen's glorious dark, chestnut hair came from his mother, Rachel.

Later that evening he and Noola were chatting about Mageen's experiences in London.

'Judging from what she said, she didn't form any sort of romantic attachment over there.'

'It's obviously going to take a bit longer for her to trust anyone enough.'

'Do you think she ever will, Noola?'

'I hope so ... someday.'

* * * * *

Bill and Harry were now twenty, but one of the most dramatic developments during those intervening years had been that Bill, when it came to time to choose whether or not to go to university, had dropped something of a bombshell. The whole family regularly had holidays together. A visit at least once a year to their villa in Monte Carlo was a must and they all loved going to the beautiful old house in Oughterard, in County Galway, where Milo's grandparents had lived in their retirement. However, every year Milo made a point of taking the twins away with him for an all-male holiday. He

124

felt this was important. It created an atmosphere of letting down of hair away from everyone else. Before Tommy had joined the RAF he was always included in this trip. Noola would do likewise with the girls and in each case the young people were allowed to choose the location. It was a very successful tactic.

When Bill and Harry had been in their final year in school, their parents had never been given any reason to doubt that they would go to Trinity together, following in the footsteps of their grandfather and his twin and then their father. In the year following Izzy's abduction, it was the long weekend in May and the boys had chosen Oughterard, where the salmon fishing was second to none, for their special time with Dad. Milo, whose antennae were finely tuned to his children's moods, however well disguised, realised that something was bothering Bill. Whatever it was he was absolutely certain that Harry knew about it. The boys were so close that, even if Bill hadn't confided in him, Harry would have been aware of his brother's anxiety. This was confirmed when, on the last day of their holiday, after their evening meal, Harry made a very thinly disguised excuse to go to one of the local pubs.

'Like to come with me anyone?'

'Not this evening, Harry.' Bill's reply was rather hasty and Milo realised that this had been agreed between them.

'Dad?'

'No thanks, Harry. I think I'll stay here with Bill and enjoy this lovely fire.'

Although it was May it was still cool in the evenings and a fire had been lit in the comfortable sitting room, creating an atmosphere conducive to intimacies. Milo poured drinks for them and then they sat for a while not saying very much.

'Game of chess?'

'Er – no thanks, Dad.'

By now Milo's imagination was running riot. What was wrong with the boy? Well whatever, he wasn't going to rush him. His biggest worry was that Bill had discovered he had some dreadful illness and didn't know how to tell him. Please, God, don't let it be that, he prayed. Anything but that!

'Dad, there's something I need to discuss with you.'

125

'Go ahead, Bill.'

'Well I'm worried about it. I've made a decision about my career, but I'm so afraid that you'll be disappointed.'

Relief washed over Milo. It wasn't some awful terminal disease. Anything else he could cope with.

'Bill, it's your life and the choice as to where or how you want to make your career is entirely up to you. Why on earth do you think I might be disappointed?'

'Because it's far away from anything you might have hoped for. It will mean I won't be joining the family firm, making a career in stockbroking.'

'That's perfectly all right. As I just said it's *your* life, the choice is yours.'

'But you may not like it!'

'For goodness' sake, Bill, what on earth are you trying to tell me? I can't imagine what you could choose that I wouldn't like!'

'I want to train to be a priest.'

Of all the things Milo might have imagined, that would not have been one of them. But, when he thought about it, perhaps it wasn't such a surprise. From the time they were old enough to think for themselves, all five children had been allowed to make their own decisions as to whether they followed their mother or their father in which church they went to. Bill and Sarah had chosen to go to the chapel with Noola and Maggie. Mageen, Harry and Izzy went with Milo, Tommy and Aunt May to the church in the nearby village, which had been attended by Butlers for generations. However, quite often the whole family went together to one or other. It was an unusual arrangement for the times and not an easy one for some, but was accepted by all concerned and outside interference was not tolerated. Bill had always had both respect and affection for old Father Callaghan and Milo knew they had often spent time together discussing religious issues, but Milo had never suspected that his son might be considering a career in the church. There was silence while Bill waited in trepidation and then his father voiced his thoughts.

'That is a very brave decision and I suspect it hasn't been an easy one for you. I'm quite sure you've thought it through very carefully

126

and probably discussed it with Father Callaghan, but are you fully aware of all that you will be sacrificing?'

Bill's relief was overwhelming.

'Yes, Dad.'

'Truly? We Butlers tend to be a pretty virile lot. You'll be foregoing a happy married relationship, physical as well as emotional, and having children.'

'I know and I haven't rushed into the decision. I've agonised over it for a long time, going round and round the arguments for and against. You're right I've talked to Father Callaghan but I've also talked it through, over and over again, with Harry. He's been so patient – never got short-tempered with me for going on and on about it.'

'Good! I'm glad you could do that and good for Harry, but I would have expected no less, the two of you being so close. So you'll be applying to Maynooth?'

'Yes.'

'Well at least it's only down the road so we will see you from time to time!'

'Yes, of course. And, Dad, . . . thanks!'

'For what, Billy Boy, for wanting you to be happy and follow your own inclination? God bless you and grant you happiness in your decision. It's such an important one.'

The floodgates opened. Bill, greatly to his relief, now felt free to talk to his father in depth and at length about his calling: his wish to dedicate his life to God's work. They talked on for a long time and Milo was impressed and proud of his son's courage of his convictions. He also realised that this was no sudden or spur of the moment decision. It *had* been thought through long and carefully, obviously agonised over as Bill had said.

When told to the rest of the family, this news was greeted with varying responses. Noola and Maggie were delighted, although they had the same concerns about the sacrifices Bill would be making. However, like Milo, they reckoned that it was Bill's life choice and he must be very aware of all that. Not so, down-to-earth, outspoken Mageen, who, having grown up with Tommy just a few years older and the twins three years younger, had no inhibitions in saying what she thought to them, even if about intimate topics.

'Good heavens, Billy, you mean a big husky fellow like you is choosing to go through the rest of your life without any sex. You must be mad! You'll never stick it.'

'*Mageen, really*! That's a most inappropriate comment to make. It's verging on being coarse.'

'No it's not! For goodness' sake, Mum, he's my kid brother. We've said much worse things than that to each other.'

'Well I don't want to hear about them, thank you, and please reserve them for private conversations between you.'

Bill was trying so hard not to laugh but not succeeding.

'It's okay, Mum. It's our Mageen just being herself. I'm not offended. And, Mageen, I've thought it all through very carefully indeed and my convictions are strong enough to make me willing to forego all that.'

'Well, good luck to you. I'm glad you've found something that you feel so strongly about but sad I'll never see you with children of your own.'

'Thanks, but, after all, there are plenty of Butlers to keep the family name and business going.'

Quieter and somewhat more reserved than Mageen, Sarah was hugely impressed. She was very proud of her older brother and told him so.

* * * * *

By the summer of 1965 Bill was well into his studies and Harry was at university reading for a degree in maths and economics. He, like Mageen, wanted to make a career in stockbroking, much to Milo's relief and delight, for with two members of the family having this ambition, the future of the family firm was assured. Like his father and grandfather before him Harry was a great sportsman, with rowing his forte. He was a member of several rowing teams having his university colours in this sport. Bill was also maintaining his sporting prowess and with him too there was much emphasis on water sports.

Sarah, at nineteen and just a year younger than the twins, was also at university. She had opted to read for a degree in natural

128

sciences and was especially keen on botany. She was fascinated by the orchid collection started by Grandpa Tom and was now working with Maggie to maintain and develop this. One unexpected aspect of her life at university was that, like her brother, she had joined Trinity Boat Club and was having as much success in the women's teams as was Harry in the men's. This was a first for the family and as her trophies joined those of generations of the Butler men in the library, so Milo's delight and pride in her grew. It was the icing on the cake of her academic successes. Tommy and her brothers were equally delighted and Uncle Paddy, who also had his colours for rowing, cheered her on and hoped his own daughter, Orla, would follow in Sarah's footsteps.

Izzy, now fourteen, attended a highly regarded independent girls' school in the city. Thanks to a huge level of support from those around her she had recovered well from her ordeal and now very rarely spoke of it. An unexpected legacy of her traumatic experience was that she had developed a remarkable resilience in coping with stress. Her musical talent had blossomed and, having won a number of prestigious awards, she was now becoming recognised locally as outstandingly gifted. A sparkling career in music seemed a certainty. Her other great love was horses and she was a highly competent horsewoman. This she had inherited from Milo's mother, Rachel, and he sometimes worried that Izzy might, like her, be killed or injured in an accident.

When the news came through of Tommy's engagement to Isabel a great wave of excitement rippled through the whole household at Riverside. Mageen, Sarah and Izzy had been invited to be bridesmaids, the fourth being a close friend of Isabel's from her schooldays. The wedding was to be in Cyprus.

'Mum, why will it be out there?'

'Why not, Izzy?'

'Because I thought Tommy would want to get married here in Dublin with the reception beside the river. It would be so wonderful. We could have a great big marquee out on the lawn.'

'Ah, but Isabel's parents live in Cyprus at the moment so she'll want to be married from her parents' home. That's the tradition anyhow.'

129

'That means when I get married the wedding will be here?'

'Certainly.'

'Good! So we'll all be going to Cyprus in September?'

'Yes! As many of us as can manage it.'

Chapter 18

The wedding ceremony took place in the garrison church in the RAF base. Tommy and Isabel looked like a couple from a fairy tale. They both had fair hair and blue eyes and with her small stature, and white dress, beside Tommy, Isabel looked like thistledown. He was much taller and looked splendid in his RAF uniform. As best man, and since it was in a British military base, Milo was entitled to wear an RAF uniform too and Tommy had persuaded him to borrow one for the occasion. Chuck had slight difficulty finding one to fit someone of his height and breadth of shoulders, but did manage it in the end. Milo looked superb, his dark colouring creating such a contrast with his fair-haired brother, albeit the black curls were now liberally sprinkled with grey, especially around the sides where it formed grey wings. As the years had gone by he had become ever more like his father, to the extent that looking at him sometimes made Maggie catch her breath.

The reception afterwards was in the Officers' Club. Chuck and Liz were highly delighted about the whole thing.

'Hey, Milo, we're all members of the same wider family now. I can hardly believe it. And Joe and Helen have been able to get here too. It's just like old times – takes you right back!'

They were having a glass of champagne together and Chuck was happy and full of bonhomie.

'It does indeed, Chuck. But while we've a few moments to ourselves, can I say how grateful I am at your acceptance of Tommy, given the background.'

'Poor Tommy. I felt so sorry for him and he was so honest: gave us every opportunity to object strongly. Said he would understand if we did.'

131

'Isabel is a remarkable young woman too. Not to have children is a very big decision for any girl to make.'

'Milo, for all we know, Isabel mightn't have been able to have any children anyhow. How would Tommy have reacted to that? I don't doubt for a moment it would be exactly as Isabel has reacted to his dilemma. As for us? We're just delighted she's found such a remarkable young man. And we do have two sons, so maybe one day we'll have grandchildren anyhow. We'll accept whatever fate sends us, as we all did during the war!'

'Thanks, Chuck, and I gather Liz feels the same way?'

'Absolutely. But let's be realistic about this. It wouldn't have made one bit of difference what Liz and I had thought about it. Isabel loves him. She was determined to marry him and would have done so in spite of anything we might have said. Now, let's forget it and enjoy this uniting of our families. I'm so tickled about it. We should find Joe and do some reminiscing. Oh and by the way! There are so many young men on the base here who have heard your story and can't wait to meet you and Joe. I'm sure you'll spare a couple of hours to chat to them. There'll be an awful lot of questions to answer so stand by.'

Milo grinned.

'Delighted! Who ever minded talking about himself?'

It was a wonderful day all round. Much to Izzy's delight the bridesmaids were consulted in the choice of their dresses. However, the climate dictated that long dresses would be a mistake and it was essential that the material should be very light and absorbent, for September temperatures in Cyprus are still high. A fine blue cambric proved to be acceptable. Milo got a huge kick out of being best man and gave a highly entertaining speech.

On the strong recommendation of Tommy and Isabel, after the wedding some family members went off to spend a few days in Famagusta, to be followed by a visit to Kyrenia before returning home. Bill had not been able to stay and Aunt May with Paddy and Aoife Flynn had also needed to get home, but Maggie joined them.

Because of the ongoing conflict between the Greek and Turkish Cypriots, members of the United Nations peacekeeping force were much in evidence all over the island. The men came from Europe,

Canada, Australia and included a contingent from Ireland. They met some of these and were highly entertained to discover that the Irish troops were considered to be very good at keeping the peace between the opposing factions and, as a result, were often placed in the most volatile border areas separating them. Even off duty all members of the UN forces usually wore their uniforms and their blue berets were a familiar sight everywhere.

The family had done their sightseeing and visited Smokey Joe's. This was something they would talk about for years afterwards, determined they would return someday to repeat the pleasure. It was so different from anything they had previously experienced. It was very hot so the tables were outside, on a beaten earth floor, beneath a magnificent vine, which spread over the whole of the outdoor area of the restaurant. It was covered with an abundance of luscious red grapes which hung suspended over the tables, ripe and just begging to be plucked and eaten. The tables and chairs were village style and there were opportunistic cats, many of them strays, hungry and poised ready to take advantage of any dropped morsel or a surreptitious handout from the diners. On this occasion everyone decided to forego the steaks in favour of a "meze", the wonderful meal where the dishes kept coming long after everyone had eaten way beyond their capacity. The dips came first, accompanied by fresh, crusty, locally baked bread. Tzatziki, humous, tahini and taramasalata were included, all new to the family. Then there were seafood dishes, including calamari, never eaten by any of them but sampled with delight. Red and grey mullet were there too. All sorts of local meat dishes followed: lamb kleftico, pork kebab or souvlakia, chicken, sheftalia and so on. And with it all a huge bowl of Cyprus salad, containing more new experiences for the palate: feta cheese and coriander added to the more usual lettuce, with slices of the huge and very flavourful field tomatoes and small, sweet cucumbers. Then the abundance of fruit: figs, warm and fresh from the tree, sweet melon and watermelon and, inevitably, grapes: huge pink/red grapes fresh from the vine. The whole meal was accompanied by bottles of local and very palatable wines. It was something of a gastronomic marathon.

'Oh, Mum, I think I'm going to burst.'

133

'Sarah! That's not the most elegant way of expressing yourself.'

'I know but it describes exactly how I feel. I won't need to eat for a week.'

Maggie, an excellent cook, was really impressed with it all and quite determined that she would get some of the recipes and try them at home.

They had also visited Nick's wonderful fabric shop, where Isabel had bought her wedding dress material. She had been introduced to Nick and his shop by a teacher friend, who lived in Famagusta, and had met his wife, Tassoula, and the rest of the family too. Tassoula had done a lovely job in making the dress for her. Nick's shop was worth a visit not just for the variety and richness of the fabrics, but also for the collection of beautifully carved Cypriot dowry chests on display, as well as other items of local artistic significance.

On their last evening before moving on to Kyrenia they were all sitting in the bar of the most popular hotel in town, where they had a suite of rooms. They were chatting in a very relaxed way, sometimes exchanging greetings and comments with the fairly numerous UN representatives. Two more of these arrived. Looking exceptionally smart, they removed their blue berets and moved over to the bar to order drinks. They were just two more amongst many so no one took particular notice of them until they turned around, drinks in hand, to find a place to sit. The Butlers were the far side of the large and very full room with only Milo and Noola facing the bar. Noola looked up as they turned and catching sight of them dropped her drink. They caught sight of her and Milo at the same moment and stopped in mid-step.

'Begorrah! If it isn't the Butlers! I don't believe it!'

Milo gaped at them speechless and the rest of the family swung around in their seats to face them. Then Izzy shrieked with delight and leapt up, weaving her way through the tables towards them as fast as she could, and launched herself at them, arms spread wide.

'Bertie! Jack! Oh how brilliant. How absolutely brilliant and you both look *gorgeous* in your uniforms!'

'Well! If it isn't little Izzy. And *you've* grown into such a beautiful young woman.'

For once in a way Mageen was speechless but also slightly

134

embarrassed remembering her comments to them when they had first met. Izzy was right. They did look gorgeous and she swallowed a large mouthful of her drink. Looking at her granddaughter's face, Maggie smiled inwardly with satisfaction. She looked at Noola and the message flashed between them telepathically. At long last, perhaps the grieving was over.

They all rose to their feet and, dragged over to the table by Izzy, the two men were overwhelmed with the welcome they were given. Prior to Jack and Bertie leaving Riverside it had been agreed that first names were acceptable all round so the greetings were very relaxed and informal. And, of course, the two didn't miss a trick, they never did. Most important of all for Jack, Mageen wasn't wearing any rings.

'Well, well, well. Bertie, Jack, and we never did know your surnames.'

'No, and I'm afraid we can only talk generalities here, Milo. We need a very quiet corner somewhere.'

'We've taken most of the top floor and there's a lovely sitting area facing out to sea. We can go up there. We've plenty to drink there too.'

'Perfect.'

As they made their way to the lift Milo hung back and caught Jack by the sleeve.

'When you left we still didn't know who was behind the abduction. Did you ever hear the end of the story?'

'No. It was out of the question for us to make any attempt at further contact, much to our regret may I say. What happened?'

Milo told him as briefly as possible.

'No! Freddie? Incredible! I never would have suspected. We all thought it might be some faction of the IRA, but thinking about it, while I don't like what they do, abducting young, vulnerable children somehow isn't quite their style. And poor Mageen. How awful for her.'

'She went through a very rough time of it but I think she's all right now. Doing really well in the world of finance. She won't have anything to do with men though, I mean in terms of a serious friendship.'

135

'But Izzy is marvellous. You'd never know she'd had such an appalling experience.'

'Yes, I know. She recovered from it remarkably well *and* is making quite a name for herself in the world of music.'

'Does she mind reference to what happened?'

'No. She's comfortable talking about it. Even at the beginning she didn't mind. I think she talked it out of her system which was great. The only nasty legacy is she still has nightmares. At first she had them frequently but now quite rarely. She still dreams she's back in that cellar all alone. We got her a big dog, a Kerry Blue, which she named Jolly. They're good guard dogs and she sleeps in Izzy's room, actually on her bed, which has helped a lot in making her feel secure.

'Okay, Milo, while I talk to the rest of your family would you put Bertie in the picture too, please. I wouldn't want Izzy upset but I wouldn't want Mageen upset either by references to the ghastly Freddie.'

Harry and Izzy were the only two present who didn't know that the two men hadn't, in fact, been members of the Southern Irish security forces. Looking at their shoulder flashes it quickly became obvious to Harry that there was something here that he hadn't been told about. They were in the Scots Guards, no less. It was no secret that these were amongst the most highly trained men in the British Army, with a longer and more rigorous training than most. Tough, almost certainly paratroopers at some stage, and whatever else he could only guess. He said nothing but Izzy put them on the spot. In her forthright way she was very like Mageen.

'But why haven't you got shamrocks on your uniform, Jack? All the other Irish soldiers do.'

'Ah, well you see, Izzy, we joined the Brits.'

'Oh! Does Uncle Sean know? If he does I bet he was sad that you left.'

'He knows that we didn't stay.'

Bertie distracted her.

'Hey, Izzy, I hear you're a fabulous pianist. I've never heard you play.'

She was thrilled to bits and launched into her favourite topic.

136

Jack made sure he spoke to some of the other members of the family before he worked his way around to Mageen.

'I truly didn't think we'd ever meet again, Mageen.'

'I didn't either, not in my wildest dreams. I feel embarrassed that I didn't know the full story about what you did for us all before you left, so I never had a chance to thank you.'

The laughing blue eyes crinkled up.

'Well, I'm here now and the most wonderful thank you would be if you would have dinner with me tomorrow evening. Come to think of it, why not spend the whole day with me tomorrow? We've got a couple of days' leave, which we had planned to spend here and I'd love to show you some of the sights. No strings, Mageen. Just two friends spending some time together?'

She smiled her wonderful smile and suddenly the old Mageen sparkle was back. Noola and Maggie, who had been surreptitiously watching, looked at each other knowingly.

'That would have been lovely, Jack, but I'm afraid we're all off to Kyrenia tomorrow.' She sounded genuinely disappointed.

'Well, let's see what we can do about that.' He thought for a moment. Bertie was regaling the rest of the family with stories about the kinds of problems that sometimes faced the UN troops. When there was a gap in the conversation he called across to him:

'Bertie, the whole family is going across to Kyrenia tomorrow. How would you feel about joining them?'

Bertie had been aware that Jack had found Mageen attractive when they were at Riverside, so now, anxious to help his friend, he didn't hesitate.

'Sounds like a marvellous idea to me. I love it over there and we haven't been for a while.'

'Milo, Noola, everybody, would that be all right with all of you?'

'It would be wonderful. Oh how exciting!' Izzy didn't wait for anyone else to reply. She was afraid someone might throw cold water on the idea and, for Mageen's sake, Noola was too.

'I'm sure we all feel like Izzy. We'd love to have you come along with us.'

'Good. That's settled then.'

As the evening had progressed they discovered that Jack was, in

137

fact, Jock MacLellan and Bertie was Ben Cohen. Neither one was ever known by his real first name when on an assignment, they were always Jack and Bertie and that's how the whole family would think of them for evermore. They had been to school together and joined up together, but this had only been revealed when they had decided that their episode in Dublin would never be discussed outside the family, not even by outspoken Izzy. She was so excited when she heard all this.

'Oh, you mean you really came to Riverside as *spies* to help to rescue me?'

'Not exactly, Izzy, but something like that. But you must keep the secret or we could be in deep trouble.'

'I'll *never* tell anybody, promise, and I'm *very good* at keeping promises.'

'That's true, Bertie, she's extremely good about not telling secrets too, and wild horses wouldn't drag it out of her if she thought it would harm the two of you.'

Afterwards, in the privacy of their bedroom, Milo and Noola were discussing the extraordinary turn of events.

'It never struck me that Bertie was Jewish, and yet it should. I suppose with his dark hair and eyes he doesn't look all that different from Mammy and me. The only real difference is the slightly darker skin. Even then it's not that pronounced.'

'It wouldn't strike any of us even to comment on it, Noola. We have a large Jewish population in Dublin and there were quite a few in school with me. They're such a well-established part of our community.'

'That's true and so I love hearing Chaim Hertzog speaking with his unmistakable Irish accent. Tell you what, though. Bertie is very handsome and I'd swear that little minx Izzy was actually flirting with him.'

Milo burst out laughing.

'Indeed she was, Noola, my love. Our Izzy is growing up fast. Now come on. Let's get into that bed. This hot climate has a strange effect on me!' He gave her a husbandly whack across the backside.

'Strange effect? You must be joking! You're just your usual randy self, my darling.'

138

'How could I be anything else looking at you wandering around with almost nothing on?'

Harry lay in bed with the evening's events also whirling around in his mind. Quite aside from the debt of gratitude the family owed them, he was hugely impressed with the two men. He had decided that they couldn't be that much older than he was and the completely crazy thought occurred to him that he could somehow follow in their footsteps when he qualified. Something about them sent two ideas churning around and around in his thoughts: SAS and Mossad. He wasn't all that far out.

Chapter 19

They made a leisurely start the next morning, heading north. They had to cross the rugged looking Kyrenia Range and pass through the slightly restricted Turkish territory en route. However, for non-Greek Cypriots this wasn't too much of a problem, although all except the UN were advised to travel through the zone in a special convoy.

Mageen and Sarah travelled with Jack and Bertie and the rest of the family in the car behind. Izzy was highly indignant.

'Why can't I go with Bertie... and Jack?'

'Because I say so, my girl, and stop making those big goo-goo eyes at Bertie.'

'*Mum!*'

'I mean it! You're going to make a show of yourself if you're not careful. You're only fourteen and compared with you he's an old man. So don't embarrass him.'

'Oh! Well I suppose I *am* allowed to *talk* to him!'

Milo was trying so hard not to smile but Izzy could see the twinkle in his eyes. Good old Dad, she thought, for some time having abandoned the "Daddy" form of address of her earlier childhood.

What nobody spotted was that Bertie found gentle, reserved Sarah most attractive. Her nut-brown hair, dreamy grey eyes and love of all things in the natural world were so appealing to him, but he was a past master at hiding his feelings.

As a botanist, the first thing that had made an impact on Sarah had been the wealth of subtropical plant life, so very different from that of temperate Ireland. She had seen some similar plants on visits to the Riviera but not in the same profusion. Hibiscus and oleander formed borders along roadsides and residences; passion flowers rambled unchecked over the sides of walls and buildings, and many others bloomed in abundance. But the shrub that impressed her most was the bougainvillea, in its various colours and liberal growth. She saw a particularly spectacular example of the red variety tumbling over a whitewashed wall and creating a lasting image in her mind's eye. She had taken rolls and rolls of photographs and had chatted to Maggie about the possibility of growing some of these plants at home.

'What do you think, Granny? You're the one who does so well with the orchids and they're tropical. Would any of these grow in our conservatory?'

'I can't see why not, darlin'. In fact the passion flower might even grow outside on a south-facing wall, well sheltered. Maybe we could persuade some bougainvillea and hibiscus to grow in the conservatory too. We can always try. After all, the peaches and grapes are quite happy there.'

They made their way through the mountain pass and arrived in Kyrenia. They checked into a hotel on the seafront and, since they all felt hot and sticky after the journey, the decision to go for a swim was unanimous. A legacy of living by the river, they were all highly competent swimmers. Maggie and Noola wore one-piece suits and both were in great shape physically both internally and externally. The three girls wore bikinis which displayed all their charms to splendid effect, much to the appreciation of Jack and Bertie. Izzy was small for her age, relatively undeveloped as yet and still fragile looking. But Jack had to try hard not to gawp at Mageen's superb figure and covered his discomposure by challenging her to race him, swimming over a set distance. She won which disconcerted him even more, since he was a pretty accomplished sportsman in most pursuits.

'Hey, Mageen. Now you've something else to thank me for!'

'What are you talking about, Jack?'

'Well, I just let you win that race.'

'You cheeky devil! I'll duck you for that.'

She chased him down the beach and her parents and Maggie

141

watched contentedly. Whether anything came of the flirtation or not, it was doing her so much good to be able to relax and enjoy a man's company after so long.

Jack and Bertie took them to the highly recommended Harbour Club for their lunch. The temperatures in the middle of the day were still high and the siesta was a part of daily life here in the hot season, a habit which they were all happy to emulate. Afterwards they went to the village of Bellapais to look at the remains of the Norman abbey there and sit under Lawrence Durrell's Tree of Idleness, drinking strong, sweet Turkish coffee and eating the locally made Turkish delight. Without exception, they fell in love with this idyllic place. In fact the dramatic scenery of the whole area impressed them. They could quite see why the various castles and forts had been built along the rugged line of the hills, understanding its aesthetic and especially its strategic attraction for the Crusaders, led by Richard Coeur de Lion.

Jack and Bertie impressed the others by their ability to order their coffee in Greek, conversing easily with those serving them and in relaxed exchanges with the locals sitting at nearby tables.

'You're so clever, Bertie, and Jack too! Did you learn Greek at school?'

'No, Izzy, Jack and I are pretty good at picking up other languages fairly quickly, enough to make ourselves understood. In a way it's part of our job. We speak several languages fairly fluently. We both speak French and Spanish. Jack can speak German and I can speak Italian and, of course, Hebrew. We've picked up enough Turkish to get by in that too!'

'Gosh, that's amazing! I can only speak a little Irish and French. We're learning Latin at school too but I wouldn't *ever* be able to speak it.'

'Don't worry, Izzy, people don't usually speak Latin now as an everyday language. It's been replaced by Italian.'

* * * * *

Bearing in mind what Milo had indicated about Mageen's reluctance to become emotionally involved, very wisely, Jack decided not to

142

rush things. When the opportunity presented itself, he had a quiet word with Noola.

'Mageen didn't refuse me flat when I suggested she might have dinner with me, even spend the whole day with me. How do you think she would react if I suggested we had dinner this evening, just the two of us, and would you and the others mind? I don't want to frighten her away.'

'First of all, no, the rest of us wouldn't mind at all and if anyone does I'll sort them out! I should give it a try. Her response to you so far has been more relaxed than I've seen her with any man for a long time. I'd say just one thing to you though. *Please* don't hurt her, Jack, and that leads me to ask you an important question. I do need to know if you're married, because if so then we stop the whole thing here and now. I can't watch her go through any more heartbreak.'

The blue eyes crinkled and twinkled again.

'No, Noola, I'm neither married nor engaged. In fact I haven't even got a girlfriend. Quite frankly, since I met her I haven't had much interest in anyone else. Never in my wildest dreams did I think that I would meet her again and that she would still be unmarried. She's the most beautiful girl I've ever met and I do love that open, forthright nature of hers too.'

'What a relief. Then go ahead and take your chance and I don't need to tell you to go gently, you've already been quite sensitive in your approach.'

He laughed aloud.

'Had I been around twenty-five years ago, I'd have given Milo a good run for his money. You're a gorgeous woman too.'

'Get away with you, Jack, you're a flatterer.' But she was pleased. What woman wouldn't have been? He laughed again.

'Your daughter is very like you.'

Noola forewarned the rest of the party, so that when Mageen apologetically mentioned to her parents that Jack had invited her to a dinner for two, they said it was a lovely invitation and she should accept.

'You don't mind us going off by ourselves?'

'Of course not, Mageen. So long as you don't take Bertie with you it'll be fine. Otherwise you'll have Izzy either scratching your eyes out or insisting she goes too.'

143

Mageen laughed delightedly.

'I had noticed and Bertie's so sweet with her.'

Jack took Mageen back across the border to the Ledra Palace Hotel in Nicosia. The meal had been extended well beyond the usual time taken to eat a dinner and both young people seemed reluctant to finish. Jack was so careful not even to touch Mageen for fear of her putting up an invisible barrier, but he felt sure that she was responding positively. For her part she was beginning to wonder if she really was attractive to him. At some moments he seemed to be on the verge of reaching out to take her hand but each time he seemed to draw back. He certainly had her guessing but the real reason for his apparent hesitancy never occurred to her.

The more she saw of him the more she liked him; more than that, was strongly attracted to him. How did she let him know without appearing to be a brazen hussy? In fact, she started to feel quite piqued. Did he not really find her desirable? Had he but known it he couldn't have adopted an approach better designed to ensure that when he did make his move there would be no question of rejection.

They drove back to the hotel in Kyrenia. It wasn't all that late and neither was in a hurry for the evening to come to an end. There was a half-moon and the stars hung low in the sky, so bright and clear it seemed as if you could reach out and pluck them from the navy-blue canopy of the heavens. The air was balmy and the quiet susurration of the waves breaking gently along the shore was almost seductive. It would have been difficult to find a more romantic setting.

'Walk along the beach?'

'I'd love that, Jack.'

So they kicked their shoes off and set out leaving two sets of footsteps that became closer and closer together in the wet sand. He reached out a tentative hand which was entwined readily with firm, warm fingers. The footprints turned in towards each other and they stopped. With his free hand he lifted her chin and gave her a gentle and undemanding kiss on the lips. Her response produced something that ran through them both in a great wave of emotion. She wound her arms around his neck and they stayed locked together for quite a long time. Jack was left with no doubts whatsoever. He had most definitely found the woman he wanted to

144

spend the rest of his life with. But, he asked himself, did Mageen feel the same way? Would she trust again? He knew he must still tread carefully.

Mageen hadn't felt that delicious floating feeling for so long but she kept a grip on her emotions. She was frightened. She remembered the old Irish saying "fool me once shame on you, fool me twice shame on me".

When they finally agreed they should say goodnight he accompanied her to her bedroom door, gave her one last kiss and saw her safely in. Then he made his way to his own bedroom, feeling elated at the way the evening had gone. Mageen was feeling exactly the same way.

* * * * *

The family was due to return home two days later. Mageen and Jack spent the whole of the next day close together and both seemed to be only vaguely aware of the others in the group. They, in turn, pretended not to notice anything out-of-the-way. The two of them had dinner together again but, since it was the family's last evening there, they'd agreed they would join the others after they had eaten. Towards the end of the evening Jack made his decision.

'Mageen, could you stay on for a bit longer? In a sense we've only just met and I'm almost panicking at the idea of having to part from you so soon.'

She gave him such a happy smile.

'I'd love to, Jack, but I'd have to ask my boss if I could have a few extra days!'

'Oh! Could you phone him?'

She laughed in amusement.

'No need, Jack. He's sitting over there and I don't honestly think he'll say no. I've taken almost no time off since I started in the job and he's said several times that I'm entitled to holidays just like every other member of staff.'

'Of course! I'm an idiot. I completely forgot.'

They made their way over to where the others were sitting chatting. All of a sudden Mageen felt rather shy.

145

'Dad, could I have a word?'

'Of course. Come and sit down.'

'No – away from everyone else.'

He eyed the two faces, rosy with happiness, and moved out onto the balcony. She hesitantly made her request and looking at her face Milo couldn't do other than say yes, even though he had misgivings which he voiced to Noola and Maggie later.

'Do you think she'll be all right? Supposing it all goes wrong, won't she need someone of her own nearby?'

Noola nodded. 'I know what you mean. I'm a bit concerned about it myself.'

'Maggie, would you stay behind with her, ostensibly just keeping her company?'

'Now look here, you two. Mageen is twenty-three years old. She spent time alone in London and came to no grief. You're asking me to be the biggest gooseberry in history and the answer is no! Just imagine how *I'd* feel, never mind the young couple.' She smiled at them and her tone softened.

'I love her too, you know, but you must let go eventually and in my view now's the time to do it. He's a grand young fellow and you've made sure over the last couple of days that you've milked Bertie dry of every possible bit of information about him and his background. And Bertie's no fool. He knows exactly what you've been up to and he's played along. It's a totally different kettle of fish from the last time, when we never actually checked on anything we were told, but trusted and took it all at face value.'

They thought about this in silence. Then Maggie carried on.

'What Mageen went through, coped with and rose above will have made her into a very strong person, someone well equipped to deal with any such difficulties in the future. She'll maybe hurt just as much but she'll come through. Believe me, I know!'

'Thanks, Mammy. You're right. We must let go.'

146

Chapter 20

Two years later Mageen and Jack were married. She'd taken some persuading and at times they'd almost quarrelled about it, because she kept procrastinating. But Jack, with remarkable forbearance, simply refused to give up. He was quite determined that he was eventually going to marry her and he didn't care how long it took or how much persuasion. After their engagement, her visit to his home in Scotland was something of an eye-opener for her. His parents were delighted that, at last, he had found a girl he wanted to settle down with but also one who was so eminently suitable in every possible way. They hoped that Jack's older brother, Alasdair, would soon find someone equally suitable, but so far he didn't seem to be at all interested in girls, although delighted with his brother's choice. He liked Mageen a lot.

Jack's father, Ewan MacLellan, was the Clan Chieftain and was like an older edition of Alasdair. Jack was more like his mother, an elegant woman with the same laughing blue eyes and sandy hair. What tickled Mageen no end was that all three MacLellan men were very competent at playing the bagpipes.

'Can we have pipers at our wedding, Jack?'

'My darling Mageen, we can have whatever you want at our wedding.'

'It would be marvellous to have you playing the pipes down beside the river, in your kilt. Will you do that for me someday?'

'Of course.'

She fell in love with the Highlands and, indeed, with Jack's family, who couldn't have made her feel more welcome. She loved their home too. It was something of a formidable Scottish stately

147

home, but nevertheless warm and comfortable throughout. This was thanks largely to the introduction of electric night storage heaters, well camouflaged and designed to ensure they didn't harm the fabric of the lovely old building.

'We never could persuade Jock to bring home any of his girlfriends, Mageen. He always had some excuse. But now we couldn't be happier to welcome you into our family.'

'Thank you, Mrs MacLellan. You've made me feel so much at home here.'

By now Mageen was fully in the picture as to what Jack's job involved, and while she wasn't too happy about the risk factor in some aspects of this, she accepted that this was what he loved doing. After all, it was how they had met in the first place, so how could she object? Marrying him would also mean leaving Ireland and living on or near a military base with him wherever that might be. Well that was part of the deal in any marriage she argued to herself and while she would be sad to leave Riverside, from what she could understand, mostly they would be based in the UK, and that wasn't so far away.

On the eve of their marriage, true to his word, Jack played his pipes for her. He had plotted with the rest of the family to have the pre-wedding drinks party down by the side of the river and the weather didn't let them down. While Mageen's attention was deliberately distracted by the bridesmaids, he had slipped away, put on his kilt and then walked across the lawn, towards the river, playing his pipes. The haunting sound drifted across on the still air as Jack gradually appeared out of the gathering evening mist, making him look as if he was floating. Everybody there fell silent, almost transfixed, and all would long remember that magical experience on the banks of the Liffey. Mageen, in particular, carried it with her for the rest of her life.

The wedding was a splendid family gathering, with relatives from all sides, some who hadn't seen each other for many years. To those not in the know, Mageen and Jack had met in Cyprus: a holiday romance, which was not altogether untrue. Mageen made an incredibly beautiful bride, positively glowing with happiness. Milo, walking her down the aisle on his arm, had a great big lump

148

in his throat, while Noola and Maggie surreptitiously wiped their eyes. Sarah, Izzy, Orla Flynn and a college friend of Mageen's were bridesmaids.

To Izzy's bitter disappointment Bertie hadn't been able to make it, so Alasdair had stepped in to be Jack's best man. Everybody was surprised and highly delighted when Jack, Alasdair and their father, in kilts, played the bagpipes at an agreed point during the reception, in a huge marquee on the lawn of Riverside House. But the biggest surprise of all was that Sean Flynn's son Oisin, unknown to most, had learnt to play the Irish bagpipes and by pre-arrangement joined the three Scotsmen, wearing the wonderful saffron Irish kilt. It was yet another experience to remember. Mageen's wish had been more than fulfilled.

Sean was thrilled to bits at the turn of events and, when he got a chance, had a discreet word with Jack.

'Never in my wildest dreams did I imagine some day you'd become a member of the family. I couldn't be more pleased. I'd still give you a job any time, at the drop of a hat.'

'And I'd be thrilled to work with you again, Sean, but I'm afraid it's not likely to happen.'

'No, I know, but I'd love to hear about a few of your other exploits sometime.'

'Well we've decided that we'd like to go to Connemara for our honeymoon; I've never been there and Mageen thinks I'd love it. We'll be back here for a couple of days before we go across to where I'm based. Perhaps Noola and Milo could be persuaded to host a dinner at Riverside for the group of those "in the know" and we could have a good chat then.'

'Just the job. Look forward to that.'

* * * * *

After the young couple had gone and the celebrations had finished, Tommy, on leave from the RAF station in the east of England where he was now based, asked Milo if they could have a few quiet words together before he and Isabel went back. The library was the unspoken agreed meeting place. They settled down comfortably and

149

chatted about the wedding for a short while before Tommy, quite anxious about Milo's reaction, very hesitantly got around to what he wanted to say.

'Lo, you know Isabel and I agreed that we wouldn't have any children?'

'Yes, Tommy. Have you changed your minds?'

'Oh no. Not at all. But I've been having thoughts about another possible way round this.'

'Yes?'

'It would mean you agreeing to something... something a bit – well, different.'

Milo was at a complete loss as to what he might be trying to get at.

'It's very hard on Isabel not having children of her own. So I was thinking...'

'What are you trying to say, Tommy?'

It came out in a rush.

'Well, you're my brother and if she had your child it would be almost like having mine and I do know there's no health problem of any kind in the Butler family.'

Milo stared at him in astonishment.

'*What?* What on earth are you *saying* to me? You *can't* be suggesting that I get into bed with your wife. *For God's sake, Tommy.* Have you gone stark raving mad? What about Isabel's feelings on this, not to mention Noola's? I can't believe what you're asking me.'

Tommy burst out laughing.

'Oh, for goodness' sake, Lo. No! Of course I wouldn't make such an outrageous request.'

'Well then, what *are* you suggesting?'

'It seems some women have children by use of sperm donation. I'd be willing for us to have a child using this method but not by some anonymous donor that I knew nothing about. I'm told that great care is taken over the choice of donors but what guarantee would there be that there isn't some genetic problem nobody knows about? It could be out of the frying pan into the fire. What I hoped was that you might be willing to be a donor for Isabel and me. Actually I suppose it's really for me!'

150

Dead silence. Milo gazed at him, completely speechless. Tommy didn't rush him, determined to give him plenty of time to get used to the idea.

'Let's have a drink, Lo.'

'Make mine a *very* large brandy while I think this through *very, very* carefully.'

Milo was really shaken. He got up and walked around the room, taking generous swallows of his drink. It was the most bizarre request that he'd ever had in his whole life and he simply didn't know how to respond. For quite a considerable time he paced about trying to decide what he should do. He prayed silently for some guidance. Suddenly he wondered what his father's response would have been if *his* brother had asked him to do something equally difficult. How I wish I could talk it over with Dad, he thought. Then the answer came to him, he didn't quite know where from. I'll bet Dad would have agreed to help his brother out, even if it was something as strange as this. He went back to his chair and sat down again.

'Have you talked this through with Isabel?'

'Not yet. I didn't want to raise her hopes in case you didn't agree.'

'Because you're my brother and for that reason only, I think I might go along with this. But first I must talk it through with Noola. You'd expect me to insist on that!'

'Goes without saying. And if you both agree then I would have to talk it through with Isabel. She might refuse, but somehow I don't think she will. I've a strong feeling she would agree but only because it's being kept in the family.'

'You must love her an awful lot to be willing to do this for her, Tommy.'

'I'd make any sacrifice for her!'

Milo suddenly grinned delightedly at him.

'Can't you just hear Maggie! "Jesus, Mary and Joseph. What an outrageous idea. Are you fellas out of your minds?". But she's such a supremely *human* human being in the end I feel certain she would understand and wish us luck.'

'I'll be in your debt for ever, Lo, even more than I am already.

151

You've been as much a father as a brother to me and those are debts I can never repay.'

'Tommy, let's allow ourselves to get a little bit sentimental here. I love you as much as I love my own children, but I'm so tickled that you're my brother too. Cheers!'

They both took large swallows of their brandy. No more words were necessary.

Milo and Noola talked it through at length and in depth. Then they talked it through again with Tommy. In the end, Noola said she thought it would be worth a try, deeply sympathetic to the young woman who, because she loved Tommy so much, had been willing to forego having children. But all three agreed that it must never be told outside themselves and Isabel, although she would want to talk to her parents about it and . . . perhaps they might include Maggie in the secret too.

They did tell her and waited with interest for her reaction. She thought about it for a while and it wasn't what they had expected.

'That's a very remarkable thing to agree to do, Milo. God bless you. It can't have been an easy decision.'

Later when he had a chance to talk to her on his own he brought the matter up again.

'Actually, Maggie, I personally had another motive for telling you the story. I tried so hard to imagine what Dad would have done in the circumstances: if he had been asked to do something so strange for his brother. Quite suddenly I felt he would have said yes. You knew him so well. Do you think he would have done it?'

To his surprise her eyes filled with tears. She blew her nose hard and swallowed.

'Milo, darlin', I've no doubt whatsoever that he would have agreed.'

It really is extraordinary the way history repeats itself, she thought. She wished she could tell him the story about his father and uncle but didn't feel she could betray the man she had loved so much.

* * * * *

It took some time for Isabel to take on board all the implications

152

and discuss it with her parents before making her decision. Chuck and Liz were as taken aback as Milo, but, after lots of thought and talking it around and around, they told Isabel and Tommy that they weren't against it but emphasised that it had to be their decision, and theirs only. Privately they were tickled at the idea. First of all it would mean Isabel would have a longed-for child. Like Tommy they hadn't missed the hunger in their daughter's eyes when she looked at others with babies and young children. And the huge bonus would be that Milo would be the father, another Butler and not some anonymous man: someone whose family and background they knew so well and someone they admired greatly.

* * * * *

It was unconventional but in the end it worked. Milo and Noola went across to England rather than try to achieve this unusual goal in Dublin's small community, where, however careful they might be, such a story could easily leak out with no intended malice aforethought. But even across the water the unusual proposal didn't go through without some obstacles being placed in the way. They thought they might have to go further afield, where the rules were less stringent. However, in the end, and after spending an almost obscene amount of money to get what they wanted, it all happened. Fortunately it was highly successful and they didn't have to go through it all a second time. To the relief of everyone Isabel became pregnant at once, with one fertilised egg surviving. No woman could have been happier.

'Darling Tommy, thank you for being willing to do this for me. Because you've made it possible, I feel that it has created an even closer bond between us and strengthened my love for you. I feel so very happy.'

'And as we've said so often, Isabel, it's all in the family!'

Nine months later, almost on the dot, Isabel went into labour late in the evening. As soon as he had seen her comfortably settled in the maternity unit of a local hospital and was assured she was absolutely fine, an ecstatic Tommy phoned Riverside. Noola answered and when she heard the news called to Milo. She looked at him and grinned, handing him the phone.

'Someone has exciting news for you.'

'Lo, it's starting, and so far everything's fine.' Tommy couldn't disguise his excitement.

'Wonderful. Any idea how long it will take?'

'Well, from what I hear nobody can ever tell that. But she's in the early stages. I must go back to her but I'll keep you in the picture.'

'We'll make arrangements to go over immediately. Good luck – I hope it goes without any hitches.'

It took longer and was more difficult than anticipated but Tommy stayed by Isabel's side throughout, holding her hand until chased out of the way by the sister in charge, just before two identical little blond-haired, blue-eyed girls were born. Even at so early a stage they looked exactly like Isabel, although in time the eyes would turn green. This was fortunate, for children with Butler black curls and such very fair-haired parents might have raised some eyebrows and drawn fatuous jokes about milkmen. Excitement bounced backwards and forwards in more phone calls across the Irish Sea.

'Wonderful! Congratulations! Good that Isabel and both babies are fine. We've been fidgeting all night, Tommy. Neither of us could sleep, but we'll be with you later today.' Noola sounded so delighted.

In the event twins were no surprise for they had been accurately diagnosed quite early in the pregnancy, with delight all round that the one egg had split into two healthy foetuses. As well as occurring in the Butler family, by coincidence twins had cropped up in earlier generations in Liz's family. Isabel could hardly miss and it was such a perfect solution.

Milo and Noola duly arrived and couldn't wait to see the twins. Later, while the two of them were having a celebratory drink together, Tommy couldn't resist pulling Milo's leg.

'You've now got seven children, Lo!'

Milo looked at his brother's face. There was no emotion there other than delight and happiness.

'No, Tommy. They're *your* little girls, not mine. I'm just so tickled

154

that I was instrumental in some small way and it all worked out. You both look so happy.'

'We are, Lo. Actually I do feel they're really mine. They're the greatest gift we could have been given. Thank you!'

Chapter 21

1972

Izzy at twenty-one was now an internationally recognised pianist. She had won many prestigious competitions and was booked to give a series of concerts in the USA starting the following spring at Carnegie Hall. Occasionally young musicians who had shown outstanding talent were given an opportunity to appear at this prestigious venue early in their careers. Izzy really appreciated how lucky she was to be given the chance to play there. Noola had diffidently offered to go with her for the entire tour. She didn't want to give the impression of being over-protective, or of being reluctant to allow her daughter to be independent, so she had left the final decision on this to Izzy.

'I know you and your agent are perfectly capable of looking after you, Izzy, and I don't want to cramp your style, but I'd love to have a look at America myself. What do you think about my coming on tour with you as a companion?'

'I'd *love* you to come with me, Mum. What about Dad? I realise he wouldn't be able to come for the whole tour, but I'd love him to be there too when I play at Carnegie Hall. That's going to be one of the high points of my career.'

'I'm quite certain he's planning to be there – as if he'd miss one of his daughter's greatest moments. No, he'd have to get back but I'd like to stay and travel on with you.'

'That would be great, Mum. Do you think Granny might like to come too? She's never been there either, has she?'

'I think Granny would be thrilled to bits. What a lovely idea, Izzy.'

* * * * *

156

Bill had completed his preparation for priesthood, was ordained and then, totally unexpectedly, decided he wanted to join the Irish Army as a chaplain. He was to take up his duties and start the necessary military element of training in the late autumn. There was great hilarity in the family that there would be one member in the British Military and one in the Irish, not to mention a son-in-law in the British Army.

'Hey Bill, what a pity you and Tommy will never meet up, or even you and Jack on some assignment or other. Wouldn't that be such a laugh?'

'Yes it would, Izzy, but not a chance.'

Fate had other ideas.

Harry, after his short-lived flirtation with the idea of attempting to become a member of the SAS, had eventually decided that his real interest lay in high finance. Like Mageen, he had spent time at the London Stock Exchange and had decided that the adrenalin charge he got from this was as powerful as any he would get from a career in the military. He had inherited a real flare for stockbroking and settled in as his father's right-hand man with ease and dedication. Milo was vastly relieved. He would never have pushed any of his children to follow in his footsteps, but with the departure of Mageen he had desperately hoped this would be Harry's choice.

Unlike Bill, Harry, at twenty-eight, was quite happy to indulge his masculinity. Like his forebears he was a big, powerful and dramatically handsome man and had no intention of living like a priest. He went through girlfriends with impressive speed and wasn't always as kind as he might when he got tired of them and wanted to end the relationship. He insisted that he had no intention of tying himself down with a wife and family for some time yet. He was simply determined to enjoy life to the full. As a result, to those who didn't know him well, he gave the impression of being rather self-centred. However, he was devoted to his family. He idolized his father, admiring and respecting him; he adored his mother and there was nothing within his power that he wouldn't do for his twin brother or for the three girls.

Both his parents, but his mother in particular, worried about his cavalier attitude to women and the careless way in which he cast

157

them off. He had brought home only two of his lady friends, both very pleasant, but he had obviously decided that neither was the right girl for him. After a phone call from one very upset girl, Noola spoke to Milo about it.

'What's the matter with him, Milo? He could have his pick of the girls and he doesn't seem to be bothered. He's been quite unkind to some of them too and I don't like his attitude. The last one has been on the phone, obviously in tears, asking to speak to him and he was quite unpleasant, telling her she's to stop pestering him. It's certainly not the example he gets at home. Do you think we should have a word with him?'

'I don't like his behaviour to women either but we can't do anything about it. He's twenty-eight years old and he's not going to take the slightest bit of notice of anything we say. Trouble is he's had it all his own way. But let's just wait and watch. I've a strong feeling that one of these days he'll fall hard for someone who'll treat him in exactly the same way and then he'll know how it feels.'

* * * * *

Just a year younger than the twins, Sarah had sailed through and got a first-class degree at Trinity College. She was invited to stay on in the botany department to follow a course of research for her PhD and do some lecturing. This had been completed successfully and she was now a full-time lecturer in University College Dublin. She had cultivated a remarkable range of subtropical and tropical plants in the conservatory and they were so successful she had persuaded Milo to extend the building further. She was now engaged to Dai Thomas, someone she had met as a fellow student. He had come from a university in Wales and also followed a course of research in the same botany department. Eventually he had been offered and accepted a full-time lectureship in Trinity. He was steady and reliable, and like many of his countrymen, was a great raconteur. He also had a lovely dry wit and a wonderful rich baritone voice. If he'd been hand-picked for her he couldn't have suited Sarah better.

When they had first met, from Sarah's point of view, their interest in each other had been purely academic. She was totally

158

absorbed in her subject and Dai was attractive to her purely as an equally dedicated professional. Having such a keen interest in common couldn't have been a better basis for a friendship, but, quite quickly, Dai's affection for this lovely-natured and very attractive young woman grew almost without his being aware of it. He found he wanted to spend more and more time with her and not just talking about botany. They discovered they had other things in common such as their interest in classical music. The Butlers for generations had enjoyed serious music and Sarah was no exception. Like others in the family she had a lovely singing voice, and had been given some basic training, although following music as a career had never been in her mind. Dai came from the Welsh valleys where music was an essential part of life.

Dai's first visit to Riverside was, ostensibly, to see the wonderful collection of plants Sarah was cultivating in the conservatory. He had worked hard to bring her around to issuing this invitation. His visit was a resounding success. Not only did Sarah suddenly realise she liked him for reasons other than their shared interest in plants, the whole family fell for him in a big way. He had a pleasant, open face, with the black hair and grey eyes not unusual amongst his fellow countrymen, and not uncommon amongst the Irish too. In fact he could have been related to the Butlers, except the hair was straight and he was shorter in stature, although what he lacked in height he made up for in breadth of shoulders. The family especially loved his disarming honesty about his mining family background, putting it to them in his lovely lilting voice and in typical Welsh fashion.

'Dirt poor as a family we are. Father, grandfather and back for generations they've been miners. I was lucky. Won my scholarship to the grammar school and then was offered a place at the University of Aberystwyth. Got a good honours degree and then the offer of a grant to do research at Trinity.' He paused and with a slightly embarrassed smile added. 'Dad and Mam were so proud.'

'I bet they were and still are, Dai. Good for you! Not only that but I gather you can sing too.'

He laughed delightedly.

'Oh, Mr Butler, Bach! There are very few Welsh who can't sing

159

and we all love it. At Aber they seemed to think my voice was good and I was given the chance to have some training. There's lucky I was.'

Dai had been slightly apprehensive about meeting members of this wealthy family and was vastly relieved to discover that social distinctions were of no consequence whatsoever to the Butlers. The friendship between him and Sarah developed into a deep and abiding love which took them both rather by surprise in its intensity. Neither had ever before met anyone to whom they had been so attracted both mentally and physically.

Having realised that the family would have no objections whatsoever to his marriage to Sarah he proposed to her. When she accepted joyfully, he didn't make a point of the fact that he couldn't afford to keep her in the style to which she was accustomed. Instead he quoted from Yeats' wonderful poem about the Cloths of Heaven:

'Had I the heavens' embroidered cloths...
I would spread the cloths under your feet:
But I, being poor have only my dreams;
I have spread my dreams under your feet;
Tread softly, because you tread on my dreams.'

This touched her more than any protestations could possibly have done.

'Dai, my darling, I couldn't care less how much or how little worldly wealth you have. I just love you for yourself and I'm pretty sure you know that by now.'

With a gentle prompt from Milo, Tommy asked the couple if they would be willing to move into the East Wing and live there on a caretaker basis. He emphasised that this would mean such a lot to him. From an earlier suggestion of his Aunt May and Maggie both had their own private apartments there. It was an ideal arrangement, with both near enough to each other and the rest of the family if they wanted company but also having complete independence. However, he explained that Aunt May and Maggie were getting on a bit and he sometimes felt that they needed a young

160

couple close by so they didn't feel too much responsibility for looking after his home.

The East Wing was big enough for Sarah and Dai to have their own self-contained, fully equipped area, just as the two ladies did. The young couple were delighted to accept this arrangement, since, apart from the many other advantages, it meant they could continue Sarah's work in the conservatory and she could keep up her rowing without any difficulty. It would also give them plenty of time to find a house of their own that they really liked, if possible not too far from the river, this to be a wedding present from Milo and Noola.

* * * * *

The wedding was to be in the summer holidays and plans were well underway. Sarah was over the moon because Bill would be able to conduct the marriage ceremony for them. The idyllically happy Mageen and Jack were coming with their two small boys and Tommy and Isabel would also be there with the twins, now almost five years old. They had decided to stay for a couple of weeks after the wedding, since it was some time since they had been to Dublin and had a lot of catching up to do. They had made a brief visit three years previously, when Grandfather Featherstone had died, and Tommy understood from Bob's widow, Deirdre, that his grandmother was now very frail indeed. He wanted to see her to say goodbye as it were. He also needed to talk business with Milo, who looked after all his financial investments and kept an eye on the East Wing.

Riverside was so big there was no difficulty in accommodating any guests who needed somewhere to stay, including Dai's family. His sister Megan, Izzy and the twins were to be the bridesmaids, with Mageen's little son Ewan to be a pageboy and wear his kilt. It was another dream wedding, with the weather being kind, and the surprise at this wedding was that Dai sang for Sarah, happily accompanied by Izzy on her baby grand piano, moved into the marquee for the occasion. He sang several love songs finishing up with "You Are My Heart's Delight", which produced gentle tears of happiness from Sarah.

161

They had decided that they would like to go to Cyprus for their honeymoon. After that first visit Sarah had hoped she would get back again someday. This seemed the perfect opportunity and an ideal romantic location for a honeymoon but also she looked forward to introducing Dai to the wonderful plant life there. By coincidence, Tommy had managed to wangle another posting to the island. He and the family would arrive back there briefly towards the end of Dai's and Sarah's visit.

Chapter 22

A couple of days after the wedding Milo and Tommy managed to have some time together, as much to talk business as anything.

'Everything all right, Tommy? I must say you and Isabel look so happy and the little girls are a delight. I do love the way they still call me Lolo and hope that will never change.'

Tommy beamed with pleasure.

'It's wonderful, Lo. We're very happy. It's all worked so well. I've actually decided I'm going to have a vasectomy which will mean we'll never have to worry again about an accidental pregnancy. I kept putting it off because I didn't much like the idea, but one of my fellow officers had the procedure and told me it's easy. I had an appointment to have it done a couple of weeks ago but then decided to postpone it until after the wedding.'

'Ouch, Tommy, I don't like the idea at all. Do be careful. Is there any fear something might go wrong?'

'I gather none whatsoever.'

'Well, good luck to you. Rather you than me.'

A week later Tommy's grandmother died. She had had a series of strokes and one final major attack ended her life. It was sheer luck that Tommy was with her at the time and they had been communicating after a fashion before it had happened. She could say enough to let him know she knew him and was glad he was there. He felt so sad for her. Life had not been easy and she had had many difficulties to cope with. At least she had met the twins and seemed to be so excited at having great-grandchildren. She never knew the truth.

Having been left executor of his grandmother's estate, Tommy needed to see her solicitor. They went through her will together. She had little to leave and when she had been putting it together with Tommy's help, he had insisted that she should leave everything of any monetary value to Deirdre and her daughters. Not only did he not need anything of that nature, once he had reached adulthood he had given her substantial financial help.

To his surprise, the solicitor gave him an envelope addressed to him which had been attached to the will. On the outside was written "To be read when you are alone". He looked at the solicitor in surprise.

'I didn't know anything about a letter.'

'No, your grandmother insisted that you should not be told about it until after she had died and I had to honour her request.'

Full of curiosity, Tommy went back to Riverside. There were few people about and most of those were down by the river or scattered in various places around the house and grounds. Milo hadn't yet returned from the office, so he sat down, alone, in the library to read the letter.

When Milo arrived home he found him sitting slumped in a chair beside the empty fire grate, head in hands. The letter lay on the floor beside him.

'Tommy?'

He raised a tear-streaked face. He said nothing, simply lifted the letter from the floor and held it out to his brother. Milo read it through and then read it again very slowly.

Darling Tommy,

This letter is being written by me with your grandfather's help to ensure I get the facts right. I'm going to tell you a story which I wanted to tell you many years ago but, for reasons which I will give you, I was not able to.

Before your mother was born, your grandfather and I lived for three years in quite a remote part of Scotland. We had wanted a child but it hadn't happened. We lived quite close to an orphanage run by nuns and one of the little orphaned girls there was old enough to be allowed to come and do some housework for us. The nuns were pleased because they trusted us and felt it was preparing her for a job outside the convent when the right time came. The girl would never tell us how it happened, but we suddenly discovered she was well advanced in pregnancy and was terrified. She hadn't told the nuns. We persuaded her to allow us to see the Reverend Mother with her and tell her the situation. The poor lady was horrified. This had happened to the child while in the care of the convent. The girl wouldn't even tell the priest who the father was. After long hours of discussion it was agreed that the girl would stay in our house and the doctor attached to the convent would attend the birth. There were serious complications and although the baby survived, the girl died. We were very keen to adopt the baby but, to protect the convent, they would only agree to this under certain very strict conditions. We had to agree that we would sign a solemn oath, sworn on the bible, that we would never reveal to anyone that the child was not our own.

We had to move away from the area very quickly and because the neighbours were few and far between we managed to keep the secret. Eventually, of course, we came over here to live.

Your grandfather and I swore that oath but if you are reading this it means we are both dead, and we felt that death would release us from it. In the light of what happened afterwards we felt it only fair to tell you the story, but we would ask that you don't tell Deirdre and her two girls.

That baby was Bob. Looking back afterwards and with hindsight we came to the conclusion that the father was one of the men who worked in the convent gardens. We had met him a couple of times and thought he was a very strange man.

Then our beautiful Angela, your mother, was born and we felt that we had been rewarded for giving the little boy a home. All this means, of course, that you are in no way whatsoever related to Bob and no doubt this will be a great relief to you, especially as it means you and your two beautiful little girls are in no danger of developing any mental disorders.

I have no way of describing to you how it has distressed us over the years not being able to tell you. But it was such a binding oath and you know how we always felt about things like that.

165

God Bless you our darling Tommy and your lovely family. You brought us nothing but joy and we love you so very much. Now you can relax and be happy, knowing you have nothing to fear.

Your loving grandparents.

Both had signed it.

'Oh dear God! This makes me feel *so angry*, Tommy. The stupid old fools. How could they *do* something like this to you? Surely there are times when anyone could justifiably be released from an oath and especially in the circumstances involved here. They say that they loved you so much, yet not enough to release you from such a burden of worry. How *wicked*. May they rot in hell!'

'Oh no, please don't say that, Lo.'

'I do say it and I'll never ever forgive them for what they've done to you – not that it'll worry *them*. I just can't understand them.'

'But I can. You remember how very devout they were. They would never have been able to bring themselves to break an oath actually taken on the bible. I'm not exaggerating when I say the distress of doing such a thing would have brought on a stroke or heart attack.'

'What you're saying to me is they loved themselves and their convictions more than they loved you. When I think of the heartache this has caused you, completely unnecessarily, I feel totally outraged.'

'Poor old things. You know, Lo, they had a rotten deal all round. This child that they adopted, out of the goodness of their hearts, murdered the daughter they loved so deeply. And all that happened after that: Wendy developing mental problems, and then Bob's involvement in the abduction of Izzy as the final straw. It must have been a relief when he was killed. I do feel very sorry for them and at least they did tell me in the end. Even the idea of breaking their oath after death must have been hard for them.'

'Well all I can say is you're much more of a real Christian than I am. In your place I could *never* find any reason to excuse or forgive them.'

166

'Drink, Lo?' Tommy managed a bleak smile. 'Do you remember the last time we sat here and I suggested a drink?'

Milo thought for a minute and suddenly grinned broadly at him.

'Yes, I do, Tommy. And, you know what? That makes me think of something else!'

'What?'

'You can have children now with no worries any more. If my memory is correct Isabel's only thirty – same age as Mageen. Yes, Tommy, I'll have a big drink, but it's going to be champagne! And please don't keep me waiting too long to become an uncle again.'

'Oh, Lo! I so nearly had that vasectomy. Somebody was watching over me when I decided to postpone.'

All of a sudden they were both laughing. They couldn't wait to tell the news to Isabel, Noola and Maggie.

Chapter 23

It was early November. Bill had started his army career and was passing through the city on an errand in connection with this. He had suggested that his father, Harry and Sarah join him for lunch in the nearby Hibernian Hotel, a favourite with the family and convenient for the workplaces of all three. Milo was unable to join them and the other three agreed to meet in the hotel foyer.

Bill got there slightly early and wandered around the lobby area while he waited. He wasn't in uniform but was wearing his dog collar. A very attractive young woman came into the hotel and seeing Bill did a double take. She walked up to him, stared in obvious disbelief and then slapped him hard across the face. He backed away from her in astonishment, rubbing his jaw.

'How dare you! You're a disgrace to that collar you're wearing. You certainly never let on to *me* that you were a priest. In fact I think it's disgusting the way you behaved with me and never pretended. I'm going to report you to the archbishop and serve you right.'

At that moment Sarah arrived and, completely unaware of what was going on, hurried across to Bill, reached up and kissed him and apologised for being late. The other woman looked at her in astonishment.

'And who are you?'

'Oh hello! I'm his sister.'

'Is he really a priest?'

'Of course he is – carries out all the functions of a priest. I was so thrilled because he was even able to marry me in August.'

'*What? He married you?* And this was allowed? I don't believe what I'm hearing! A priest carrying on with me the way he did and now I find he's married to his sister. I think I must be having some sort of a nightmare. Please tell me this isn't happening. You're both *disgusting!*'

Sarah looked at her in astonishment. Whatever was the matter with this strange girl? In the meantime Harry had arrived and, undetected by the other three, walked silently across the carpet. He heard most of the last part of the exchange.

'I think perhaps you owe my sister and brother an apology, Marie.'

She whirled around and was bereft of words. Standing before her was the mirror image of the man in the clerical collar. As realisation dawned on her, her legs almost gave way and she had to clutch hold of the desk. Harry's face was suffused with anger to the extent she was actually frightened. Bill, on the other hand, realising the girl's mistake, felt sorry for her.

'I'm so sorry, Father, and your sister. I didn't realise Harry had an identical twin and one who was a priest. I feel so embarrassed.'

'Please don't worry, Marie. Lot's of people confuse the two of us. Oh and by the way, I married my sister to her husband Dai Thomas.'

Looking at Harry's face, Sarah also felt sorry for the girl, who now turned to Harry.

'I need to talk to you, Harry, *please.*'

'No! I've already told you there's nothing more to say. So go away and stop pestering me.'

The girl disappeared fast.

'That wasn't like you, Harry.' Bill looked at him quizzically.

'No, it wasn't. I've never heard you speak to anyone like that before and she seemed quite a nice girl.'

'Oh for goodness' sake, Sarah. I made her no promises but she's become a nuisance. Keeps phoning the house and the office. I've had to ask the switchboard staff to tell her I'm not available. I just can't get rid of her. We had an enjoyable *affaire* so far as it went but I've made it absolutely clear that it's over. It's unfortunate she happened to come in today when you were here.'

They went into the restaurant and had their lunch but it took a while for the atmosphere to relax.

* * * * *

169

Not long after that, on 26 November 1972, there was the first of a series of four terrorist attacks in the centre of Dublin. It happened outside a cinema showing a late film, close to Burgh Quay and not far from O'Connell Street. Nobody was killed but forty people were injured, some severely. Shock reverberated not only through the city but also through the whole country. Nothing of this nature had happened in the city since the 1920s.

'Dear Lord, Noola, I hope we're not going to get sucked into the kind of problems those poor souls in the north are having. Thank God no one in the family or on the staff was in that area at the time.'

'Not very likely I think, Milo. So far as I know no one here goes to a late night showing of a film. Do you think this is an IRA response to the government's move to clamp down on their activities down here?'

'We'll probably never know. Let's just hope it's a one-off, but it's making me feel uneasy.'

'Me too! But what can we do about it? We can't stop going into town because we're worried about more explosions. It's a big place and there's no knowing where they might attack next – if they *do* attack again.'

Five days later two more car bombs exploded, both again in the vicinity of O'Connell Street. This time two people were killed and 131 injured.

'I thought that incident five days ago would be a one-off.'

'No doubt everyone hoped so, Noola, but now I wonder if we're in for a spate of them.'

'Interesting though. Just as the bombs went off, they were debating that bill to bring in special powers to combat the IRA.'

'Yes, and as a result the bill went through when many thought it would be defeated.'

'So maybe not the IRA this time?'

'Maybe not. Perhaps the Ulster Volunteer Force was using the leverage of terrorist attacks to get the bill passed.'

'And all those innocent people injured and a couple killed, going about their business, getting on with their lives. These attacks are *so* cowardly.'

'That's war, Noola, of whatever kind. Innocent people invariably get hurt.'

'But it's so wrong and unfair. How would we feel if a member of our family or our staff was injured or killed?'

'It doesn't bear thinking about. Pray to God there'll be no more of it now that they've achieved their aim, assuming that's what it was all about.'

Milo's prayer was not answered. On Saturday afternoon, 20 January 1973, when the streets were crowded with shoppers, a fourth car bomb detonated in the same place as one of the earlier explosions, close to O'Connell Street. This time one man was killed and fourteen others were badly injured. Although a cousin of Mickeen Flanagan's had a slight cut from flying glass, no one from Riverside itself had been there at the time, any necessary shopping having been completed earlier in the day and far from the area of the blast. To the relief of everyone, there were no further terrorist activities for the rest of that year and into the start of the next year. It looked as if things had settled down again and the prayer had been answered, albeit slightly late. However, that wasn't to be the last of the attacks in Dublin.

Chapter 24

1973

A few months after the explosions in the city centre Izzy went off to the USA for her concert tour, with her first appearance, as planned, being at Carnegie Hall. Originally she was to be accompanied by her parents and Maggie, but Mageen, Sarah, Bill and Harry were so determined to be there for such a special high point in Izzy's career, that they all made whatever adjustments were necessary to their various commitments and arrived in time for the big moment. To her bitter disappointment Aunt May had a nasty dose of flu and wasn't able to attend.

As was expected the concert was a sell-out. The whole family was bursting with pride. Sitting waiting for the concert to begin they chatted quietly.

'Who would have believed that our unplanned, unexpected child, and the one who was so frail when she was little, would have become an international star? I can't believe that I'm truly sitting here in Carnegie Hall, waiting for her to start playing Rachmaninoff.'

'It's a weird feeling, Milo, and this is going to sound so silly – but *I* feel nervous and *I'm* not the one who's going to be performing.'

'I do too, Noola darlin', but don't we always feel that way when we're at Izzy's concerts?'

'Yes, Mammy, but never quite so much as I do now.'

Milo laughed.

'And I thought I was just being an over-anxious dad.'

Overhearing him, Harry also laughed.

'Since you've admitted it, I must say I'm nervous too, I'm certain we all are!'

It was a resounding success and there would be rave reviews the next day. After the concert there were celebrations well into the small hours. Afterwards Milo and Noola, with enormous pride and pleasure, reflected on Izzy's success.

'It's unbelievable, especially when you consider all she went through.'

'You know, Noola, I'm convinced that surviving and recovering from that appalling experience has made her into a person who will cope with anything life may throw at her.'

'Yes, my darling. Just like Mageen, only Izzy's experience was even worse. It's a wonder she came out of it sane and normal.'

'Well she certainly did and it looks as if this is only the beginning of her success.'

'Let's hope and pray for that.'

Inwardly he couldn't help reflecting how proud his father would have been of this gifted grandchild. I wish you knew, Dad, he thought to himself. But then, maybe you do – you who, I'm quite convinced, protected her when she so needed you. Maybe I'm becoming a nutter!

Milo, Bill, Harry and Sarah had to return home, but Noola and Maggie stayed with Izzy for the remainder of her tour and revelled in the whole amazing experience. Izzy's last concert was scheduled to be in Minneapolis where she was to play with the prestigious Minnesota Orchestra. For several days leading up to the concert they stayed in a big comfortable hotel close to the concert hall, this allowing rehearsals with the orchestra. Izzy developed an allergic reaction to something, she wasn't sure what, but the old familiar rash broke out. At a small, privately owned pharmacy nearby, recommended by the receptionist at the hotel, she asked for some of the lotion which she knew would help. The pharmacist had difficulty finding exactly what she wanted and called the owner/manager. A good-looking man came to speak to her and looked at her with delight.

'You're Iseult Butler, the pianist, aren't you?'

'Yes, I am,' she answered, with pleasure at being recognised, although this was becoming quite a common occurrence. However, she hadn't expected a pharmacist to recognise her, although she couldn't quite think why.

'I'm going to your concert tomorrow and really looking forward to it.'

'Thank you. I hope you enjoy it.'

'I know I will. Now let me see what I can find that will get rid of that rash. Something not needing a prescription.'

He searched around and found a lotion for her.

'I'm pretty sure this will do the trick.'

'Thank you so much.'

She got out her purse to pay.

'No, no. Please, it's on the house. It's not every day I've the pleasure of serving an internationally recognised pianist.'

'That really is very kind. Thank you.'

He was tall and slim with crew-cut silver hair, blue eyes and a warm smile. He also had a closely trimmed beard and moustache, in colour a little darker than his hair. He had a very sympathetic aura about him and she liked him.

'We'll be having a celebration after the concert. As a thank you for your generous gesture would you and your wife like to join us?'

'I'd love that but I have no wife.'

Why did that make her feel pleased?

'I don't know your name.'

'I'm Jed Seabourne.'

'Well, Jed, if there's anyone else you'd like to bring along that would be fine.'

'No. It'll just be me and I look forward to that.'

Like all her other concerts it was a huge success, with a standing ovation for Izzy. Much to her delight Jed turned up afterwards for the party. They got along like a house on fire and Noola and Maggie liked him too, finding him very sociable and easy to talk to. He seemed almost old fashioned in his manners and attitude generally and he didn't have too strong an American accent which, perhaps, could have made him difficult to understand at times to the untuned ear. However, he was obviously a lot older than Izzy and, in a way, they were quite glad they were going home soon, for she seemed to be more than a little taken with him. Remembering her attraction to Bertie, it occurred to Noola that Izzy seemed to have a preference for older men and wondered if they gave her a sense of security perhaps not given by younger men. It was getting late and the party was winding down. Izzy felt free to spend a little more time with Jed, having been meticulous in talking to all the other guests and indeed revelling in the generous accolade for the final concert of her tour.

'Sorry I haven't been able to spend much time with you, Jed, but I'm so pleased you came along.'

'So am I, Miss Butler.'

'Oh, my friends all call me Izzy and I'd be happy for you to do the same.'

'Thank you. I feel honoured to be regarded as a friend.'

'Well, you were so kind to me yesterday how could I regard you any other way?'

'If you've nothing special planned for your last few days here I'd love to give you a guided tour of our places of interest. Did you know we've strong connections around here with Hiawatha and Minnehaha?'

'No, although we were very excited at seeing the mighty Mississippi. We've been so taken up with my concert arrangements here that we haven't had much time for sightseeing.' She paused for a moment. 'But I would *love* to have a guided tour given by someone who lives locally and knows the places worth seeing. I'm sure my mother and grandmother would be delighted too. Give me a few minutes to talk to them. I won't be long.'

He made his way over to the bar, hardly taking his eyes off her, while she spoke earnestly to Noola and Maggie. She put the proposal to them.

'I really would love to have Jed show us the sights. What do you think?'

They looked at the eager, anxious face. Izzy had worked so hard; had had an exhausting tour and not that much time to do what she really wanted. Concert after concert; rehearsal after rehearsal; daily practice for hours. She wasn't asking much of them and somehow they couldn't refuse. They liked Jed but still had those reservations. However, they'd soon be home and she'd probably forget him quite quickly.

'You don't want to go and have a quick look at California, perhaps San Francisco for a few days?'

175

'I really would rather stay here, Mum.'

'All right, sweetheart, why not? What about you, Mammy?'

'I'm just happy to be with you both, wherever it may be in this fascinating country.'

'Mum, Granny, you're wonderful. Thank you.'

The radiant face was their reward. She hurried back to Jed.

'Yes, they're happy to accept your offer.'

He gave her a marvellous smile and joined Noola and Maggie.

'Thank you both. I feel so privileged to be allowed to act as guide to an international star and her family. In fact I'm really excited.'

'Can you get time off at such short notice?'

'Well, actually I own the pharmacy and have an excellent assistant manager who I trust. I rarely take time off so I feel quite comfortable asking her to look after things for a few days.'

They were there for their last three days and found it genuinely interesting, with Jed as a wonderful guide. He behaved impeccably and didn't try to push anything with Izzy. They couldn't have faulted him, although he said very little about himself and they didn't want to pry. So on the last evening Noola and Maggie agreed that they would back out of dinner and leave the two of them to have some time to themselves. Izzy felt so comfortable in his company and had longed for a chance to have him to herself, so was highly delighted. Jed felt as if he had been given a million dollars.

Neither would ever forget that evening. He took her to a restaurant in a highly recommended hotel where there was live music and dancing. He wanted to know all about her and in her forthright way she chatted away about her family and Riverside and the family's great love affair with the River Liffey. In turn he told her how he'd been to college, but decided he would like to try running his own business. How hard it was at first and how he had sometimes worked eighteen hours a day to pay off the outstanding loan to the bank, not minding what he did: labouring, working in bars and so on. But now he had almost paid off the debt and would soon own the business outright. He felt quite proud of his achievements. His foster parents had been dead for some years. He had no known relatives and didn't want to pursue any enquiries in that direction in case he found they weren't what he might have chosen.

176

'Is that very selfish, Izzy?'

She thought for a moment.

'No. Actually I can understand. I've heard of people discovering they had relatives who they would have preferred not to know.'

'Izzy, these have been the most wonderful few days of my life. I can't remember when I've been happier. Would you be willing to keep in touch? I know we live far apart and I'm a lot older than you but I'd be really sad to lose all contact. Could we be penfriends?'

He seemed almost wistful. She didn't hesitate. She'd been hoping he might make some suggestion of this kind.

'It's been such a happy time for me too. I'd love to keep in touch. The penfriend idea is great. Then if I come back for another concert tour we could meet up again or you might even come to Ireland for a holiday.'

'Well, you just never know. Now how about a dance?'

'Yes. That would be lovely.'

He took her in his arms and she had the weird feeling that she had come home, this was where she belonged. They danced slowly around the floor and she nestled her cheek next to his. They didn't speak – words weren't needed and afterwards, in true gentlemanly fashion, he took her back to her hotel and said goodnight, with a brief peck on the cheek. He didn't dare to wait for her to suggest a nightcap, for he wouldn't have been able to refuse and he was frightened where it might lead. There was no way he was going to risk being tempted any further or, more to the point, compromising Izzy.

Next morning he drove them to the airport to see them off, courteous and considerate to the last. They said goodbye reluctantly, but Noola didn't extend an invitation for him to stay at Riverside if he came to Dublin. She was still much too concerned about the obvious age gap between him and Izzy and was relieved there was such a big distance separating them. Moreover, much as she admired the United States, she was rather appalled at the idea of Izzy possibly emigrating to America. She simply didn't want one of her children so far away from her. The UK was quite far enough. Later Izzy would look back on 1973 as such a happy year.

177

Chapter 25

In June of that same year Isabel gave birth to a little boy. She and Tommy were ecstatic and the twins were apparently vying with each other in trying to help with the new baby. This time the child did have typical Butler black curls but very blue eyes. They called him Milo after his uncle. Not long afterwards, to everyone's delight and by a remarkable coincidence, Bill was posted to Cyprus with a contingent of the Irish UN Peacekeeping Force and so was able to report back first-hand on the new member of the Butler family.

Being so good-looking Bill was often the target of female interest, something he had been accustomed to from his teenage years. But while he enjoyed the company of the girls, and even flirted gently with them, he had never ever stepped out of line with his vows. However, being a normal red-blooded man, he was not by any means immune to feeling the appeal of members of the opposite sex and, during his brief stay in Cyprus, he was put to the test in a big way when he found himself strongly attracted to a very beautiful Cypriot girl.

He met Androulla at a social function hosted by one of the UN groups to which some of the Irish contingent had been invited. Local dignitaries had also been invited, including Androulla's father who was a member of the Greek Cypriot Government. She had characteristic Mediterranean dark eyes and hair and a perfect smooth, olive complexion. She was also highly intelligent and Bill found her extremely good company with her quick-fire repartee, a ready wit and an impressive knowledge of current local and worldwide politics. She had recently completed her studies to be a lawyer at the new University of Warwick, so it was no surprise that her English was perfect, spoken with a delightful trace of a foreign accent, which added to her attraction. She appealed to him powerfully, both emotionally and intellectually, more than any other girl he could remember and he quickly picked up the fact that she was responding to him in the same way.

The evening came to an end and Bill had spent more time with Androulla than protocol would have dictated. Even though he had occasionally made the supreme effort to go and mingle socially with the other guests, time and again he drifted back to her. When they were saying goodbye, in a very brief aside out of hearing of anyone else, she had made a comment that had disconcerted him:

'I'm sorry that you're a priest, Bill. I do understand what that means – it's best if we don't meet again.'

He was on the verge of saying he was sorry too; of saying he'd love to meet her again, all his instincts telling him that she would readily agree to such a suggestion, but he pulled himself up short and bid her and her parents a formal farewell.

He was so sorely tempted. Typical Butler it had taken the briefest time for him to lose his heart completely to this lovely young woman. He had never been in love before. He had found some girls extremely attractive but had never really loved any of them. Now I understand, he thought to himself. I didn't fully appreciate before what I was sacrificing. Dad's right. We Butlers are a virile lot and now, for the first time, I truly realise what I've forsworn. I've been so self-righteous in believing I knew what it was all about and that it wasn't such a difficult thing to do: to forego my natural instincts. Now I'm being tested and what am I going to do? Fall at the first fence? Give up everything I believe in? Give up being a priest? But, oh God, I want her desperately, in every sense of the word. I want to be with her; spend all my time with her; to enjoy her company as much as I know I would; to have the joy of looking at her; to make love to her.

It hurt so much. He wasn't convinced he could withstand the temptation. He spent most of that night and was to spend many hours afterwards on his knees, in agony of mind, praying for strength and courage to honour his vows.

More than two thousand miles away to the west Harry knew.

179

Like the earlier generation of Butler identical twins he and Bill could feel each other's emotions and more than anything else they could feel each other's pain and distress. Harry couldn't sleep a wink. He tossed and turned. He tried reading a book, but it was no good and instinctively he knew something was wrong with Bill. It came to five o'clock in the morning and he couldn't stand the anxiety any longer. He knew that by then it would be seven o'clock there and everyone on the base in Cyprus would be up and about with many having started their day's work. So he telephoned and asked to speak to Bill urgently, explaining that he was his brother calling from Dublin. He didn't have long to wait, for Bill was close by having cup after cup of coffee in the dining room. Concerned that something was wrong at home, he hurried to take the call.

'Hello, Harry. Is something wrong?'

'Not here, Billy, but I know something's very wrong with you – I haven't slept a wink. What is it? Can I do anything?'

'Bless you, Harry, I wish you could but it's something I've got to sort myself and not something I can talk about on the phone.'

'I could go out there for a few days. Perhaps just talking about it would help. Dad wouldn't mind if I took a few days off and I needn't say why, just that I'd like a bit of time with you out there.'

There was a brief silence.

'Bill?'

'Sorry, Harry, I was thinking about your offer. You know that would be great. Regardless of my problem it would be so good to see you and would help me a lot.'

'I'll get there as soon as I can. With any luck in the next day or so.'

Bill was vastly relieved. He had decided that he didn't want to talk about the whole thing with anyone out there, not even a fellow cleric. Had he been at home he might have gone to Father Callaghan and unburdened himself to his old friend and mentor, but there was no one like that here. It would be such a help to have Harry, someone he knew he could trust implicitly.

Harry arrived the next day. When he had asked, as casually as possible, for a few days leave from the office to spend a bit of time with Bill, he didn't fool his father for a second. Milo, having watched

180

them growing up together, knew the extraordinary telepathy between them. Maggie had told him the story of how that same closeness had saved one of the earlier generation of twins from a particularly awful death when he was buried alive in the First World War. His brother had refused to give up digging for him because he had known, by that same strange telepathic communication, that he was still alive. Now, when Harry was leaving, Milo simply said to him:

'I hope you can help him, Harry, whatever the problem is.'

Harry smiled.

'We can't hide anything from you, Dad!'

'Well, not much when it comes to matters involving the closeness of you two. Anything else I wouldn't be too sure about.'

Having his twin there really did help Bill through the next few difficult days. Harry listened patiently while Bill talked it through and he made sympathetic comments. However, never once did he try to influence him in his decision. Womaniser that he was, in no way was he going to try to persuade his brother to walk down the same path, for he knew that the guilt he would suffer in doing so would destroy him. In any event he felt very strongly that the final decision must be Bill's.

They had a good time together, Harry doing everything in his power to take Bill's mind off his worry and with some degree of success. Then the day after Harry returned home the October or "Yom Kippur" War broke out and despite their very short stay there, the Irish unit in Cyprus was transferred to the Sinai Desert, for peacekeeping duties in the area separating the Israeli and Egyptian forces. This kept Bill so preoccupied he had little time to dwell on personal problems and it built on the coping process started by his brother's visit.

Once they had settled into their new base, as a member of a neutral military force Bill was able to visit both countries. He had intended to visit the Holy Land while in Cyprus, but now this was even closer. Like any tourist he couldn't have failed to find it fascinating, but as a Christian in holy orders he was deeply moved to think that all the places he was walking in had probably been trodden by Jesus Christ. He also found the sights in Egypt so

181

interesting and had time to visit the Valley of the Kings as well as the Pyramids at Giza and the museum in Cairo, with its amazing remains of all kinds but especially those of Tutankhamun. He felt sad that it had been a war that had given him such opportunities but fully appreciated it all nevertheless.

It took time but he recovered and was very thankful that he had managed to resist such a strong temptation to abandon his vows. However, one thing he did firmly resolve was that some day he would return to Cyprus, perhaps on leave, to stay with Tommy and family, for, like so many others who visited this magical island, he had fallen in love with it and wanted to see more. He now felt he could do that without opening up the sore spot again.

Chapter 26

Early in 1974 the family at Riverside heard that Isabel was expecting another child in September. At almost exactly the same time Sarah and Dai, with great delight, announced that Sarah was expecting their first child in the October. There were celebrations on both sides of the Irish Sea and all worked out well because Sarah would be able to finish the academic year and so not let down her students in mid-course. The baby would be a first grandchild in Dai's family.

Milo and Noola were thrilled to bits at the idea of all this expansion of the wider Butler family and Maggie and Aunt May were also highly delighted.

'With Sarah and Dai living in the East Wing, at last we'll have a grandchild living close to us. Oh, Milo, I'm so excited.'

'So am I, Noola. It'll be good to have another little one nearby and with any luck it will be the first of many trotting around Riverside again. And you know what? I'll be able to teach him to row! I'll get such a kick out of that.'

'Interesting! You're assuming it'll be a boy!'

'Well whichever – I'll still be able to teach him or her to row – stop splitting hairs, Noola.'

* * * * *

On 17 May Sarah was hurrying along South Leinster Street, making her way towards Trinity, where she had arranged to meet Dai in the car park just inside Back Gate in Lincoln Place. Within minutes of each other, around 5.30 pm, three car bombs exploded in the heart of Dublin City, one of these in South Leinster Street. Sarah was one of many hit by the blast. She was hurled into the middle of the street, slammed into the side of a car, bounced off it and was thrown under the wheels of one coming in the opposite direction.

Dai, waiting in the car park, heard the explosion and with many others from inside the college flew flat out towards the disaster, his heart in his mouth and praying aloud:

'Please, God, don't let my Sarah be there. *Please*, God, don't.'

He arrived at the scene of carnage and searched frantically, calling her name over and over again. Eventually he spotted her quite distinctive dress where she was lying in the middle of the street, one leg trapped under the wheel of the car and the contents of her briefcase scattered around her. She wasn't moving but she was breathing. She was also haemorrhaging but as yet, so far as he could see, not heavily. He knew he mustn't try to move her for fear of aggravating her injuries. He knelt down beside her and spoke to her but no response. He put his jacket over her and shouted over and over for medical help, most especially an ambulance. One of his own students heard him and, recognising the Welsh voice, made her way through the piles of debris to offer what help she could. Gemma was a determined young woman and, horrified at the sight of Sarah so badly injured, ran off and refused to give up until she got paramedics to the scene. Given the numbers of injured needing help this was a major achievement but she felt justified in pushing for help since she reckoned the only people with injuries worse than Sarah's were dead.

The nearest hospital was not too far away and when the ambulance got there no effort was spared to save her life. The family at Riverside received Dai's distressed call and in a remarkably short space of time Milo and Noola arrived. They had heard about the explosions on the evening news but it never occurred to them that a family member might be caught up in the disaster. Usually by this time in the evening Sarah and Dai were home. Like Dai they were frantic and desperately anxious to speak to the doctor but Sarah was in surgery and there was nobody who could tell them anything except that they were fighting hard for her life. Once in a while somebody would come out of the operating theatre and, looking grave, would simply say they were doing their best to save her.

Maggie, Harry and Izzy arrived as quickly as they could get there and the mutual support helped them all.

After five hours the lead surgeon came to speak to them.

'It's been touch and go but we think she's going to make it.'

Having borne up with amazing fortitude, some of those waiting shed tears of relief. Dai spoke to the tired looking man.

'Thank you and your whole team, you must all be exhausted, but we're all so grateful. Can you give us the details? All we know is that her leg was trapped and she seemed to be haemorrhaging from several different places, including the side of her head.'

'Well, first of all I'm so sorry to tell you she lost the baby, which is probably no surprise to you in the circumstances. Then we found her spleen was ruptured and we had to remove that. The rest of the time we've spent working on her leg. It was in a very bad way and we thought we'd have to amputate but we've managed to save it. Unfortunately she'll walk with a limp for the rest of her life, but she still has the leg. Luckily the head injury was superficial – just needed a couple of stitches, so there's no fear of brain damage. But one way and another she did lose a great deal of blood. Fortunately we had a good supply of her blood group in store.'

There was a stunned silence while they all took in what they had been told.

'So it's likely to be a long, hard recovery?'

'I'm afraid so. We'll have to keep her in here in intensive care for as long as it takes and then we'll need to keep a close watch on the early stages of recovery. It may be some time before she can go home again and she'll be in a lot of pain, perhaps for a long time.'

'When can we see her?'

'You can certainly have a look at her, but she won't regain consciousness for quite a while. In fact you can sit with her and wait for her to come around. It would be reassuring for her to see familiar faces when she does wake up. But I should warn you. Initially, while the anaesthetic is still working she won't appear to be too distressed. That will come later and that's when she'll really need you there.'

Only a few weeks before the explosions across the city Bill had returned from Sinai after the statutory six months of his tour of duty. Having taken end-of-tour leave he wasn't in Dublin at the time of

185

the explosions but cut short his holiday in Cyprus and came flying home as fast as he could when he heard what had happened to Sarah. He was a huge support to everyone and they were all so glad to have him there, especially Sarah. He didn't care how much time he spent with her, day and night, talking to her, praying with her and giving comfort and encouragement to her and the rest of the family. While desperately upset, nevertheless, he appeared calm and utterly dependable at all times. Dai hadn't really had a chance to get to know him previously but now developed a sincere respect and affection for this completely selfless and dedicated man.

'I know how much it has meant to Sarah and the rest of the family to have you here, but you'll never know how much it has helped me personally. I'll never forget it, Bill.'

'Thanks Dai, but she's my much loved sister and I would have done no less. Just keep praying that she makes as full a recovery as possible.'

Sarah did start to recover, helped by having some member of the family beside her day and night. They all wanted to help and not just visit her but take their turn in watching over her and keeping her company. She was in a private ward and the staff moved a temporary bed into the room so that whoever was there at night could get a little sleep. At first Dai refused to leave her, regardless of who else was there, but as she progressed she insisted that he went back to college and his students. Concerned colleagues had been trying to fill in for him, willingly taking on the extra workload during his absence.

A month later Sarah was allowed to go home but only on the understanding that she had the care of qualified nurses day and night for another two weeks. She was a shadow of her former self, but she had endured and she had made it. One of the most cheering pieces of news for her and Dai was that the consultant gynaecologist said, in spite of all she'd been through, she should still be able to have children. She was so pleased that Dai felt it helped to speed up her recovery.

Many others who had been caught by the explosions were less fortunate. Altogether twenty-three people died instantly, a high proportion of these young women, with some bodies mutilated beyond recognition. The casualties that fateful day in May, including those of a similar bomb which exploded in Monaghan, were greater in number than on any other single day throughout the so-called "Troubles" of the twentieth century in Ireland.

Chapter 27

Six weeks after the car bomb attacks a well-dressed woman, wearing black and carrying a small child, arrived at the Butlers' stockbroking office asking to speak to Harry Butler. The secretary on duty at the reception desk asked the usual question of visitors.

'Have you got an appointment?'

'No, but I need to speak to him urgently. Otherwise I'd like to see his father, either will do.'

'I'll see what I can do. What's your name?'

'Mrs O'Connell.'

She came back and said Mr Harry was with a client but Mr Milo Butler would see her. She was ushered into Milo's office and he stood up to greet her, smiling at the child. Something about the little boy niggled at him.

'Good afternoon, Mrs O'Connell. I'm Milo Butler. How can I help you?'

'It was really your son I needed to see. But he's not available, as usual.'

This puzzled Milo.

'You've tried before?'

'Oh no. But my daughter did many, many times and he refused even to speak to her. Letters were returned unopened and never would he agree to see her in here.'

'So how can I help you?'

'My daughter, Marie, was killed in the bomb blast in Talbot Street in May. This little boy is hers. He's also your son's child.'

Milo stared at her speechless, looked at the child and then realised what it was that had bothered him. The child could hardly have been more of a Butler. He had the black curls, exactly like his own two sons, but in this case the eyes were very dark brown, just like Noola's and Maggie's.

'I had no idea and I'm sure Harry didn't either. I'm so sorry you lost your daughter like that. My own daughter was badly injured, crippled in fact, and lost her baby the same day, so I can imagine how you feel.'

The woman's face softened.

'I'm sorry, Mr Butler. That must have been a dreadful shock too. As for Harry knowing about the baby! Of course he didn't. As I just explained, he cut off contact of any kind, so in the end Marie decided she had to cope without him. Luckily she had us. But now her father has had a stroke and is severely disabled, brought on, I'm certain, by all that has happened. I'll have a full-time job looking after him for the rest of his life and I can't possibly look after the child too. It's too much at my age and we can't afford to pay for help. So I've brought him to his father. He'll have to take responsibility for him now and he can certainly afford to get someone to care for him. I'll miss the little fellow and hope I'll be allowed to see him sometimes, after all he is my grandson and I do love him. But I want the best for him and I can't give him that.'

She had tried so hard not to weep but the tears threatened and the lower lip quivered. Milo couldn't but admire her dignity in very difficult circumstances. Looking at the child he didn't doubt her story for a second. He was in a state of some shock himself but recovered his composure quickly.

'Harry must come in and discuss this and I can assure you that any arrangement made will include giving you access to the little boy. Come to think of it he's my grandson too. What's his name?'

'Johnny, after my husband.'

He stooped down beside the chair and spoke to the child.

'Hello, little Johnny. I'm your other grandpa!'

Puzzled brown eyes looked at him and then the child buried his head in his grandmother's shoulder.

'Home, Gangan, home.'

'He still believes his mother is at home somewhere – toddles around the house calling her. She used to play a game where she hid

189

and he had to find her. Now when he can't find her he cries and cries for her.' She couldn't stop a couple of tears spilling over. 'I miss her too.'

'He's going to find it very hard parting from you and your husband and in such a short space of time after losing his mother. Poor little boy. When Harry is here we'll have to work out a way to handle this with the minimum of distress for him.'

'Thank you, Mr Butler, and may I say I don't understand how a sympathetic and understanding man like you could have produced a son so hard and uncaring as Harry. From Marie's description of him he seems to care for nothing but himself and enjoying life.'

'I can't tell you how sad I am that you see him in this light but in the circumstances I can see why. He's been a good son to us, one who has given us many reasons to be proud of him. He's never been anything but kind and considerate to other members of the family too. One thing is certain, he must put right this dreadful wrong insofar as he can.'

Milo called the reception desk and asked that Harry should be sent in immediately he was free. He saw no reason for trying to soften the shock for him. He had brought it all on himself through his almost inhuman behaviour and it had landed on his father out of the blue, something for which he was in no way to blame. For the first time in his life he felt really ashamed of one of his children.

The door opened and Harry came in.

'You wanted to see me?'

'Yes, Harry. This lady here is Mrs O'Connell. She actually came here to see you but you weren't free at the time so I've been speaking to her.'

Harry turned and smiled at them rather puzzled. The name was not uncommon and he didn't make any connection. He barely glanced at the child.

'Good morning. How can I help?'

He was all charm and pleasantness and Nora O'Connell was incensed. This was not the side he had latterly shown to her daughter, although she could see how he must have originally charmed her off her feet.

'I've come to make arrangements for you to give a home to your

190

child: the child Marie had after you decided you didn't want to have anything more to do with her. You, of course, having got everything you wanted from her long before he was born.'

Every trace of colour drained from his face. He stood there staring at her and the child, trying to take in the appalling implications of what she had said. She continued:

'And please don't try to deny he's yours. Just take a good look at him and then go and look in a mirror. The only difference is the colour of the eyes. Maybe someone in your family has dark brown eyes? Aside from anything else you were the only man Marie was ever seriously interested in and I'm quite convinced that she had never been intimate with anyone else. She simply wasn't that kind of girl. Did you know she was only nineteen when you met?'

At last he found his voice. He knew what she had said about Marie was true; she *was* sexually inexperienced when they had started their relationship. But she had told him she'd been to Belfast and got a supply of the contraceptive pill. What had gone wrong? Just above a whisper he answered her.

'No. I had no idea. She said she was twenty-four and I believed her. But where is she? Why hasn't she come here with you?'

'She hasn't come with me because she's dead.'

Now he felt sick.

'*Dead*! Oh I'm *so* sorry – I had no idea. How?'

'In the explosion in Talbot Street a few weeks ago. Johnny was fourteen months old.'

'How dreadful for you and poor little Johnny.' He paused as this all sank in. 'What can I do to help?'

Thank the good Lord, Milo thought inwardly. He's going to show that underneath that apparently hard-baked exterior he is at heart a decent human being. Much more like the man we know at home.

Mrs O'Connell explained what she expected Harry to do and why. They spent a long time talking it through and in the end reached agreement that Johnny would go to live at Riverside House. A nanny would be employed to look after him for as long as was necessary. She agreed that, for a short time, the person employed would live in the O'Connell house, even though conditions would

191

be very cramped. This would give Johnny time to get to know and like her before being taken away from his grandparents. To make the transition as easy as possible for him, during this interim period he would be taken to visit Riverside daily, so it and the people there would become familiar to him.

It was also agreed that Mrs O'Connell could visit Johnny without restriction and because this would be difficult for her and impossible for her husband, Johnny would be taken to see them at regular intervals. Nora O'Connell was vastly relieved. She was still angry with Harry and would never forgive him but at least he was trying hard to face up to his responsibilities and had done so without the bluster and denials she had expected. She had come ready for a fight and argument and there hadn't been any.

Throughout the discussion Johnny, blissfully unaware that his whole future was being decided, had slept peacefully in Nora's arms, sucking his thumb and clutching his favourite soft toy. Looking down at the little child the hard shell around Harry's heart, the one he had deliberately developed to protect him from wanting to enter into a serious relationship with any woman, suddenly started to crack. This little boy is my son, he thought; *my son* and suddenly he was the one close to tears. He had never imagined he could feel such an intense wave of emotion and one quite different from his feelings for his parents and siblings.

'Would he mind if I held him?'

It was asked rather hesitantly. Nora had watched the different emotions flitting across his face and felt more than ever that she had made the right decision for Johnny. Awful as he had been to her daughter he would care for the child. She was now convinced of that.

'You can hold him, but since he doesn't know you he'll probably cry.'

She passed Johnny gently to him. The child stirred slightly but then nestled into the comfortable, protective arms cradled around him without waking. The hard shell completely disintegrated and Harry didn't dare to speak for fear of breaking down completely and making an exhibition of himself.

Looking at Harry's face Milo felt slightly better. A measure of

192

justice had been done, albeit rather late in the day. However, that evening, with Noola present, he didn't pull any punches with his son. He had put her in the picture and she was even more appalled than he had been by the whole story. Rarely really angry, Milo was furious and he put his earlier thoughts into words.

'It's the first time ever that your mother and I have actually felt deeply ashamed of one of our children. We completely fail to comprehend how you could treat anybody like that. Is there any way in which you can excuse yourself? And please don't tell us that you're twenty-nine years old and it's your life and your business. It has been *made* our business and especially it's been made *my* business. Not only was I completely mortified but my heart went out to that unfortunate and, indeed, courageous woman today who bore all her problems with such dignity.'

Harry made no attempt to justify his actions or offer any excuses. His face was colourless and he looked quite gaunt.

'I realise there's no way I can ever apologise adequately to you both but especially to you, Dad, who had to be directly involved today. Thank you for helping to make arrangements for Johnny to come and live here. Would it be easier for you if I moved out and set up my own place, with a nanny for Johnny? I'm prepared to do that. I'm so sorry that you're ashamed of me, but I can't blame you. In your shoes I'm sure I'd feel the same way. I'm sad that I'm such a disappointment to you both.'

'You're only a disappointment to us in the way you've behaved in this matter and in the way you treat women generally. We find your attitude to them appalling. However, in all other ways you're not a disappointment, and there have been times when we've been very proud of you. What's more, there's no way we could fault your behaviour and attitude to members of the family.'

'Thanks, Mum.'

'As for moving out, there's no need to do that. We would miss you if you left. I also feel it would be better for Johnny to be here with the rest of us. Just don't do this to us again.'

'I promise I won't, Dad.'

Talking it all through afterwards, Noola expressed a slight concern.

'I wonder how Sarah will take all this. She's lost her baby and now another Butler baby will be joining the household. Do you think it will upset her, almost rub salt in the wound of losing her own?'

Milo thought about this new slant on things.

'A lot will depend on how it's handled. Living in the East Wing, she won't have to come into contact with him all that often, especially since he and his nanny will have their own quarters in the old nursery area, on the top floor. But who knows? If she wanted to help out with him from time to time it might be the very thing that will speed up the healing process and compensate her in some small way for her loss. And just think of Maggie's reaction! Yet another little motherless boy in the house and this time it's her great-grandson. She may have turned eighty but she's still very spry and active. I bet she'll want to be involved!'

'I'm quite certain she will and don't forget it makes us grandparents again too. But now you'll have a little grandson living here and you can teach him to row and other water sports, just as you did your own children. What about that for a thought?'

Milo smiled at her.

'True, but I wish it hadn't happened quite the way it did – Sarah's accident and Marie's death.'

So Johnny joined the family at Riverside. Harry legally adopted him and in no time at all he became the darling of the entire household and a supreme delight to his father. Harry was a changed man in terms of appreciating the immense joy of having your own family.

Chapter 28

Bill had used the remainder of his official leave helping to watch over and support Sarah during the earlier critical part of her recovery. Being based in Ireland for the moment meant that he was able to return to duty at the official appointed time and still visit her regularly. In fact he spent most of his free time with her. However, after some weeks his commanding officer, noticing how strained he was looking, decided he would regard Bill's time spent with his traumatised sister as a sort of compassionate leave and suggested he went back to Cyprus to finish his broken holiday there. He agreed readily, and Tommy and Isabel were delighted that they would have a first-hand report on Sarah's progress.

He arrived on 12 July 1974 just three days before the ruling Greek Military Junta sponsored a coup organised by the new EOKA 'B' faction, overthrowing the legitimate Cyprus Government and deposing the Greek Cypriot President, Archbishop Makarios. These extreme right-wing EOKA supporters made particular attacks on any Greek Cypriots who were loyal Makarios supporters or those with strong left-wing sympathies. The Turkish Cypriots were also natural targets. There was no particular panic for those staying in the military bases, but there was considerable alarm. Those with any understanding of the political situation knew well that the mainland Turkish Government wouldn't stand by and see their fellow Turks in Cyprus wiped out, especially if they called for help.

At that particular moment Tommy, Isabel and family with Bill were enjoying a few days in Famagusta, introducing Bill to the delights of this resort. With its romantic associations it was a favourite haunt for the young couple. They had, of course, been to visit Nick's fabric shop and, later on, called around by invitation to have an evening meal with the family. Daughter Maria was there, home on holiday from her course of language studies in a college in Oxford. They had had a marvellous evening with a superb meal. They had also had the unmissible visit to Smokey Joe's, where Isabel and Tommy had become engaged. They little thought that within a few weeks the whole of this community would disintegrate and disappear forever in its existing form, with Famagusta becoming an abandoned and ravaged ghost city.

As soon as the coup occurred Tommy and family with Bill headed back to Akrotiri immediately, "just in case", and as things turned out this was a wise decision. With his Irish passport and army ID there was no problem allowing Bill through with the family and he had taken the additional precaution of donning his clerical collar with a khaki shirt. He carried these with him wherever he went since there was always a chance he might need them. Tommy returned to full-time duties and the whole military community was on the alert for emergencies or any escalation of the crisis.

As the rumours filtered in about the behaviour of the leaders of the coup, in rounding up and executing people who were their particular targets, worries grew for Cypriot friends and colleagues. Tommy was busy and preoccupied with the emergency, planning strategies for evacuations in the worst-case scenario, and to an extent the whole of the military community became involved, including wives. Bill did his best to help out by entertaining the twins, Lizzie and Vicky, now six years old. This wasn't difficult for they adored him and were very happy to spend as much time as possible with him. Characteristically for children of that age they subjected him to minute scrutiny. After one such inspection, Lizzie commented on something that hadn't occurred to him previously.

'Isn't it fun, Bill? Our hair is blond and yours is black but we have green eyes just like yours. Daddy and Mummy have blue eyes.'

It was strange and set him thinking. After dinner that evening he and Tommy were having a nightcap together after Isabel had gone to bed. Tommy was tired and they were drinking the brandy sours Cyprus was famous for, so he became quite mellow.

'Lizzie made an interesting observation earlier today, Tommy.

196

The twins have green eyes. Where do they get them from – are there green eyes in Isabel's family? Strange thing is they're such an intense green and exactly like mine.'

Without stopping to think Tommy answered him.

'Of course they're just like yours, they're Lo's eyes.'

'Now come on, they can't be *Dad's* eyes. He inherited them from his mother and you're in no way related to Granny Rachel. You've got your own mother's very blue eyes.'

Tommy suddenly realised what he had said. There was no way he could backtrack. Bill was looking at him in such an odd way.

'Okay. Serves me right. That's what comes of drinking brandy sours when I'm tired! They *are* his eyes. He's their real father.'

Bill was dumbstruck.

'But... how...? Why?'

'Right. I'll tell you the whole story but I'm trusting you, totally, never to tell anyone else.'

'Tommy, I'm a priest. I don't betray confidences but now I'm intrigued and, knowing you and Dad, I'm certain it's not what it sounds like on the face of it!'

Tommy smiled at him.

'No. It was all absolutely above board and completely moral, I promise you.'

So he told him the whole story, which took quite a while. Bill was so surprised but his reaction was not quite the unequivocal forgiveness response that Tommy would have expected from a priest.

'I'm inclined to agree with Dad. I think it was a dreadful thing for your grandparents to do to you, not to tell you the truth when they realised Bob had such a problem. Surely they must have realised you would worry sick about it, especially getting married. And it shouldn't have been impossible to get released from an oath in the circumstances. They could have gone back to the orphanage or even written to them and explained the problem. I'm sure they would have released them from their vow of silence, maybe with some conditions.'

'Well they did eventually tell me, even if a bit late in the day. But it all worked out in the end.'

197

Bill was silent for a moment then he grinned broadly.

'As our American friends would say, well whadaya know – I've got two more sisters. How lucky that they look so like Isabel! But it's marvellous that it was all discovered in time for you to have children with an easy mind.'

'The twins will always be so special to me. All right so genetically they aren't mine but after all they're Lo's and they solved quite a problem for us. I love them so much – just as much as our baby Milo.'

They chatted on for a while and then Bill made a decision.

'Actually I'd like to share a confidence with you too, Tommy, and a worry, but again for your ears only, although I suppose I wouldn't mind if you told Isabel, she's such a sympathetic soul and is not likely to blab about it.'

'You have my word. We'd both respect a confidence.'

'When I was based here briefly that time, before we were transferred to Sinai, I met a wonderful girl, Androulla. To be honest with you I fell in love with her deeply and unreservedly. She was the most amazing girl I ever met and the only one I was ever really in love with, heart and soul. It took every ounce of self-discipline and control not to throw up everything for her and I knew, instinctively, and actually from something she said, that she felt the same way.'

'Oh, Billy, how dreadful for you. And nobody else knew?'

'Harry knew by instinct that I had a problem and came out to help me through. You know how we're so tuned into each other's feelings!'

'Thank goodness. But is it still difficult for you?'

'I thought I was over it, had come to terms with not being able to be with her and so was fine to visit here again. Now I know I'm not over it because I'm worried silly about her.'

'Why?'

'Her father is a staunch Makarios supporter and we know the stories that are being circulated about them: they're being rounded up and disappearing. It may be rumour or it may not, but you can see why I'm concerned. Are such hostilities likely to extend to families too?'

'Who knows? But there's nothing we can do about it, we can't interfere!'

198

'I'm wondering if I couldn't go out and see what the situation is. I could visit her home. She told me exactly where she lives. Not far from the Ledra Palace Hotel in Nicosia. I could get a rental car and nobody would be any the wiser. I could be just another tourist.'

'I'm not too keen on the idea. It could be very risky. Tell you what, why don't we sleep on it and have another chat about it tomorrow? I'll try to think of some way it could be done with a minimum of risk.'

'Fair enough! It's too late tonight to do anything about it, but thanks for listening.'

'You know I'd do anything in my power to help you, Bill.'

'Yes, I know that, Tommy.'

'What have you in mind beyond ensuring she's safe? Have you changed your mind about a long-term commitment?'

'No. I'll stick by my original decision to honour my vows, but I just want to be sure she's all right and give any help I can, if it's needed.'

'You'll go through all that agony of mind again.'

'I know but that's the way it has to be if I'm to retain my honour and a shred of self-respect.'

They talked on for a long time. Bill told Tommy all about Androulla and her family and seemed to get some relief for his feelings by doing this.

The next morning, Saturday, 20 July, they awoke to the news that mainland Turkish forces had landed in the north of the island, in support of the Turkish Cypriot community. They were fighting their way south, presumably towards Nicosia, which would be a natural target for them. This was to be fortunate for many who, as a result, survived the depredations of the leaders of the coup. But it was unfortunate for a great many more who suffered devastating losses of all kinds and some of the abuses so often associated with any invading army. With this initial invasion began the first phase of the carving up of the island into two distinct areas, a division that was to last for the foreseeable future.

Greek Cypriot refugees from the invaded northern areas of the island started to stream southwards and with them unsavoury stories about the invading Turks. In the south of the island, fearful of reprisals

199

from their Greek neighbours, Turkish Cypriots started to flood towards the British base at Akrotiri for protection. The British Forces Broadcasting Service went on air twenty-four hours a day, keeping everyone in the picture as best they could. Bill now became frantic with worry about the fate of Androulla and didn't stray far from the radio. They heard that a British Military rescue convoy was being organised to go as far as Nicosia to the various areas where British civilians and any tourists were concentrated and he decided that, if necessary, he could use the protection of the convoy to get Androulla to the base. Tommy was completely opposed to this new idea.

'No, Bill, you can't do it. It's far too dangerous. The island is now at war for heaven's sake! Anyhow, surely Androulla and family will have moved out knowing the Turks have landed and will certainly head for Nicosia. You could get there only to find she's gone. No doubt you've tried phoning her?'

'Over and over again but no luck. Communications seem to be chaotic which is no great surprise in the circumstances. I think there's a strong possibility that her father has been rounded up during the early days of the coup and they won't move out until he comes back or they find out what's happened to him.'

'That's pure speculation, Bill. They could still have moved away and you could run headlong into trouble.'

'But I must find out. I must know that she's all right. Look, Tommy, I'll put on my dog collar and khaki shirt and pants. If you could find a blue beret for me that would pass for the UN variety, that'll be all the protection I'll need.'

'I can't let you do this.'

'You can't really stop me – I'm going to find her. If you don't feel you can get me a beret, so be it, but I'm convinced it would help.'

'Of course I'll try to find you a beret, but if anything happens to you I'll feel guilty for the rest of my life.'

'Nothing will happen to me and there would be no reason to feel any guilt. It's my decision and against your advice and judgement. Please, Tommy, help me in this.'

'Okay. All I ask is that you wait one more day. Maybe this first assault will be a sabre-rattling affair and the EOKA faction will back off.'

This didn't happen. The attack by the Turkish army continued through Sunday and now there was no hope of persuading Bill to wait. Tommy had told Isabel the story. She felt so sorry for Bill and offered to lend him her own car for the journey, an ageing but reliable Ford Taunus, with the rare advantage of a bench seat in the front. Tommy did find him a blue beret, but declined to tell him where or how. It took time to arrange everything, with Bill champing at the bit, but by Monday morning he was ready to set off, in a car well provisioned for his needs on the journey and, as recommended in the broadcasts, flying a small Union Jack fixed to the front of the car. He had spent some of the waiting time minutely scrutinising detailed maps of Nicosia and working out the best route to Androulla's home and this was now firmly fixed in his mind.

'I owe you both! Isabel, you're a gem and, Tommy, you must know how much I appreciate all this.'

'Just come back to us safely and if need be bring Androulla and her family back with you. We'll make some arrangement to accommodate them here on the grounds they're friends of yours and thereby friends of ours.'

'Bless you, Tommy!'

'Do try to tag onto the convoy if you can. According to what we're hearing from BFBS, the Turks don't seem to have got as far as the city yet.'

'Yes, but the house and family could by now be in an occupied zone, which makes me really uneasy. On the other hand I could be just ahead of the invading forces and get them out in time. You know what happens to women when an army invades. It doesn't bear thinking about.'

'I sympathise and I'm quite frightened for you. God go with you, Billy.'

'He'll look after me, I know that! Thank you both for everything.'

They waved until he was out of sight.

'Poor Bill. What a dilemma for him. I'm quite sure Androulla fell hard for him too. How could she have helped herself? Like the rest of the Butler men he's very handsome but he's such a lovely person too.'

'True! I think it's time to start praying really hard, Isabel.'

Chapter 29

Armed with as much information as possible about the timetable for the rescue convoy, Bill travelled eastwards through Limassol then turned north towards Nicosia. He missed the convoy but the journey was without incident. However, the traffic coming out of the city was very heavy, with people fleeing away from the advancing Turkish forces.

Wearing his blue beret and dog collar, as planned, nobody challenged him but when he was getting close to the capital, he could hear gunfire. He headed northwards and west of the Ledra Palace Hotel to Androulla's home. The sound of the gunfire was much louder now but as yet, much to his relief, no sign of Turkish troops. He drove up to the house, jumped out of the car and ran to the front door. He knocked hard but there seemed to be no signs of life. He didn't know whether to be worried or relieved. He hammered hard again but no response. He ran around to the back of the house and peered in the windows and saw a movement.

'Androulla, it's Bill. Are you there? Please open the door.'

The back door burst open and she flew into his arms.

'Oh, Bill, Bill. We thought the Turks had arrived. What a relief. But how did you get here? Why are you here? I thought you were thousands of miles away in Ireland.'

The tears were streaming down her face and he wrapped his arms around her and held her close.

'I've come to take you all out of here to the British base where I'm staying with relatives. They're expecting you. But why are you still here in this dangerous place?'

'My father. He was taken away and my mother refuses to go

until he comes home. I've a horrible feeling he won't be coming home but I can't persuade her to go.'

'I suspected that might be the situation, but they're getting very close; we must go at once. That gunfire sounds as if they're just down the street. I'll try to persuade your mother to come with us. Please understand if I put things to her quite bluntly. That may be necessary.'

They went inside where Androulla's mother was sitting on the sofa as if carved in wood, not moving, just staring into space. He sat down beside her and took her hand.

'Mrs Nicholides, you must come with us at once. The Turkish army is almost on the doorstep. There's not a moment to lose. If you refuse to come with me then Androulla won't come either. You know what could happen to her and, yes, to you too when they arrive here. Would you like to watch your daughter being raped, maybe many times? Invading armies can be very brutal.'

She looked at him with sudden comprehension in her eyes. She still said nothing but nodded, patted him on the hand, got up and went with her daughter to collect together a few things.

'*Please hurry*, Androulla. They sound very close. I'll go and start up the car.'

Androulla, anticipating the possibility of eventually persuading her mother to move out, had collected together and packed a few essential items, so they were very quick and he hustled them into the car. He put Mrs Nicholides in the back with the bits and pieces of luggage so that Androulla could sit beside him. He drove off at speed, heading to where he would have a chance of joining the convoy, for he knew his timing was right. It wasn't far and at last he felt he could relax a little. It was then that machine-gun fire raked his side of the car. Sitting behind him Mrs Nicholides was killed outright with a bullet to her head and several bullets slammed through the metal of the door and into Bill's side. Androulla was untouched.

There was only the one burst of fire, no more and he thought it must have been sheer chance and bad luck that they'd been hit. At first he felt only a thump in his side but he knew he had been hit and that once the numbness of the first shock had worn off the

203

unbelievable pain would kick in. He was determined to keep driving until they were safely away.

'You all right, Androulla?'

'Yes.' She sounded as if she was verging on hysteria. 'But my mother has been hit. I think she's been killed.'

'I can't stop yet.'

'I know, Bill, I know!'

The pain started and he knew he wouldn't be able to go on for long. When he thought they were out of any firing line and very close to the convoy route he stopped. He was grey in the face with the agony of his injuries.

'I've been hit, Androulla, and I can't go on. Change places with me and keep driving towards the British base at Akrotiri. My uncle is in the RAF there, Squadron Leader Tommy Butler.'

'Oh, Bill, no! I didn't realise you'd been hit.'

'Come round and take my place. I'll try to slide over – can't get out.'

She hurried to do as he asked and was appalled to see how much blood was on the seat and dribbling down onto the floor. She leant across, stroked his face gently and kissed him.

'Stay with me, my darling Bill, I'll get you to some place where you'll get help.'

Trying to control her feeling of hysteria, she too drove as fast as she could and very shortly she reached a major junction and stopped. By sheer chance their timing was spot on. The convoy was approaching. Tears streaming down her face, she leapt out and waved frantically for them to stop, using Bill's blue beret. It worked. One of the leading trucks pulled in to the side and stopped, and waved on the rest of the convoy. An armed guard, a sergeant, jumped down from the back.

'Are you in trouble, Miss?'

'Yes, *please hurry*.' She was almost screaming. 'We were shot at. My mother's dead and my friend's in the car, badly injured. This is his beret.'

The guard hurried to take a look at Bill. Added to the blue beret, the Union Jack on the front of the car, the clerical collar and khaki all had their effect.

'Oh my God. I'll do what I can, Sir.'

Bill was now barely conscious. Pain and loss of blood had taken their toll. The soldier, once given the details by Androulla, ran back to report to the others and they radioed directly to Akrotiri for help, emphasising that the injured padre was nephew to Squadron Leader Butler. They got a call back remarkably quickly, saying a rescue helicopter would be on its way with medical help within minutes.

In the meantime, one of the civilian passengers in the truck, who was a nurse, realised there were injuries and jumped down and ran to the car to see if there was anything she could do. She took a horrified look at Bill and started doing her best to give him first aid without disturbing him too much, not wanting to aggravate his injuries if possible. She grabbed everything she could find amongst the luggage in the car to staunch the bleeding from his side. She realised that he had been badly injured internally and called back to the truck for the emergency first aid kit. She was so relieved to see that, thanks to it being an army kit, there were some ampoules of morphine there and talking to him all the time she explained that she was going to give him an injection of morphine. He nodded weakly.

'It'll ease the pain, Padre.'

The sergeant hurried back to the car.

'Akrotiri is sending a helicopter for you, Sir. Hold on there, it won't be long. As the crow flies it's not far.'

Androulla had got back beside him in the car and was sitting as close as she could, holding his hand. The morphine did ease the dreadful pain quite considerably, enough for Bill to be able to say a few words.

'Don't think I'm going to make it, Androulla.' He paused to gather his strength a little further, enough for the words he needed to say to her. 'Love you so much. Since the day we first met. Sorry – couldn't do anything about it.'

The tears were streaming down her face again. Her dead mother was in the back of the car, her face now covered over, and the man she loved seemed to be dying in front of her eyes. She got her arms around him as best she could without hurting him and he laid his head on her shoulder.

'I have loved you so much too since that first meeting. Felt I couldn't live without you. And now you're so badly injured and all because you loved me and wanted to rescue me. I'll never forgive myself.'

He smiled the wonderful Butler smile.

'You must. If I die now I'll be dying in the arms of the woman I love. Can't ask better than that. Please kiss me and then pray with me.'

She did as he asked, and, having been to college in England, had some familiarity with the prayers he was muttering, barely audibly. As he prayed he made a valiant effort to reach his breast pocket but his hand slumped away, too weak to complete its quest.

'What are you searching for, Bill?'

'Rosary,' he whispered.

She found it in the pocket and wound it around his hand, which seemed to comfort him.

The sergeant was right. Rescue helicopters were on standby and in a remarkably short space of time the rescue team was there and, even more remarkably, Tommy was on board. There was enough space in an adjacent car park to land and the paramedics and Tommy were at the car in seconds.

Tommy tore open the car door.

'Bill, it's Tommy. Can you hear me?'

The head nodded.

'They're going to lift you out and carry you to the chopper. We'll have you back in the hospital in no time. Just hang in there.'

'Too late! Androulla?'

'Yes, she's here and we'll take her too. Don't worry.'

They lifted him out as gently as possible onto a stretcher and into the helicopter. Tommy spoke to Androulla.

'Come with us. I'll make arrangements for the car to be driven back to the base and for your mother to be taken to a mortuary.'

Heavily sedated, Bill did last until they reached the base at Akrotiri. The hospital staff were waiting for them and he was lifted onto a trolley and straight into the operating theatre where they did their very best for him. Tommy had asked for a priest who came and gave him the last rites after the surgery and from then on Tommy,

206

Isabel and Androulla never left his side, with full support from Padre Johnson. Just as the sun was setting he came to briefly. Androulla held onto one hand, Tommy the other. He smiled and then gathering every scrap of energy he could muster he simply said:

'Love you all . . . Harry!'

Then he whispered his last words:

'*In manus tuas Domine*. Into thy hands, O Lord,' and he was gone.

The three of them were devastated. Hard as he tried, Tommy couldn't prevent the tears from rolling down his face. Quite aside from his own distress he now had the appalling task of telling Milo and Noola what had happened.

Afterwards, the Chief Medical Officer at the hospital spoke to them.

'I'm so sorry. We did our very best to save him, but he didn't really have a chance. The bullets tore up his liver and part of his intestines. He must have been in the most frightful pain. How he lasted any length after being injured like that is extraordinary, never mind surviving until you got him here.'

'Thank you all for what you tried to do,' replied Tommy. 'I suspect sheer will power kept him going. He would have felt strongly about being with the family and having the last rites if at all possible.'

Chapter 30

Harry had been restless all day on Sunday. He couldn't settle to anything and, having spent quite a lot of the morning with little Johnny, eventually suggested to his father that they should go for an afternoon row in the double skulls. Milo never turned down an opportunity to maintain and hone his rowing skills and was delighted to join Harry. They had a good workout and then Harry had gone to spend some time with Sarah, in the ongoing efforts of all the family to keep her spirits up and help her recovery. He still had the fidgets and Sarah noticed.

'Something wrong, Harry?'

'No. I just can't seem to relax today – don't know why.'

Like the rest of the family she was aware of the uncanny closeness of the twins and just wondered.

Everybody had heard about the Turkish invasion of the north of Cyprus the previous day, just as they had heard about the New EOKA coup that had taken place five days previously. Knowing that Tommy and family with Bill were safely lodged in the RAF base they had no concerns about family members. However, feeling so restless, Harry now began to wonder if there was something bothering Bill. It was the only way he could account for his mood. On the other hand he was sure Bill would phone him and tell him if something was wrong with anybody. Maybe it's got nothing whatsoever to do with Bill, he argued to himself.

He didn't sleep too well and next morning felt quite rough. Obviously I'm going down with some sort of summer flu, he thought. From the time he arrived in the office he felt tense, then, quite suddenly, he got a severe pain in his side. His worry about

Bill returned. As soon as Milo was free he went into his office.

'So sorry, Dad. I feel very rough. I thought I was coming down with something yesterday and I honestly can't keep going. I've got a bad pain in my side. There's no way I can see clients.'

'It's most unlike you to be ill but I must say you do look rough. Don't worry. I'll make arrangements to share you clients between the rest of us. Perhaps Paddy would take a look at you. Are you all right to drive home?'

'Yes. I'm sure I'll manage.'

Even though he knew how often it happened, totally absorbed in his work, it didn't strike Milo that Harry might be registering something wrong with Bill. Harry got home within the half hour to find that Noola was out, which disappointed him since he would have been grateful to share his worries with her. The pain suddenly started to ease until it was a dull ache and then stopped, but he still felt dreadful. Anxiety about Bill grew until he had no doubt whatsoever that something was very wrong with his twin. He spoke to him aloud:

'What is it, Billy? What's happening to you?'

He decided to call Tommy's direct line in Akrotiri but could get no answer. This worried him even more, although he realised they must all be very taken up with the crisis. He now felt desperately tired and wandering into the sitting room sank into a comfortable armchair facing across the lawn and down towards the river, his and Bill's favourite view from the house. He drifted off into a light doze and then woke with a start. Someone had called him. He felt as if his heart was being torn in two. Something inside him seemed to die and he knew. He leapt to his feet and cried out loud again:

'Oh, Billy, Billy, what's happened? You haven't left us, Billy, *please, please no.*'

He ran to the phone. He tried to contact Tommy again but no luck so he called Milo on his restricted private line and spoke to him, trying hard to hold down his feeling of panic.

'Dad, I'm not going crazy, but do you remember when I was ten, Sarah and I went climbing and I fell out of the old chestnut tree and broke my arm?'

'Yes – but...?'

209

'And do you remember that, although he was out in a canoe with Tommy, Billy knew I'd broken it, even which arm I'd broken and felt so much pain he had to stop paddling?'

'Yes, I do, Harry. What are you trying to tell me?'

'I know that something dreadful has happened to him. I've tried to call Tommy, but I can't get any answer and I don't know what to do.'

Milo didn't doubt him for a second.

'I'll be home as soon as possible. Keep trying to get Tommy. See if you can get a general number for RAF Akrotiri and turn on the radio and television to see if there's any news that might help.'

Milo suddenly remembered he had a number for Chuck Wilson, now back in the UK, and he called him. No answer there either, so he headed for home as fast as he could. Harry was waiting for him with a face that would have made a ghost look animated.

'Oh, Dad. I can't get through to anybody. I just know something awful has happened.'

'I believe you, Harry. We'll keep trying until we get through to somebody. And I do understand how you're feeling.' He put his arm around Harry's shoulders. 'He's your twin brother but he's also my son.'

Harry told him the full story of his dreadful day and ten minutes later the call came through.

'It's Tommy. Is that Milo?'

'Yes, Tommy, and we know that something pretty dreadful has happened. It's Bill, isn't it?'

'I'm so very sorry, Milo, to be the one to tell you this.'

'He's dead?'

'But how could you have heard already? It only happened within the last hour. I called you as soon as I could.'

'Harry knew. I think he felt it exactly at the moment it happened.'

Exerting every possible element of self-control he could muster, he listened to the details. Before Harry's eyes the life seemed to drain out of his father and he knew he would watch the same thing happen to his mother, with similar effects on the rest of the family.

210

Chapter 31

Tommy brought him home but Isabel and the children were not able to travel with him. According to the MO her advanced pregnancy made it most inadvisable. Tommy never told how he managed the extremely complex arrangements and wouldn't be drawn on the subject, but Milo and Noola realised that, given the conditions and circumstances, it couldn't have been easy.

Grieved as he was Tommy knew that his feelings couldn't approach those of Bill's parents. However, as he had predicted, and in spite of Bill's insistence that he should not feel so, his sense of guilt was devastating. Understandably, after he arrived at Riverside, as soon as the three of them could snatch some time together, Milo and Noola had wanted to know the full details about the whole tragedy. On the phone he had glossed over Bill's reason for being in the area of conflict, saying that, following the Turkish invasion, Bill had gone to rescue a Cypriot family he had become friendly with when on UN duties there. Now he held nothing back, confident that, given what had happened, Bill would forgive or indeed support the betrayal of his confidence. When he had finished the story he was silent for a moment, then, his voice cracking with weariness and emotion, he continued.

'You can't imagine my sense of guilt. I'll never forgive myself that I wasn't able to dissuade him from going on this mad venture. But I couldn't convince him that it was so dangerous.'

'Stop beating yourself up, Tommy. He loved this girl, Androulla, and that was the beginning, middle and end of it. He gave his life to save the woman he loved. She must be quite a girl to have affected our Billy that way. Someday I hope we'll meet her.'

211

'Milo's right, Tommy. Bill wouldn't want you to feel this way. From what you've told us he made it clear nothing you said would stop him and, like the rest of the Butlers, he was a very strong-minded man.'

Tommy looked at these two people he loved so much and who, in spite of their shock and grief, were trying to make him feel better. Although he had expected them to look pretty rough, when he saw them on arrival at the house he was very shaken. They had always carried their years so well but both had aged a decade since hearing the news.

'Here you are trying to ease my guilt when you're so devastated. Bill was such a supremely unselfish man and it's so obvious where he got it from. Thank you both.'

His parents insisted that Bill should be buried in the family plot in the old churchyard, but did agree that the funeral service should be in the Catholic chapel that he had attended growing up. There was a full military funeral with an Irish Army guard of honour. Father Callaghan was in attendance and had especially requested that he would be allowed to give the eulogy, which was readily agreed to by the family, since they knew how much this would have meant to Bill.

Milo read the lesson, one of his own choice. Knowing it to be a special favourite of Bill's he read from St Paul's letter to the Corinthians all about love, but then added a piece at the end from the Old Testament, explaining it was the passage from King David's lament on hearing of the death of his son, Absalom, and that this expressed so well how he and Noola felt.

'And... thus he said, O my son Absalom, my son, my son Absalom! Would God I had died for thee, O Absalom, my son, my son!'

* * * * *

Tommy stayed for just a couple of days after the funeral, torn between supporting the family at Riverside and getting back to Isabel, whose condition concerned him. The family assured him that they understood he must return to his wife as soon as possible and

212

in the circumstances wouldn't expect otherwise. He had, however, come to a decision and before he left for Cyprus told Milo about it.

'I've given this a lot of thought, Lo, and I've decided it's time I came home. I'm going to resign my commission and, if you'll have me, join the family firm. I do have experience: those holidays learning the job and making pocket money weren't lost. I'll need to have a refresher period but I don't think it would take long to get back up to speed.'

'Now just a minute, Tommy. This has been brought on by your feelings of guilt. You're blaming yourself for this tragedy and trying to compensate. I would be *delighted* to have you working alongside me but I'd much rather you didn't make this decision now.'

'Oh, but...!'

'No, Tommy, hear me out. Go back and wait at least another couple of years. That will give you time to come to terms with what has happened and will make certain you're not making a life-changing decision for emotional rather than rational reasons. You're still only thirty-six and, from the time you were old enough to think about a career, you've wanted to fly planes. There's plenty of time. You could join me a bit later, just about the time I'll be looking to wind down a bit, when it'll be a real godsend to have you there.'

There was silence while Tommy digested this and Milo didn't hurry him for a response.

'You're right. I would be making an emotional decision. I'll put it on hold for the moment, but I think I'll be coming home sooner rather than later.' He smiled. 'Not only do I miss the family, I really miss Riverside and the old Liffey too with all it means to people like us.'

'What about Isabel? Will she be happy to settle here permanently? She might want to be nearer to her parents.'

'Isabel *loves* Riverside and has always made it clear that she would be happy here. You know we're a bit like you and Noola. So long as we're together that's what matters and this is where I would have a job earning our crust! There's the children's education too. Do we upheave them every few years or send them home to boarding school? I'm not that keen on either idea.'

'No, well I take your point.'

213

'And think about it, Lo! Chuck and Liz will have even more excuse to visit us and imagine the great times we'll have together. I hear Joe's coming back too and will be living in his family home across the river. It'll be like old times.'

'Yes, and it'll also be like old times for Joe and Paddy and me. Paddy's highly delighted too that Joe's coming home.'

'There's something else.'

'Yes?'

'I'd love our children to grow up here close to the rest of the family. I suppose I'm being a bit clannish!'

'There's nothing wrong with that.'

Chapter 32

Tommy had hardly returned to Cyprus when Isabel went into labour and on 5 August another little boy was born. They agreed that he should be called Thomas after his father and both grandfathers. He was to be known as Tom to save any confusion, so once more there were Butler brothers called Tom and Milo, but this time they were not twins and not really much alike in looks.

Just nine days later, as negotiations were in progress in Geneva to come to an agreement about the situation in Cyprus, the Turkish Army suddenly and completely unexpectedly renewed its offensive and swept southwards to occupy an enormously expanded sector of the island. When they arrived at Famagusta they found it totally deserted, so instead of stopping at the edge of the existing Turkish enclave, as they had in Nicosia, they took possession of the whole town. The Greek Cypriots, too frightened to stay, had fled, including all the town's officials. Most went to the British base territory in and around Dhekelia for safety. They little realised that they would be refugees for the foreseeable future and indeed too long for some of them, who would not live to realise their dream of someday returning home.

Stories filtered through to Akrotiri about how people had to flee with only what they stood up in and eventually first-hand experiences were told which confirmed this. As the days and then weeks went by and it became obvious that there would be no return any way soon, people started to move westwards, finding accommodation in towns such as Larnaca and Limassol. The RAF offered transport back to the UK for students who were in the middle of university or other higher education courses and this was

215

when Tommy, who was helping with these arrangements, unexpectedly came into contact again with Maria. She was accepting the offer to get her back to Oxford to complete her course of studies. Her family's story was fairly typical of what had happened to the majority of the refugees and she told Tommy that whole story.

'We had no real warning. Some people heard a booming noise and didn't realise it was heavy gunfire. Whole families drove out to the high ground south of Famagusta to see if they could get a view of what was going on. In the meantime, the Turkish tanks swept in and cut off the town and those families never got back. It was hot so they were dressed in very light clothes. That's all they had.'

'But what about you, Maria? Is that what happened to you and your family?'

'Not quite. We didn't go out to see what was happening but something said to me by a friend I met in the street bothered me. So I packed up a few of our valuables and hid them "just in case". We did manage to snatch a few other basic items but then we had to go too – in a hurry!'

'So you got to the British area at Dhekelia?'

'Yes and we lived there under the olive trees at the village of Ormidhia within the safety of the base boundaries for a week.'

'But where's the family now?'

'We had relations in Limassol and they contacted us through the broadcasts from the British Forces radio, urging us to join them. My grandmother and my brother's small baby were not well so we were glad to be able to go there.'

'Are the banking restrictions a problem for you?'

'No! Luckily my father had a fair amount of cash he had taken from his shop. Like others, since the coup he had not left any money in the shop overnight. I've got money in my bank account in Oxford, so for the moment we're all right. We're luckier than some!'

'I'll try to get to see Nick and Tassoula. I'm very glad we're at least able to give you a lift back to Oxford. Is there anything else we can do to help?'

'No thanks. I'm all right for the moment. I left some things in Oxford so I'll get by. But how's Isabel? Did the baby arrive safely?'

'Yes. Imagine you remembering in spite of all your many

216

problems! She had a baby boy just before the Turks started their second offensive. A blond-haired, blue-eyed boy like his parents.'

'Congratulations. I'm so happy for you both. Please give her my love.'

Chapter 33

June 1975

The whole family grieved deeply for Bill, but support from within and from the wider family helped them to come to terms with what had happened. Added to the shock of discovering he had a child, whose mother was dead, the effect on Harry of losing his twin was quite devastating. He withdrew from the social scene completely and seemed to have given up all liaisons with the opposite sex, although there was some speculation as to how long that would last. He spent quite a lot of his free time with Sarah, especially when Dai was unable to be there for any reason, such as being away on field trips. Sarah was having to cope with the double grief of losing a brother, to whom she was devoted, hard upon the heels of her accident and loss of her baby. She and Harry now grew very close.

Harry also spent as much time as possible with Johnny. To his great delight, far from upsetting Sarah, as had been feared possible, she and Johnny adored each other. He was getting an unbelievable amount of pleasure from teaching his son to become familiar with all things to do with the river and watching Sarah doing likewise. The little boy was proving to be crucial to the recovery of both and at Riverside generally a great joy to everyone. He was now more than two years old and rapidly developing into quite a character. The trouble was he was getting thoroughly spoilt, not only being the apple of his father's eye but also the delight of his grandparents as well as Sarah. So there was never any shortage of willing childminders when his nanny was off duty.

Nanny O'Donovan was something of an enigma. She was efficient in every possible way. Johnny adored her and it was obvious that the feeling was mutual. There was no way she could be faulted in her care or affection for the child. What was almost offensive to Harry was her appearance. Anybody less feminine he couldn't imagine and above all he admired femininity in women. Any girl he had ever had a relationship with, however briefly, had been very attractive. Furthermore, the women in the family all presented themselves as undeniably, even aggressively, female.

Cathy O'Donovan was always spotlessly clean, nobody could have argued otherwise, but attractive she definitely was not. Her lifeless, almost dusty-looking hair was always scraped back into a tight bun, held in place with a thick black net, so that its colour was difficult to tell. She wore the ugliest black, wire-framed glasses he had ever seen on anyone and used no make-up. Her clothes were practical in the extreme, which, given her job, was understandable. She always wore wide-legged garments akin to workmen's overalls and thick Aran sweaters, or, in warm weather, what looked like oversized men's shirts. The unattractive outfit was finished off with flat laced-up shoes. This all gave her the appearance of being both frumpy and shapeless. The clothes didn't look exactly cheap but their dull colours enhanced the all-over drab appearance.

Whenever Harry visited the nursery she faded into the background, although always stayed within calling distance. He presumed this was a determination on her part to be tactful and give him time to have his child to himself. She reported to him on a regular basis. During these contacts she maintained a polite, professional distance, always referring to him as Mr Butler or Sir. There was nothing to dislike but there was nothing much to make her appealing either and, given he had never seen her crack more than a small smile, he sometimes wondered at Johnny's deep affection for her.

Cathy had been with the family now for almost a year. She had her own self-contained flat on the top floor next to the nursery, where she could entertain friends or family on her days off, this a clear understanding. She rarely did this, tending to go out visiting instead. She had a large family of her own and seemed very close to them. She was the youngest of seven children and some of her older nieces and nephews were much the same age as herself.

Occasionally Harry had to go away on business trips for the

219

ever-expanding family interests and Cathy was always informed of this, since it meant he would not be visiting Johnny or be present for her to report on the child's progress. Well aware of his reputation, she wondered if he was always alone on these trips, but, she argued to herself, that was none of her business. In spite of being out of circulation on the social scene, the rumours still circulated and the gossip was sometimes quite malicious. There was a certain element that, for reasons of personal gain, made sure this was maintained at particular levels in Dublin society.

On one of these occasions Harry had gone away on the Saturday morning and Cathy was starting a weekend off. Johnny was with his beloved Aunt Sarah and Cathy was expecting one of her nieces for dinner. She had, as always, gone to a lot of trouble, cooking Gill's favourite coq-au-vin and setting a beautiful table, complete with crisp linen, candles and a small arrangement of flowers in the centre. The flat was very tastefully furnished, a budget having been set aside for her to use for this purpose. She had brought in some of her own personal possessions too, such as pictures and ornaments and her favourite Waterford glass. She had also spent her own money on putting the finishing touches, most especially a variety of judiciously selected potted plants, all chosen and cleverly placed to complement the décor of the living area. The ambience she had achieved was remarkable; elegant but relaxing and soothing to the senses.

Having completed all the arrangements for the meal, she had opened the wine and left it to breathe while she showered and changed. She had quite deliberately left the door slightly ajar so that Gill could walk straight in when she arrived. The bell rang and she called out from the bedroom.

'Come straight in, sweetheart, and help yourself to a glass of wine – it's on the sideboard. You're nice and early. I wasn't expecting you just yet but I'm nearly ready.'

There was no answer. She combed her newly washed hair into place, finished her toilette and inspected herself in the mirror. She was content. Then she hurried into the sitting room and without stopping twirled around.

'Bought this dress last week and I'm delighted with it! What do you think?'

220

She stopped and laughingly raised her eyes to look at Gill. But it wasn't Gill. To her absolute horror it was Harry. It would have been hard to say which of them was more surprised. They stared at each other speechless. Harry couldn't believe his eyes. The voice belonged to Cathy but nothing else added up. Standing before him was one of the most attractive women he had ever seen. She had shoulder-length glossy hair the colour of warm, dark chocolate, shot through with russet tints. These caught the light giving the impression of being natural rather than artificially created. The eyes, hitherto hidden behind those hideous glasses, were huge and the colour of spring violets and her make-up, skilfully applied, made the most of this feature. She was wearing a pale blue dress that had a closely fitting bodice and a skirt which fell just below the knees in graceful folds. Shapely legs were enhanced by elegant high-heeled shoes and the whole outfit set off to perfection a beautifully proportioned slim figure. For her part Cathy was taken completely off guard and said the first thing that came into her head and which she realised, the minute she'd said it, sounded so silly.

'But you've gone away!'

He smiled and found his voice.

'I didn't get away. The flight was grounded and I got tired of hanging around the airport for hours. So I came home. I'll try again tomorrow.'

'Oh! But Johnny's not here. He's with Sarah.'

'I know. I've come with a message from your sister. She couldn't get through to you on your private line. It must be out of order. So she rang the house and I took the call. She was most anxious to get the message to you.'

'Oh dear! Is something wrong?'

'She says you're not to worry. Your niece cut her foot quite badly on some broken glass and your sister's taken her to have it stitched up. She doesn't know how long she'll be but she'll call you later on. Your niece won't be able to drive so she'll take her straight home afterwards. She's very sorry about the dinner.'

'Poor Gill. But my phone's not out of order.'

She went over to check to find the handpiece had not been returned firmly on the cradle.

221

'You might be sure. The one time it was important!'

They stood and stared at each other for a few seconds. Cathy suddenly remembered her manners.

'Thank you. Sorry you had to trail all the way up here with the message. Would you like to have a glass of wine? You'll have heard me invite you to help yourself, but I see you didn't take up the offer!'

The atmosphere relaxed and he laughed.

'Er – yes. Yes, I'd love a glass of wine.'

'Well do sit down.'

He lowered himself into one of the comfortable armchairs and she handed him his wine. She poured a glass for herself and sank into the other chair, crossing those shapely legs. His eyes were now brimming with merriment.

'I didn't answer your question.'

'What question?'

'You asked me what I thought of your new dress!'

'Oh, so I did. Well, as you must now realise the question wasn't meant for you so you're not obliged to answer.'

'But I'd like to. I think it's one of the most attractive I've seen for a long time.'

'Thank you, Sir.'

'Oh please! You're off duty now. Couldn't you manage to call me Harry? And may I call you Cathy – off duty?'

She hesitated. She wasn't at all happy with where this was going. Knowing his reputation she had worked so hard to make herself look as unattractive as possible, and now it had all been wasted. She wasn't sure whether she wanted to laugh or cry.

'Well I suppose yes, to both – for now.'

'Fine, and may I also say I think what you've done with this flat is remarkable. It too is so attractive. You seem to have real flair.'

'Thank you again.'

'Since your niece won't be here for dinner would you like to come downstairs and have a meal with me? My parents and Izzy are out and Kitty has been given the evening off because of that, but I'm sure I could find something for us. There's always lots in the fridge.'

'That's very kind but I won't waste all that work I put into producing the meal. I'll eat it myself.'

She hesitated. After his invitation it seemed almost churlish not to reciprocate. There was plenty of food for two.

'It won't be up to your usual standard I'm sure, but would you like to share what I've made? It's all ready: even the table, as you can see.'

'That would be delightful. I'll go downstairs and fetch some wine. At least let me make some contribution to the feast.'

'That's a kind offer but there's no need to go all the way down to the cellar. As you can see, I've more than one bottle ready there on the sideboard. We were going to celebrate our weekend off in style.'

They were both surprised at how much they enjoyed the evening and, even though it was well into the small hours, were sorry when it came to an end. They had laughed a lot and the first time she relaxed enough to allow herself to smile broadly and without restraint, he suddenly saw why Johnny loved her so much. A smile like that made the sun seem almost redundant.

She was away for the rest of the weekend but when she returned on Sunday evening, ready to resume duties the next morning, there was a bouquet of beautiful flowers in a vase of water outside the door to her apartment. An accompanying card thanked her for a most enjoyable evening and delicious meal. Having written him a formal note of thanks, she kept his card tucked away in her desk, something she made a habit of doing, especially if it was one she particularly liked. In the meantime Harry had left for the busy schedule of meetings planned for the week ahead. Neither mentioned their evening together to anyone else, each with personal reasons for not doing so, but this would prove to be a great mistake and something both would later regret.

* * * * *

The whole week he was away Harry couldn't stop thinking about Cathy. Why on earth did she dress in that appalling way for work and why did she never, when off duty, change into anything less ugly, except in the privacy of her own apartment? The more he thought about it the more he realised he knew very little about her. His mother and Johnny's other grandmother had interviewed her

223

and he knew she came highly recommended as a fully qualified children's nurse. Noola, ever efficient, had made sure that she had spoken personally to those who had written references for her. As she explained, this was essential for someone who was going to have full care of Johnny and also live within their household. When interviewed she had been simply dressed and neatly turned out. Noola too had wondered at her strange way of presenting herself when working in the house and, knowing Harry's reputation, arrived at exactly the right conclusion. She reckoned that Cathy was a very smart girl. Harry would *never* be able to make out that she had set her cap at him.

Now, at last, the truth burst on Harry too. It took him a while for he was unaccustomed to girls trying to keep him at bay. Quite the reverse. He did tend to get chased and, as his parents had commented to each other, he was thoroughly spoilt. For someone to set out to make herself unattractive to him was a new experience: in his eyes akin to outright rejection.

At first he felt quite piqued, then that turned into real annoyance and eventually into full-scale outrage. What a cheek this girl had! Whatever made her think that he might be even *slightly* interested in her? The nerve of her, to go to such lengths to make herself look almost unsavoury to him. The *unmitigated conceit*! She had been *assuming* that he would find her attractive unless she went to such lengths. Well he had news for her! She wasn't his type at all. He wouldn't have been even remotely interested in her, even dressed up to the nines... or would he? Wasn't it time to be really honest with himself? When not absorbed in business affairs, he had thought of little else all week. But why? Was it just that she had deliberately set out to deflect his attentions away from her indicating, so clearly, that *she* was in no way attracted to *him*?

Cathy had done the one thing guaranteed to arouse Harry's interest in her and that was diametrically opposed to what she had intended. She had a boyfriend to whom she was engaged. They didn't make this public. They couldn't afford to get married just yet and both were saving as hard as they could to collect the down payment for a small house. Cathy's job with accommodation attached was ideal, for it meant money wasn't being wasted on rent.

Sam Dwyer was a petroleum geologist and his current job was abroad, with a prospecting company in South America, where he was being very well paid and had an allowance for living expenses. Even if they had been married, Cathy couldn't have gone with him, for the area where he was working wouldn't have been suitable for women.

At the time of her interview for the job at Riverside Cathy had not been engaged. She was very much in love with Sam and had hoped he would ask her to marry him, but there had been no indication that he wanted a long-term commitment. Just a few weeks previously, before he left for Columbia, he had proposed and they agreed at that point not to have an official engagement. He was on a two-year contract, so Johnny would be heading for five years old by the time he came home again, almost old enough to start at kindergarten and, as the only child in the house, he needed to mix more with other children.

She salved her conscience with that thought. She was also quite certain that, any time she left, Sarah would immediately step in and offer to act as a substitute mother. This would be an ideal arrangement and, she knew, would be accepted as such by everyone concerned, but most especially by Harry. Not only were Sarah and Johnny devoted to each other, but furthermore there was no sign of Sarah becoming pregnant. She and Cathy were good friends and she had confided her disappointment at not having a child of her own. Of course she mustn't make assumptions or count chickens, but it should all work out beautifully, without Johnny feeling in any way abandoned.

* * * * *

So far as anyone else in the household was concerned, nothing had changed. To Harry's disappointment, Cathy returned to her duties caring for Johnny looking exactly as before. He resumed his visits to the nursery but no more frequently and Cathy reported to him as usual, observing all the previous formalities. She gave not the slightest indication of their having spent such an enjoyable evening together.

225

This annoyed him even more. Well if that's the way she wants to play it, he thought to himself, then so be it. In any case he had no intention of embarking on a new relationship with anyone for the foreseeable future. He had plenty to keep him occupied and interested, without all that. Nevertheless, whenever he saw her, he didn't see the frumpy shapeless creature she dressed herself up to look like, but the lovely girl he had seen that evening in her apartment. His interest in her didn't diminish; it grew until it became almost an obsession, but he still managed to hide his feelings. For the moment he must content himself with at least being able to see her daily, even if she kept herself so remote and so formal.

For her part Cathy was honest enough to admit to herself that she did find Harry a very attractive man, but her love for Sam never faltered. She waited for him to come home mustering every ounce of patience she could manage. Nevertheless, she looked forward to her contacts with Harry, and, she argued to herself, there was nothing wrong with that.

This state of affairs continued for some months. The only person who sensed something was eating Harry was his mother. She wondered if it was some woman but, unusually for her, didn't get anywhere near the truth. She didn't know for certain that he wasn't seeing anyone, although she thought not. So what was it? She watched him covertly.

Chapter 34

1976

The following January Milo and Noola decided to hold a New Year Ball. Since Bill's tragic death, naturally enough there hadn't been any sort of family celebration and they felt it was time to end the period of mourning by doing something that would involve the whole family and which, they hoped, would give pleasure and cheer everyone up. As always, by family tradition, members of Riverside staff were invited, with caterers and other temporary helpers brought in to release them from their duties.

Much to his delight, Jockser was included in the invitations. He couldn't quite believe this and was shy about accepting, worrying about what he would wear and all sorts of other imagined difficulties. Since joining the household after Izzy's abduction, Mickeen and Kitty had taken him under their collective wing and he had blossomed socially, proving to be anything but the "eleven pence halfpenny in the shilling" suggested when they had first met him. A small flatlet created for his use at the end of the stable block had also made a huge difference to his way of life. He took a great pride in keeping it neat and tidy and no longer felt the need to wander. If ever this urge arose he would simply go and sleep in the hayloft above the stables. Now, with the encouragement of the Flanagans, he accepted the invitation and, as it turned out, had the most enjoyable evening that he could remember in the whole of his life.

Cathy's invitation included a partner. Completely unexpectedly, and to her great delight, Sam had managed to get a couple of weeks' leave to come home for Christmas. His fare was paid for by a grateful employer, highly delighted with the success, so far, of the oil-drilling operations. She would be able to bring him as her partner to the ball and she was over the moon. She decided to splash out on a very special evening dress, and blow the tight budget she had stuck to in the interests of saving. She knew the Butlers would all look really elegant and she wanted Sam to be proud of her.

She decided to change at her sister's and arrive at Riverside with Sam, as a couple, rather than have him arrive alone to meet her there. When they got to the house the door was opened to them and they stepped into the superbly decorated hallway where the family had gathered to greet the guests. A fire was burning in the enormous fireplace at one end, creating a warm and comfortable atmosphere for the arriving guests. As they crossed the thickly carpeted floor, Noola and Milo turned to welcome them and, just like Harry on that June evening, for a few seconds they didn't recognise Cathy. They too were rendered speechless. It was reminiscent of the Cinderella story, a real cliché, the rather dull-looking nurse had been transformed into a veritable princess. She was wearing a beautiful, and obviously horribly expensive, delicate lavender-coloured evening dress. It set off her own colouring to perfection, most especially her eyes, which picked up the colour of the dress. But she didn't have to wait to meet her handsome prince; he was right there by her side, quite tall, fair-haired, slim and very good-looking. The word "Adonis" sprang unbidden into Noola's mind. What a remarkable looking couple, she thought, which echoed what was crossing Milo's mind. As they welcomed the two of them and Sam was introduced, Harry turned around and, before he had time to wipe it off, Noola caught the fleeting look on his face when he saw Cathy. She also saw the envious and almost venomous look he shot at Sam, but knew it was unlikely anyone else but her would have noticed. However, when introduced he was his usual charming self.

So *that's* what the trouble is, Noola thought. Well I'm blessed. But when did he ever see her dressed other than in those frightful drab clothes, she wondered. Surely he could never have found her attractive dressed like that. Oh, Harry, is it retribution at last? I thought it had to come and it's justice, but you're my son and I can find it in my heart to feel quite sorry for you. Unrequited love is a

228

dreadfully painful thing and I should know, having loved your father for years when he hardly realised I existed.

It was a most successful evening. Harry hadn't invited a partner, but had suggested to Izzy, also without an escort, that they should partner each other, something she readily agreed to. Making sure she was not too obvious about it, his mother watched him and silently congratulated him on his strict observance of the courtesies to all their guests. He laughed and joked with everyone, he danced with many different people including members of the staff and to an extent was the life and soul of the party. He even persuaded Sarah to have a turn around the floor with him, accepting no excuse about her leg and, in the event, she managed very well. There was no hint to anyone as to where his heart lay and how devastated he must be feeling to see Cathy so totally absorbed with another man. Noola was convinced that even Cathy herself couldn't possibly have thought he had any particular interest in her, but in any case she was much too taken up with Sam to notice much about anyone else. The girl was obviously completely smitten and, looking at Sam, Noola couldn't blame her. The Butlers weren't the only stunning men in town.

She worked her way over to Milo and took his hand.

'Well, my gorgeous husband, how about asking your favourite woman for a dance?'

They wrapped their arms around each other, and Noola decided to mention her suspicions to Milo.

'Well if you'd told me yesterday that you had such an idea I would have said your imagination was working overtime. Now I think it could be possible, but has he ever seen her looking like this before? If not I don't see how it could have happened, knowing our Harry.'

'He must have but we never heard about it. Very curious!'

Towards the end of the evening, but well before the last dance, Harry danced with Izzy and then steered her over to where Sarah and Dai were talking to a very animated Cathy and Sam. Using every ounce of charm he spoke to the visitors.

'Would Miss Cathy O'Donovan be willing to dance with me and would Mr Sam Dwyer mind if I took her away from him for a turn around the floor?'

229

Accustomed to being the most handsome man in the room, Sam recognised a rival when he saw one. He had to admit to himself that Harry Butler, being tall, dark and very handsome and with those intensely green eyes, was a remarkably attractive man. However, he had no doubts whatsoever as to where Cathy's affections were rooted and, anyhow, he didn't have any choice but to agree to Harry's request.

Harry took her in his arms for a slow foxtrot and wondered if she could hear his heart beating so fast. He had waited all evening for this moment and felt as if he was shaking. He looked down at her and smiled. She smiled back and his heart raced even harder.

'If I may pay you a compliment, I think you look incredibly beautiful. I had begun to wonder if I had imagined that girl I spent such an enjoyable evening with last summer.'

'Thank you. You look very handsome yourself. The girl of last summer had to return to duty and go back to a strictly professional relationship with her employer. Anything else would have made it impossible for her to continue working here.'

'Oh! I see.'

He then did something he had never imagined in his wildest dreams that he would do. Afterwards he realised that he had behaved like a gauche, lovesick youngster, blurting out his feelings with none of his usual suave restraint. Where had Harry, the smooth operator, got to?

'Cathy, I love you. Will you marry me?'

She was taken completely off guard. That was the last thing she was expecting and she had to pause to collect her thoughts before replying.

'Well, Harry, that's such a huge compliment – the greatest compliment any man can pay a woman, but I'm afraid I must refuse your lovely offer. You see I love Sam. We're unofficially engaged and hope to marry as soon as we've saved enough for the down payment on a house. That could be a couple more years yet.'

He tried so hard not to show his bitter disappointment: had he been a woman he thought he would have wept. He could almost feel his heart breaking. Noola saw some of the joy disappear from his face and wondered what had taken place between them.

230

'If you hadn't met Sam, do you think I might have had a chance?'

'I love you, Harry, just like I honestly love all the Butlers. You're an amazing family and I've been so happy here. But I'm not *in* love with you. My feelings are more like those I'd have for a brother. I'm in love with Sam. If this makes it difficult for you to have me in the house, then I must leave.'

'Oh no! Please don't do that. Johnny would be heartbroken and he's already had so much upheaval in his short life. I must put his needs first. If anyone goes away it should be me. I'll work out a plan, for I can't possibly stay and cause you embarrassment.'

'That would also cause heartbreak for Johnny. No. I'm sure we're both capable of returning to our strictly formal relationship in the interests of your little son.'

'Fair enough. Thanks, Cathy, but do you think you could improve on the drab appearance?'

She laughed delightedly.

'I think I could manage that, Harry.'

The music came to an end at that moment and they rejoined the others. Harry was devastated but later it occurred to him that, since he clearly hadn't frightened her off with his gaucherie, there was still hope and he refused to give up. The one advantage he had over Sam was that he was on the spot, while Sam was soon going far away again.

Chapter 35

Following the drama of Johnny being introduced into the household, there was someone who thought considerable financial advantage could be taken of Harry's philandering activities and various liaisons with the opposite sex. He decided to bide his time, however, and not rush in too quickly after Johnny had been accepted as Harry's child, in case it would be seen for exactly as it was: opportunist cashing-in on someone's now proven reputation as a womaniser.

Tim Kelly had been taken on as a member of the grounds staff just two years previously and a year ago Breeda, his niece of fourteen had, at his instigation, been offered light weekend duties in the house to help her to make a bit of pocket money. Daughter of his widowed sister, Aine, she was a pretty girl. She was also quiet and a competent worker and made no ripples in the household. She had left just after Christmas, at the suggestion of her uncle, this being part of a very carefully worked out strategy. Then Tim himself had left in the New Year.

He had kept careful watch and methodically recorded his observations of Harry's comings and goings. He took every opportunity to make sure Harry's reputation was not just maintained but grew, and to this purpose he was quite prepared to make up juicy stories if necessary, albeit without a shred of evidence to back them up. It was now February following the New Year Ball and over eighteen months since Johnny had arrived at Riverside. Tim decided to make his move. With the full connivance of her mother, who saw that there could be a lot to gain financially, he had coached Breeda carefully throughout her time in the household and

232

felt they couldn't fail in a bid to make a lot of money out of their employers. He engaged a solicitor and a letter was sent to Harry accusing him of having seduced Breeda which, given her age, constituted statutory rape.

The case would be taken to court. Of course Harry could settle out of court but the implication was clear to anyone that he would be expected to pay punitive damages for the whole nasty case to be kept quiet. It was blackmail. Once he had recovered from the initial shock, Harry was outraged at such a suggestion and had no intention of agreeing to the disgraceful proposal. He took the whole matter straight to his parents. They were equally outraged.

'Well, Harry, there are some things you could be accused of and which I wouldn't dispute, but seduction of a minor is not one. I really can't see you stooping to that.'

'Thank God for that, Dad. I certainly would never think of doing such a despicable thing. I'm going to fight it all the way and, if necessary, right into court.'

'Good, for if you decided to pay up, that, in itself, would be seen as an admission of guilt.'

'True! But I suppose there are some who would do that rather than have a public court case, which, even if their innocence is proved, leaves a nasty taste.'

'Right. We'll get the best solicitors in the country.'

'I know that my behaviour in the past has brought this on me. I just deeply regret that the family has to get tangled up in it too. I'll do my best to confine the unpleasantness to myself.'

'Sometimes being wealthy can be a heavy burden. I had hoped the ghastly incident when Izzy was abducted would be the end of it but here we go again – people trying to extort money from us.'

'I'm *so* sorry, Mum.'

'Harry, I'm convinced that with people like these they would have tried something on even if you'd lived the life of a monk. We'll all stand by you.'

He was almost in tears.

'Thank you both. That support is going to mean so much to me over the next few weeks or even months. If somehow they manage to give convincing evidence, I could be sent to prison for a period.

233

I'm certain, if there's any shred of doubt, the girl's word would be taken against mine.'

Afterwards Noola and Milo were talking about this unpleasant and completely unexpected turn of events.

'Is there to be no respite for us, Noola? First Izzy and Mageen, then Sarah and Bill, not to mention Tommy. Then Harry's child and now this. Do you think we're cursed in some way?'

'I think nothing of the kind, Milo. You're understandably depressed at the moment. Izzy is now a very strong person because of what she went through and is a highly successful and internationally recognised pianist. Mageen is so happily married and settled with her two boys and little girl and that came out of what happened to Izzy. Sarah has made a remarkable recovery. Her limp is barely perceptible and I'm convinced in time may disappear altogether. It's amazing what they can do these days.'

'True, and, come to think of it, Tommy couldn't be happier.'

'Yes! Then Bill. Well, he died looking out for other people: typical of our wonderful son. I think we've many reasons to be proud of our children and, except for Bill, to be thankful for the way things have turned out. All right, Harry had an illegitimate child but look at the joy Johnny is to us all. Like you, I don't believe for a second that he would have done such a thing. He's always been able to have his pick of the girls. With the notable exception of Cathy, they've thrown themselves at him. He would *never* have needed to chase after a little fourteen-year-old who was helping in the house.'

'That's true.'

'I'm so glad that you're standing by him, Milo. He's going to need our support in the biggest way possible.'

'Of course I'll stand by him! I remember when a serious accusation was made against me and my father didn't stand by me. I can still feel the acute heartbreak of knowing he thought I'd lied to him.'

'I do remember, darling, but that worked out too.'

'You are a remarkable woman, Noola. Whatever would I do without you? Somehow you always manage to pull the positive out of any situation.'

'Of course. Otherwise I'd go mad – maybe even become a depressive.'

234

'Well it'll be interesting to see what they produce as evidence. They must think they've something pretty convincing.'

* * * * *

The story was that one evening Harry had been on his own in the house. Breeda was coming to the end of her Saturday evening duties and was clearing the grate and setting the fire in the cosy den beloved by the family and much used when on their own in the house. Just as she was finishing up he had come into the room with a bottle of wine in his hand and invited her to join him. The girl was flattered and accepted, the implication being that nobody would expect her to refuse someone like Harry Butler. Not accustomed to alcohol she quickly became befuddled. She remembered more wine being opened and then Harry had taken advantage of her inebriated state and seduced her. A full description was given of what had transpired, with no thought to sparing anyone's blushes and especially not Breeda's.

Harry's solicitor sent back his answer. He made it quite clear that this would *not* be settled out of court and that, unless there was rock solid evidence for the accusations being made, the consequences for the accusers could be very serious. Amongst other details, evidence of very specific timing of the incident would be expected.

The timing aspect bothered Harry slightly. He wondered if he would be able to remember details of his movements for every day over the past year. When was the girl maintaining that this happened? She had left before Christmas, so obviously before that, but exactly when? If a long time previously, why had she waited until now to come forward with this ridiculous story? Since Bill's death, and he had retired from the social scene, he had been the only family member in the house on more than one occasion, so he really could have a problem. On the other hand there were usually other staff around until well into the evening, so it would be difficult to maintain that he had been absolutely alone in the house at any time. He would have been acutely concerned had he known that Tim knew exactly when. It was so carefully recorded in his diary.

Tim was taken aback and his sister more so. They had been

235

certain of an out-of-court, very quiet settlement, without Breeda's name being dragged through the mud, although, given her age, she would have a degree of protection from publicity. Tim and her mother had banked on this, although they worried that certain elements of the press couldn't be depended upon to keep her identity a secret. They had been absolutely confident that the last thing the Butlers would want would be for the case to be made public. However, Tim was so sure of himself, so confident that his information was foolproof, that what he had recorded so meticulously was correct, he was determined he would go all the way through with it. Anyhow, if he didn't, now that the accusation had been made, he could be the one being sued.

As was expected, it took quite a while for the case to be put together on both sides. During this time neither side chattered about it, both aware of the dangers of doing this: either could destroy his case by broadcasting evidence and counter evidence. Milo, Noola and Harry decided that, until absolutely necessary, and a court case became inevitable, they would keep it between the three of them. They agreed there was no need to worry the rest of the family, none of whom need be involved in any way.

* * * * *

The weeks dragged by and although Harry always became completely absorbed in the considerable demands of his work, nevertheless, there were few times out of the office when he was able to get the nasty business out of his mind. He tried to fill every minute of these hours. He entertained Johnny, concentrating on developing his ability in water sports. He also started teaching him to ride. He rowed often with Milo and Sarah, who was coping admirably, determined that her leg should not handicap her in this favourite sport. He spent time with Izzy listening to her practising and rehearsing and sometimes accompanying her when she needed an escort for one of her musical events. He was surprised at her lack of interest in the many young men who had seemed attracted to her but whose approaches were rebuffed. This man she had met in America must be something very special to have held her interest

236

from such a distance. With all this activity, at the end of each day he fell exhausted into his bed, far too tired to lie awake worrying, which was the object of the whole exercise.

He and Cathy had resumed their formal association with one another, neither referring again to the evening of the ball. He did his very best to ensure that he in no way embarrassed her, and never put a foot out of place, but his feelings for her didn't diminish.

He was looking so unhappy and stressed out that Noola and Milo took pity on him. Somewhat to his surprise, they suggested inviting Cathy to join the three of them in a game of Bridge. They covered up their subterfuge well. They made the suggestion one evening when they were sure there was no one else who could make up a four.

'We'd love a game of Bridge, Harry, but it's only the three of us this evening. Is there anyone else you can think of who might join us?'

'No, Dad. All the others have gone to the theatre so it's just us at home.'

'Oh, what a shame! Is there anyone else you can think of who might like a game, Noola?'

'Well no one springs to mind. Oh . . . but wait a minute! I wonder if Cathy would be interested. What do you think, Harry? Does she play Bridge?'

Harry was stunned. She was never far from his thoughts and this was heaven sent. And *he* hadn't made the suggestion! Looking at his parents he wondered just exactly how much they suspected. He should be used to their powers of perception by now. As boys growing up he and Bill used to think they had second sight. But he was completely convinced that he had covered up his real feelings so well.

'I've no idea, Mum.'

'Well, I'll go and ask her. She could join us and pop up from time to time to make sure Johnny was all right.'

Cathy was surprised but, in truth, delighted. Friendly as the family and staff were, there were times when she felt a bit isolated. She was good at entertaining herself but she loved company and this invitation from Noola, in person, was great.

237

'I'd love to join you, but I haven't played for a long time and I'm a bit out of practice. I might spoil your game.'

'Not at all! We don't take it very seriously. It's just a bit of fun and entertainment. We don't spend ages after each game analysing it, I promise you.'

'In that case, yes. I'd love to join you.'

Harry looked happier that evening than he had for a long time and his parents were glad they'd thought of the small deception. Cathy played a very respectable game partnering Milo, while Harry and Noola played together. Everyone enjoyed the evening and Cathy was invited to join them again on some future occasion, an offer which she accepted with real pleasure.

Not long after that Cathy asked if she could have some of her accumulated holiday time to go and join Sam for the month of July. At long last his company had moved to a less hostile area and she would be able to stay in a nearby hotel, close to him. They planned to make their engagement official. She offered to recommend a suitable temporary nanny, a friend of hers who was also a qualified children's nurse, to care for Johnny, but much as she suspected, Sarah asked to be allowed to take him under her wing. All fell into place nicely. Cathy felt comfortable at having made her request and left for Brazil at the end of June.

Harry was not all happy. Cathy going away was the last straw especially since his case was about to come to a head. On the other hand he was glad she wasn't going to be there to witness his possible complete humiliation. He felt absolutely miserable. He couldn't sleep and was eating almost nothing. He had lost so much weight over the months leading up to this he had started to look emaciated. In the end he was actually relieved when the court case began, just a few days after Cathy had left.

Chapter 36

June 1976

Izzy had stayed closely in touch with Jed. They corresponded regularly and from time to time they spoke to each other by phone. Her parents often wondered what the attraction was. She had known him for such a short time, and had had little person-to-person contact with him. Noola had described him to Milo and on that basis he was just as puzzled as her mother.

Izzy couldn't persuade Jed to come over to Dublin for a holiday. He was worried about his business, which was going through a tricky patch and he didn't want to leave it, even in the hands of his very competent store manager. Could Izzy not come back to Minneapolis instead he asked.

Her life was hectic. The life of a concert pianist was not an easy one and she was fully committed to a programme of formal and informal concerts and rehearsals, not to mention the hours of practice she had to put in as well as giving music lessons. Fortunately she loved it, otherwise it could have become very tedious. In the end she decided that she owed herself a holiday and agreed that, providing Jed could arrange for her to have access to a piano for the essential practicing, she would go over there for a break. She had to make the point to him very strongly that she must practice regularly, just like an athlete or sportsman needed to workout, otherwise, like them, you "lost form" as she put it. Her plans meant she would be away during the time Cathy would be on holiday with Sam. As in Cathy's case, Harry was glad Izzy wouldn't be at home when the nasty affair became public as was now inevitable, although the whole world would know eventually.

Jed was so excited. He couldn't wait to see her again. So that she

239

wouldn't feel compromised he asked very close friends if Izzy could stay with them. That way not only would they be chaperoned but there was also a piano in the house. The Earles were delighted to oblige. They were genuinely fond of Jed, who regularly babysat for them and helped around the house and garden in his free time. Their three children adored him and they all regarded him as an additional member of their family. They were pleased that he had found someone he obviously liked a lot and hoped that, at long last, he might be thinking of marriage.

Jenny Earle couldn't believe her luck. Privately she hoped Izzy might be persuaded to play as a surprise guest at a charity concert her Women's Sorority were organising. The charity was one which was raising funds for "distressed musicians" and there were surprising numbers of them. What could be more appropriate than to enlist Izzy's support.

'Oh, Jed. How exciting. We're going to have a famous musician staying with us!'

'Yes, and she's very self-effacing about her talent – never makes a big deal of it!'

Izzy was tickled at Jed's old-fashioned attitude but so appreciated his desire to protect her reputation. This also helped Milo and Noola to feel happier about her planned trip to the Twin Cities. Jed was obviously no fly-by-night wanting to take advantage of a much younger girl and indeed a wealthy one too. Izzy was accumulating quite a fund of savings on her own account, as well as having the legacy from her grandparents. She would be quite a "catch" in that respect, for any man. She had matured into a lovely young woman. She had large trusting eyes with the wonderful strawberry-blond hair which had deepened a little in colour as she had grown up. She had remained slight of build and still had that fragile look, which, with her pixie face, added greatly to her attraction. She had a ready smile, which always made her look like a slightly mischievous sprite.

Butler to the core, Izzy had fallen in love with Jed and, so far as she was concerned, that was it. Nobody else got a look in. Milo and Noola wondered what would have happened if Bertie had suddenly appeared on the scene again but that was not something they could

240

contrive. So far as they were concerned, he would have been a more acceptable choice, if it came down to her having an interest only in older men. At least they knew all about him. Even more important, they liked him a lot and trusted him.

* * * * *

The great day dawned and on arrival in Minneapolis Izzy's eyes searched around for Jed. They spotted each other at the same moment. Both ran and outstretched arms were wrapped around each other.

'Oh, Izzy, Izzy, I thought this moment would never come. I can't tell you how excited I am to see you again. And you look as beautiful as ever.'

'Jed, it's so good to see you too. You haven't changed a bit, although why would you? It hasn't been all that long!'

'I know what you mean though. You wonder if you've remembered accurately. The photographs help but they're no substitute for the real flesh-and-blood person. If you're not too tired, I'd love to take you somewhere special for dinner. I don't want to share you with anyone else just yet.'

'That would be wonderful and I'm definitely not too tired. Are we going where I think you might be taking me? The hotel where you and I had our first dinner together?'

'Oh! You guessed. I'm almost disappointed.'

'Don't be. Anywhere you took me would be so special. But what about your friends? Don't they mind if we're a bit late? I don't want to seem rude when they've been so kind.'

'They don't mind at all. In fact they came up with the idea which was perfect, because I felt the same way as you about suggesting it.'

It was such a memorable evening. They talked non-stop and were really disappointed when the time came for Jed to take Izzy to meet her hosts. The welcome she got from adults and children alike made her feel so much at home she was delighted that Jed had arranged for her to stay with this warm-hearted family in congenial surroundings. However, Jed was such a favourite with them all and there was so much excitement at having Izzy as a guest, the two got little or no time to themselves. In the end Izzy decided that, pleasant as it was, she would like to have Jed to herself for at least a couple of days and put this to him.

'Could we slip away for a couple of days, just the two of us? They're such lovely people and I do appreciate their warm hospitality but I'd like us to have just a little bit of time alone together.'

'Yes, it's been a bit overwhelming. How about we fly across to Las Vegas? It's such an interesting and exciting city, I'm sure you'd love it.'

'Let's go as soon as we can without giving offence.'

Two days later they flew off to the great gambling Mecca. They hadn't booked in anywhere but Jed said there would be no problem finding somewhere to stay. They found a very upmarket hotel and Jed asked for two single rooms. At dinner that evening Izzy challenged him.

'Don't you find me attractive, Jed?'

'You're the most attractive woman I've ever known, Izzy.'

'Then why the separate rooms?'

'Perhaps because I love you too much to take advantage of you.'

'Maybe I'd like you to take advantage of me!'

'No, Izzy.' He paused. 'Never in my whole life have I loved and wanted anyone so much, but there's no way I can agree to our becoming lovers. You don't know the whole truth. There are things about me that you should know and when you do I think you'll change your mind.'

'There is absolutely nothing that you need to tell me. I know everything about you that I need or want to know.'

'You can't!'

'But I do, Eddie. I knew from the moment you took me in your arms on the dance floor that first evening we went out together. I looked into those gentle blue eyes and knew I had come home: I was where I wanted to be forever more, safe and protected. I was a little girl again with the man who had defended me against evil people; who had looked after me; who had saved my life.'

He looked at her for a few moments, shaken and bereft of speech. She continued.

242

'I realised that some arrangement must have been made for you to disappear and come to live here with a new identity. I was glad, because I often wondered what had happened to you, but all Uncle Sean would say was that you were all right. In the end I gave up asking.'

'How can you possibly feel this way about me, Izzy, knowing what you know? I was one of your abductors – much as I bitterly regretted that from the moment we snatched you, but by then·it was too late to back out.'

'Look at it this way, Eddie. If it hadn't been you they would certainly have found somebody else. Very likely he would not have been such a sympathetic person, one who would have cared for me as you did. In fact I could have been so much worse off and I would probably have died.'

'But why on earth didn't you tell me you had recognised me that first time we met out here?'

'I was afraid you'd feel morally obliged to stop all further contacts and I didn't want that to happen. I was so thrilled to have found you again, alive and well.'

'I honestly can't understand how you don't hate me, let alone love me.'

'But I do love you, Eddie, very much. The question now is what can we do about it?'

'Nothing, my darling Izzy. There's no way we can marry, for then your family would have to know who I really am. I can never go back to Ireland. Inspector Flynn was so kind to me. He arranged for me to disappear and gave me financial help to make a new start here, with a new identity. I don't know how he managed to arrange it all or where he found the funds – maybe from his own pocket. I promised him I wouldn't try to return.' He paused again and with a break in his voice continued. 'I get so homesick sometimes. It breaks my heart to think that I'll never again set eyes on dear old Dublin. But it's my own fault. I brought it all on myself. What a fool I was to do the things I did.'

'Oh, Eddie! Now I want to cry for you.'

'Don't do that! I don't deserve it from you of all people. Aside from the fact that I love you so much, the contact with you has

243

somehow allowed me to keep in touch with home. You know, I think I fell in love with you all those years ago, when I thought you were the bravest little girl I had ever met, incarcerated in that foul cellar and coping with it all with so much courage.'

They talked on turning the whole problem around and around. He told her the full details of his sad story, being brutally honest, holding nothing back: details which could not have been given to her as a child, but which he had told Sean all those years before. When he finished the story, explaining how he landed in so much trouble in the first place, trying to help the underage, pregnant girl, Izzy was indignant.

'But her parents *asked* you to help her. It wasn't your idea. Were *they* not sent to prison too?'

'No! They denied any knowledge of the whole thing. Made out that the girl had approached me unknown to them and they knew nothing about it.'

'How dishonest! But what about the girl herself?'

'She was terrified and backed up her parents. She even denied that she had told me the pregnancy was the result of being raped by her uncle. I hadn't a chance. It was my word against hers and everyone believed *her*.'

'So that really led to everything else: rejection by your family; hard labour; a miserable existence when you were released.'

'Yes, Izzy, then succumbing to the temptation to get the money so I could go far away and start again. How stupid can you get! And of course you know the rest of the story – no one knows it better.'

Izzy did understand Jed or Eddie feeling he could never return home.

'Well, if you can't go back to Ireland I could come to live here instead.'

'No, Izzy. There'd still be the question of my true identity and that could cause a split with your family. I could never agree to that. Equally you can see that I can never agree to our becoming lovers. Somehow that would seem like compounding the original crime I helped to commit.'

'If we get married here then I will come to live here and nobody at home need ever know who you really are. After all, where I live is

244

my choice. My parents would be the first to agree with that, even though they'd be sad that I was so far away. My sister got married and moved away from Ireland. I wouldn't be the first in the family to do that. Dad's brother, Tommy, moved away too.'

'Too many problems, Izzy. How are you going to explain to your parents that you want to get married here, in fact can't get married at home, as would be usual and expected?'

'If we get married here, tomorrow, there would be no more to be said. The whole city seems to be geared to spur of the moment marriages: marriage parlours everywhere. Mum and Dad would be disappointed not to have been here for it but they're very flexible people and would accept it.'

'No, Izzy. I can't let you do this to them. It's not fair and getting married in haste like that you'd almost certainly live to regret it. Compared to you I'm almost an old man, with a really disreputable past. And what about your career?'

'My career can be continued from anywhere. I don't have to live at home for that.'

'There's no way I can agree to rushing into this Izzy, much as I'd love to do as you've suggested. It might not be illegal but to me it would be completely immoral.'

'But, Eddie . . . '

'Let me finish, Izzy, please. I've had to work so hard to make a new and decent life and I've lived very strictly on the straight and narrow. I paid such a high price for my mistakes and deservedly so. I was determined that never again would I do something that I knew was wrong, but now I'm beginning to feel that I was very wrong to want to pursue our friendship. I honestly didn't intend it would get to this stage with both of us. I just so loved and valued the contact with you. I'm obviously still such a fool, for I thought we could be very good friends and nothing more, on a sort of uncle and favourite niece basis.' He paused. 'I didn't foresee that we would fall so deeply in love.'

'You know, Eddie, just like you think you fell in love with me when I was eleven years old, I'm convinced I fell in love with you too at that dreadful time. I came to depend on you totally. I remember so well the day you brought me the ice cream and

245

chocolate and then when you put your arms around me to protect me from the dreadful Willie.'

'And I remember your wonderful smile when I gave you that chocolate.'

'Then you saved my life and I was so glad when Uncle Sean told me you hadn't died.'

They had hardly touched their starter course and now the waiter approached and asked if they were ready for their main course, so they stopped talking while the food was eaten and the delicious looking steaks arrived.

'Let's concentrate on our food, Izzy, and think while we're eating. Then after dinner we can do a bit of gentle gambling – a pity not to make the most of being here!'

They had a wonderful evening. Eddie won the jackpot on one of the fruit machines while Izzy lost all she gambled. They laughed a lot and agreed that they would sleep on their problems and discuss them further in the morning. However, true to her Butler heritage, Izzy had by now made up her mind exactly what she was going to do to precipitate things and nothing was going to stop her.

Chapter 37

The day for the court case to open dawned at last. It transpired that Harry was supposed to have committed this crime of statutory rape the previous June. The reason given for the time lapse between the event and the accusation being made was that Breeda had been frightened of reprisals and had not mentioned it until pressed to tell her mother what was worrying her so much. She was not sleeping, had lost weight and couldn't concentrate on her studies. Frank Maloney, Harry's counsel for the defence, challenged this idea strongly, asking if her treatment by the Butlers had been such that she would expect them to take some sort of revenge. It was admitted that she had always been treated well but she was of a nervous temperament and would worry about imagined difficulties.

Martin Corrigan was the prosecuting counsel and he spared Harry nothing. He made the most of parading his reputation as a womaniser and the fact that he had an illegitimate child. Forewarned by the counsel for the defence, Frank Maloney, this was no surprise to Harry or the rest of the family.

Since he hadn't been told in advance of the date of the supposed event, Harry had taken his diaries for the past eighteen months to court with him. He asked permission to check his diary and this was allowed, the diary being presented as evidence for the defence. He could understand why his solicitor hadn't been given the dates in advance. There was to be no chance of his cooking up some story and finding willing "witnesses" to provide a would-be rock solid alibi. His solicitor, Frank Maloney, knew very well that Harry would never stoop to such a deception. He would never give false testimony and especially not under oath. However, as he pointed out, the people bringing the case to court were obviously judging Harry's possible behaviour by their own standards.

With overwhelming relief he discovered that he could account fully for his activities on the evening suggested for his crime. But this was quickly followed by dismay, for this was the evening he had spent with Cathy. Not only was she out of the country but he most definitely didn't want her involved in these unpleasant proceedings.

Counsel for the prosecution openly sneered at him about this.

'Oh, so we now have some mythical person you maintain you spent the evening with, but you don't wish to say who that person was?'

'Not at this point.'

'Is there anybody else who can testify to this?'

'No.'

'You never mentioned it to anyone?'

'No.'

'Why did you feel the need to keep it a secret?'

'I didn't want to give rise to undue speculation and I had no idea whether or not the other person would want it talked about. Anyhow, I don't report my *every* movement to others.'

'So you don't want to involve this woman – it's obviously a woman – and nobody else can support your story?'

'I believe some members of the household staff may be able to bear witness to the fact that I was not in the main part of the house during the time I'm accused of being with the young girl.'

'For example?'

'Possibly Mickeen Flanagan, the estate manager, or Kitty Flanagan, the cook-housekeeper.'

'*Loyal* employees, dependent on the family for their living?'

'Yes, but honest and truthful to the core. Neither would dream of lying, even out of loyalty to the family and I wouldn't expect them to do so.'

'Very honourable I'm sure!' The cynical tone and the sneer were even more pronounced.

Counsel for the defence appealed for an adjournment at this point to give reasonable time to call in the Flanagans and this was granted. The court was to reconvene next day.

248

Milo and Noola had been with Harry every step of the way and with him had felt the wear and tear on their nerves. They didn't look quite as gaunt and ill as Harry but the strain showed almost as much. They were vastly relieved to know there was somebody who could testify to his innocence. At home again after their stressful day they were discussing the proceedings amongst themselves.

'Who were you with that you don't want to mention?'

'It was Cathy, Mum, and there's no way I want to drag her into this whole unsavoury business.'

'*Cathy?*'

'Yes!' and he told them the whole story.

'And you just sat and chatted until the small hours?'

'Yes, Dad. Strange as it may seem to you, knowing my reputation, that was all. We had a great evening together. We both enjoyed it, which is why the time went by without our realising how late it was.'

'But you never told a soul?'

'No, nobody. What I said in court was absolutely true. I didn't want anyone jumping to the wrong conclusions and I didn't know whether or not she wanted it mentioned. We didn't discuss that at the time.'

'I wonder if she told anyone.'

'I suspect not, Mum, and maybe for the same reasons. She wouldn't have wanted Sam to hear about it and have any reason to wonder if anything had happened between us.'

Noola looked at him for a few seconds and then spoke very gently.

'And now you love her too much to want to do anything that might hurt her, or harm her relationship with Sam?'

Harry gave her a bleak smile: his parents' intuition again.

'Yes, Mum, that's exactly the problem.'

'Well, we'll just have to hope Mickeen or Kitty can help.'

'It's such a long shot but worth a try. Should I talk to them on my own or do you think we should discuss it with them together?'

'It might be a good idea if the five of us sat down together and talked it through and it's essential that we wait until Frank Maloney joins us. He should be here shortly.'

249

Mickeen and Kitty, in full and indignant knowledge of the accusation against Harry, and having been put fully in the picture, were quite happy to join them. They, and indeed the rest of the staff, had grown to dislike and mistrust Tim Kelly and were glad when he left. The part he was playing in all this did not entirely surprise them, although Breeda's connivance in the whole thing did. Both had liked the girl.

Harry now asked them if by any chance they remembered the evening, the previous June, when he had come home unexpectedly, having supposedly gone off to London. He reminded them that the rest of the family had been out for the evening and Kitty had been given the evening off, since no family dinner had been needed.

At first, neither could remember the evening in question, but, having talked it around, Kitty had a thought.

'Mickeen, do you remember that evening when you came in a bit late – you'd been talking with Jockser in the stables? You said Mr Harry had come back and I wondered if he'd be wanting a bite of dinner after all?'

'Oh yes, I do remember!' He grinned at Harry. 'You drove your car down the drive at your usual breakneck speed, otherwise I mightn't have noticed.' He turned to the others. 'Kitty was in the middle of cooking our meal so I went over to find out, but there wasn't a sign of him anywhere. I looked all around the house. I even went up and knocked on his bedroom door but he wasn't there.'

'And when you came back and told me, we decided that he'd probably gone over to see his sister in the East Wing so we looked no further. The only problem is I can't be sure if it's the right evening.'

'I can't be sure either, Kitty. All I can remember for certain is that it was June when the evenings were so light. Perhaps you can think of something that might pinpoint it for us, Mr Harry?'

'No! I wish I could.'

'Well it's a good, positive start. Is there any way we can narrow it down a bit? For instance how often have you returned home when you were supposed to have gone away on a business trip, Harry?'

'I can only remember one other time, Frank, and it was just before last Christmas.'

'Yes! I remember, but that was in the morning and you were home by midday. You and I had lunch together.'

'That's right, Mum, but I can't think of any other time, certainly not within the last couple of years.'

'It's an excellent start. On the one hand there's no certainty about the specific date, but there's enough evidence to narrow it down to that particular incident. Are you certain that there are no other times when your flight was delayed or cancelled and you had to return home?'

'I'm certain, unless my memory's playing me false.'

'And you're adamant that, for the moment, you won't reveal the one witness who could clear your name once and for all?'

'Not unless I'm really driven to it.'

'There is one other thing that's just struck me, Frank. I should have thought of it before.'

'Noola?'

'Unless something extraordinary happens, we don't usually have fires in the small sitting room in June. I can't remember the day when it last happened. So why would Breeda be clearing out the grate and setting a new fire, if there'd been no fire and no one was expected to be in the house? Yes, Breeda sometimes did late duties but that wouldn't have been one of them at that time of year.'

'Marvellous! It's still not solid evidence but it could be enough. It'll be hard to refute it.'

'Thanks, Frank. That makes me feel a lot happier. And, Mum, you're brilliant!'

'Delighted I thought of it!'

They all talked around the problem for quite a while and then Frank and the Flanagans left. After they had gone, Harry voiced his anxiety to his parents.

'I know Frank's pretty good – the best, but their solicitor's good too and he'll twist everything Mickeen says: he'll tie him up in knots!'

'Well, as Frank said, if need be your mother can testify about the fire.'

'Yes, and I'd be glad to do so.'

'Thanks, Mum.'

251

They planned and talked on late into the night.

In the meantime, Mickeen told Jockser the whole miserable story. Jockser listened carefully and when Mickeen had finished Jockser was very thoughtful, obviously trawling his memory.

'I remember that evenin', Mickeen – the evenin' Mr Harry came screamin' back up the drive when we thought he was away. Shure wasn't that the day I cut me hand so bad and had to go and ask Dr Flynn to patch it up for me. It was handy havin' him up there in The Lodge: it meant I didn't have to go to the hospital and shure I don't like them places. D'ye not remember? It was Kitty who suggested that I ask him to take a look at it and he did a grand job on it too.'

'Begob I do, Jockser. I'd forgotten that. But I don't suppose you'd remember the date.'

'Shure of course I do! Wasn't it me birthday – I wouldn't forget *that*! Mrs Butler and Kitty were so good to me. Kitty made me a cake and the two of ye gave me presents. Mrs Butler gave me grand presents too from her and Mr Butler: a lovely new coat and new shoes and some money. They're real dacent people!'

'Would you be willing to tell in court about Mr Harry coming home unexpectedly that evening, Jockser?'

'Well I wouldn't be too keen on the idea, but for them I'd do it so I would.'

Chapter 38

The dreaded day dawned. As predicted, Martin Corrigan did, to some extent, tie Mickeen up in knots, but Frank did a good job too and Mickeen's testimony sounded feasible, especially when he explained that Jockser was able to tell him, quite specifically, what the date had been. However, that, as Martin pointed out, was drawing on somebody else's memory of the date and not his own.

True to his promise, Jockser went along and gave his testimony and wasn't the pushover that Martin expected him to be. He stuck doggedly to his story and Frank suggested that, although there would be no official record of it, his evidence about the date he cut his hand could, possibly, be corroborated by Dr Flynn. However, Martin questioned Jockser closely about his employment by the Butlers, especially what his life had been before that. He made much of the fact that he had previously been a vagrant. Then, for both Jockser's and Mickeen's evidence, in turn, he tried his best to cast doubt on the veracity of what they said, suggesting that loyalty to the Butlers would colour what they maintained and ensure they remembered the incident. Mickeen became quite angry at this assertion.

'Anyone who suggests that I would lie under my oath on the Bible better be careful, for when the truth of this is confirmed – and it will be – then I'll sue him for slander.'

Jockser leapt to his feet and, quite out of order, shouted: 'And so will I! I wouldn't lie under oath either.'

The judge reprimanded Jockser who sat down looking mutinous.

For a moment Martin was taken aback. He was surprised at this coming from Mickeen and Jockser. Milo and Noola smiled and Milo whispered to Noola:

'That shook him! Good for them.'

Frank then called Noola to give her evidence about the lighting of the fire. However, when pressed by Martin for factual information on this, regarding that particular weekend, she admitted she was unable to give any specific date, which showed that she, certainly, wasn't prepared to lie under oath, even to save her son. However, what she said challenged Breeda's story and added strength to Mickeen's evidence about nobody being at home that evening.

The trial took several days more, with the evidence for and against Harry going around and around. Tim Kelly and Breeda stuck doggedly to their version of the story, in spite of the evidence against them. Finally they reached the stage of summing up, starting with counsel for the prosecution. Martin did a competent job, and it wasn't looking good for Harry. Oh yes, he agreed, there was some evidence to suggest that Harry hadn't been in the house at the time he was supposed to have seduced Breeda, but then how reliable was that evidence? Wasn't it all a bit circumstantial and given by *loyal* employees? He really larded that particular point. He spun it out and dragged it on and got to his trump card.

'And, members of the jury, as to the idea that he was with some anonymous person for the evening, someone he *apparently* doesn't want to compromise, well I question that story. *Who* is this mythical person? *Where* is this mythical person?'

'I'm right here!'

There were gasps all round. At the back of the visitors' seating area Cathy stood up. The court erupted: there was pandemonium.

'Thanks be to God,' Noola said quite audibly to Milo who put his arm around her and held her close. He knew she would weep tears of relief and he felt like joining her. He looked across at Harry and his son's expression said it all.

The judge banged his gavel hard on the desk and when order had been restored he questioned Cathy.

'Who are you, Madam, and why have you not come forward before?'

'I'm Catherine O'Donovan. I'm nanny to Johnny Butler and live

254

in a flat on the top floor of Riverside House. I haven't come forward before because I arrived at the airport from Brazil only two and a half hours ago. I got to the court half an hour ago, when I slipped into the back row here.'

Martin tried to object, but the judge cut him off allowing her to continue.

'You asked two questions, Mr Corrigan and, unorthodox as it may be, you're getting your answers.'

'I only heard about this case yesterday and got here as fast as I could. I had to rush to the local airport hoping I'd get a seat. I got the last one!'

Frank immediately called for an adjournment which, in the strange circumstances, was granted, while Cathy insisted that she wished to be accepted as a witness and didn't need to have a break and a sleep to recover from the long journey. Much to Noola's and Milo's amusement she had scraped her hair back, donned the ugly glasses and wore no make-up. She had somehow got hold of her original working outfit and really looked the part of the unattractive, rather prim nanny, which she had so carefully cultivated. There was no way whatsoever that Martin Corrigan or indeed the jury members could, by any stretch of the imagination, think that Harry Butler, with his reputation, would have wanted to embark on an *affaire* with her.

The feeling of relief emanating from Harry seemed almost tangible. The face that had been grey and gaunt with hopelessness and despair had now turned pink with relief and new optimism. He had tried so hard not to have Cathy involved but was vastly relieved to see her, knowing that now he would be completely vindicated and he needn't feel guilty: it had been her choice to come forward.

Martin objected strenuously but the judge decided that, given her story, he would allow her to testify, assuring Martin that, if he wished, he would be able to resume his summing up afterwards. Eventually Cathy took the witness stand and told the whole story, clearly, calmly and in detail. Questioned by Martin about her memory as to the exact date she responded:

'I've no doubts at all. My sister and my niece will be able to confirm it if necessary, and if you insist on written evidence there

255

will be the hospital record of her treatment. She had to go back several times, for the cut became infected. The full details must be there.'

'Oh, we'll check all right, Miss O'Donovan.'

'Please do! But my niece is in the visitors' gallery. She can corroborate my story if you wish. But actually I do have another item of evidence.'

'Indeed! And what might that be?'

'Mr Butler sent me some flowers and a thank you note for the evening. I usually keep such notes or cards for some time. That card will still be in the desk in my flat. I haven't been back there since I arrived but, if need be, I can produce it. It is dated. My niece could go to my flat now and get it if you wish.'

Her unshakable calm rattled him and his questioning became more aggressive and verging on the offensive.

'What is your relationship with Henry Butler?'

'Strictly professional: employer and employee.'

'So why did you spend the whole evening together? You yourself have testified that you didn't part company until the small hours of the morning.'

'No particular reason. We were just eating dinner and talking. I've explained in detail – we found we had lots of interests in common.'

'And nothing else took place between you?'

'Such as?'

'Did you get into bed together?'

'Most certainly not!' The expression of outrage on her face brought the flicker of a smile to some faces.

'Are you in love with Henry Butler?'

'Objection!'

'Sustained! What point are you trying to make, Mr Corrigan?'

'Your Honour, it could explain Miss O'Donovan's wish to defend Mr Butler.'

'It *is* irrelevant, Your Honour. May I speak?'

'Yes, Mr Maloney.'

'Objection! I haven't finished my questioning.'

'Sit down, Mr Corrigan. You'll be given your chance to resume. Continue, Mr Maloney.'

'Whatever Miss O'Donovan's feelings, and regardless of what they were doing, the fact is Henry Butler spent the evening in her flat, which clears him completely of the accusation made against him. She can even produce a dated thank you card written by him. He couldn't have been in two places at once. Miss O'Donovan has been able to give, very specifically, the time he arrived in her flat, which is earlier than the time he is said to have been with his accuser. Miss O'Donovan was surprised at what she thought was the early arrival of her niece and looked at her clock. What she has said tallies exactly with the evidence of Mr Mickeen Flanagan and Mr "Jockser" Connolly – the evidence upon which counsel for the prosecution poured so much scorn! All the evidence against him has now been shown to be false, and what was dismissed as circumstantial or the invention of loyal employees has been proved to be the truth. The whole case has disintegrated.'

The judge looked at Cathy for a long moment.

'Miss O'Donovan, before I make a final statement, is there anything further you'd like to add?'

'Yes, Your Honour, there is. I'm surprised at Breeda. From what little contact I had with her I found her to be honest and honourable and I'm amazed that she agreed to making such a contemptible, false accusation. Something that, if accepted as the truth by the jury, could have sent Mr Butler to prison and branded him as a paedophile for the rest of his life. That's really wicked. I can't help wondering if someone else pressured her into doing such a thing.'

At this Breeda burst into tears. She realised that their case had collapsed and was intelligent enough to understand that she and her uncle could now be in deep trouble. She leapt to her feet.

'She's right! She's right! *He* talked me into it.' She pointed at Tim who also leapt to his feet.

'Shut your mouth you little fool.'

'No I won't shut my mouth! I didn't want to do it but *you* persuaded me. *You* said we'd make a fortune out of it and now we're in bad trouble. I'm sorry, Mr Harry. I'm *so* sorry – it was a terrible thing to do!'

257

Chapter 39

Izzy had arrived home during the final week of the court case. She was outraged by the accusation made against Harry. She never doubted his innocence for a second and, like the rest of the family, gave him her full and unreserved support. She was indignant that she hadn't been put in the picture before the whole thing broke but understood Harry and her parents not wishing to worry any more of the family than necessary, in the hope that the accusation would be withdrawn rather than risk having it brought to court and shown to be untrue. Even at this late stage Mageen and Tommy hadn't been told for the same reason: why worry them unnecessarily?

Izzy strongly suspected that her parents knew who the anonymous witness was. She and Sarah talked about it and they decided they would try to persuade their parents to tell them. They pressed them for the information and, since it was so far into the trial, they saw no reason not to tell the girls, providing they didn't pass it on to *anyone* else. They readily agreed to this and were as surprised as Noola and Milo had been when they heard who it was. They applauded Harry's desire not to implicate Cathy. However, they hadn't promised anything about not contacting Cathy. They were surprised that she hadn't already heard about it via the grapevine, since the newspapers were having a field day about the whole case, and not least the fact that there was a witness who was to remain anonymous. There was some outrageous speculation as to the identity of this person, especially that, of course, Harry must be protecting the reputation of some married woman. They were both certain that if Cathy had heard she would have come straight back to bear witness to his innocence. But then if nobody knew it was

Cathy why would anyone contact her about it, especially if this was difficult?

Sarah knew where Cathy was staying. It was a big, well-known hotel and she had promised to give Cathy a call every so often to let her know how Johnny was getting along. Sarah had found it exceptionally difficult to reach her by phone, but now she and Izzy called and called, persisting doggedly until eventually Izzy managed to catch her, but it was virtually the eleventh hour.

When Cathy heard the whole story she was appalled and especially when she was told that the next day was likely to be the summing up. The plan was she would get her seat on the next possible flight, phone her sister and ask her or her niece to go to the airport to meet her next day and take her directly to the court. She also asked Izzy if she could collect her working clothes from her flat and take them to her sister's house. Izzy was delighted to do anything at all to help.

'You really are brilliant, Cathy. I can't thank you enough. I hope this won't cause any trouble for you.'

'No problem, Izzy. I'm just so glad you told me. Poor Harry! I'm so touched that he wanted to protect my reputation. But he needn't worry, I think I'll manage that.'

So Cathy turned up at court just in time and, clever girl, looking almost like something out of a horror film.

* * * * *

Apart from Harry's complete vindication, the outcome of the trial saw Tim Kelly being convicted of perjury and sent to prison, with Breeda being let off rather more lightly because of her youthfulness. There was an enormous celebratory party at Riverside House to which family and friends, who had been supportive throughout, were invited. Jockser, the Flanagans and especially Cathy were the guests of honour. Mickeen took Milo aside and made a suggestion to him.

'You know Shamus is going off to a job in America next month and we'll need a new assistant estate manager?'

'Yes, Mickeen.'

259

'Well, I wondered what you'd think about giving Jockser a chance; give him a sort of trial period as assistant. He's so reliable and actually nobody's fool and I think he'd do a good job.'

Milo was delighted. He'd had a similar thought but coming from Mickeen, who worked closely with Jockser, this was much the best way of getting to it.

'It's a great idea, Mickeen. By all means give him a chance, but do let him know it's just a trial period both ways! That's only fair. He might prefer it that way so he won't feel awkward if it's too much for him and he wants to go back to the way things are at the moment.'

'Right you are, Sir. Will you make the offer to him or will I?'

'You ask him first and if he accepts I'll confirm the arrangement.'

Aside from being eternally grateful to her, and expressing this in the most heartfelt way, Harry and his parents were really curious as to how Cathy had found out about the trial. All she would say was that someone had phoned her and the story had come out during the conversation. Nothing would persuade her to tell more than that. She had returned to Brazil after the trial to finish her holiday there and they had delayed the party until she had come home. Harry had insisted on reimbursing her for the not inconsiderable expense of the return fare from Brazil and any other expenses incurred by her unexpected trip home. At the first possible opportunity he grabbed his chance to have a private word with her.

'Can I ever thank you enough for what you did for me?'

She looked at him and with dancing eyes teased him.

'Probably not!'

He was so taken aback at the unexpected response, then looking at her impish smile he burst out laughing.

'Cathy O'Donovan, you're incorrigible! Seriously though, I really do owe you. I wish there was something I could do to express my huge appreciation.'

'No need, Harry. There's no way I'd see anyone falsely accused and condemned if I had the means of proving his innocence. Neither would you, would you?'

'You know the answer to that.'

'Johnny's looking well. He does love Sarah.'

260

Harry took the hint and veered away from the subject.

'Yes, he's in great form. How was Brazil? I'm sure you found it a fascinating experience.'

'Yes, I even managed to have a look at the rainforest area, which is amazing. And Rio is incredible.'

'Sam all right?'

'Yes, fine.'

'Is the engagement official yet?'

'Er… well no, not yet.'

'Everything on course?'

'There are slight complications which we need to sort out. Sam's contract finishes quite soon and he'll be coming home. That'll make it easier. But thanks for asking.'

Again he took the hint and changed the subject even though he was dying to know more. What exactly was wrong? Was it his job, the money, the relationship or what? Well, he'd just have to wait. It was bound to come out in time.

'Another glass of champagne?'

'That would be lovely.'

Talking to his parents when the guests had gone, Harry told them that, from his conversation with Cathy, he thought that she and Sam might have financial worries about getting married.

'Is there some way we could help? For instance could we offer them an interest-free loan for a down payment on a home? The offer couldn't come from me for obvious reasons, but, Mum, how would you feel about mentioning it to her? She might feel more comfortable if it came from you.'

'I'd certainly be willing to help, but I think we shouldn't rush into this. I'd hate to offend her by having her think we're trying to repay her in some way.'

'Yes. I suppose you're right.'

His parents were thoughtful for a few minutes for his attitude to Cathy puzzled them. They knew he loved her, genuinely and sincerely, but here he was trying to help to promote her marriage with Sam.

'Harry, there's something we don't understand here and would love you to explain it to us.'

261

'I'll try.'

'Well, as we've told you before, over the past years we've been rather shaken at your attitude to women and your treatment of those you've dated, not least Marie, Johnny's mother. It seems so out of character. Did something happen to make you behave towards them in this way?'

He was silent for so long they prompted him.

'Harry?'

'Sorry! Yes, Mum, something did happen years ago, something I find painful and embarrassing to talk about.'

'Oh! Well, we can leave it for now.'

'No. I think the time has come to tell the two of you and get it off my chest. It'll probably go some way to explaining my sometimes appalling behaviour, a lot of which I now feel ashamed about. But it's late! Are you sure you don't want to go to bed? You must be tired.'

Milo raised his eyebrows at Noola who shook her head.

'No, we're fine, quite comfortable here in the den, so let's finish off this champagne. It'll probably help you to tell us about it.'

'Thanks, Dad. It will!'

There was another long silence and this time his parents didn't try to rush him. Then he took a deep breath and started.

'It all happened shortly after I started my degree course at Trinity. One of the other junior freshmen students brought along his sister, Emily, to a party and even though she was three years ahead of me – just into her final year – I fell for her hook, line and sinker.'

'Ah! We Butlers tend to make a habit of that!'

Harry smiled briefly.

'I know, Dad. I've noticed! Well she was extremely attractive and others were vying for her attention but I was really pushy and asked her to have dinner with me. She laughed and said she'd think about it. In the meantime, as I found out later, she got all the information she could about me and, indeed, the family background, from various friends of mine, especially Chris, an ex-school friend. One thing she definitely discovered was that we were wealthy. I hadn't been able to take my eyes off her the whole evening and Chris teased me about it unmercifully. At the end I went over to her and repeated the invitation and she accepted.

262

'*You* made no enquiries about *her?*'

'No, Mum. I didn't care who or what she was. I was totally bewitched. From then on I made a complete fool of myself. I didn't quite "stalk" her but very nearly. I used to hang around where I thought she might be. I couldn't think of anything or anyone else. It was pathetic. Looking back now I can't *believe* I behaved so stupidly.'

'Give yourself a chance, Harry. You were only just eighteen. You'd been to an all boys' school and, aside from the girls in the family, you hadn't had that much close contact with the opposite sex. You were, in a sense, ripe for the plucking!'

'You're so right, Dad, and oh boy, did she ever take me for a complete sucker! She had a very close friend and the two of them connived over the whole pathetic business. Whenever I took her out to dinner, and it was regularly, she insisted on the most expensive restaurants. Then her friend would turn up, by the way unexpectedly, and Emily would insist that she joined us. Then the two of them would order all the most pricey items on the menu, including top quality wines and, of course, I paid.'

'How often did this happen?'

'Just about every time we went out, Mum. I realised that she had no interest whatsoever in me personally. Any time it was supposed to be just the two of us, her eyes would be searching around the room looking for friends or acquaintances who could join us. Looking back on it now, I obviously bored her stiff.'

'And there was no romance?'

'Not a chance. The most I ever had from her was a chaste kiss.'

'And you didn't get fed up with this treatment?'

'No, Dad. As I said I was totally besotted. I just wanted to be with her, regardless of the fact that there was obviously no return of feelings. Pathetic, isn't it?'

'No, Harry. It's happened to other people before now. But where did it go from there?'

'She started asking me to buy jewellery for her. Not quite as obviously as that, but she would stop at jewellers' windows after our meals and say how much she would love certain items. Needless to say I fell over myself to buy what she wanted. I suddenly realised she was getting me to buy things her friend wanted too, but even

263

though I knew that, and knew they were laughing at me behind my back, I somehow just couldn't refuse her. Thinking about it afterwards I realised what I was trying to do was to buy her affection and we all know that doesn't work!'

'What a pair of absolute bitches!'

'I can think of worse things to call them now, Dad. The dreadful thing was that I couldn't cure myself of my feelings for her. It was as if I was addicted, like someone hooked on a drug. I ran through money like water. I spent all of my allowance from you, which was always generous, and even used as much as I could lay my hands on from Grandpa's trust. It's a good thing the capital was tied up until I was twenty-one or a lot of that would have disappeared too. There were a couple of occasions when I actually ran out and couldn't even buy my lunches.'

'What happened about your work or your training? I don't remember you neglecting your rowing.'

'No, I didn't, Dad. The times when I could see her were limited. She made sure of that! At least that meant I could get on with my boat club activities, although I did find concentrating on work difficult.'

'And you told nobody?'

'No, but you'll not be surprised to hear that Bill knew by instinct that there was something wrong. Every time we met he asked me several times if I was all right, but I didn't tell him until it had been going on for nearly six months.'

'What was his reaction?'

Looking at his father's angry and outraged expression, Harry had to smile.

'He looked exactly like you do now, Dad. He was furious. He insisted that I cut loose from her, but I was almost afraid of her by that stage. I didn't know how to do it, for I knew enough about her to realise she would be livid at losing her tame meal ticket. I'm not sure what I thought she would do, but I was so scared of being made to look a complete laughing stock if she spread the story of what a fool I'd been.'

'So what happened to end it? Did Bill help?'

'Yes, Dad, he came up with a great idea.'

264

He hesitated and a reminiscent smile spread across his face.

'Well, for goodness' sake don't keep us in suspense. What did he do?'

'What Granny told us Grandpa and his twin used to do when they were boys!'

'Do go on – I'm intrigued!'

'He suggested that we swap places for a dinner date, but with other strategies to be in place first. I was to take her out for dinner as before and note what she said about a piece of jewellery she liked or wanted. I was to let him know and he was going to do something but wouldn't tell me exactly what. Then he would take my place on our next date and present her with the gift.

'I did exactly as he suggested. Then I prepared him in every way I could think of to take my place. I knew she wouldn't spot it wasn't me because she had never scrutinised me closely, so any slight physical differences she wouldn't notice. But he needed to know the kind of thing we usually talked about, or more accurately what she talked about, for I never got much of a chance to take part in the conversations and anything I did say I'm convinced she didn't even listen to!'

'Oh, Harry!'

'It's all right, Mum. I'm well over it now, except for regretting being such a fool.'

'So what happened next? I can't wait to hear what Bill did.'

'He went to the jewellers where I had bought most of the items and saw the manager, Mr Macken. Of course, we're very well known there so it wasn't difficult getting an appointment to see him. They chatted and the manager told Bill the staff had noticed that I had, recently, been buying a lot of expensive jewellery. Incidentally, Bill had made sure Mr Macken knew which twin he was speaking to. He told him, in confidence of course, how I was being ripped off and they worked out a plan together.'

Harry paused to take a mouthful of his drink. He savoured the memory of what had happened next.

'Don't keep us in suspense.'

'Sorry, Mum. Bill borrowed my clothes, made sure our haircuts and everything else matched and went off to meet Emily for dinner.

He arrived early and spoke to the head waiter then was shown to a table in a quiet corner, with subdued lighting. Emily arrived, late as usual, and took her seat. Before the friend arrived, as he knew was inevitable, he gave her the beautifully wrapped jewellery box. He got a perfunctory thank you and the wrapping was torn off and the piece admired in a cursory fashion, and, with a satisfied smirk, put into her handbag. Bill told her that she should have it insured, and suggested getting a valuation certificate for this purpose from the jeweller. Well it seems that, at least, produced a reasonably warm smile. Then the friend turned up as predicted. Neither spotted that it wasn't me!

'I had told Bill that I had taken to ordering the least expensive items on the menu for myself and drinking water, in the hope of getting through just the one bottle of wine and keeping the cost down, so this is what he did. Emily and friend ordered lobster thermidor starters, then roast pheasant, followed by a meringue confection and cheeses to finish with. They had cocktails before the very expensive wine came, and when they had finished they ordered liqueurs. The cost of the whole thing must have been fantastic. When they had finished, Billy excused himself and they assumed he was going to pay the bill. Actually he was but, by prior agreement with the head waiter, his bill had been prepared separately from the bill for the two girls. He paid for himself and left.'

His parents burst out laughing. Milo clapped his hands in delight and continued to chuckle with amusement for some seconds.

'Good old Billy. This is the best laugh I've had for a long time.'

'Oh that wasn't the end of it. He had managed to persuade Mr Macken to go to the restaurant and eat there with his wife, at Bill's expense, and to sit close to the front reception desk. Mr Macken joined in with delight for he was indignant at the story about my being so suckered. He told Bill afterwards what happened.'

'I can't wait!' Noola was still smiling.

'I'm getting there, Mum. When Bill had left, the waiter handed the two girls their bill. They were totally thrown. They said that the man with them had gone to pay their bill but he explained that Mr Butler had paid his own bill and left. It seems they became quite violently angry and then, when they saw the amount involved, almost hysterical. They had nowhere nearly enough money to pay. They were standing at the desk frantically turning out their pockets and their handbags, but couldn't find anything like that amount. They asked if they could return and pay the next day, but the manager said he couldn't allow that.

'Then Emily thought of offering the new necklace as security, but the manager was sceptical. He said he didn't know anything about the value of such things. Mr Macken was sitting close by as arranged, and at this point he intervened politely saying he was a jeweller and perhaps he could help. The two girls almost fell on his neck. He inspected the necklace and gave his verdict: "Very pretty but I'm afraid it's paste. Not worth very much, a few pounds at the most." Well it seems they nearly fainted off. "Are you *sure*?" Emily asked him. "Oh yes," he said. " It's not unusual for such items to be copied in paste". This was quite true and what Bill had asked him to do. Then Emily tore off a brooch she was wearing, another piece I had given her, and asked Mr Macken what it was worth. He was brilliant. He looked at it closely, made a long face, shook his head and handed it back, simply saying "sorry!". No comment as to its value, so no lie was told. In the end one of them had to wait in the restaurant while the other went all the way back home and got a cheque book.'

'Brilliant! Well done, Billy!' Milo was still grinning broadly. 'How did it all end? I bet she tried to hit back.'

'Oh yes. The very next day she found me in the college café and threw a paper bag at me. She screamed at me that I was a cheating son-of-a-bitch and how dared I treat her like that. "What are you talking about, Emily?" I asked her, looking as perplexed as possible. "You know damn well," she shouted. "How dare you abandon us in that restaurant last night!" I smiled in apparent astonishment and said to her "But I was out all evening with the boys in the pub. Ask any of them!"

'Well, she called me an impressive number of names, including liar, but what seemed to enrage her most of all was the jewellery, because after Mr Macken's performance, she took it for granted that everything else I had given her was paste and it was all bundled into

267

the paper bag she'd thrown back at me. She was very stupid not to allow herself to cool down before she did anything like that. If she'd been a bit more controlled about it she'd have gone to another jeweller, asked to have it all valued, and discovered that, aside from the necklace, it was genuine.

'She completely dismissed that story about my being with friends in the pub for the evening for she never bothered to check up. Obviously she "knew" I was lying. I was so nervous during the whole incident I actually felt physically sick, but I stuck to my guns and kept my cool, which Bill had said would be so important.'

'But I don't understand. Why didn't Bill simply put the whole idea to you and let *you* have the satisfaction of carrying out his plan?'

'Because he realised, quite correctly, that I was too emotionally involved and even too frightened of her reaction to go through with it.'

'So she was the one who looked the fool in the end! Did she ever find out the truth? Oh I do hope so!'

'Yes, Mum. Trinity Ball was a fortnight later and Bill suggested that he and I went and took Mageen and Sarah. Mageen was still recovering from Freddie and not wanting to date with men and Sarah didn't have a boyfriend, so both were delighted at the idea. It was perfect for Bill too – in training for the priesthood. And you know we had a marvellous evening: just four Butlers together.'

'I remember that well and thinking that it was such a good idea all round, even without knowing your story.'

'The lovely part was that we were at the main Trinity Ball venue and Emily and her friend, with their partners, were there too. You should have seen the two girls' faces when they saw us. First the identical twin bit of it and then there we were with two beautiful girls, and we all know that Mageen actually is stunning. Neither had ever met either Mageen or Sarah and they didn't look anything like us, so there was no hint that they were our sisters. As I said, Emily took no interest whatsoever in my family other than the money aspect.'

'And that was the end of it?'

'Not quite. Bill couldn't resist it and I didn't try to stop him. He went across the ballroom to speak to Emily and friend. He

268

introduced himself, saying they had met before, just once, and he thanked them for such an interesting evening. Then he said "and by the way, Emily, that jewellery that you threw back at Harry in a paper bag, it was absolutely genuine – the real stuff! I do hope you enjoy your evening." Then he turned his back on her and walked back to us before she had time to react.

'They were too far away for Mageen and Sarah to hear what was said and they just assumed he was greeting friends he hadn't seen for a while. I distracted their attention as best I could, so they never knew.'

'Did you ever come into contact with her again?'

'No. She very carefully avoided me. She took her final exams and went off to Canada, where, it seems, she had a boyfriend she eventually married. He'd been there in the background all the time, but needless to say neither she nor her friend had bothered to mention this to me.'

'But it all took its toll?'

'Oh yes. And how! It took me quite a while to get her out of my system. Bill was marvellous. He helped me every way he could think of, but it left me so utterly, even savagely bitter and with a basic mistrust of all women outside the family. I was determined that I would take my revenge on the whole lot of them and never allow myself to become emotionally involved with anybody. I would just use them as she had used me. I deliberately grew a cast-iron shell around my heart.'

'Oh, Harry! But I can sympathise to an extent.'

'But only to an extent, Dad. I should have grown out of it. Risen above it, but I didn't. And now I'm so ashamed of some of the things I did. Most especially how I treated Marie.'

'Well I understand that but at least you've shouldered your responsibilities there, and you never for a second tried to deny your involvement.'

Harry laughed.

'With Johnny looking every inch a Butler, I could hardly do that. But in any case, I'm completely devoted to him, as you know. He's the one really good thing that came out of the whole sorry business. It was Johnny who cracked the shell.'

'And then poor Bill was killed and you didn't socialise for quite a long time.'

'No, but Cathy happened and saved me from possible dreadful retribution for the way I had behaved to all those poor girls.'

'And now you want to "do the decent thing", in spite of the fact that you've fallen so hard for her and you would be helping her and Sam to bring forward their marriage. That will ensure that you've no chance with her.'

'I know, Mum, but that's how I feel I must play it now. I'll not do anything calculated to come between them. Aside from everything else, I owe her such a lot.'

'Does she know how you feel?'

'Yes. I told her, but before I knew she and Sam were unofficially engaged: that things were so serious between them.'

'Oh dear! It's such a sad story all round. But thank you for telling us. It does explain everything.'

They were all silent for a while and then Milo made what he thought was a sensible suggestion.

'It's very late and I think we should go to bed and sleep on it all before deciding how to play it. As Mum said earlier, we need to be very careful we don't look as if we're trying to *pay* Cathy. That could be the ultimate insult, but I can see the logic in offering her an interest-free loan.'

'I agree with your father but are you sure that's the problem?'

'No, Mum, but there's a strong chance it could be and, of course, I can't ask her.'

'Okay. Then let's talk again tomorrow.'

Noola had her own private feelings about what Cathy's problem could be, but they remained just that – private! However, a few days later there was a letter from Androulla. At long last she had accepted the very warm invitation, given several times by Noola and Milo, to come to Dublin sometime, stay at Riverside and meet Bill's family. It was now almost three years since Bill had died in Cyprus. Noola, in particular, thought this should be a really interesting visit. Since Bill had fallen in love with her at first sight, how would his identical twin react to her and, indeed, how would she react to Harry?

Chapter 40

August 1976

In late August, a few weeks after Harry's trial had finished with such a satisfactory outcome, Izzy contacted Sean Flynn and asked for a private meeting with him, in his office for preference. Sean was consumed with curiosity. Why all the secrecy? However, Izzy was a great favourite of his so he was more than happy to oblige. He knew she had been back to the USA for a second visit but he didn't know why. He had heard in a vague way that she had met some man there and had been keenly interested in him. Since no big deal had been made out of this it never struck him that her visit to him might be connected in some way.

They exchanged family news, with Sean saying how glad he was that Harry had been vindicated and they chatted for a while about the ins and outs of the case.

'What a lucky thing that Johnny's nanny turned up in the nick of time! I wonder who it was alerted her to what was happening when Harry had made it clear he didn't want to compromise her.' His eyes twinkled.

'Yes, it was really remarkable, Uncle Sean.'

'All right, Izzy, now what is it you really wanted to talk to me about?'

'Okay! On my first concert tour of the United States I met this man in Minneapolis. We connected in a big way, kept closely in touch ever since and I went back to Minneapolis specifically to meet him again.'

'Well, I'd heard you'd met someone there. Is there a problem?'

'His name is Jed Seabourne.'

For a few seconds the bell didn't ring and then it burst on Sean who Izzy meant.

271

'Oh Jesus, Mary and Joseph, Izzy, no, please no! You know who he is?'

'Yes, Uncle Sean, and now I need your help. I want to marry him, but obviously there are huge difficulties.'

'You just can't do this, Izzy. What does *he* have to say about it?'

So she told him the whole story, holding nothing back and especially Eddie's insistence that there was no way they could go down that road.

'Poor eejit! I always felt he had made foolish mistakes but was essentially a decent man. This proves my point. It's a complete non-starter.'

'No, Uncle Sean, it's not! You see I'm pregnant.'

'Oh Jesus, Izzy, no! But you said he wouldn't agree to your becoming lovers.'

'He wouldn't but I laid a deliberate trap for him. All my fault, not his. The evening before we returned to his friends' house in Minneapolis we said goodnight and he said he was going to have a shower and go to bed. Our bedrooms were next door to each other with adjoining balconies. When I heard the shower running I climbed over the rail, took off my clothes and slipped into his lovely, double bed.'

'And he didn't have a chance?'

'Well no, not really!'

'You are an absolute minx, Izzy!'

'Yes, I know, Uncle Sean. But, what I'd really like to know is, could he slip in here so that we could have a very quiet wedding, strictly close family? He said you told him he could never return, but knowing you, I'm quite sure his new identity is completely legal and his passport too.'

'Oh yes. It's been done before and doubtless will be done again in the future. It would have to be legal or he would never have got into the USA. The biggest problem about his coming back here is that he might be recognised. Then the ketchup would really hit the fan! So far as his family and friends are concerned they think he's dead. With his more than willing compliance, we deliberately allowed everyone to think that so he could slip away and make a new start. He's done well too by the sounds of it.'

272

'But he's unrecognisable now.'

Sean was silent for a few moments while he thought through the likely complications.

'Do your parents know anything of this?'

'Not that I'm pregnant, but they do know that I feel very strongly about Eddie, although not who he is.'

'I think the next essential step is that you tell your parents all about this. It's not fair to keep them in the dark, although I hate to think of the shock it's going to be for them. And they've had plenty of those recently. Then, if it would help, the four of us could get together and talk the whole thing through. Meantime I'll try to work out some sort of solution that might be acceptable to everyone.'

'Sorry to cause you all this trouble, Uncle Sean. But I really love him so much. The thought of going on through life without him doesn't bear thinking about.'

He looked at the anxious face and his heart went out to her. What a ghastly dilemma for her. After all, it wasn't *her* fault that she was abducted and that was how she came into contact with this man in the first place.

'I'll do my very best, Izzy.'

'I know you will.' She hugged him. 'I do love you, Uncle Sean.'

'Get away with you, girl, before you have the eyes out of my head!'

* * * * *

Izzy waited until she had a chance to have her parents to herself. They were sitting in the cozy den after dinner, drinking coffee and watching a play on television. The warm, deep gold-coloured curtains had been closed; the fire had been lit against the slight chill of the autumn evening and the atmosphere was relaxed. When the play ended she asked if she could discuss something with them. They had felt her tension and both had realised that there was something she wanted to talk to them about but had waited for her to broach the subject.

'Of course, Izzy. But wait for just a minute while I pour us another cup of coffee.'

273

Noola poured the coffee and settled back into her comfortable armchair.

'Away you go!' Neither she nor Milo had the remotest idea what was coming.

'I want to get married.'

'Oh! All right. I take it this is to your American friend?'

'Yes. But it's not quite as straightforward as that.'

'You mean he's so much older than you and lives in Minneapolis, which means you would be moving a long way from home. This will be difficult for us to adjust to. It's so very far away, but if that's what you want, well, so be it.'

'There's quite a lot more to it than that, Mum.'

'Oh? Like what?'

'Jed Seabourne. Did you like him?'

'Yes. Granny and I both did, very much, but the age difference seems to me is too great. Granny thought that too. However, if you're really certain that you love him enough then how can I object? He feels the same way?'

'Oh yes. Very much so, but there are other problems.'

'Now I'm intrigued!'

'Jed's original name is Eddie: *Doctor* Eddie Conran.'

The penny dropped with Milo first and he leapt to his feet in protest.

'No! *No, no, no.* You just can't do this, Izzy. My darling child, think what you're saying.'

'I know, Dad, the whole story – everything. He's held nothing back.'

Milo sank back into his chair and, as with Sean, she then told them the full story, making it abundantly clear that Eddie himself had the same objections as they had.

'I've been to see Uncle Sean and talked it through with him. He thinks we *might* be able to work something out, but wanted me to tell you both the whole story first.'

There was a long silence while Noola and Milo digested all this. Izzy waited patiently for their reaction. Eventually Milo, trying his best to stifle his dismay and revulsion at the whole idea and remain as rational as possible, gave his response.

'Much as I love you, Izzy, and always will, no matter what

274

happens, I just can't agree to having this man in our home, not ever. There's much too much history between us.'

'But, Dad, . . . '

'No! I want to make a suggestion. I'd like you to agree to wait for a year before taking such a big step. Then if you still feel the same way we'll think about it again. Perhaps your mother might feel she could go to a quiet wedding in the USA, but I'm afraid I can't cope with it. What do you think, Noola?'

'Waiting for a while does seem to be a good, sensible compromise, although I'll still have huge reservations about it for a number of reasons.'

'But I can't possibly wait a year; I'm pregnant!'

'Oh my God! But you said he categorically rejected any suggestion of all that!'

'Yes, he did,' and she told them just as she had told Sean, then added, 'It was the only way I could make sure he would eventually agree to our getting married. Even then I couldn't be sure I would become pregnant. It's all my doing not his. *Please*, Dad. I love him so much and from my early teens I've had wonderful visions of getting married here, with a reception in my own home by the river.' Now the tears were rolling down her cheeks. 'I so want it to be here, however small and quiet, but if not then I'll just have to go over there, on my own if need be, and get married in Minneapolis.'

Milo and Noola were really shaken. Neither knew quite how to react.

'We need just a little time to think this through, Izzy. We love you and we'll support you as best we can. If Dad feels he can't go to your wedding, wherever it takes place, then I'll certainly go but I must say I do understand how he feels. He laid his life on the line in his attempt to rescue you from this man and his fellow villains. He could have been killed like some of the others out there at Powerscourt Falls.'

'I know, Mum, I know, and I'll *never* forget that. You two and Eddie are the three people I love most in the world.'

'As I said: just give us a day or so to get used to this idea and see how we feel then. I think we'll talk it through with Granny. Would you be happy for us to do that?'

'Yes, of course.'

275

Chapter 41

As on many evenings, Maggie joined the family for dinner the following day. Noola had told her that she and Milo wanted to have a private chat with her afterwards and she was intrigued. Dramas in this family had become quite a commonplace occurrence and she wondered what had happened now.

They were in the intimate and comfortable atmosphere of the den again and Noola and Milo between them told her the whole story, with Milo still adamant that he wasn't able to come to terms with the situation.

'No wonder my hair's almost completely grey, Maggie, and Noola's too come to that. I keep hoping that we'll have a break from it all, a lovely, long period with no more problems, but one after another they keep coming.'

'That's true, Mammy, it can be very depressing sometimes,' added Noola. 'And although aside from Bill the various other problems have sorted themselves out, I'm afraid now we've an unfortunate first: a young, single girl, pregnant and needing to get married in something of a hurry. *That* hasn't happened before in either family, has it?'

Maggie looked at the two of them for quite a long few moments, making up her mind as to exactly what she should tell them.

'Sorry, Maggie! We shouldn't have landed it in your lap quite so bluntly. You're obviously shocked.'

'Well, before answering that, I want to say first how much I admire you both and how you've coped throughout all the problems and difficulties that have been thrown at you, none of which you deserved. As for being shocked, no! Astonished, yes, about who this

276

man is that our Izzy has fallen in love with. It reminds me of that film, *Casablanca*: what Humphrey Bogart said about Ingrid Bergman walking into his bar. Of all the pharmacies in the world that Izzy could have walked into it had to be his! It makes you wonder about "fate" doesn't it?'

'But you're not shocked about Izzy being pregnant?'

'No, I'm not. Perhaps it's time to tell you both some of the family secrets and in the circumstances I feel sure I would be forgiven by those no longer with us. You see, Noola, I was pregnant with you before Billy and I got married and we did indeed have to get married in a hurry.'

'*Mammy!* And I never knew!'

'Of course you didn't. It's not something I would have boasted about, most especially in those days – complete disgrace for the whole family!'

'Poor Maggie! That must have been so difficult for you. At least Billy really loved you and did want to marry you. Otherwise what an awful dilemma for you! But, you know, I've a feeling Granny Butler would have stood by you. She was very devoted to you.'

'You're absolutely right, Milo, she would and once said as much, but that's not the end of the story.'

'What more can there be to tell?'

'Sorry if it upsets you, Milo, but your own mother was pregnant with you before she and Tom were married.'

'*What?*'

'Oh yes! That's why they got married so quickly after he returned at the end of the war and why they went and stayed in the villa at Monte Carlo until after you were born. Ostensibly it was to give Tom a chance to recover both physically and emotionally, having had his twin die in his arms and being severely injured himself.'

Speechless, Milo and Noola stared at her.

'It probably happened quite a lot in those days. Young people in love frightened, each time they parted, that they might never see each other again and with good reason – I don't need to tell you what the casualty rate was. So, both of you, don't be too hard on Izzy. And, let's face it, although like you I'd prefer it hadn't

277

happened, there's not the stigma that there used to be. Anyhow, don't tell me that you two didn't hop into bed together before you were married, because knowing you both so well I'd find that really hard to believe. So that's that part of the problem out of the way. The rest is a bit more difficult I know.'

'There's no way I can agree to having any contact with that man, Maggie.'

'Okay, Milo, fair enough. I can understand how you feel. It's an awful lot to ask of you. But think of this. If Izzy goes out to Minneapolis, gets married and dies giving birth to her child how would you feel if you had refused to have any part of the whole thing? I know it doesn't happen so often these days but it *does* happen. She's only a little scrap of a thing and there could be all sorts of complications. After all, she didn't *ask* or plan to fall in love with this man.'

'But, Maggie…'

'Milo, as Izzy herself has pointed out, more than once, if it wasn't for him then she wouldn't be with us today. You and Noola did finally agree with Sean's suggestion that he should be allowed to slip away.'

'Yes, and to add insult to injury we gave some financial support to help set him up in a new life. The irony of it!'

'You're angry, Milo, and understandably so. I would suggest that you take a few days to cool down and think this over before you make a final decision as to how you'll play it, a decision you might regret later if made in haste.'

'Well whatever the decision, in the circumstances we can't spend too long making it.'

'That's true, Noola darlin', and if it's all right with you I'll have a chat with Izzy myself. The girl needs to know she has somebody who's unequivocally on her side regardless of the circumstances.'

'That would be great, Mammy, but she does know that, unhappy as I am about it, I will stick by her; go to her wedding and be there when she has her baby.'

'She knows I'll always stand by her too. I've told her as much, but I do have my limits. You know I feel almost betrayed! Isn't that silly?'

278

'No, Milo darlin'. It's completely understandable but something's just struck me that may take any decision out of all our hands.'

'Oh?'

'How is Eddie going to complete the details required on a marriage certificate here? Details about his parents' names, his place of birth, etc.? Because of all that I'd say it would be impossible or at the least extremely difficult for him. He can't use his real name, he's supposed to be dead!'

* * * * *

Izzy eventually agreed that, quite aside from all those complications, it would look very strange indeed if she had a "hole-in the-corner" wedding at home. Not only was she too well known to get away with it, but also it would look especially odd considering the big celebrations there had been at Riverside for Mageen's and Sarah's weddings. Milo came up with what, in the end, even Izzy thought was a good compromise. They would go to some exotic location to get married. That was becoming increasingly fashionable and for someone who was a celebrity it wouldn't seem too strange. It would fit the "star" pianist image. It could be done very quietly and the world told much later. They talked it through with Sean and he agreed that Eddie could slip into the country for a quick few days later, perhaps after the baby was born, so that Izzy could at least have a family celebration at Riverside both of her marriage and the birth of her child. They'd have to keep it as small as they dared so as not to raise too many eyebrows, but the big question now was would Eddie agree to the plan?

Izzy tried to break the news of her pregnancy to him gently but he was still very shaken. So far as he was concerned there was no argument that they must get married but he was all too aware of the complications involved and the reservations of her family were completely understandable to him.

'No wonder they're shocked and shaken, Izzy. I would be in their place. I'm shaken myself, even though the thought of marrying you is wonderful. Don't for a moment think it doesn't give me the

279

greatest pleasure. And then the added delight at the idea of being a father, something that in my wildest dreams I didn't think could ever happen for me, given my history. I just don't deserve all this good fortune.'

'Well, I'm very relieved to know that you're happy about it. What about this quiet wedding idea?'

'It makes so much sense. But let's forget about somewhere exotic. How about we go back to Las Vegas? As you yourself pointed out there's ample provision there for spur of the moment weddings. They're not unusual there and would raise no eyebrows around here.'

'And it's where it all happened! That's a brilliant idea and, don't forget, for us here Las Vegas does sound quite exotic, even really exciting.'

* * * * *

In the end Milo, taking on board the points made by Maggie, did decide to go to the wedding with Noola and Maggie. So far as the world was concerned they were going to meet Izzy's fiancé and even other members of the family weren't put fully in the picture. With excitement and anticipation, all assumed the wedding would be at Riverside. Mageen was quite determined that Jack would take leave and they would all come over for the big day. That put the final seal on the sense of the wedding taking place abroad, for Jack was one of the few people who would, with his training and astuteness, undoubtedly recognize Eddie, however much altered or disguised he might be.

In spite of his deep reservations and prejudices, Milo found himself warming to Eddie. They had a long heart-to-heart during which Eddie made it clear that he understood well how he and Noola must feel and that he had not planned or intended that things would work out as they had. However, he also made it abundantly clear how utterly devoted he was to Izzy and his whole existence from then on would be dedicated to the care of her and their child.

'I'll do everything in my power to make her and keep her happy. As you know, I would give my life to protect her.'

280

'Yes, well you've already proved that, Eddie – I must get used to calling you Jed now.'

Eddie's friends, especially the Earles, were disappointed at the sudden wedding in Las Vegas, but accepted it with a good grace and insisted on giving a huge party for them when they returned to Minneapolis. Izzy and Eddie agreed, on the understanding that there would be no publicity relating to Izzy's celebrity status.

The other members of the Butler family were astonished and, like Eddie's friends, disappointed at being denied a wedding celebration, especially one at Riverside. However, they too accepted with a good grace and when word of Izzy's pregnancy filtered through no more was said. However, they all looked forward to meeting "Jed".

Chapter 42

Androulla arrived at Riverside in October, two weeks after Milo, Noola and Maggie returned home from Izzy's wedding. Wanting to make her feel really welcome, in circumstances which they realized could be quite stressful for her, Noola and Milo both went to meet her at the airport. When they had spoken on the phone Androulla had asked how she would know them and Noola had assured her that she would have no difficulty in identifying Bill's father.

They, in turn, had no problem in recognizing the lovely young woman, described to them in detail by Tommy and Isabel, with eyes so dark they looked almost black and raven-coloured, shoulder-length hair. Both could see at once what had attracted Bill. Milo, in particular, was taken aback at her effect on him and found he had to dampen down his very male response to her.

Even though she had been forewarned, Androulla was surprised at Milo's strong resemblance to his son. He was exactly what Bill would have looked like in another thirty or so years' time. She was touched at the warm welcome given to her and felt comfortable with both of them from the outset.

When they arrived at Riverside, like many before her, on first seeing the splendid old house she was so overwhelmed that for a few minutes she was lost for words. The entrance to the estate was graced by huge, antique, wrought-iron gates where, set slightly back from these, Paddy and family lived in an elegant lodge. The long, almost straight drive gave an unimpeded view of the house, which, although originally a large Georgian edifice, typical of it's kind to be found scattered all over Ireland, had been sensitively extended by different generations to accommodate changing needs. One of these

282

extensions was a large conservatory which, she would discover later, housed a number of specimen shrubs and plants familiar to her from her homeland.

To left and right stretched parkland. On the right this gave way quite quickly to a copse of trees, while to the left horses grazed and ornamental trees were displayed to full effect. Close to the house were beautifully tended and groomed flower beds and although it was October, there were still roses, chrysanthemums, michaelmas daises, begonias, and dahlias, with other survivors of the summer flowering season.

'What a beautiful place. I've never seen anything quite like it, even in the area where I live in Stratford, and there are some pretty impressive places around there. I feel quite overwhelmed. Its upkeep must take an army of staff.'

Milo laughed in delight at her reaction.

'Not quite an army, Androulla, but it does take a lot of hard work to maintain.'

She was equally impressed with the interior of the house, like Jack and Bertie noting and appreciating the quiet good taste in evidence everywhere. She too recognized the many valuable antiques in both furniture, furnishings and ornaments, all judiciously placed to display them to best advantage.

She was shown to her room, the windows of which overlooked the beautifully sculptured lawns, sweeping in terraces down to the river. After she had washed and changed she came down for tea in the sitting room where the whole family had assembled to meet her. As well as Milo and Noola, Maggie, Aunt May, Sarah and Dai were there. Harry arrived slightly later, leading Johnny by the hand. When Androulla saw him, again in spite of knowing what to expect, her face drained of all colour. Noola, spotting her distress, put her arm around her.

'I don't think I need to introduce Harry and this is his son, Johnny. Harry, Johnny, this is Androulla.'

To everyone's keen delight, Johnny, a very sociable child, held his arms out to give her a hug.

'Hello, Loola, I'm Johnny!'

The slightly strained atmosphere completely relaxed and everybody laughed.

283

'Well, Johnny, I'm delighted to meet you and even at such a young age you certainly know how to make a girl feel welcome!' She stooped down and gave him a big hug, which was returned with enthusiasm. She continued. 'It obviously runs in the family and I do love the name Loola.' She smiled at them all. 'It sounds very like Noola!'

'Ah, well I'm really Finoula but when my brother, Paddy, was little he couldn't manage that and called me Noola, which stuck. I'd now feel quite strange if anyone called me Finoula, although I do like the name.'

Harry looked at Androulla with undisguised interest. He gave her a warm smile.

'Somehow I feel I know you well enough to give you a hug too – that's if you don't object.'

The colour returned to her cheeks and deepened.

'Of course I don't mind.'

Everyone started talking at once and Androulla immediately felt drawn into the heart of this delightful family. She would have expected nothing less of Bill's relatives, especially having already experienced the kindness and sensitivity of Tommy and Isabel. The likeness between Milo and Tommy also fascinated her, for although their colouring couldn't have been in greater contrast, their facial features were remarkably similar.

So close to Milo and so finely tuned to his every mood and feeling, it didn't escape Noola that he found Androulla fascinating. For the first couple of days it seemed he couldn't take his eyes off her and he concentrated all his attention on her whenever she was in the room with them: much more so than his duties as host would demand. In fact at times, if she wasn't around, he deliberately sought her out. Noola knew she was being unreasonably bothered about it but she couldn't help herself. However much she told herself that she knew she had first place in his heart and always would, nevertheless she fretted. So much so that in the end she *had* to talk to somebody and her mother was the obvious choice. She went to have a cup of tea with Maggie when she knew she would find her on her own. She talked about all sorts of things never quite able to get to the point. In the end Maggie did it for her.

284

'Noola darlin', what's bothering you?'

'Oh, Mammy, you always know don't you?'

'You're my child, darlin', and we've always been very close. And however long we both live, you'll be my child, even if you're an old woman yourself before I go.'

'I know, Mammy.' Then she told her exactly what was bothering her.

'I'm being so silly, but I just can't help it. I suppose if I'm honest with myself, it's real green-eyed jealousy. Trouble is, I still love him so much. That's never faltered and I'm frightened he might be falling for someone else – the younger woman! And I have to say, looking at her, I can't blame him for finding her attractive. The strange thing is I was sure it would be Harry who would fall for her, but so far that doesn't seem to have happened.' She paused for a moment. 'But I've noticed *she* can't take her eyes off *him*, which is also understandable, given how she felt about Bill.'

Maggie looked long and hard at Noola, obviously thinking how best to respond to her worries.

'When you and Milo became engaged to be married do you remember what I said to you?'

'I've never forgotten it, Mammy. You said to remember always that marriage is no insurance policy against ever finding anyone else attractive, but that what matters is how you handle it. If the marriage has a solid foundation, based on genuine, enduring love, it will be nothing more than a passing fancy.'

'Right! Now are you going to tell me that you've never looked at another fellow and thought he was a bit of all right? Because I can think of a few I thought were dishy, even "fancied" but that was as far as it went. Exactly the same happens to the men I can assure you. Now Milo may be at that sort of age but I don't believe for a second that he's having one of those mid-life crisis things you hear so much about. Remember, I know him almost as well as you do. From the time his natural mother died, when he was eight years old, I took the place of a mother to him.' She paused to take a mouthful of her tea.

'I strongly suspect what's fascinating him is that this is the woman his son died for. He's curious to find out what it is about her that engendered that sort of feeling in Bill. And maybe he does find

285

her attractive, but you know perfectly well that he's committed to you heart and soul. There was never another woman he was really in love with and there never will be. Anyhow, if he fancies her and still loves you the best, still wants you more than anyone else, that's the biggest compliment he could pay you. Sorry about the long "give out" but I needed to say it to you and I hope it has helped.'

'Thanks, Mammy. It's helped a lot. I'll just have to be so careful that I don't give myself away and behave like a jealous wife.'

'You won't. May I make a suggestion?'

'I'd love it.'

'Go out of your way to be especially friendly to her – you'd do that anyway! Take her shopping; take her out for lunch; sightseeing; to a show: I bet she'd love to go to our famous Abbey Theatre. There's so much to do that won't be a problem. I can come with you for some of the outings. I'd enjoy that. The three of us could go across to Oughterard for a couple of days. The west of Ireland is always well worth a visit. And talk to Milo about her, but most important encourage *him* to talk about her. At least that will bring everything out into the open: let him get it out of his system.' She paused for another mouthful of her tea, thought a minute and then went on.

'And don't forget the other side of this coin. I imagine Androulla desperately needs to talk about Bill. Encourage her. After all, you're his mother. Who better for the poor girl to let her hair down to? Especially given she lost her own mother, and indeed her father, at the same time that Bill died. She really has been through it.'

* * * * *

For her part Androulla's feelings were really confused. So much so that she wondered at the wisdom of her visit. She had felt desperately guilty about Bill's death but, in spite of knowing she had been the cause of this, time and again she had been encouraged to visit Riverside and then welcomed with such warmth by the whole family. Milo and Noola had immediately become mother and father figures to her and she couldn't help reflecting what wonderful parents-in-law they would have made if circumstances had been

286

different: if it had been Harry she had met instead of Bill and they had fallen for each other in the same way.

She felt irresistibly drawn to Harry. He was Bill in every possible way – in looks identical: that was to be expected. What hadn't occurred to her was that they would be so alike in every other way. The smile that went all the way to his eyes; the quirky grin; the way he threw back his head when he laughed; his mannerisms in general; the inflexions in his speech; the way he used his hands when explaining something. It was all Bill and it hurt. She had to keep reminding herself that this truly wasn't Bill.

Harry had expected to feel angry and resentful towards the woman responsible for the loss of his twin. Instead he found he felt desperately sorry for her and went out of his way to be kind to her for, aside from all her close personal losses, he was aware that she must carry that awful burden of guilt. And he really respected the courage it must have taken to come here into what could have been the equivalent of the lion's den: right into the heart of the family she was responsible for depriving of son and brother. However, regardless of his feelings of sympathy and admiration, emotionally he was still totally committed to someone else.

Yet another interesting response to Androulla's visit, and the family's reaction to her, was experienced by Cathy. She watched Harry's attention to the beautiful visitor and was surprised at her own feelings about that. To her amazement she found she too was jealous. Whatever is the matter with me? She asked herself. I'm engaged to Sam and he'll be home soon. I really love Sam . . . don't I? Being brutally honest she had to admit that things hadn't gone too well between them towards the end of her visit to Brazil, after she had raced home to be a witness to Harry's innocence. She had told Sam the whole story openly and honestly but since then she had sensed a slight coolness in him. She wondered if he really believed that there had been no intimacy between her and Harry on that now famous evening they had spent together. She supposed she couldn't blame him. He had met Harry and knew he was a very attractive man.

She mused on for a long time questioning her own feelings. Why was I so desperate to race back to his rescue? Why was I so worried

287

that he would be convicted and sentenced to a period in prison? After all, I knew perfectly well he would appeal and I could have come forward then. But no! I completely panicked, dropped everything and flew to his defence. Why? Has Androulla's visit made me face the rather painful truth? Who it is that I *really* love? How would I feel if I had a letter from Sam calling it all off between us? To her astonishment she realized that she wouldn't mind at all. Worse, she would actually be relieved. It would leave her free. Oh, Cathy, Cathy, she agonized. What's the matter with you? Are you really so fickle?

The more she thought about it the more she realized that she had started to feel this way since that New Year's Ball when Harry had declared his love for her. That was when the rot had really set in and maybe even before that. He had never once afterwards referred to his feelings for her by even the slightest hint. Had that disappointed her? Perhaps. But one thing was certain: he hadn't put a foot out of place in his behaviour towards her. He couldn't be accused of "pressing his attentions on her" as the saying went.

Then she had another thought. Had Sam sensed this change in her feelings towards him before she had herself? Quite possibly. Well, now she must do the honourable thing. She must end the engagement with Sam and find another job. There was no way she could openly declare herself free and willing to embark on a relationship with Harry. Much better she should cut her losses and go far away, preferably abroad, where she could view things rationally from a distance. One of her brothers, who was quite a bit older than her, lived in Boston and she knew he and his wife, Maura, would give her a warm welcome if she wanted to stay with them for a few weeks. At least she would know somebody there to start off with, which would make the break from home a little easier. She would write her resignation to Noola and Harry and she would ask Maura about the possibility of a job over there. She had saved enough to tide her over for a while between employments and Johnny would be well catered for within the family.

* * * * *

288

Noola followed her mother's advice and made a big fuss of Androulla, so much so that a considerable bond developed between them. She became fond of the girl and was genuinely sorry when the time came to say goodbye to her. She felt she would like to give her a memento of her visit. She discussed this with Milo. He was delighted at the idea and suggested that they might give her an item from his mother's collection of valuable jewellery. They chose an antique ruby ring, which they felt complimented Androulla's dark colouring.

When they presented her with this on the day she was leaving, they told her it was something of a family heirloom which they wanted her to have in memory of Bill. She burst into tears.

'This is the most wonderful gift I've ever been given. I will always value it because of its associations. Thank you both so much for such a generous gesture. I so wish I *was* a member of your family. I'll never forget your kindness to me.'

'But we feel you *are* a member of our family and we all hope you'll come back and visit Riverside again. There'll always be a welcome for you here.'

'Thank you, Noola.'

Milo and Noola took her to the airport and waved her off on her journey back to Stratford-upon-Avon, where she had a partnership in a legal firm. She invited them to visit her there and enjoy the interesting town, and especially its famous theatre. She had noticed their keen interest in arts of all kinds, which was evident around the house as well as in their preferred non-sporting leisure activities. They assured her they would accept her offer. Two days later an enormous bunch of flowers arrived with a card that said: "With love and appreciation from Androulla".

Noola, following Maggie's advice again, had not by the slightest hint betrayed her anxiety to Milo. The evening Androulla left they were getting ready for bed in their big, comfortable bedroom. She had put on her most glamorous nightdress and, relaxed and happy, was looking her very best. Milo had donned his dressing gown after showering. He looked at her with a big, appreciative grin and put his arms around her.

'Do you know something, Noola?'

289

'In particular?'

'You are still the most attractive woman I've ever known. Even at our great advanced ages I find you the biggest turn-on imaginable. What's more, I've yet again witnessed your kindness to someone who needed sympathy and support. I love you so much I don't quite know how to tell you.'

Her eyes filled with tears. How could she ever have doubted him?

'Well I can assure you the feeling is absolutely mutual and I can think of one way you'll undoubtedly try to let me know.'

'Most certainly. But aside from that, I want to give you something. I thought I'd like to get you a special present. You deserve it so much.'

He pulled a small gift-wrapped package from his pocket and handed it to her, with a kiss.

'That's with so much love.'

'Thank you, my darling.'

She unwrapped it carefully, trying so hard not to tear the attractive paper, and opened the oblong box. Inside was a dainty, gold Rolex watch, set around with diamonds and with a solid gold strap. Noola was accustomed to being given generous presents by Milo but this took her breath away. For a few seconds she was lost for words.

'Oh, Milo. I'm not sure I really deserve this.'

'You most certainly do and I hope you will wear it as often as possible.'

She gave him such a happy smile.

'You need have no doubts whatsoever about that.'

Chapter 43

Cathy waited for a couple of weeks after Androulla had left and then, in late October, handed her letters of resignation to Noola and Harry. She wanted to be certain she wasn't making a hasty decision. She had written to Sam breaking off their engagement as gently as possible. It was something of a bolt from the blue for both of her employers. They hadn't had the slightest idea she was thinking this way. She had asked to see them together to give them the letters rather than leaving them on the hall table, where letters for posting were placed.

'Cathy! What a surprise. Has the wedding been brought forward?'

'No, Noola. It's time for me to move on. Johnny will be fine. He'll be off to school before too long and if you feel you need another nanny for him, I've a good friend I can recommend. I'll stay until you get everything settled for him. You know how grateful I was for your offer of a loan so that Sam and I could buy a house, but all that's on hold for the moment.'

'Have you got another job to go to?'

'No, but I'm planning to go abroad for a while. I thought I'd try Boston. I've a married brother living there. It would be lovely to be with someone from the family.'

Harry was really shaken. His reaction was much as his mother's: he too assumed the wedding was being brought forward. He listened to the exchange between her and Noola and was puzzled that no real reason for her leaving was being offered.

'Have we upset you in some way, Cathy? I hope nothing has happened to make you unhappy here.'

291

'No, truly I've been so happy with you all from the time I first came here. I just feel it's time for me to have a look at the rest of the world before I finally "settle down" as it were. The visit to Brazil whetted my appetite.'

That was all true. Not the real reason behind it but close enough: she must get away so as she could view everything from a distance. Harry was about to argue further but got a warning look from his mother so said no more. Noola, perceptive as ever, had a pretty fair idea what it was all about.

'I'm really sorry you're leaving us. But could I suggest a compromise?'

'Of course.'

'Why not take six months off, rather like a sabbatical? We'll keep your flat for you and you can leave your belongings here. I know Sarah would be only too happy to take on Johnny for a while. We could get some temporary help if need be. I'm sure Harry wouldn't object to that arrangement.'

'No, I'd be quite happy with that. Please think about it, Cathy.'

'You're very kind. It does sound like a good compromise.'

Truth to tell she was delighted. It seemed the perfect solution. It would allow her that break but it wouldn't cut her off completely from the family.

Three weeks later she had it all arranged. She spent her last evening with her own family having put them in the picture, explaining that the romance between her and Sam was over and she was going to America. However, other than to her sister Noreen, she made no mention of Harry. Noreen had been more like a mother than a sister to her, since Cathy's mother had died shortly after her birth. Cathy had shared her whole dilemma with Noreen, who had supported the idea of her going away for a while to clear her mind.

Noola manoeuvred things so that Harry took Cathy to the airport. Carrying her cabin luggage for her he walked her to the departure gate where they stopped to say goodbye. He hugged her and gave her a light kiss on the cheek.

'I'll miss you but I do hope everything works out for you, Cathy. If ever you find yourself footloose and fancy free, remember I do love you so much. My feelings haven't changed since I first told you

292

that. In fact they've grown stronger. I'll always be here for you if you need me.'

'Oh, Harry. Thank you. I'll miss you too. In fact I'll miss you all.'

She almost ran to the gate, afraid he would see the tears in her eyes. She turned to wave and stopped. Shoulders slumped, he had such a forlorn look. Unbelievably, Harry Butler looked almost like a lost, small boy, reminding her strongly of Johnny when he was about to cry. She walked back, put her case on the ground, reached up and, hands on his shoulders, gave him the lightest brush of a kiss on the lips.

'Actually, I've realized I love you too, Harry. Sam and I are no longer engaged. But I'm so confused I need time to sort myself out.'

He folded his arms around her and almost squeezed the breath out of her. His smile seemed to light up the whole departure area. He didn't embarrass her by kissing her passionately in public even though he ached to do so.

'You've no idea what a happy man you've made me. I'll be waiting but not patiently. Don't make it too long. And don't forget, Johnny will miss you too!'

Now the sunny smile was hers.

'I promise I'll come back.'

* * * * *

Harry's elation was obvious for all to see. As soon as he arrived back home from the airport he hurried down to the dock at the riverbank with a new spring in his step. Although it was mid November, the weather was mild enough for the family to gather there for tea. Johnny spotted him before anyone else and ran to meet him. Harry swung him up in his arms.

'How about a row in a boat, Johnny, before it gets too dark?'

'Yes please, Dad, and Grandpa and Sarah too?'

'Of course.'

Milo, Noola and Maggie were grinning from ear to ear. They exchanged knowing looks with each other. At long last things had turned the corner for Harry.

'He's a real sucker for punishment, Harry. He's already been out with his grandpa.'

'Yes, but I want to go out with you too, Dad. And I want to do some rowing. I want to row in The Liffey Descent with you and Grandpa and Sarah next year.'

'Good for you, boy!' Milo was so delighted to have such strong evidence of his grandson's love of the river.

'But you don't know how to row yet.'

'Yes I do, Dad. Grandpa and Sarah showed me how.'

'Let's all go then and we'll see what you can do.'

Sarah was smiling happily but declined the invitation to go out in the boat again.

'I think I'll pass this time, Harry. Uncle Paddy has warned me not to overdo it.'

He looked at her in surprise and noticed there was a special glow of happiness about her.

'Is there something I don't know about?'

'I've only just had it confirmed. I'm expecting a baby in about seven months' time, around next June. Dai and I are so excited. But I've been told by all the medics I must be very careful.'

He put Johnny down and gave her a big hug and thumped Dai on the back.

'I'm so happy for you both. We must all look out for you now, Sarah. Hey, that means two of my sisters are pregnant. I wonder what Mageen's up to – perhaps it's catching!'

Later that evening Milo commented to Noola:

'For once in a way we're free of crises. At long last all members of our family seem to be happy. I'm almost afraid to say it in case I'm tempting providence.'

'I know what you mean but let's just enjoy it while we have it. I haven't seen Harry so happy for some time, even happier than after the trial ended so well for him. Clearly something happened when he was saying goodbye to Cathy.'

'It looks like that. Your manipulation of her departure arrangements obviously worked.'

Chapter 44

Harry survived less than a month without Cathy and couldn't stand it any longer. He just had to see her and hear her tell him again that she loved him. He had begun to wonder if he had imagined it. He had written to her and had an answer but both had steered away from anything very personal, other than telling her how much he missed her. He decided he would go to Boston without telling her in advance. He could go first for a quick visit to see Izzy in Minneapolis, for he had missed her too. He realized that her first Christmas away from home would be quite tough for her.

He asked his father if he could spare him for a week or so and Milo agreed without asking any questions. However, later that evening, having their pre-dinner drinks, he decided to come clean and tell his parents the story.

'So I'm going over unannounced to try and persuade Cathy to come back with me. Apparently she's been doing occasional relief work at the local children's home, as a volunteer, so she wouldn't be letting anyone down.'

'I don't think either of us would try to dissuade you, Harry, and may I say I would be thrilled to bits to have Cathy as a daughter-in-law.'

'Hear, hear. And what a good idea to start off with a visit to Izzy. She'll be so excited at the thought of seeing a member of the family. Would you take a few Christmas presents for her?'

'Of course, Dad.'

Within a couple of days he was off. He did tell Izzy that he was on the way. She was very excited, but curious as to his real reason for a sudden visit to the States so close to Christmas. He was delighted

295

to meet Jed at last, whose true identity he didn't know, since this had been kept strictly within a closed circle. He had a wonderful few days with them and was sorry his visit had been so short. Jed had a heavy cold and chest infection but didn't let that prevent him from giving Harry a warm welcome and being an excellent host. To Izzy's delight the two men got along famously and she was equally pleased when she heard the reason for his visit to Boston. He told her the whole story.

'Oh, Harry, I'm delighted! I love Cathy and to have her as a sister-in-law would be wonderful.'

'Thanks, Izzy. I hope she's open to persuasion to come back to Riverside with me. But when are you and Jed coming over to see us? Everyone's dying to meet Jed and I know they'll like him too.'

'We hope to go across after the baby is born and then everyone can meet both new members of the family. You really like Jed?'

'Yes, I do, Izzy. I find him a really sympathetic kind of person: there's nothing about him *not* to like!'

'That means a lot to me, Harry.'

* * * * *

Harry moved across to Boston. He had booked into a hotel quite close to where Cathy's brother lived. Then he called her.

'Harry! How lovely to hear you. Is everything all right?'

'Yes. I was calling to invite you out to dinner.'

'I'd love it but it would be rather a long way to go just for dinner.'

'It's only a few steps around the block.'

'What?'

'I'm just around the corner in the Hilton Hotel.'

'*Harry!* How?'

'Oh, the usual sort of way these days. I flew across.'

'I'm so surprised. I almost don't know what to say!'

'Well, you could say yes, or I could come over there and abduct you!'

They had an evening together that neither would ever forget. Harry had made prior arrangements with the hotel staff, telling them it would be a special occasion. A table had been prepared in a

296

quiet corner, where the lighting was subdued and the atmosphere romantic. The pianist had been asked to play some of his favourite songs such as "In the Still of the Night", "I Get No Kick From Champagne" and "The Way You Look Tonight", songs particularly appropriate from Harry's point of view and he knew Cathy would get the message.

At the end of the meal, little of which either of them ate, by prior arrangement a bottle of Moët & Chandon Champagne was brought to the table in an ice bucket. After it had been poured and they had toasted each other Harry produced a small box and handed it to Cathy. She opened it to find a beautiful sapphire ring, set in diamonds. It was impressively large without being vulgar. She raised eyes to him that rivalled the champagne in their sparkle. He came around the table and knelt down on one knee beside her.

'My darling Cathy. This time I trust I'm not embarrassing you by saying if you've nothing else in mind for the next fifty or so years will you marry me?'

'Thank you, Harry. I can't think of anything I'd rather do for the rest of my life than be married to you. The answer is yes.'

He slipped the ring onto her engagement finger, then took her in his arms and kissed her while the delighted staff in the restaurant applauded enthusiastically. They had waited in anticipation and were not disappointed.

'It fits as if it had been made specially for me!'

'Of course. It *was* made specially for you.'

'But how did you know the size of my finger?'

'Ah, I've ways of finding these things out. The important thing is do you like it? I took a bit of a risk and wondered if I should have allowed you to choose your own ring.'

'I love it and it is very much the kind of ring I would have chosen, although I would never have dreamt of being given one so beautiful. Sapphire is my favourite stone. Now you'll tell me you knew that too!'

'As I said, I've ways of finding out and I was correct in guessing that you would wear a blue dress this evening, not unlike the one I saw you in that famous evening – the time I discovered you were such an attractive woman!'

297

She didn't take too much persuading to go home with him. Her brother and his wife were disappointed that they weren't going to have her with them for Christmas after all, but were very excited to be the first to be told the news of the engagement. Even better, they took a genuine liking to Harry who exerted all his charm to make himself seem a worthy husband for Cathy. Like Izzy, they were sworn to secrecy. Harry and Cathy both wanted to be the first to tell the rest of their families the news.

*****

Harry had carefully planned their return to Riverside to coincide with pre-lunch drinks on Sunday. He and Cathy had already made a quick visit to her sister to tell her and the rest of her family there the news, but had asked them not to tell anyone else just yet and explained why. Both were concerned at having any publicity about their engagement, since they wanted to avoid, at all costs, any leak to the press that they were going to get married. They didn't want speculation as to whether or not a romantic liaison had started before his trial, which could raise questions about Cathy's evidence, despite the fact that the whole false accusation had blown up in Tim Kelly's face. Now the O'Donovans, but especially Noreen, were jubilant at the news and they all had a celebratory drink together before Harry and Cathy moved on to Riverside.

By tradition Sunday lunch was the main meal of the day at Riverside to leave the staff free for the rest of the day, and also by tradition as many members of the family as were anywhere around the house joined one another for this unfailingly special occasion. As often as not there were additional visitors, friends who would otherwise have had a lonely Sunday. On this particular occasion, as well as Milo and Noola, Maggie, a frail but sparky Aunt May, Sarah, Dai and Johnny, had all gathered in the elegant sitting room, where a roaring fire had been lit, brightening up a rather dull December day.

Harry and Cathy arrived, unannounced, holding hands and radiating a happiness that seemed to add further warmth to the atmosphere. Everyone became aware of their presence at the same

298

moment, but Johnny got to them first. He hurtled across the room.

'Dad, Cathy! You're home, you're home,' and he promptly burst into tears. Harry gathered him up into his arms where he buried his head in his father's broad shoulder.

'Hey, I thought you'd be pleased to see us, but here you are crying!'

'Don't tease him, Harry. Come and give me a big hug, Johnny. I'm so excited to see you too.'

He wriggled down and ran into her outstretched arms beaming through the tears.

'I was lonely for you, Cathy. I'm glad you're home.' From early on she had asked that he wouldn't call her Nanny and he was comfortable with calling her Cathy.

As she hugged the child, the engagement ring became highly visible and everyone in the room spotted it. All of them were now smiling broadly and the atmosphere became positively festive.

'What a wonderful surprise! Welcome home you two. And by the looks on your faces and that ring on Cathy's finger I'd say you've got something wonderful to tell us!'

'We have, Mum. I've proposed to Cathy and she's accepted. Hey, Johnny, how would you like to have Cathy as your mum?'

'Oh yes please. Can you fix that, Dad?'

'Thanks to Cathy I can. She and I are going to be married. Are you really pleased?'

To their consternation fresh tears started to flow.

'So you won't go away and leave me again, Cathy?'

'No, little one. I promise that if I go away it will be only for a short time. Trust me, Johnny.'

'But now at bedtime will you sing to me like Sarah and Dai?'

'I'll try! What have they been singing to you?'

'The song about all the angels around my bed and sometimes Dad joins in too.'

'I don't know this song. Could you sing it for me?'

The tears were rapidly replaced by a broad smile.

'Yes, but Sarah and Dai must start and then Dad and I can join in like we usually do.'

Dai willingly gave the lead with Sarah and Harry quick to join in. Then the child's voice was raised, and he sang the wonderful words set to Humperdinck's haunting music, absolutely in tune and without faltering:

'When at night I go to sleep
Fourteen angels watch do keep
Two my head are guarding
Two my feet are guiding
Two are on my right hand
Two are on my left hand
Two who warmly cover
Two who o'er me hover
Two to whom 'tis given
To guide my steps to Heaven'

It brought lumps to the throats of the other adults and was a scene that Johnny would remember until he was an old man.

'Where did you learn to sing like that, Johnny?'

'Dai taught me first then Sarah helped. But you can sing too, Cathy, I've heard you.'

'Not so well as you but I want you to teach me that song. It's lovely.'

'Well done everyone, but now I think it's time to celebrate. When is the great day to be?'

'Neither of us wants a long engagement, Mum, so we hope it will be around Easter time. But it will need to be a quiet one with absolutely no publicity and we don't need to explain why.'

'Indeed not, but congratulations. May you have many happy years together.'

Everyone added their good wishes and Milo went and found a bottle of champagne to toast their future. In a whispered aside to Noola he muttered:

'He's settled at last! Thanks be to the Good Lord.'

'Yes, and with somebody we all like so much. What a wonderful Christmas present!'

300

Chapter 45

1977

Although Izzy greatly missed her family, she and Eddie were idyllically happy living in a leafy district on the edge of Minneapolis/St Paul, or the "Twin Cities", in an elegant house her parents had given to them as a wedding present. Fortunately she was kept so busy organizing everything to do with their new home that she didn't have too much time to dwell on her homesickness. With characteristic American hospitality, her neighbours rallied around and quickly made her feel a part of their community. Izzy's interest in her music never flagged and this helped too. Eddie's wedding gift to her had been a baby grand piano and she played happily, both for practice and pleasure, giving an occasional informal concert but carefully keeping out of the limelight. Like her mother before her, her pregnancy wasn't easy so she had the perfect excuse not to get involved in a programme of either formal or informal engagements. This limit on social activities also helped her to adjust to calling Eddie "Jed" when they were in company.

As the months passed by she became rather concerned about Eddie. He was looking tired and what her grandmother would have described as "washed out". Through the severe months of winter weather he seemed to get cold after cold, the infections always sitting on his chest and causing him to cough a great deal. It was one such infection he had been suffering from when Harry had visited them. It was now late February and the baby was due in April. Izzy put it all down to his anxiety over the approaching birth. She kept pressing him to go to the doctor but he had insisted that he didn't need to, certain that once the warm summer months came he would be fine again. Then one day, when the home help was off ill, she was sorting their clothes to run through the washing machine and noticed that one of his handkerchiefs had quite a lot of blood on it. Having grown up in Ireland where tuberculosis, although now curable, was still feared, she immediately panicked, for this was one of the dreaded symptoms of that disease. She phoned him at work and insisted that he go immediately to see the doctor. Hearing the panic in her voice he agreed at once.

Eddie had known all too well what the symptoms could be but was trying to treat himself, refusing to accept that the blood was more than the result of a damaged throat from all the coughing. However, Izzy's fear had communicated itself and he did go at once to see his doctor, who immediately sent him to a consultant in the famous Mayo Clinic not too far away from Minneapolis. Izzy insisted on going with him and he was glad to have her there. A whole range of tests was run and in due course the news was broken to him. This time he had quite deliberately chosen to be on his own with the doctor, not telling Izzy that the results were through.

'I'm sorry, Jed.'

'It's all right, Doctor, I've a fair idea of what you're going to tell me. It's tuberculosis, isn't it?'

'No, it's not.'

'Oh! But the symptoms?'

'Yes, they're the signs of TB but I'm afraid it's something more serious.'

'I don't think you need to go on.'

'There's no easy way to break this to you, Jed. I'm afraid it's lung cancer and well advanced.'

'Dear God! And my wife's expecting our first child in less than two months' time. How long have I got?'

'With luck just a bit more than that. It's an unusual type, but one we're seeing more and more. It's mesothelioma caused by exposure to asbestos. Did you ever work with asbestos?'

Eddie thought for a few seconds.

'Yes. I'm pretty sure there was quite a lot in the buildings I was helping to demolish years ago, when I was doing labouring jobs to earn some extra funds.'

This had happened when he had come out of prison and had

302

been desperate for employment of any kind, so long as it was a job bringing in enough to allow him to scratch a basic existence.

'Unfortunately quite a small amount of exposure is all it needs and then it can lie dormant for a very long time. It can suddenly start to grow and by the time it's detected it's usually too late for help. As a pharmacist you probably know all this.'

'Yes.' And as a one-time doctor he knew a lot more than he could admit to. He knew exactly the unpleasant end he was facing. What worried him even more was Izzy and how he was going to tell her that he had been handed a death sentence. Thank God she had a supportive and closely knit family she could go to when the worst happened. A thought suddenly struck him and he gave a bleak little smile. His child would grow up in Ireland, in dear old Dublin, after all.

He tried his best to break it to her gently but the shock was too much and she went into premature labour. He called Riverside and told them that the baby was coming early but not why. Milo, Noola and Maggie got there as quickly as they could, but not before a tiny but perfectly formed and healthy baby girl was born, late in the evening on St Patrick's Day 1977. Izzy's emotions were totally confused, a mixture of immense joy at the safe birth of their child but complete heartbreak at the knowledge that Eddie would be with them for such a short time to share that joy. Over and over again she had asked him the same question.

'You're sure there's *nothing at all* that can be done?'

'No, my darling, it's much too far advanced and galloping away.'

For a few days the arrival of his child gave him a very short new lease of life but he slipped back and started to deteriorate rapidly. Milo, Noola and Maggie were horrified when they were told the story. All three were adamant that they would stay as long as necessary to give their support. Milo now had complete confidence in Harry's ability to run the business on his own for some time if need be, so there was no mad urgency for him to return to Dublin. His youngest and most vulnerable child needed him and he would stay for as long as it took. His respect for Eddie grew as he watched him cope with a terminal condition but also struggle to help Izzy to come to terms with what lay ahead.

303

'I'm so sorry, Eddie, and may I say how much I admire the way in which you're coping with such devastating circumstances. As you can imagine, I was totally opposed to your marriage to Izzy, but you've obviously brought her so much happiness in the short time you've had together and for that I want to thank you. It's tragic that it has to end in this way.'

'You'll never know how much those words mean to me and especially from you – I don't deserve your kindness. Thank you, Milo.'

'I wouldn't wish what's happening to you on anyone, Eddie.'

'You're a remarkably forgiving man. You and Sean Flynn are the most decent men I've ever known.'

* * * * *

Eddie went downhill with frightening speed after that. The cancer was so aggressive and in the end spread right through him in a matter of days. It got to the point when the hospital staff could do no more for him and gave him the option of going home for the last few days of his life. He agreed readily and full-time nursing help was installed, with a doctor on constant call.

While he could still speak, albeit with difficulty, he told Izzy how lucky he thought he was to have found her again and discover that she loved him.

'Because of you, my darling Izzy, the little girl I stole away, I've had such a happy end to my life. I've never loved any human being as much as I love you. In the short time we've had together, you've been the joy and light of my life. And to top it all you've given me the greatest gift possible, our child – our very *Irish* child!'

A severe fit of coughing interrupted what he was saying but then, making a supreme effort, he went on with dogged determination.

'In spite of the mess I made of my early years, I feel my life has now been fulfilled. I'm just desperately sad that I have to leave you, but so grateful that you have such a wonderful family to support you.'

'I love you too, Eddie, so much, but you know that and I do feel

I was given such a gift too in meeting you again. What were the chances of that happening? Extremely remote, but I'll forever be glad that it happened and even that I trapped you into marrying me.'

He managed a smile, coughed some more producing the inevitable bloody flux, then struggled to answer.

'Would all the traps in life were so delightful and had such a wonderful ending. If you hadn't trapped me, you wouldn't be here with me now, by my side at the end. I'm a lucky man.'

As long as he was able to speak he kept telling her how much he loved her. He asked that his ashes should be taken back to Ireland and scattered somewhere in the Dublin Mountains that he had loved so much when growing up. He slipped away from them at dawn just three weeks after the birth, with Izzy's arms around him and his little child by his side. They had agreed to call her Patricia, an inevitable choice given her Irish heritage and the date of her birth. At the request of Eddie, she was formally registered at birth as Patricia Butler on the grounds that Seabourne wasn't his real name and he admired the Butler family so much. Trisha Butler would eventually become quite a formidable character.

Chapter 46

In the circumstances Harry and Cathy's wedding was postponed. It went without saying, and needing no discussion, that they would wait until everything had been sorted out for Izzy and she was safely and securely installed back in Riverside House. As always, the whole family rallied around and she was given huge support. In the unbelievable pain of her grief, her little daughter was an immense consolation. She had inherited Izzy's small build but was also tiny because of her premature birth and the fact that she needed almost constant attention meant that Izzy had to concentrate all her energies on her. This was helping her through those horrific early days. She would not entertain the idea of employing a nanny to help and give her a break.

'You know I'll give you a rest any time you need it, my darling Izzy. I would be delighted to share in the care of my newest and very precious grandchild.'

'Thanks, Mum. At the moment I'm all right. Trisha is keeping me so busy she's helping to save my sanity, but if I get beyond managing or really need a rest I'll take you up on the offer. It's just so good to have you close by.'

Johnny was fascinated by the new member of the family and was happy to sit beside Izzy and look at the baby. He even tried talking to her.

'You'll be quite safe here, Trisha. I won't let anyone hurt you. She's so small, Izzy. Will I be able to hold her soon?'

'Quite soon, Johnny. She'll love that.'

'Do you think she's very sad that she hasn't got her dad?'

'She's too little to understand that yet. And although her daddy isn't here there are lots of other kind men to look out for her, like you and your dad and Grandpa and Dai.'

He thought about all this for a few moments.

'I didn't have a mum. She died too. But now Cathy's going to be my mum and I'm really happy. I love Cathy.'

'We all do, Johnny.'

Inevitably Izzy's music was also crucial in her coming to terms with losing Eddie. When not tending to Trisha's needs she wheeled her pram into the room where her piano was kept and she played away. She found it fascinating that as long as she was playing the baby never cried, just lay there, apparently quite content to be entertained in that way. In time her heart and soul began to heal and she started to come back to life but it was a long, slow process.

* * * * *

Three months after Izzy returned to Riverside with Trisha, to everyone's delight Sarah gave birth to a little son, which she and Dai unanimously agreed would be called William.

'Bill was such a special person I feel that would be a lovely memorial to him.'

'Thanks, Dai, I'm so pleased you feel that way.'

The others in the family were equally pleased and the arrival of the little boy seemed to give particular pleasure to Izzy. As the birth became closer she had spent increasing amounts of time with Sarah and this, like her music, had helped her greatly in coming to terms with her bereavement.

After this excitement and the baptism of William, Izzy had a long chat with Harry and Cathy and insisted that they should go ahead with their wedding.

'Please! It would give me a lot of pleasure to see the two of you married and after all, for the best possible reason, you never intended to have a big wedding. Now it would be obvious to the outside world that it wouldn't be appropriate to have a big celebration. We could also let it be known that I've pressed you to go ahead with it, in spite of my being in mourning.'

307

'Bless you, Izzy. That's such an unselfish thought. What do you think, Cathy?'

'Somehow it doesn't seem quite right. Are you sure, Izzy?'

'Yes, Cathy. I can't wait to have you as my sister-in-law and I get the feeling that Johnny can't wait to have his new mum.'

There was a question mark over where the wedding breakfast should be held. All agreed that a hotel would be too public and Cathy felt reluctant to impose such an event, however modest, on her sister and family, even though their home was pleasant and roomy. In the end, having discussed it with Milo, Noola suggested to the couple what she thought was a good solution.

'In a way you could consider this as your home, Cathy. After all, you've lived in your flat upstairs for some years now. How about having a reception here on the kind of modest scale you and Harry had planned? The family would be delighted.'

'Oh, Noola. What a generous offer. That would be wonderful and my family would be delighted too. Noreen suggested that she could provide some refreshments but I know it wouldn't be easy for her. She works full-time and looks after a big family. It would be such a relief to her to know it would be here.'

Milo and Noola had met Noreen and her husband, Colum, and had liked them a lot. Now all four put their heads together with Harry and Cathy and worked out the details for the big day.

It was a September wedding and the plan was to keep it strictly family and very close friends. However, by the time all the Butlers, the Flynns and the O'Donovans were included it was quite a crowd, even before any friends were added.

Harry was highly delighted that Mageen, Jack and their three children were able to get over for a few days. Their little daughter, Rachel, born in 1972, and now aged five, was thrilled at the idea of being a flower girl, with Johnny, at four and a half, as pageboy. Cathy's niece, Gill, was to be bridesmaid.

It started as a lovely misty autumn day and later the sun came out turning the view towards and beyond the river into something akin to a backdrop for a movie, with the trees dressed in their full autumn splendour of tawny colours: red, yellow, orange, gold, russet and brown. Not wanting to risk the weather suddenly turning nasty, and

308

since the numbers could be accommodated inside without difficulty, the reception with wedding breakfast was being held indoors. The windows of the house faced across the beautifully manicured lawns to this artist's palette of colour and the view was breathtaking.

Harry and Cathy made an idyllic looking couple, both such beautiful people. Noola's and Milo's delight with the turn of events almost rivalled that of the young couple.

'I don't remember ever having seen Harry so happy. Just look at him! He can hardly drag his eyes away from Cathy, let alone move from her side. It's almost as if he's afraid she'll disappear in the proverbial puff of smoke.'

'Yes, and she so obviously returns his feelings in full measure. They remind me so much of us on our wedding day. Do you remember, Noola?'

'Now do you really expect me to answer "no" to that question?'

'Well, reassurance is sometimes so good.'

'My darling, gorgeous big eejit. I love you so much.'

Milo burst out laughing, reminded vividly of the first time she had called him a big eejit – the evening he had, at last, told her that he loved her and asked her if by any lucky chance she felt the same way.

* * * * *

At Cathy's special request, Harry took her for their honeymoon to East Africa where neither had been before. They came home full of enthusiasm for the incredible sights they had seen and experiences they had had in the Maasai Mara and Serengeti. They had even managed to get to the top of Mount Kilimanjaro.

'Gosh, Dad, Mum, I can't think why none of us ever thought of going there for a holiday before. The wealth of animal life is unbelievable. I know Dublin Zoo does a good job, but it's just not the same as seeing them in the wild, as they should be, and in such numbers.'

'We must go, Noola.'

'I'd love to. Perhaps next spring when Izzy is feeling a bit better. I wouldn't want to leave her just now.'

309

* * * * *

Harry and Cathy settled happily into their new accommodation. As soon as they had announced their engagement, discussions had taken place as to where they would live. Harry wondered if they should have a place of their own away from Riverside but, having talked it through previously with Noola, Milo suggested an alternative to him.

'Riverside House is so big and, if you leave, there'll only be the two of us with Izzy and Trisha rattling around in it. It's our intention to sign it over to you in trust once you're married. This has been done for generations as a means of reducing inheritance tax and someday you'll probably do the same for Johnny. Supposing, for now, we turn the whole of the top floor into a self-contained flat for you, incorporating Cathy's flat. It would be very spacious: ample room for you and a family and with the library and games rooms to use as and when you want. Then when the trust comes into effect, we may well do what Gran and Gramps Butler did and retire to Oughterard. Alternatively we could simply swap accommodation. What do you think?'

Harry thought for a few moments but it didn't take him long to decide.

'That's such a great offer, Dad. Thanks. I'll talk it through with Cathy, but I can't see her objecting. For me it would be marvellous to stay and still be close to the river. I'd love that for Johnny too and indeed any other children that may come along. And I hope you will both stay here after retirement. With separate, self-contained accommodation we won't get under each other's feet and Oughterard, lovely as it is, would be quite far away from your children and grandchildren.'

'Thanks, Harry. I think it's very likely we will opt to stay but we'll wait and see how it all works out.'

310

Chapter 47

1982

The five years following Eddie's death and Harry and Cathy's marriage were relatively peaceful at Riverside, much to the relief of Milo and Noola. Aunt May had turned ninety, Maggie would soon reach the same age and the rest of the family knew that, although both were in good health, they would have to say goodbye to them soon. Aunt May, although frail, still had all her faculties. Maggie was still feisty and although suffering quite badly from arthritis was determined not to allow that to get in the way of anything she really wanted to do.

Trisha and Will were the best of friends with Johnny, now aged nine, taking very seriously his responsibilities as the oldest. He was also highly delighted at having a brother and sister of his own, Orla aged four, called after Cathy's mother, and little Henry, aged three, after his father but called Hal to avoid confusion. Milo and Noola were so pleased to have five grandchildren running around at Riverside and when Mageen and family visited there were three more. To Milo's delight they all were what he referred to as "water babies", following in the Butler tradition of loving and being outstanding at water sports. Mageen and Jack's two boys, Ewan now fourteen and Alasdair at twelve, like their Butler forebears, were already remarkably good oarsmen, this not only being in their blood, but also encouraged from birth by living close to a Scottish loch. Rachel, at eight, was holding her own too and competing successfully with Johnny in handling an oar or paddle.

It was March 1982. Jack had taken some leave and he, Mageen and the children were looking forward eagerly to spending the Easter holidays at Riverside. The children were all at independent

311

schools so although Easter Day was quite late, not until 11 April, their schools had broken up for the holidays on 31 March. The next day the family had piled into the big, comfortable S-Class Mercedes and headed for the ferry to Dublin.

Jack, however, was uneasy. There had been news of the Argentinian flag being raised by metalworkers on South Georgia, a British territory close to Antarctica and not all that far from the Falkland Islands. In response, the British naval vessel, HMS Endurance, had been dispatched from Port Stanley in the Falklands to investigate the incident. Jack knew that Britain had also dispatched submarines to the South Atlantic from various locations, but he had not had his leave cancelled or been put on "standby" so he didn't postpone his holiday plans. However, his uncanny sixth sense, acquired from all his training and experience, together with an astute political awareness, was making his finely-tuned, intellectual antennae tingle with apprehension.

The family arrived at Riverside tired but happy after a long journey and they were given an ecstatic welcome. They had a wonderful celebratory dinner, cooked to perfection and served by Kitty and her team, with the whole family present around the enormous dining table. Milo noticed that Jack wasn't his usual relaxed self and after the meal gradually manoeuvred his way around the sitting room to where he was sitting.

'Everything all right, Jack?'

'To tell the truth, I'm a bit on edge, Milo. I don't like the smell of things happening in the South Atlantic. Where the Falkland Islands are concerned I don't trust Galtieri's motives one little bit and I'm not alone in that.'

'I take your point. Strange stories have been filtering out about large numbers of his own Argentinian citizens disappearing.'

'Yes, and the intelligence is that those tales are true. Before he became President of Argentina he was a very senior member of the ruling Junta. The "Death Squad" reported directly to him and at that time left-wing sympathizers were being rounded up and taken away. There were mass executions and, so I've been told, torture was quite commonplace.'

'What a lovely man – shades of Nazi Germany!'

312

'Well you can see why I'm not inclined to trust a man like that, nor indeed those in power around him. There's more to it than that though. It seems the economy is something of a disaster too and what with that and family members disappearing without trace the people are becoming restless – or so we hear!'

'So this business in South Georgia could be just the prelude to a much bigger and more serious act of aggression which could distract the people from the other problems?'

'Absolutely! For some time now Argentina has had eyes on the Falklands. Trouble is they would be able to get troops there much more quickly than we could and the islanders are not very well equipped to defend themselves. The Argentine Junta knows that, but also *must* know that nuclear subs are on their way in response to the South Georgia episode – it's been leaked by our own press for God's sake. It's a pity some politicians can't keep their mouths shut! So what would you and I do in his place?'

'Ah! You think he might be panicked into a sudden attempt to invade the Falklands. But might he not be just sticking his toe in the water to test the reaction of the Brits? He hasn't actually landed troops on South Georgia has he?'

'I don't know but I wouldn't be surprised to find he has infiltrated some military personnel in there, amongst the civilians who raised the flag.'

'What happens if he *does* invade the Falklands?'

'Good question, Milo. Somehow I can't see Maggie Thatcher sitting doing absolutely nothing while they get themselves well entrenched there, as efforts are made to work out some sort of diplomatic solution. I bet the Falkland Islanders will want a very rapid response too. They certainly won't be happy at being taken over.'

'Hmm! So where does that leave you?'

'If it happens I'm certain I'll be on the way in no time.'

'You reckon your special skills would be required "up front" as it were?'

'I feel the chances are pretty high. After all, ours is considered to be one of the "crack" organisations for small group infiltration behind the lines, surveillance and, if need be, swift and decisive

313

action. Usually very effective! But, in these particular circumstances, the clincher will be that I speak quite reasonable Spanish. Actually, so does Bertie. That's a skill in pretty short supply at the moment amongst our people.'

'Presumably needed for questioning prisoners effectively, which would put you in at foot-sloggers level, regardless of rank?'

'Exactly.'

The next day the BBC announced that the Falklands had been invaded and were now occupied by Argentinian forces. Broadcasts by the invaders, claiming to have taken possession of the islands, were confirmed on the afternoon of 2 April. Within hours Jack received the expected call.

'Jack – it's Bertie. Can you get here pronto?'

'Yes. Tonight?'

'If you can manage it! There's a lot to do in a short time.'

'Sure. I'll get there somehow.'

'Let me know the details. I'll have transport waiting.'

Jack found Mageen and told her he wanted a word in private. There was nobody in the library so they closed themselves in there and he told her. Mageen, accustomed to Jack's sudden calls to duty, was outwardly remarkably calm.

'I'll pack up everything and we'll be ready to go home in no time.'

'No, Mageen. I think you should stay here for the rest of the holiday as planned. I'm certain we'll be off to the Falklands very soon and I think it would be best for you to stay here where you'll have the support of your family.'

She put her arms around him and he drew her close.

'I would like to be with you until the last possible moment. You know the agonies I go through every time you have to go away on some assignment or another. I don't want to be a silly, clinging wife, so I do try not to nag at you about your job, but you must know how I feel.'

'Mageen…'

'No wait, Jack. There's another thing. I think Ewan is beginning to suspect that you're not simply a regular member of the Scots Guards. He's a bright lad and he's probably worked out for himself what you do. He hero-worships you, both the boys do, as you know,

314

but sometimes I see the worry in his eyes too when you're away. It's very touching. He goes out of his way to keep me company as much as possible at those times – almost as if he's watching over me.'

'Well done, Ewan! Would it make you happy if I retired from soldiering?'

'Yes for me, but not for you. I know you'd be miserable doing a desk job.'

'When this latest skirmish is over we'll talk about it again. I'll be forty-five next month so maybe I'm getting to the point where I should think about alternatives. Not necessarily a desk job though!'

'That would be wonderful for all of us. Thank you, my darling.'

'But I'd still like you and the children to be here for as long as possible while I'm away.'

'All right. If it will make you happier we'll stay but, whatever happens, the children will have to go back to school at the end of the holidays.'

'Let's cross that bridge when we come to it. But now I must get away at once.'

Later that evening Mageen and the children took Jack to Dublin Airport. Given that members of the British forces needed to keep a low profile in Southern Ireland they were all acutely aware of the need for discretion, so the goodbyes there were rather muted. The more deeply personal farewells had been made before leaving the house. Now all managed to maintain the proverbial stiff upper lip except little Rachel who couldn't stop the tears from rolling down her cheeks. Jack gathered her in his arms.

'If you have to go to war you will come home safely to us, Dad, won't you?'

'No problem, sweetheart. Your dad's a tough guy you know.'

'I know, Dad, but I so hope you won't have to go.'

All this was said in little above a whisper, Rachel, even at that young age, being alert to the dangers.

Back at Riverside Milo and Noola were trying to explain to the younger children why Jack had to leave so suddenly and, with the other adults, were doing their best to distract their attention. When they had a moment to themselves they were at last able to voice their considerable alarm.

315

'I feel so much for Mageen in particular, although all three children are old enough to understand the dangers.'

'I can feel for her perhaps even more, Milo. I remember vividly how I felt when you went off to join the RAF in 1942 and I was pregnant and so sick I couldn't go over there to be close to you.'

'Well at least she's not pregnant and unwell unless I've missed something?'

'Not as far as I know, but the children will need support too. We must think of as many ways as possible to keep their minds occupied.'

'It'll be difficult to drag them away from the news reports. In fact we'll be glued to them ourselves.'

Chapter 48

The day after the invasion of the Falklands, the Argentinians invaded South Georgia. As he had fully anticipated, Jack, as part of an SAS contingent, set sail for the South Atlantic with the British Task Force, on 5 April. They all knew the 8,000-mile journey by sea would take several weeks but transporting large forces of men and military equipment that great distance by air was not an option, not least because there were no suitable and available runways close to the Falklands. The small airport in the capital, Stanley, was already in the hands of the Argentinians.

Throughout the journey the men trained intensively, both physically and mentally, for the job they were facing, the huge decks of the aircraft carrier giving great scope for exercise. They were heading into winter in the southern hemisphere and the Falklands, lying far south, would be having freezing temperatures and long hours of darkness. They were aware they would have little or no cover or protection from the elements and at times would be in isolation, but, having undergone intensive training in similar territory and conditions, they felt prepared for surviving and doing the task ahead of them.

They also had to be given some up-to-the-minute first aid training, in case they were injured with no help in the offing. This included ensuring they all remembered or learnt how to inject themselves with morphine and how to attach a saline drip, each being given a supply of both as part of a comprehensive first aid kit. In addition, each team of four always had one member who had been given quite an intensive medical training course, enabling him to cope with a wide range of injuries.

* * * * *

317

The Falklands War 1982

Route taken by Task Force April 1982

318

The Task Force was well on its way by the time the school holidays had ended and Mageen and the children had returned to mainland Britain in time for the new school term. Although the concern and support from all at Riverside had been unflagging, nevertheless, in a way Mageen was glad to get back to the UK, since she felt she would get any news with an immediacy not possible in Dublin, but also huge mutual support there too, intensified by a fellow feeling.

As Milo had predicted it had been hard to drag everyone away from the television and radio, but especially Mageen and her children. Day after day they followed the stories of progress made, both with the fleet of ships moving south and diplomatic efforts to avert a full-scale war. Wives of men who had sailed with Jack and Bertie had managed to keep Mageen up to date with news from and about the men on board ship.

Goodbyes at Riverside had been highly emotional for everyone, completely lacking the laughter and banter usually accompanying such partings.

'You're sure you wouldn't like us to go back with you, Mageen? You know Dad and I would be more than happy to go if it would help, even if only with the driving!'

'Thanks, Mum, but not yet. I don't mind the drive, after all I do have company. Let's wait and see what happens. If things get difficult then maybe I'll take you up on that offer.'

'Well you know you only have to ask.'

'I know, Dad, and thanks. It's great to know you're right there behind me.'

'Always, darling girl!'

'Me too,' added Maggie. 'I'll come over to you at the drop of a hat if I can be of any help. I may be nearly ninety but I'm still active enough to be useful.'

'I know, Granny, thank you too.'

* * * * *

The ships of the Task Force called at Ascension Island, that isolated pile of volcanic rock, normally a quiet spot with not a lot going on there. Now there was maximum activity, twenty-four hours a day,

319

and here the ships refuelled and replenished other items needed for the remainder of their journey south. The evening they sailed on again Jack and Bertie were having an after-dinner drink with Steve and Geoff, the other two members of their team.

'That was an interesting visit, Jack.'

'It certainly was, Bertie. I thought our Yankee cousins were keeping a determinedly neutral stance in this affair.'

'I think we all did but look what happened back there!'

'Exactly. They're helping to replace our fuel and other supplies.'

'Good for the Yanks.'

'You mean "God Bless America", Bertie?'

'Maybe even that!'

Everyone joined in the laughter and glasses were raised in an appropriate toast then the discussion continued, others joining in.

'I wonder if the Argies will agree to some sort of diplomatic settlement and avoid an all-out war.'

'Somehow I doubt that, Steve, especially if our lads manage to retake South Georgia as planned.'

'Do you doubt that for a moment, Geoff?'

Geoff grinned broadly.

'Course not! Any day now.'

'And then? All-out war?'

'Well actually they've already committed an act of war by their invasion.'

'Yeh, Geoff, but it still may not come to an all-out war as such.' Steve sounded uncertain. 'When faced with the reality of our combined forces they may decide to opt for a peaceful solution.'

'I can't see them backing down given the huge loss of face that would mean. No, I'll be amazed if it doesn't come to a full conflict, especially with so many on both sides primed and ready, almost itching for something decisive to happen!'

It would be some weeks before the news came through that the United States was now officially giving their support to the British efforts in the South Atlantic, especially in terms of supplies at Ascension, including weaponry. Ronald Ragan had got fed up with Galtieri and his ministers' continual refusal to give way and compromise in the intensive diplomatic efforts at negotiating a settlement. In the light of all that, on 20 May, Margaret Thatcher's government published the Falklands White Paper, which ended the negotiations. Now it was war – officially.

However, well before that happened, by 1 May the ships of the Task Force had arrived within helicopter reach of the islands. After dark, Jack and Bertie, with members of their SAS squadron, were ferried to the west side of East Falkland Island. Sea King helicopters, with advanced night-vision equipment, made possible this essential night-time movement of troops. The men were in their four-man patrol groups and their job was reconnaissance of the inland areas, where they were to hide and report on Argentine troop positions, movements and any other information of value.

They had all been well briefed and knew that they would have a long trek, or what the Marines called a "yomp", to reach their objectives, carrying very heavy backpacks, loaded with supplies and ammunition. It was an extremely difficult assignment in really hostile weather conditions and across territory which, having no trees or bushes, had little or no cover.

'Oh, God!' said Bertie as they stood in the biting wind and loaded themselves up for their trek. 'Why do we volunteer to do things like this?'

Unseen in the dark, Jack grinned.

'Come on, Bertie, you know you enjoy every minute of it – it's become a way of life for both of us. The adrenalin rush is addictive!'

'Right this minute retirement seems an awfully attractive idea.'

'No way – not yet anyhow!'

They trekked with the other two members of their patrol group, for many difficult, weary hours, a lot of the journey being uphill. They arrived at their destination and had to dig shallow "hides" in rocky ground that had just a thin covering of topsoil: not the ideal conditions for ensuring they were well concealed. However, although almost at exhaustion point, being well trained for extreme adverse conditions, they managed to achieve all this before daylight, scraping niches to lie in and camouflaging themselves as best they could.

Then, exhausted as they all were, only three of them were able to fall asleep, for at all times somebody had to be on watch or "stag", each taking his turn. By dawn all were awake, aroused partly by

321

being freezing cold and wet from lying in the waterlogged ground. They did some more surreptitious sorting of their equipment, had something to eat and drink from their ration packs and set about their observations of the Argentine encampment below them which was just coming to life. Then they spent the rest of the day, hour after hour, lying still, powerful binoculars trained on the foot soldiers carrying out their various military duties. From time to time helicopters flew over the exact spot where they were hiding and they lay without even twitching, knowing that if they were spotted and attacked they were on their own and must fight their way out of trouble unaided. Twice a foot patrol came very close to where they were concealed, but they weren't spotted.

When darkness fell again they discussed in whispers what they had observed.

'They don't seem to be a very disciplined lot do they, Jack?'

'They certainly don't look exactly jumping with joy at being here. In fact they all strike me as looking rather miserable.'

'Yeh – freezing cold and wet like we are – even our training conditions in Wales were never as awful as this!'

'Well I know, of necessity, we're a scruffy looking lot but the rest of our military look very smart when in uniform on duty. Those men on duty down there look scruffy even in their uniforms.'

'Their officers look smart though.'

Bertie thought about that for a minute.

'When they put in an appearance – yes.'

'But they don't seem to care what their men look like on duty. Surely being clean and smart when on duty is a part of discipline in *all* armies.'

'You'd think so but apparently not down there.'

They stayed out in this inhospitable territory for several days and nothing they saw changed their opinion that the ordinary infantry were quite an apathetic lot, even rather sad. Stories would be told later of how neglected some of these men had been by their officers – left out on duty in remote areas, more or less abandoned in that appalling winter weather; with out-of-date equipment; without adequate food and with uniforms only fit for summer conditions.

322

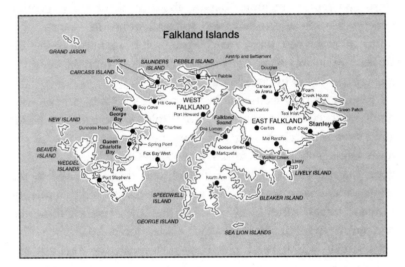

Falkland Islands

Chapter 49

Jack and Bertie's team sent back their reports regularly, from time to time moving their location, as directed from headquarters on board ship. The reports included details about some of the Argentine helicopter bases which had been spread around the islands. This information helped their own Harrier pilots to make successful strikes and destroy some of the helicopters, so limiting the ability to move Argentinian troops around the islands.

Eventually they were called back to their ship to be briefed for a different special operation. They were told of the concerns about attacks from the air during and after the planned landing of the main contingent of British forces close to San Carlos. Air strikes from Pebble Island, north of West Falkland, and therefore close to the approach routes and this landing area, were considered to represent a major threat, for it was believed that there were substantial numbers of Argentine ground attack aircraft located there.

The plan was to send in a team to eliminate the threat. A full assault on the base would take place, with diversionary attacks from the ships of the Task Force.

Jack and Bertie were to be a part of the assault team and they took off from their aircraft carrier, again in a Sea King helicopter. Unanticipated gale force winds made the whole exercise far more difficult than expected, not least for the aircraft carriers of the Task Force attempting to get close enough for the Sea Kings to be able reach their intended landfall. However, using their passive night-vision goggles they landed, of necessity, some distance from their target, to ensure the minimum chance of detection. The men, laden with all their assault equipment, then had to march a considerable distance to reach the target area. They had been split into two groups, one to provide ground support in the form of covering machine-gun fire, aimed at the settlement where they knew most of the Argentinian forces were sheltering from the weather. The other, for the actual assault, included Jack and Bertie.

As they jumped down from the chopper the full force of the wind hit them. It was even worse than conditions they had so far experienced.

'As Mageen would say, Jesus, Mary and Joseph! It's going to be one helluva walk in this gale before we reach the action!'

Bertie's reply was whipped away on the wind.

'I don't believe it! I've just trodden on a dead penguin.' Poor things, he thought. I know there are large colonies of them all over the island and once our assault gets going in the morning we'll disturb them in a big way.

After a punishing march of almost four miles they reached the point from which they could overlook the airfield and they settled in to wait for zero hour. Eventually, before the first pale light of dawn brightened the sky, tension reached boiling point. Bertie whispered to himself:

'Come on boys – where's that covering fire?'

The words were hardly out of his mouth when all hell broke loose from the guns of one of the off-shore battleships, while the machine guns of the ground support group started up simultaneously. On all sides the Argentinian forces were kept pinned down, while gunfire from the cover team and the battleship destroyed the fuel and ammunition dumps.

'Scots Wha Hae, Bertie, we're off.'

They tore down and along the runway, crouched low, and as they reached the aircraft on their assigned side they attached plastic explosives with quite short fuses. As instructed, they made sure they fixed them to the same part of each plane so that any surviving parts could not later be collected and cobbled together into replacement machines. They then attacked the planes with their various firearms doing considerable damage, including shooting away the undercarriages on some.

The team as a whole managed to place the explosives on all the targets, including the radar installation, without any opposition from the enemy. It was only after the job had been done, and the assault team started to withdraw, that the Argentinians responded and began pursuing, firing at the retreating men. However, in the return salvos, the officer leading them was killed and the counter-attack disintegrated.

As they ran back towards the helicopters, surprised at how little real opposition they had met, suddenly a mine, detonated by remote control, exploded close to the fleeing men. They were all showered with mud and Bertie grunted, dropped his assault rifle with it's attached grenade launcher, but stooped to pick it up, on the run, with his left hand.

'Okay, Bertie?'

'Yeh – shoulder's hit. I'll manage.'

He continued running and Jack and Geoff flanked him with Steve behind until well clear of the airfield. Then they insisted on carrying his rifle for the remainder of the journey, since he still had to cope with the rest of his load. They reached the helicopters without further mishap and the whole team was lifted back to the battleship.

Much to Bertie's chagrin, his injury was enough to mean he had to have a few days out of front-line action, especially as it was his right shoulder, and, being right-handed, this handicapped him in firing any weapon.

'Come on, Doc! Surely you could patch me up enough to allow me to carry on with the others.'

'Yes, I could but you might damage it again, even more seriously, and then you'd be out of things for the duration.'

'But I'm letting the others in my troop down.'

'You'd let them down very badly if you had to do some sudden fast firing and couldn't. It could put everyone at risk.'

'Suppose so,' he agreed, reluctantly. Then turned to his friend standing by:

'Sorry, Jack. Please tell the others I feel rotten about it.'

'You needn't! I'm going ahead with the contingent that's been given the job of creating a diversion during the landings. There'll still be plenty to do after that as we head towards Stanley, so you'll

326

be able to join us later.' He grinned. 'In time for the final victory parade!'

Jack was part of a group of SAS personnel to be transferred by Sea King from his ship to another in preparation for this task. They had to circle the ship until its landing spot became available and while doing this disaster struck. Suddenly and without any warning the pilot seemed to lose control and the helicopter plunged towards the sea.

'What the hell's happening, Geoff?'

'Dunno, Jack, but looks like we're in deep shit.'

'Oh God, and we've no life jackets.'

The disintegrating helicopter struck the water violently and many were killed instantly. Others died shortly after that. Only one third of the men survived, all with multiple and mostly severe injuries. Some of them managed to cling on to a small life raft that had inflated automatically. Jack was one of these and someone was clinging on beside him.

'Geoff?' he shouted. Silence and a barely recognisable voice shouted back.

'It's Steve – I think Geoff's bought it. You okay?'

'Can't feel my legs. Arms working. You?'

'One arm's useless but my legs are all right. Looks like we'll die of exposure.'

Fortunately, one of the other ships was close enough to manoeuvre alongside and a plucky young crew member dived into the icy waves and managed to swim the men to the ship where they were lifted as carefully as possible on board.

Jack's back was broken and his pelvis was in a mess. His war was over. They patched him up as best they could on board the ship. Then, with the others who had been badly injured he was transferred, by helicopter, to the big hospital ship. This had been equipped especially for the Falklands conflict with state of the art medical facilities and the most highly qualified medical personnel that the military could provide. The surgeons did their best to treat his injuries, but on his future prospects for being able to walk their verdict was couched in very reserved terms. The senior medical officer on board spoke to him about it.

327

'They'll be able to do much more for you back at home in a hospital that specialises in spinal injuries. It's amazing what can be achieved these days. I can't honestly give you any sort of definitive answer at this early stage as to whether or not you'll walk again. I'm sorry!'

Grey in the face from pain, Jack looked at him, and summoning up a ghost of a smile gave his reply.

'I'll walk again, Sir. Have no doubt about that!'

The surgeon looked at him and smiled.

'You know I really do believe you will.' But in his heart of hearts he was not very optimistic and shared this with a colleague later.

'If that man ever walks again it will be a miracle.'

* * * * *

Back on the base in England news was being sent regularly about the events 8,000 miles away. Mageen was reluctant to leave the house in case anything significant was reported. She suffered from a strange paradox of emotions, on the one hand clutching at all sources of possible news, but at the same time almost afraid of what she might hear or be told.

When Bertie's injury was reported to her, sorry as she was to hear of it, she was, nevertheless, relieved first that it was not serious and then that it wasn't Jack. If the two of them get away with that we'll all be happy, she thought. She wondered about contacting Bertie's ex-wife but, since they had never been very close and his injury was relatively minor, she decided against it. She had liked Rebecca well enough but, because the marriage had lasted such a short time, she had never got to know her really well. Their one child, Josh, now ten, lived with his mother and, like her own two boys, he idolized his father. Rebecca had tried to make the marriage work but couldn't cope with the constant anxiety and strain when Bertie was off on one of his special assignments.

Shortly after the news about Bertie, Mageen had a telephone call inviting her to drinks with the Brigadier and his wife. This was not unusual. Jack was very senior within his regular regiment. Brigadier Gordon was his superior officer, but as well as being fellow officers, the men and their wives were good friends.

328

'Lovely to see you again, Mageen.'

'It's good to see you too.'

She sat down on the sofa and Jenny sat beside her. Julian Gordon poured drinks and then, as he and Jenny looked at Mageen, she knew. The colour drained from her face and she put her hand over her mouth.

'Oh no. *Please*, God, *no… no, no, no…*'

'He's *alive*, Mageen.' Jenny put her arm around her, swift to reassure her.

'But?'

'He's injured.'

'And it must be badly or I wouldn't be sitting here being told by you personally?' She got her answer from the Brigadier.

'His injuries are quite severe, but he's getting the best treatment possible. We really do have a superb team of medics out there on the hospital ships.'

'Please tell me everything – leave nothing out!'

They told her in as much detail as they could. When they had finished she was silent for a while before responding.

'So they believe the helicopter hit an albatross which broke up the engine. Oh, my darling Jack. The irony of it! To have your military career finished by a *bird*.' By now tears were running down her face and she paused while she tried to pull herself together and collect her thoughts.

'I'll go to him. I'll bring him home myself. I'm not waiting for any of the formal military procedures.'

'That's not possible, Mageen. How would you get there? Not via Ascension Island: it's far too busy with the war. And you certainly can't go via Buenos Aires.'

'No, but I can go to Montevideo. I know that route is open for bringing casualties home.'

'Well yes, but what then? A civilian flight isn't equipped to deal with stretcher cases.'

'I'll charter a plane home for him and me and then I'll have him treated in the best hospital in the country that specialises in spinal injuries.'

The Brigadier was appalled.

329

'But, Mageen, even if feasible, that would cost an unbelievable amount of money.'

'I realise that, but I'll find whatever it takes. And if I can't my parents will help me. Come to that the whole Butler family would – they all love Jack and, indeed, owe him a huge debt of gratitude. Some years ago, when my sister Izzy was abducted, he helped to save her life and with it my parents' and indeed the whole family's sanity, but I'm not supposed to tell anyone that!'

'All right, your secret is safe with us. Let's not rush into a decision while you are, understandably, suffering from shock and extremely upset. Let's think it all through carefully. In the meantime drink this.'

He handed her a large glass of brandy which she sipped slowly. Eventually Jenny tried to put the situation in perspective.

'The procedure at present would follow, almost exactly, the steps you're contemplating, Mageen. Jack will be transferred to Montevideo by one of the smaller hospital ships and yes, you're right, Uruguay *is* cooperating with us and allowing RAF transport planes to land and take off from there for bringing the injured home. The big VC10s have been adapted, with beds installed for stretcher cases. Jack will be as comfortable as is possible for the long journey and have medical staff in attendance. Then when he gets back here the Services will see to it that he has the best treatment money could possibly buy.'

'Thank you, Jenny. But I want to be with him. He needs me now as he's never needed anyone before. My uncle is a doctor. I *know* he'd come with me to look after Jack on the journey. It wouldn't be the first time he's done something like that.'

Another silence and the Brigadier, gently, put a different point of view to her.

'Have you thought how Jack might feel about all this? Do you think he would be comfortable at being given very privileged treatment, not available to his injured comrades, and only possible because his wife comes from a wealthy family? So far as I'm aware, no other family would be able to afford to do such a thing. Knowing him as I do, I think he would feel acutely embarrassed at such privilege and guilty too.'

330

By now the tears were coursing down Mageen's face again.

'You're making me feel so selfish. But I'm just desperate to be with him and look after him.'

'You're not selfish, Mageen,' answered Jenny. 'You're a woman who loves her husband and has just had a severe shock. You haven't really had time to think it all through.'

Mageen looked at them both for a few moments.

'I know you're right. Jack wouldn't be happy at being given special privileges, not available to others.' She paused and then continued. 'You told me he had said to the surgeon that he *would* walk again. Well, he *will* and I'm just as determined about that. I'll help him every step of the way. And something else! So will his children, so will the whole family, just as we did for Sarah, my other sister, when she nearly lost her leg in a terrorist explosion.'

Her two friends smiled at her.

'That's the spirit, Mageen. I bet you'll do it too! But I must say your family has certainly had its share of difficulties to cope with over the years.'

'Yes we have, Julian, but you know we all pull together and support each other to the hilt and that's a large part of the reason why we get through in the end – whatever may be thrown at us.'

* * * * *

It took some days for the hospital ship to reach Montevideo, the procedure following exactly the steps described to Mageen. Jack was under heavy sedation and slept for most of the journey to Brize Norton.

In the meantime the family at Riverside and Jack's parents in Scotland had been told the whole story. Mageen accepting their offer to come to her if or when needed, Milo and Noola had hastened across to be with her, hard on the heels of Jack's parents. They tactfully suggested that they should not go to the airport with Mageen and the MacLellans, feeling that Jack might be a bit overwhelmed if they all went to meet him. The others wouldn't hear of that.

'I think that Jack would actually be quite disappointed if you

331

weren't there. He'll know very well that you'll have come flying over to be with me when you heard the news.'

Jack's mother agreed.

'Mageen's quite right, Noola. You're like second parents to our son and he'll be delighted to see you there.'

So they waited together for him to be disembarked. He was wheeled through to them and in spite of his pain and emotional distress he was determined that he would wear a cheerful smile. Mageen ran to greet him and at least he was able to put his arms around her. She wasn't to know that she was reliving a scene very similar to that experienced by her grandmother, sixty-four years earlier, when greeting her injured and disfigured fiancé arriving home from the trenches. Try as she might she couldn't stop the tears, even though she too smiled determinedly through them.

'My darling Mageen! I'm in a bit of a mess...' He choked up and had the hardest time not weeping with her.

'Jack, I love you so much. All that matters to me – to all of us – is that you're alive and you're home. Together we'll cope with the rest. And look who's here with me to meet you!'

Then he saw his parents, with Milo and Noola and the smile came back, broader than before.

'Mum, Dad! And begorrah if it isn't the Butlers! What a welcome home!'

Chapter 50

1989

Jack spent several difficult and painful years in and out of hospital and attending a rehabilitation unit. He was offered and accepted retirement on full pension, even a desk job with the army being out of the question.

He became an enthusiastic supporter of and participant in sports for the disabled and developed into a very competent archer, this being added to his outstanding ability as a marksman. He had great respect for the attitude of his disabled fellow-casualties, their determination in coming to terms with their injuries matching his own. They were a constant source of encouragement to each other. Nothing less than "positivity" was acceptable amongst this group of courageous men and, where this flagged, they helped each other through the dark days. As predicted by Mageen, the whole family rallied around too and support was forthcoming from the MacLellans and the Butlers young and old alike.

Not long after Jack became a casualty of war, his older brother, Alasdair, had developed AIDS, and had slipped downhill rapidly. When his parents had finally realised he was homosexual, for people of their generation, they had been remarkably accepting of the fact but drew the line at inviting his male friend to their home. While this disappointed Alasdair, he didn't press the point. However, he did so want them to meet this person who was as special to him as any wife could have been.

'Please Dad, Mum, I understand how difficult the whole situation is for you and the embarrassment it must be. I'm very grateful that you haven't rejected me completely. But I would so love you to meet Rupert. Would you at least have dinner with us one evening?'

333

Mairi looked into her son's pleading eyes and couldn't find it in her heart to turn him down flat.

'Give us time to think about that, Alasdair. And we would *never* reject you completely. You are and always will be our son, whatever your gender preferences may be, and we will always love you.'

'Thanks, Mum.'

Anxious not to hurt their son unnecessarily, they did eventually agree to have dinner with Alasdair and Rupert. In spite of their reservations they couldn't but be drawn to the gentle, artistically gifted and very attractive man, who had natural charm, a sharp wit and an almost old-fashioned courtesy. Later Alasdair had to know their reactions.

'Did you like Rupert?'

'Yes, we both did, Alasdair, but don't rush us. He seems to be a delightful young man and we found him highly entertaining. Another dinner at some later date is not out of the question.'

Alasdair's eyes filled with tears.

'Thanks, Dad.'

There was one more dinner date before both men were diagnosed as HIV positive. Rupert became too ill to socialise and then the disease took him. Alasdair's decline after that was rapid. He seemed to lose the will to live and followed his partner to the grave within months. In spite of the fear and social stigma attached to the disease at the time, his parents stood firmly by him to the end. Both were at his bedside when he died, his mother with her arms around him. This made Jack, and in turn Ewan, next in line to be the Laird, a role that would keep Jack fully occupied in the future. His father, meantime, was still an active man and while he and Jack's mother grieved deeply for Alasdair, they were thankful that they had a surviving son and three grandchildren.

After the first few years of Jack's treatment, operation following operation, the surgeons explained that they could do nothing more to improve things. However, although slow, he had made some recovery and eventually could manage to manoeuvre along with a walking frame. This was regarded as remarkable progress – more than any of the medics had dared to hope for in the earliest stages and attributed, in large degree, to his dogged grit and

334

determination. However, he insisted that family support had also been a vital factor in keeping up his spirits.

At the suggestion of his parents, Jack, Mageen and their children eventually moved into the family home in Scotland. Here Jack and Ewan could learn the full complexities of running the large estate. This was a good arrangement for Jack in terms of his health too, for their home was not too far from Edinburgh with all that could be offered there in terms of medical help. Jack went regularly for physiotherapy, confident that this was helping him to improve his walking. Mageen wasn't so sure but was determined to remain positive in her outward attitude to the situation. So far as she was concerned Jack was *walking* again, regardless of how well or with how much difficulty.

Ewan, now twenty-one, was studying at St Andrews University, his Butler heritage showing in his chosen subjects of maths and economics, both of which would be useful when, at some time in the future, he took over the running of the estate. However, at the moment he was desperately keen to become a stockbroker, again following in the Butler family tradition. His younger brother, Alasdair, known as Al, had opted for a career in the army, hoping to follow in the footsteps of the father who was his great hero. He had joined Jack's Scots Guards regiment and was determined to make a success of a military career. Rachel, at fifteen, was a talented sportswoman and planned to take a degree in a related area. Jack and Mageen were so proud of all three.

Tommy had retired from the RAF the previous year when he had reached fifty. The family had grieved when Aunt May had died peacefully in her sleep four years earlier, the last of her generation of Butlers.

Maggie, well into her nineties, had moved back into the main part of Riverside, where Noola and Milo could keep a close watch over her. Dai and Sarah lived in their own home, built on a plot of land adjoining Riverside, which they had jumped at the chance of purchasing when it came on the market. With easy access to the river, Sarah was still able to enjoy her rowing activities and she and Dai were close to the large conservatory that they had continued to tend and develop since their marriage. All this had left the East Wing free and Tommy and family had moved in there.

335

Milo, now rapidly approaching seventy, had handed over the running of the stockbroking business to Tommy and Harry. Tommy had settled back into the business with remarkable ease but had, however, insisted that Harry should be the senior partner on Milo's official retirement.

'It would be so unfair for me to step in and expect to take over, after all the years you've spent helping to run and grow the business.'

'I wouldn't mind, Tommy.'

'You're generous, Harry, but I *would* mind. Aside from any other consideration, you're far more experienced than I am.'

They had all agreed that Milo should keep a few of his oldest clients, so now he spent just a couple of mornings a week in the office. This also meant he was available as an "*eminence grise*" when there were tricky decisions to be made, but it was also allowing him to retire in stages which he felt would be important.

Chapter 51

Given his ambitions, each year Ewan was encouraged to spend some weeks of the summer vac learning about stockbroking and earning some pocket money in the family firm in Dublin. When they had seen that Ewan had a natural talent for sound and clever investment, Milo, Harry and Tommy had discussed the idea of opening a branch office in Edinburgh run by Mageen and Ewan. This idea was received by all, including Jack, with enthusiasm and the wheels were set in motion for the office to open when Ewan graduated the following summer. Milo proposed that he would spend some time over there to help with the setting up of the business and this was greeted with even more enthusiasm.

'Gosh, Grandpa, that would be so cool!'

'Yes! It really would be – er – "cool", Dad!' Mageen grinned at him. 'Would you come too, Mum?'

'Do you really think I'd let him go off to live somewhere exciting like that, even for a short time, without me? Not a chance.'

The plan was that Mageen would start looking, at her leisure, for suitable premises to buy, lease or rent. Milo and Noola would then spend some of the following spring and early summer putting everything in place and there would be an opening ceremony after Ewan's finals around June or July. With plenty of time to plan, there was no urgent rush.

What was being planned much more immediately was a huge combined seventieth birthday party for Milo, Noola, her brother Paddy and Milo's old school friend and war-time partner in the RAF, Joe Malloy. The four of them were getting the best kick out of the idea, all eager to repeat their joint celebration for their twenty-first birthdays, nearly fifty years earlier. This time, by mutual agreement, it would be close to Milo's birthday in June and, as on that previous occasion, would be held at Riverside.

The children and grandchildren of all four of them had been given plenty of advance warning and told that refusals or excuses would not be accepted. Without any other guests these alone would form quite a crowd but there were lots of other relatives they wanted to invite too, as well as special friends. It was going to be a big party with plans for a large marquee to be put on the lawn between the house and the river. Outside caterers would be employed so that all staff could join the guests. The MacLellans would not be able to come over for it but Jack, Mageen and their three children would be there. Harry and Cathy would also be present with their three children. Johnny, now sixteen, was an outstandingly talented sportsman, often pursuing these activities to the detriment of his studies. Orla was eleven and Hal was ten, both also children of promise in their different ways.

Sarah and Dai had two boys, Bill aged ten and David, eight, called for his father. David, in particular, was a great musician, strongly encouraged by the whole family, especially by Izzy, although both boys, true to their Welsh ancestry, had good singing voices. Izzy's daughter, Trisha, now eleven, was a fine pianist, like her mother. However, her absorbing interest was anything to do with medicine. Her favourite game, when she was little, was nurses and doctors and at six years old she had insisted that what she most wanted for Christmas was a toy stethoscope. No one doubted that she would eventually opt to join the medical profession. Uncle Paddy Flynn was thrilled to bits, feeling that this was definitely the Flynn blood coming out but Izzy, her parents and Maggie knew otherwise. Izzy often reflected how delighted Eddie would have been.

All these members of the family planned to be there. Milo was so pleased that, not only Tommy, Isabel and their four children would be present, but Isabel's parents, Chuck and Liz, would also be able to get over for it.

Sean Flynn, much the same age as Milo and Noola, had eventually reached the rank of Chief Superintendent and was also

338

retired. He too was looking forward to the big celebration. He often met his ex-Garda colleagues for a pint after they came off duty and on one of these occasions he was told some news that really bothered him. Freddie Armstrong was out on parole. He had hoped against hope that Freddie would be kept in prison for the duration, but apparently he had never put a foot out of place and, it seemed, had become a reformed character. The word was he had become a very devout Catholic. Sean had snorted with derision at that idea. Crafty bugger, he said to himself, that's the one thing he *knows* would soften attitudes and gain sympathy with those in authority. He made an opportunity to have a chat with Milo about it.

'It's something I feel you should know, Milo.'

'Like you I'm not at all happy about it Sean, but what do you advise? We've a lot of children around at the moment. How on earth do we protect all of them all of the time? I'm at a bit of a loss as to how we should play it.'

'Well, I don't want to worry you needlessly, but there's something else I feel I should tell you. While Tim Kelly was in there he and Freddie became great buddies, doubtless founded on feeding each other's grudge against the Butlers. Tim Kelly completed his sentence long ago but, now that Freddie has some freedom, I wonder what the two of them might be hatching – grievance is something that can grow, spreading like a malignant tumour until it eats up the soul. I'm convinced that Freddie wouldn't have any hesitation in breaking his parole if he thought he could get his revenge.'

'Oh, *please* God – not *again!*'

'They may use the opportunity of your party to do something, on the basis that you'll all be preoccupied with the celebrations. In my view that's going to be the vulnerable time. So, I've asked my old colleagues if they could provide some men to patrol the grounds for the day. You remember Noel, I'm sure! He's the one who was with us out at Powerscourt that day and knows the full story. He stepped into my shoes as Chief Superintendent and he's more than willing to help.'

'Thank heavens for that. We'll keep this as low key as possible. There's no need to frighten the children but the adults should be warned.'

339

'It's what I would have suggested. I may be worrying needlessly but...'

'Yes, Sean, I feel exactly the same way. I wonder if we should cancel the party.'

'I wouldn't do that if I were you. At least if they decide to do something then, the children will all be here together, with the adults and my men to protect them. It would be almost safer if they were to try something then and be caught red-handed. That'll end any danger for the children there and then.'

'The devil of it is they both know the house and grounds so well: they know exactly where they can hide away undetected. But you're right, Sean! Let them come and do their worst and let's get it over with once and for all.'

'I suggest you move all the firearms out of the gun room and lock them away somewhere. If you and Tommy could very discretely carry small arms, and I will too, then at least we'll have some cover.'

'Jack and Bertie will be here. They're both crack shots and I'll ask them to arm themselves too.'

'Great! I'll feel even safer with those two on the job. It'll be good to see them again. Haven't seen Bertie in years – not since Izzy was abducted.'

'We're all delighted that he's able to join us. He's coming all the way from Israel.'

'Israel?'

'Yes, he's retired from the army now and is trying to settle into life there.'

'Mossad?'

'No idea, but I wouldn't be surprised if they felt his training and experiences could be useful.'

Chapter 52

The great day approached with the preparations well in hand, both for the party and for very tight security. All the adults had been put in the picture and everyone was determinedly keeping the outward appearance of being relaxed. Noola and Milo had been concerned at the effect of the news about Freddie, in particular on Mageen and Izzy, but knew it would also be of concern to Harry that Tim Kelly could be involved, so they decided to tell their three children first.

'Sorry to have to be the bearer of disturbing news about these two, especially about Freddie, girls.'

'Don't worry, Mum. It took time but I got over it. As we've said before, in some ways good things came out of it for me: I met Jack! I suspect Izzy got over it years ago too?'

'Most definitely.'

'Thank goodness for that. Harry?'

'Yes, I agree with you, Dad. If they're planning some sort of revenge attack, better it should be now when we're so well prepared for it – get it over and done with.'

'Well done! Now let's put all the others in the picture.'

* * * * *

On the eve of the party, the actual date of Milo's birthday, the close family, adults and children alike, were allowing themselves to relax with special celebratory pre-dinner drinks by the riverbank. The only incomplete family was Mageen's. So far Jack, Ewan and Al hadn't turned up and Milo refused to open the champagne until all were there.

341

'Where on earth have they got to? Do you know what's keeping them, Rachel? When I left our room Jack was almost ready and the boys insisted on helping him to get down here.'

Rachel hesitated.

'Well it can't be anything drastic or one of them would have come to tell us.'

'Maybe I should go and look for them.'

'Oh I should give them another few minutes. If they don't come soon I'll go myself and have a look.'

Then they all heard it. Drifting across on the light evening breeze came a sound Mageen remembered so vividly hearing in the same spot on the eve of her wedding. Someone was playing the bagpipes, the sound moving towards them. But then it had been Jack. So far as she knew, since his injury Jack had played his pipes rarely and only with difficulty. So who was playing? It had to be one of the boys. Lovely and with the best of intentions, for they all knew the story, but perhaps not the most tactful thing to do, for it brought home to her very forcibly that Jack would never be able to do such a thing again. This was rather rubbing salt in the wound, but she tried hard to swallow the big lump in her throat. The whole group gathered there had fallen silent, straining their ears. Then around the end of the marquee someone came marching quite steadily and Mageen was rooted to the spot. No! It couldn't be! But it was! Jack was marching towards her, kilt swinging, playing "Amazing Grace", with the two boys behind him, also kilted, carrying pipes and ready to join in. Tears poured down her face and she strongly resisted the impulse to run and throw her arms around him. Rachel took her mother's hand and squeezed it hard. All three men now playing, they reached the riverbank where Jack laid down his pipes and opened his arms. Mageen ran to his embrace, careful not to knock him over, and wrapped her arms around him tightly.

'You sneaky devils all of you! You never let on a word. When? How?'

'All those visits to the physiotherapist in Edinburgh and the exercise bike in the basement! I worked myself into the ground and the boys and Rachel helped, but we wanted to keep it as a surprise and this seemed the perfect occasion to show you what I've managed to achieve. You know, my love, I can even run!'

'You wonderful, wonderful man. My darling Jack!'

Ewan, Al and Rachel were grinning from ear to ear and Jack seemed to glow all over albeit with some hint of moisture in his eyes too. The rest of the family had been as stunned as Mageen. The secret had been well guarded. Now they all joined in the delight and congratulations.

'Wow! What a celebration we're going to have and what a birthday present. Well done! You really are an amazing man, Jack.'

'Thanks, Milo. You're not so bad yourself – a hard act to follow, as they say.'

'Let's crack that champagne!'

* * * * *

Milo and Noola had alerted all the staff as well as the rest of the family to the possibility that Freddie and Tim might try some sort of an attack. On the morning of the party Mickeen sought Milo out with news that he felt he should tell him.

'I've been trying to find out some information about Tim Kelly.'

'Thanks, Mickeen! Any luck?'

'Well, some. It seems he hits the bottle really hard. Actually he's an alcoholic. This could limit his usefulness to Freddie Armstrong.'

'Or make him even more dangerous? As we all know, some people grow really aggressive when drunk.'

'I'd say if he *is* persuaded to try anything he'll make a wreck of it. In Freddie's shoes I wouldn't trust him an inch.'

'But Freddie's clever. He might use Tim's drunkenness to create a diversion.'

'Oh! Didn't think of that. Well at least we're now alert to the kind of tricks Freddie might pull.'

'Well done, Mickeen. I'll tell Sean Flynn.'

343

Chapter 53

The evening was an unequivocal success. A small floor had been laid for those who enjoyed dancing and there was a group to play for this and some gentle background music. The huge table from the dining room, which conveniently divided into several sections, had been set out at one end for the buffet and lots of chairs from the house had been arranged in small groups for those who would find standing for any length a problem. Izzy had taken little persuasion to play during the evening and her grand piano had been moved, with great care, into the marquee. The children sang to her accompaniment and Jack, Ewan and Al played their pipes again.

There was plenty of much enjoyed reminiscing too. Milo, Joe, Paddy and Chuck Wilson relived the episode where the two friends had been shot down and rowed home, fetching up in Dunmore East then Waterford Hospital, where, by coincidence, Paddy had been working as an intern. And later the triumphal return to the squadron and the delighted reception and celebrations. Noola added her memories of Milo's unannounced return home and his creeping up on her as she paced the riverbank grieving for him.

Bertie hadn't been able to arrive until the very last minute, coming straight to the party from the airport. He, Jack and Sean Flynn also had a great session together, they too reliving the time they had met when Izzy had been abducted. Noel, although very much on the alert with his men patrolling the grounds, did snatch a few minutes to join this particular group and got a real kick out of catching up with Jack and Bertie.

One of the delights of the evening was the meeting between

Bertie and Izzy. For a brief few seconds they just stood and looked at each other, unusually for both, words deserting them. The years fell away and she was a young teenager again, arms outstretched, feet flying to greet him and Jack in the hotel in Famagusta.

'Oh, Bertie! How wonderful to see you again. It's been such a long time.'

'Little Izzy! As beautiful as ever.' She was folded into a bear-hug embrace.

They spent as much as possible of the remainder of the evening together, catching up with each other's news. Bertie was introduced to Trisha who took an instant liking to him.

'Your mum was just about your age when she and I first met.' It suddenly occurred to him that Trisha mightn't know the story. 'Has she told you about it?'

'Yes, she's told me all about meeting you and Jack in Famagusta. I'd love to go there someday.'

'I'm sure you will and you could both come to visit me in Israel too.'

'I'd *love* to do that, Bertie. Oh, Mum! Could we *please*?'

Izzy smiled broadly.

'I don't see why not if Bertie can put up with us for a few days.'

'Izzy dear. I can put up with the two of you any time and for as long as you want. I'd be delighted. How about arranging a concert tour there?'

'What a wonderful idea. I'll get to work on that!'

Noola watched the two of them with growing pleasure and commented to Milo:

'I wish Bertie had come back to visit us several years ago.'

'I'm not so sure. It could have been a bit too soon. As well as Izzy's grieving, don't forget he was getting over a broken marriage.'

And so the evening passed happily, the younger children wild with excitement at being allowed to stay up so late, and Noola and Milo, as always the perfect hosts, making sure everyone was looked after in both food and drinks, not least the Garda on duty. Although the adults, especially the men, remained on full alert, nothing untoward happened until close to the end of the evening. Milo had been quite right: in spite of all the security, both Tim and Freddie remembered vividly the detailed layout of Riverside in and out and Tim had managed to slip in on the tails of the caterers and hide away in the basement. Unfortunately for him, he found the wine cellar open and helped himself liberally while he waited for word from Freddie. He became very drunk and got fed up waiting so, with everyone out of the house, he made his way up the back stairs to the roof. Then, just as the caterers were thinking of starting to clear up, he appeared at the front parapet waving a bottle in each hand and shouting venom against the Butlers.

Noel and one of his men called up to him to come down but he just swigged more whisky and swore at them. Then staggering towards the parapet he threw one of the bottles at them and in doing so lost his balance. The second bottle flew out of his other hand as he tried to save himself, but it was too late and he toppled over the edge. Somersaulting down, he hit the stone flags below, head first, and was killed instantly.

Fortunately the party was still in full swing so nobody in the marquee on the other side of the house was aware of what had happened. Hiding the body in the bushes, Noel called for an ambulance to come without sounding its siren. Then he went to find Sean to tell him what had happened.

Milo had been absolutely right in his surmise. All this was exactly the distraction Freddie had banked on. While it was going on he managed to slip into the house, with the equipment he needed to do the job he planned. He hid himself away where he knew nobody would search.

* * * * *

The guests started to say their goodbyes and gradually the party came to an end. The caterers did an efficient job of tidying up and eventually there was nothing left for anyone to do, so the family drifted off to bed, tired but happy, for as yet Noel had kept Tim's death to himself, his men and Sean.

'Should we tell Milo do you think?'

'No, Sean. Let him have his night's sleep. Pity to spoil what was obviously a great evening. The other fellow can't have got in or he

346

would have tried some mischief by now. It looks as if he missed his chance. Do you think we overreacted?'

'No, I'm still uneasy, Noel. Don't trust him at all. Can you leave some of your lads here until the morning?'

'No problem. I'll stay a bit longer myself and we'll continue to keep an eye on the back of the house as well, although an approach from that side would be more difficult. Somehow I doubt he'd use a boat, but you never know.'

'Thanks, Noel. I'll keep you company.'

Chapter 54

By 3.00 am all was silent in the house. Nobody was stirring, everyone relaxed and happy after the celebrations. Freddie had listened to the sounds of voices fading away as gradually goodnights were said and people went to bed. Then just as the first streaks of dawn were showing, when he would need the minimum use of a torch, he crept out of his hiding place carrying two large cans of petrol. He knew precisely where to start a fire so that it would have the most devastating effect and ensure his supreme satisfaction. Adding to the likelihood of maximum effect, it would be on the river side of the house, opposite to where the duty Garda were concentrated, so if he timed it carefully and watched for any men patrolling, it shouldn't be spotted until well underway.

Like many of the other downstairs rooms, the beautiful old sitting room was lined with wooden panelling, there since the house was first built and now tinder dry. The curtains were also some years old but, being of top quality, had stood the test of time and still looked good. However, they too were powder dry. He left the door wide open to ensure a good flow of air to fan the flames, then starting with the door frame, he spread the petrol liberally along the panelling. He worked deliberately slowly, determined to do a thorough job. He pulled the curtains slightly across the windows and sloshed the petrol over them reaching as high as possible. In doing so some of it splashed onto his clothing but he didn't worry. He knew exactly what he was doing. He had planned carefully and knew, if it worked, the fire would take hold extremely rapidly and then spread uncontrollably through the rest of the house. Well before the fire brigade could hope to get there Riverside would be finished.

Any attempt to save it would be a complete waste of time and, with any luck, some of the Butlers would die with it – the more the better.

At last he felt ready. Savouring this dreamed of moment he waited for a few minutes after the latest patrol team had passed the back of the house and then he struck a match and threw it at the curtains. He had, however, done an even better job than he realised, for a lot of the petrol had flowed onto the floor and, because he had worked slowly, the air was now full of the volatile vapour. The flame connected with this instantly and the room exploded into an inferno. It caught him completely by surprise and, helped by the petrol he had slopped onto them, his clothes ignited and also his hair. He ran screaming to the door in agony hoping to escape but by now he was a human torch and the flames were licking around the door frame. He inhaled the flames making the agony more than his heart could endure and he died before he got out of the room.

Outside Sean sniffed the air.

'Can you smell smoke, Noel?'

'Yes, I can. Where's it coming from?'

'Oh, please God, no! That's what he's done – set the house on fire. If I get my hands on the bastard I'll strangle him. But where is it?'

'No matter where, Sean, take the men and run and wake the household. Get everyone out as fast as possible. I'm sending for the fire brigade and ambulances.'

That was when the flames suddenly lit up the sky at the back of the house and they realised that they had so little time to get the people out let alone save the house. The job was made more difficult by all the doors being very firmly locked and bolted, as had been recommended, in a continuing effort at security. Sean and the Garda hammered and banged at the main entrance door and rang the bell furiously. No reaction. Surely *somebody* would have been disturbed by the noise and smell.

Somebody was. Little Orla, never a sound sleeper, woke up and noticed the strange smell. Then, her bedroom facing towards the river, she saw the flames two storeys below. She ran to her parents room screaming at the top of her voice.

'Mum, Dad, wake up, oh please wake up. The house is on fire.'

Cathy and Harry stirred, at first thinking that the child had been

349

having a nightmare. But then they smelt the smoke and from their own window saw the flames lighting the sky.

'Out everyone as fast as you can. Cathy, take Orla and Hal – don't wait for anything just go down the back stairs and head for the river. I'll go along the corridor and wake Johnny. Then I'll make sure everyone else is awake and gets out.'

Harry ran and got Johnny moving. Then he almost fell down the stairs and ran along the next landing, unceremoniously throwing open all the bedroom doors and shouting at the top of his voice.

'Wake up everybody, wake up, wake up. For God's sake hurry – the house is on fire!'

Everyone responded with lightening speed.

'Make for the river. Get as far away from the house as you can.'

He could hear the men outside shouting and hammering at the door but could do nothing about it until he was sure everyone was awake and moving. The flames were now licking hungrily at the west end of the great entrance hall and he knew the worst thing he could do would be to open the door and feed in more air. He ran in the opposite direction and into the library. He closed the door behind him and then threw open the windows and called to Sean.

'Along here, Sean. I can't open the door – the flames are already in the hall. Everyone's moving out by the back stairs and heading for the river. Could one of the fire engines concentrate on the corridor connecting the East Wing to us: try to stop it spreading there?'

'Good idea! The fire brigade should be here any minute.'

The words had hardly left his lips when Harry heard the sirens of the approaching fire engines. He closed the windows and ran down the corridor connecting the main house to the East Wing to make sure everyone there was awake too. However, the noise and smell had already disturbed Tommy who was getting his family out fast. When Harry was almost at the end of the corridor he cannoned into Tommy, hurrying to make sure the family in the main house had been alerted.

'I've advised everyone to go down to the river – it'll be the safest place.'

'That's what I thought too, Harry, and they're all on their way down there. I'm wondering if there's anything can be done to minimise the spread of the flames.'

350

'They'll do their best, Tommy.'

At that moment Milo appeared at the far end of the corridor and called:

'Everyone out your side, Tommy?'

'Yes, Milo. Yours?'

'Yes. At the moment the fire is being blown westwards but will inevitably spread here too. I'm not going to take any chances – let's go!'

'Okay, Dad, but since the fire hasn't reached this end yet maybe we could save some of your antique books? We can hand them out of the window to the men there.'

'Yes, Milo,' added Tommy. 'In fact Harry could hop out and we could hand some of the books to him.'

'Are you two stark raving mad? Thanks for the thought but antique books can be replaced, you can't! Now out of here both of you and down to the river with the rest. If the flames have reached the top of the house the roof is likely to cave in any minute. *OUT*!'

Milo leaned out of the library window to have a word with Sean.

'Just get out of there, Milo, the lads will do their best.'

'The Flanagans and Jockser?'

'All out. Jockser's taken the horses and dogs safely out of the way too. Now *go*, Milo!'

He closed the library door firmly behind him and followed Harry and Tommy down the corridor to the East Wing and out that way across the lawn and down to the others.

'Everyone here, Noola?'

'Yes, Milo, as you can imagine, we've checked and double checked over and over again.'

Mickeen and Kitty and family were there too but Jockser had decided to stay with the horses and dogs. He had taken them far from the house and was keeping them as calm as he could. When one of the Garda went to check on him he was standing there with the tears streaming down his cheeks saying over and over again:

'The beautiful old house, the beautiful old house, destroyed altogether.'

* * * * *

351

The fire brigade did a remarkably efficient job with fire engines ploughing around the East Wing and across the tennis court to get to the river, from which they then had an endless supply of water. The marquee was far enough away from the house not to get caught by the flames which were being blown away from it, but the sousing by the fireman ensured it survived. Attacked from both sides the fire gradually came under control but not before the central section of roof did collapse inwards, as Milo had feared. Like the sitting room, the wood in the rest of the house was tinder dry and had fed the greedy flames. They devoured the elegant stairway which facilitated their route to the floors above. It would be some considerable time before a forensic team found what little remained of Freddie's incinerated body.

The whole west side of the house was destroyed, including the big conservatory with all its rare plant specimens. Thanks to the unflagging efforts of the firemen the flames hadn't jumped the gap between the main house and the Flanagans' home, or the stables and garages. Miraculously, and again thanks to the firemen, a small part of the east end of the main house, including the library, wasn't too badly damaged and the East Wing had escaped unscathed, but all that remained of the rest was a charred stone shell.

Chapter 55

The whole family had stood there on the banks of the river watching Riverside House dying before their eyes. Sarah and Dai had been wakened by the noise and had run across the adjoining lawns to see if they could help. They now watched helplessly with the others as the flames were gradually brought under control and eventually doused.

There was an uncanny, stunned silence. Milo and Noola were side by side in the centre of the group, with tears rolling down their faces. Eventually Mageen moved between them. She put her arms around their waists.

'Dad, Mum – our beautiful home!'

'All that matters to Mum and me, Mageen, my darling, is that everyone is safe. By some miracle nobody has been killed or injured, family and staff members are all accounted for. What do bricks and mortar or indeed stones matter compared with that?'

Looking at the stricken, tear-streaked faces all around him Milo decided he had to do something to try to raise spirits a little. His sense of humour coming to his rescue, he even managed to summon up a grin.

'And after all, we've got the horses and dogs, a boat-house and some boats and it looks as if the Flanagans' home and the East Wing have escaped! We've also got a marquee, a dining table and chairs and a grand piano – it could be worse!'

They all heard this and appreciated his effort to be positive, to lighten the mood of despair.

'And let's not forget we owe the good old Liffey a big vote of thanks, Lo. The devastation would have been a lot worse without its water supply.'

'Too right, Tommy!'

Johnny moved over to him and, now almost as tall as his grandfather, plopped an arm around his shoulders.

'You know, Gramps, you now have a very full-time job for your retirement. You've often said how some day you'd like to have the kitchen moved upstairs. Well, now you can do that and some other things that you never would have dreamt of doing.'

'He's right, Grandpa,' Ewan chipped in excitedly. 'That's a brilliant idea. You could turn the basement into a series of offices and move your staff out here to run the business from Riverside. You need only have a token office in town and with computers the technology of the future the arrangement would be perfect. I'd so enjoy working on that with you and I'm sure Harry and Tommy would too.' Both nodded their heads.

'Great idea and hey, Dad, you could also have a marvellous games room in the rest of the basement.'

Milo's smile became broader.

'Good idea, Harry. And, Noola, you and Maggie'll enjoy designing a new kitchen with all "mod cons".'

'Yes, we'll really have fun with that, won't we, Mammy?'

'We certainly will and we'd want to consult you too, Kitty.'

'Oh yes please – that'd be great!'

'And, Dad, you and Dai and I could put together plans for a new conservatory we could restock with new flowers and plants – lots of new exotics. Mickeen's very knowledgeable in that area too. I'm sure you'd like to be included in the planning, Mickeen?'

'Indeed I'd love that.'

'And Trisha and I could also design a new purpose-built music studio.'

'In the meantime you can all tuck into the miraculously saved East Wing with Isabel and me. We can easily snug up and fit you in.'

'Actually, Dai and I have plenty of space and we'd be delighted if some of you moved in with us too.'

'I wonder, Noola, if any other couple has such a remarkable family.'

She moved closer to him and slipped her arm around his waist.

'I doubt it, my darling, and no family could possibly have such

354

a remarkable man as head of it. I think I love you more this minute than I've ever loved you, Milo Butler, and that's saying something!'

He smiled even more broadly and drew her close.

'Believe me, Mrs Butler, the feeling is quite mutual.'

Author's Note

With the exception of those mentioned below the characters in this story are fictitious. Riverside House is a purely imaginary place, although at the time the story opens there were some large, privately owned properties located where I have placed the house, on the banks of the River Liffey to the west of Dublin. One of these was the original model for Riverside House, although I located the estate in a different place, using author's licence to extend the banks of the Liffey to accommodate it.

I thoroughly researched the various traumatic events described, where possible consulting with people who actually experienced these events. When I had no first-hand accounts I used published texts and researched the Internet. This has been an invaluable source of information, much of which comes in the form of original documents, as, for example, the information on the Dublin terrorist attacks and the political upheavals and fighting in Cyprus.

My thanks to Frank Brown who provided really helpful information about training for the priesthood in Ireland and Cal Clifford for details about the Irish Army element of the United Nations peacekeeping forces. I hope this organisation will forgive the addition of a fictional character to its ranks.

I was fortunate enough to have worked in military establishments in both Germany in the 60s and Cyprus in the 60s and up to 1972, so I know that what is described is authentic. A big thank you to Nicos Florentos and Maria and Vassos Stylianou. By reading the sections concerned, they have given me invaluable additional help in ensuring the situations described and traumas suffered, especially in 1974, are accurate. They have kindly agreed to allow their real names to be used as well as to being included as participants in a fictitious story. "Smokey Joe's" really did exist. My apologies for having used writer's licence again and credited him with serving a *meze*. This was not a meal habitually offered in his restaurant, but one frequently experienced elsewhere in Famagusta in the 60s. Smokey was best known for his charcoal-grilled steaks – and very good they were too.

Much appreciation also to Alan Grace for additional information on the 1974 crisis in Cyprus. Alan was there at the time, with the British Forces Broadcasting Service. BFBS provided a crucial twenty-four-hour broadcasting service during this crisis. He gave me information, for example, about the organisation of the rescue convoys after the invasion by mainland Turkish forces.

Fortunately there is a wealth of literature about the Falklands War, with a number of the books giving personal accounts. Of the many texts I consulted I found the single most useful was *The Battle for the Falklands* by Max Hastings and Simon Jenkins. I owe an especially big thank you to Alan Jones, who not only lent me a number of these texts but also read the section on the Falklands in draft and ensured that what I wrote about the SAS and their involvement in that conflict was authentic. Information about the SAS is also well documented on the Internet. My apologies to the British Armed Services too for inserting fictitious members into *their* ranks and real events. Regarding the mention of the poor treatment of the unfortunate Argentinian foot soldiers by their superiors, I first heard about this from local residents when I visited the Falkland Islands.

My knowledge of the Irish legal system is minimal, mainly because I have had no direct experiences of its processes and procedures. I know I must have made errors in the court case I have described, so apologies to anyone irritated by these and please allow author's licence yet again. I did visit some proceedings at the Irish Law Courts which were quite helpful, although not of the type I have described in the story. Neither have I any knowledge of institutions for the criminally insane, so the place mentioned of that nature is entirely a product of my imagination.

357

The biggest thanks of all must go to those patient members of my family who read the story and gave me invaluable feedback. Christabel and Jim Grant and Eileen White read it section by section as I wrote it, giving me detailed, written comments. All three read the final version more than once. This was truly "above and beyond". Christabel and Jim also gave me help with several other aspects of the novel, for which I have so much appreciation. Much appreciated too was the help given by Aileen White, Ian Grant, Lisa Grant and Fiona Pradhan who read the full version. Aileen made some very useful comments and Lisa gave written responses. Fiona's input at the final editing stage was most helpful. All of this was important in refining the story and keeping it interesting and more or less credible. Ann Searle and Janet Clough also read the full version and paid me the compliment of saying they "loved it". As before, I hope the various elements of the story, if not always likely or probable, are at least possible.

A very special thanks to Chris Bridger for reviewing the novel with, again, such useful feedback and to Janet Clough for the lovely sketch she drew for the cover of the book. The sketch she created for the cover of *The Liffey Flows On By* was widely admired and commented upon and I feel sure this will draw similar responses.